To: Jeanne

Blessings

Fran

Frances L. Peterson
Isaiah 26:3

A Tale of Two Bamboos

Frances Peterson

A Tale of Two Bamboos

By Frances L. Peterson

Frances Peterson

A Tale of Two Bamboos

Fran Peterson

Four Seasons Publishers
Titusville, FL

A Tale of Two Bamboos

A Tale of Two Bamboos

All rights reserved
Copyright©2002 Fran Peterson

This work is nonfiction. The characters are real people, some of names and identifying information have been changed.

Reproduction in any manner, in whole or in part,
in English or in other languages, or otherwise
without written permission of publisher is prohibited.

For information contact: Four Seasons Publishers
P.O.Box 51, Titusville, FL 32781

PRINTING HISTORY
First Printing 2002

ISBN 1-891929-88-7

PRINTED IN THE UNITED STATES OF AMERICA
1 2 3 4 5 6 7 8 9 10

Frances Peterson

Table of Contents

Chapter		Title	Page
Prologue		A Whole New World	1
Chapter	1	U. S. A.	2
Chapter	2	The War	17
Chapter	3	China	31
Chapter	4	Korea	92
Chapter	5	U. S. A.	120
Chapter	6	India	151
Chapter	7	Hong Kong	207
Chapter	8	Singapore	269
Chapter	9	Thailand	278
Chapter	10	Anne and Jim	314
Chapter	11	Korea	325
Chapter	12	U. S. A.	330
Chapter	13	Vietnam	342
Chapter	14	U. S. A.	373
Chapter	15	Widow	388
Epilogue			403

A Tale of Two Bamboos

In years past, Americans born and reared in the Far East were sometimes called *Bamboo Americans*. I came from a missionary family in Korea; Kedar Bryan's father was a lawyer in Shang hai, China, and we met in Yokohama, Japan. Thus the title, *A Tale of Two Bamboos.*

In a number of cases, real names are not used.

Frances Peterson

This book is dedicated to

Edward Kedar Bryan
my husband

Edwin Kedar Bryan
my first-born

Anne Bryan Helsby
my daughter

James Park Bryan
my last-born

for the many wonderful, exciting, and sometimes difficult years we had living all over the Far East in

China,
Korea,
India,
Hong Kong,
Singapore,
Thailand,
and
Vietnam

They have my everlasting love and thanks.

Frances L. Peterson

A Tale of Two Bamboos

Frances Peterson

A Tale of Two Bamboos

Prologue

A Whole New World

With one last hug and kiss for Mother, Daddy, Jim, and Molly and a pat for Lexie, the dog, I boarded the train in Syenchun, Korea, to begin a new adventure–all on my own this time. I was headed for the United States and college.

After a week of travel to Japan and some sight-seeing, my sister, Betty, and I arrived at dock side in Yokohama to board the *Heian Maru*. It was a Japanese cargo/passenger ship accommodating about 120 passengers. Margie Lutz (another college "mish kid" spending the summer with her family in Korea), Betty, and I were booked to share a cabin.

As I put a foot on the gangplank I had a strong sense of the importance of the moment. The thought came to me as I boarded the ship; I really am beginning a new season in my life. From this moment on, everything will be different. When we pull away from the dock, nothing will ever be the same. I wonder what it will be like. Will I be disappointed, or will it be better than I have ever dreamed? Being an optimist, I was sure it would be fantastic.

Gripping the handrail with one hand and my purse with the other, I made my way up the wobbly gangplank. As I neared the top I looked up into the eyes of the handsomest man I had ever seen. He was slender, of medium height, had light brown wavy hair, and the most beautiful dark brown eyes. He smiled. My heart did a double flip, and yes, life was going to be good indeed!

A Tale of Two Bamboos

Chapter 1

USA

Our stateroom was at the end of a narrow passageway. There was one upper bunk and two lowers. Guess who got the upper. Our accommodations boasted a small basin, three very narrow closets, one opening porthole, and a ceiling fan. No A/C. All other facilities were around the corner and down the hall.

We were busily settling in for the ten-day voyage from Yokohama to Seattle when the gong sounded, and a loudspeaker announced repeatedly, "All ashore who are going ashore." We locked the door and made our way to the promenade deck. Because of the *Heian Maru's* limited accommodations there were no bands to send us off or streamers to toss to those staying behind.

After a couple of blasts from the ship's horn, several officials with briefcases in hand hurried down the gangplank before it was hauled aboard, and a megaphone gave the command to release the final line holding us in place. As inches then feet and yards separated us from land, my throat tightened. It was hard to let go; yet I was filled with anticipation of what lay ahead. And that young man who'd helped me over the top step–Kedar–I didn't think I had mistaken the look in his eyes.

We stayed on deck, amazed at the mechanics of leaving a crowded harbor. Several tugs tooted and whistled as they pushed and shoved us from our berth to open water. Gradually the noise of the engines grew. One small boat stayed with us until the harbor pilot, charts and papers under his arm, boarded it from a waterline door and pulled away. Leaving the breakwater behind, we felt the engines throbbing beneath our feet and decided it was time to check out the facilities on our deck. The smell of diesel oil from the engines and boiling cabbage from the kitchen gave my stomach a twist or two, but I determined not to be seasick no matter what!

There were no showers, and since all passengers shared a few tubs, it was necessary to schedule their use. I signed up for 5:00 p.m. If I forgot, the young Japanese room stewardess appeared and reminded me where I needed to be as another expected to bathe in twenty minutes. Her search wasn't hard; the ship's northern route took us past the cold and rainy Aleutian Islands, so much of our time was spent indoors in one of the lounges. A huge tub was filled with nice warm salt water, great for soaking if you had the time, and a pitcher of fresh water was there for a rinse-off. The same young girl awakened us each morning with a rap on the door. She suggested appropriate dress for the day, depending on the temperature.

As long as the supplies lasted we tossed our used, homemade undergarments out of the porthole instead of washing them. We'd buy new ones as soon as we reached the States. There's a saying that the floor of the Pacific Ocean is paved with missionaries' dirty underwear. We contributed our share.

We were just taking our assigned seats in the dining room the second night when the headwaiter asked me to follow him.

"If you have no objection," he said, "you will be seated at another table for the rest of the voyage."

"None at all," I answered when I saw he'd given me a

place next to Kedar. I was thrilled. We'd had a few short conversations, but this move on his part was a sure sign he wanted more time with me. I could hardly contain my joy.

After we got beyond "do you know so-and-so," we began to share our hopes and aspirations for the future. The exterior reserve Kedar saw belied what was going on in my heart as I came to know him a little more each day. Always a gentleman, his dress was casual and of the highest quality.

Kedar's grandfather, Robert Thomas Bryan, was born in 1855. Following college and graduation from the Southern Baptist Theological Seminary, he was accepted by the Foreign Mission Board in July 1885. He married his sweetheart, Lulu Freeland, and they sailed for Shanghai in November. After learning the language, he preached, planted churches, built schools, translated the Bible and Christian literature into Chinese, and raised a family. The first three children were Catherine, Elizabeth, and Lulu. The youngest and only son, Robert (Bob) Thomas II, was Kedar's father.

While very young, a botched operation on Bob's right eye left it with a droop that couldn't be corrected. He was very sensitive about it and insisted all pictures be taken from the left side, where it was less noticeable.

Much to Granddaddy Bryan's disappointment, his son wanted to be a lawyer. But to satisfy his father he took all the courses required to prepare for the ministry. He then switched to pre-law.

He sailed to Shanghai upon graduation from the University of North Carolina Law School and went into practice with two others. He married Gladys Parker, daughter of Methodist missionaries, and had three children: Alice, Kedar, and Peggy. Gladys became ill with some sort of lung infection that couldn't be treated in China, so she and baby Peggy were sent back to the States. They called it TB, but they weren't sure. After she died the cause was found to be a cyst on her lung, which today would be cleared up with a short course of antibiotics! How sad.

Kedar was just three at the time and had only one clear memory of his mother, though he faintly remembered her beautiful face, blue eyes, and curly golden hair. He was playing in the yard when she called from a second-story window and dropped a toy to him.

The practice of law was going well, but the cost of keeping a sick wife and baby in the States drained Dad's bank account, so he, Alice, and Kedar lived at various times with his parents in the Baptist missionary compound or with Gladys's parents. In time Peggy returned to China accompanied by somebody who was making the trip.

In 1926 Dad Bryan married Gertrude Barndt, a math teacher at Shanghai American School. A year later he was appointed municipal advocate of the International Settlement of Shanghai, equivalent to attorney general in the United States.

His Chinese was flawless. He learned it as a child under the care of his amah then took up a serious study of the language in several dialects when he returned as an adult. After he'd mastered the basics, a scholar came to the house every day to read and discuss the classics. He was the only man of either race capable of translating the Chinese law code into English, and vice versa. He practiced in both Chinese and American courts up to World War II.

Kedar had his first year of high school at Kooling American School, but his father decided an American prep school was what he needed to ready him for college. He wrote to a half-dozen Ivy League schools, asking which high schools they'd recommend as good preparation for college. Every one wrote back naming several, but the only one listed by all was McCallie School in Chattanooga, Tennessee. He'd never heard of it; but after corresponding with the headmaster, he chose it for Kedar.

"Those were my three best years," he said, "The life

was well-disciplined, classes were challenging, and Dr. McCallie's family treated me like a son on weekends. Girls really fell for the uniform too."

Kedar returned to Shanghai for his freshman year at St. John's University and was now on his way to the University of North Carolina in Chapel Hill, a forth-generation Bryan to attend.

My family was so different from his. Born to a Presbyterian missionary family in a little town in North Korea just fifty miles south of the Yalu River, I was sixth of eight children–four boys and four girls. Daddy was an evangelist and in the early years, itinerated on foot four rugged, mountainous counties bordering the river. When roads were built he traveled by car.

Our whole life was centered in our home. We were born there. Mother made our clothes, oversaw the growing, canning, and storing of our food, taught us through the sixth grade with the Calvert System, nursed, and loved us. There was never a lot of money, but we always had enough. Daddy's philosophy was "prosperity is a state of mind, not what you have in your bank account."

Heydon was the oldest, followed by Willard. They graduated from college and McCormick Seminary and were ordained Presbyterian ministers. Both married before I came to the States. Cordelia (we called her Hunkey, not knowing it was considered uncomplimentary) was in nurses' training in Grant Hospital in Chicago, and Nathan was a sergeant in the army air corps. Betty was attending Beaver College and would go back to school after her summer at home. I came next, followed by Jim and Molly, who were still in Korea with Mother and Daddy. We were constantly challenged to do our utmost, and no dream was too outlandish to consider. Best of all, our parents loved each other, and we felt very secure.

By the time we reached Vancouver, Kedar and I'd spent hours together talking about what was important to us and sharing dreams of an unlimited future. He smoked, and I thought it was so sophisticated, though it was one of the things Daddy suggested I not do. Neither of us had any idea that some years later it would snuff out his young life.

Both of us viewed the future with optimism, open-ended and packed full of endless wonderful possibilities. We were ready to take on the world! We were going to schools a thousand miles apart and knew we'd meet new and interesting people, so our behavior was that of good friends. It wasn't until the last night that he kissed me. Wow, I wanted more; but the voyage was over.

Kedar left the ship early the next morning to visit friends before catching the train across Canada and down to North Carolina. The rest of us went ashore and toured the city before trying out several rides in an amusement park, where I encountered my first roller coaster. Enough of that. My stomach was not happy! When we returned to the ship for the 10:00 p.m. sailing to Seattle, Kedar was on the dock to say one last good-bye. I was impressed. Did he like me all that much? I was thrilled and got one more kiss too.

Heydon and Hunkey met us the next morning. They had driven out from Illinois to pick us up, and after a short visit with Nathan we headed east. Nathan looked wonderful in his uniform, and I was sorry we didn't have more time with him. He was the brother I knew the least.

In the days before interstate highways and cars with air conditioning, it wasn't an easy trip; but with every turn in the road there was something fascinating to behold. One big surprise was seeing Americans who weren't well dressed, obviously poor. I had seen many such Asians but no Americans.

Since Hunkey lived in Chicago she offered to get me outfitted for college. What I knew about shopping you could put in your eye because Mother made all our clothes. Our only stop was Marshall Fields. I was so awed by its opulence that she feared we'd never get the job done if I had to look over everything before making a choice. She put me in a dressing room, told me to stay there, and came back with armloads of things to try on. She did well with my limited budget by selecting mix-and-match school clothes that left some money for date and prom dresses.

One thing I couldn't understand was the mandated dress code. On the first of September all summer clothes were packed away, and you wore fall and winter outfits no matter what the temperature was. Heaven forbid that you wear summer clothes and light shoes even if it was in the 90s, and it was in Lewiston, Illinois, where I stayed with Heydon and Mary until mid-September when school began. Praise the Lord, times have changed.

Orientation at Knox College in Galesburg was easy. I'd been at boarding school for years, so settling in was second nature, and I loved the way everything looked so clean. With paved streets and sidewalks, shoes didn't get muddy on rainy days. Everybody was friendly and spoke English. Man alive, I thought, a breeze. There was also sorority rushing. I was a Pi Phi legacy and had lots of attention from them, but I preferred the women in Tri Delta so responded to their bid.

Classes were challenging but not too difficult. My weekends were busy with dating several men, all nice but nothing special. I got a job working in the alumni office at the going wage of thirty-five cents an hour to stretch my monthly allowance of thirty-five dollars. I landed a minor part in the musical, *No, No, Nanette*, and went out for field hockey and basketball.

From the day we parted in Vancouver, I heard regularly from Kedar. Calling was too expensive, but he wrote of the good things at school and all the excitement of being there. He always mentioned that he thought I was very special. Late in the fall he hitched a ride with a man who also had a friend at Knox. It was so good to be with someone who spoke my language, who knew and understood my past. Neither of us was interested in football, ever the passion of college students, but we followed closely what was going on in the international scene, particularly in the Far East. During Christmas vacation I visited him in North Carolina, and so it was from then on. I had a summer job at a private club in Sequenota, Michigan, and at the end of the season he joined me there.

The freedom we had when together would have tested our values to the limit had we not faced the issue and decided not to step over the line, and would remain celibate. It was a good choice.

In the fall of 1940 all Americans were ordered out of Korea by the U.S. consul general. Mother and Daddy, Jim and Molly were evacuated with the others on the *Meriposa*. At the end of that first summer they were living with Heydon and Mary in Lewiston. Kedar drove me to meet them, and they liked him immediately. "He's a gentleman and a scholar," Daddy said, the highest of compliments.

Like everybody else, I can clearly picture where I was and what I was doing on 7 December 1941. I had just come back from church and was getting ready for dinner when I turned on the radio to hear President Roosevelt's famous announcement. What would that mean for Kedar? How soon would he have to enter one of the services, and what about his parents, who were still in Shanghai? There were a thousand questions and no answers.

Some of the men signed up right away, but most stayed in school as long as they could. Kedar enlisted in the marines but wasn't called up right away. They needed officers, so the hope was that he could finish college or at least complete his major courses and enter officer candidate school.

Wanting to be together as much as possible, I went to Chapel Hill for summer school. We took full loads, but there was plenty of time on the weekends. What a difference between Knox and UNC! At Knox, Benjie, the Whiting Hall doorkeeper, checked the students in at 8:30 p.m. for freshmen and 9:00 p.m. for sophomores, but at the university you were on your own. Dorm doors were locked at 11:00 p.m. and if you weren't in on time, tough beans unless you had a friend on the ground floor, which I did.

I liked the honor system too. When exams were given you could take them wherever you chose–library, your dorm room–any place just so long as they were turned in by a given time that day.

Sunday nights that were rain free were special. We took blankets and laid them out on the ground in the football stadium to listen to "Music under the Stars," a concert of recorded classical music. There were extensive wooded areas around the campus. Sundays we took picnics, blankets, and books to a quiet place to eat and study. Once Kedar took his .22 and a few shells for target practice. He put a tin can in a tree about fifty yards away and took aim. We hadn't seen another soul all the time we were up there, so we were surprised and amused when his first shot brought forth cries all around us of, "Don't shoot! Don't shoot!"

The last week of the summer term Kedar received notice that he was to report to Quantico, Virginia, for OCS on 31 December. We began talking seriously about setting a wedding date. His parents were interned by the Japanese in Shapei Camp near Shanghai, and there was no money except for the amount doled out by Alice, his older sister, and that was for school only. He was directing a group of V-12 students on campus, for which he received a small stipend, but soon he'd be getting a regular salary from the marines.

One of our last evenings before I was to return to Mother and Daddy in St. Louis, Kedar walked me back to Alderman Hall through the arboretum. We stopped at our favorite place under a tall tree.

"Fran," he said, putting his arms around me, "We've

been engaged since February 26, and we could wait until after the war to be married. But I've thought it over, and I'm sure we can manage if we get married before I report for duty. Will you be my wife on October 31?"

"I certainly will," I answered, hugging him tightly around the neck. "I've loved you since the moment I saw you at the top of the gangplank boarding the ship at Yokohama, and marrying you will be the happiest moment of my life."

We laughed and hugged and kissed with tears streaming down our faces and didn't even notice others walking by. There was much to consider–the war was raging, we had very little money. Separation was certain and perhaps death, but we delighted in each other, and nothing else mattered. The world was there for us to conquer, and together we would. Oh, youth!

And so it was that at 4:00 p.m. on October 31, 1942, I walked down the aisle on my father's arm to exchange wedding vows with Edward Kedar Bryan.

I wore my great aunt Frances Dunlap's wedding dress, complete with bustle and train, that she had worn eighty-six years earlier. Yellowed with age, it was still elegant and fit perfectly. She was shorter than I, so to get the hem close to the floor I constructed flat sandals from inner soles and matching satin material. Mother found the exact shade of tulle and made a braided piece for the top of my head and a delicate finger-tip veil.

For his part, Kedar wrote to Dr. McCallie, headmaster of the military prep school he'd attended, and asked for a four-hundred-dollar-loan. He was quick to respond, "It gives me great pleasure to help in this way. Pay it back when you have a good, regular job after the war. If for some reason you can't, I'll count it as an investment in a fine young man." One of the happiest things Kedar ever did was to return the loan with interest three years later.

Our nuptials were modest but beautiful and well attended by church members who'd supported the Lampe family in Korea for many years. Daddy walked me down the aisle, gave me away, and performed the ceremony too. Three of my brothers were there, and my three sisters were bride's maids.

These were war years with all the attendant rationing and restrictions. Even if that were not so, Mother and Daddy lived on a stipend from the Board of Foreign Missions, and there wasn't a spare nickel anywhere. As Mother said, "We aren't poor; there is precious little for extras, but there is always enough." It really is possible to live an abundant life with just enough to get by, and they did.

Since I was the first of us four girls to be married, Mother kept strict accounts to be sure the other three would not be short-changed. In the final tally, the whole shoot'n match–trousseau, wedding, and wedding breakfast–came to just over two hundred dollars.

Molly, Betty, Fran, Mother and Hunkey

Marriage is serious business. We'd read enough and

talked endlessly about our expectations, so we thought we had most of the answers before we approached our wedding bed. We found excitement, passion, and sweet intimacy, but neither of us had any idea it was so much fun!

Mr. & Mrs. E. Kedar Bryan

"Everything goes," was the advice of a father to his young son who was getting married, "so long as it pleases both of you." We reveled in our freedom. There was laughter, playfulness, and joyful tenderness in our union.

Knowing that we were sharing it exclusively with each other made it all deep-down, blessedly wonderful.

I was surprised that Kedar wanted to go to church the next day at Clifton Heights, where Daddy was preaching. He later confessed that what he really wanted was to hear someone call me Mrs. Bryan. After lunch together we went back to my parents' apartment and finished packing the last few things before catching the train to Durham, North Carolina, and our first home in Chapel Hill.

Rosemary Lane was a pretty, shaded street of small houses. Ours was an apartment in a story-and-a-half cottage. We had half of the second floor. With wartime shortages we were happy to have a roof over our heads, and that just about describes our two-room abode. The first was a kitchen–dining room, boasting a sink, icebox, and a small table next to the window. A table and four chairs stood back under the sloping ceiling. A wood-burning stove in the adjoining bedroom provided heat for both rooms. We shared an unheated bathroom with the couple across the hall. The advantage of such a beginning? There was no place to go but up. My cooking skills left much to be desired, but armed with several good cookbooks, and a wish to impress my husband, I didn't do too badly on my two-burner hot plate and electric roaster oven. That Mother insisted I have one saved my life.

We had exactly two months until Kedar reported for duty at Quantico, and every moment was precious. I got a job in the university's alumni office while he attended classes, finishing up his major requirements. The University of North Carolina agreed to count his officer candidate and officer-training courses as credits toward his B.S. degree upon commissioning. One day in the grocery store Kedar pointed out Dr. Knolton, a professor of his who was also shopping.

"Biology isn't my favorite subject, and I just hope to squeak by," Kedar remarked under his breath. "Be sure to give him your sweetest smile. If he has pity on my having to go into the service, maybe he'll pass me." When Kedar was commissioned, he received notice from the University that his degree had been entered into the record. What a relief.

Kedar was the third-generation Bryan in Shanghai and the only son. With all the Asian culture absorbed through many years in residence, he felt the importance of having a son to carry on the family name was paramount. His future was a worrisome unknown, so putting aside all precautions, I was soon pregnant.

During OCS Kedar got only one weekend pass, but as soon as he pinned on his shiny new bars he got off every weekend, and I moved to Lynchburg, Virginia, to be near him and take advantage of base medical facilities available to dependents. This time I shared an apartment with another young woman whose husband was in Kedar's class. We took turns having the apartment on weekends and alternately going to a motel.

It was a fine arrangement, but the owner who lived downstairs was a piece of work. The rental agreement stipulated that she'd maintain all equipment, but when things broke down it took her forever to get them fixed; and something always needed attention. Most repairmen were in the army, so service was in short supply. Every time we asked when help was coming she'd answer, "Ma deah, it's not yo' fault. It's not mah fault. It's the wo-wah."

Across the hall lived another of Kedar's classmates and his wife, Chief and Hattie Jones from Mule Shoe, Texas. He was a school teacher and half-Indian, thus the name. He complained endlessly about the tough drill sergeants, ending up his remarks with, "Hell, they treat us worse than we treat the blacks in Texas!"

Selection time came for a specialty, and Kedar received orders for forward communications. The rest packed up to leave for other bases or to go overseas, but we stayed for another six weeks.

Too soon, orders came for him to join the First Marines in the South Pacific, and reality set in. I knew it was inevitable but kept dismissing the idea that he would be leaving with no assurance of ever coming back. Thousands of other wives and sweethearts were in the same boat, but that didn't make it easier to bear. I was seven months pregnant when he took me back to St. Louis to stay with Mother and Daddy. A big lump in my throat refused to go away. When we went to the station to see him off I was okay until he stepped up on the train and turned to give me a big smile and a wave before he disappeared. A wrenching sorrow took hold of me so that I could hardly get my breath. When the last car disappeared around the bend it all broke loose, and the healing flood began.

Kedar goes to war

Chapter 2

The War

Pearl Harbor, and instantly everything changed. As we emerged from national shock and rage, differing goals and aspirations were put aside, and the country turned into one gigantic body struggling for survival. There was but one purpose–destroy the enemy and save the world. No price was too high to pay.

The propaganda machine went into full gear, cranking out reasons for us to hate the Japanese, Germans, and Italians. Hollywood fell into step with movies about our brave men in uniform and the enemy that would take them from us. A number of stars went through basic training, put on handsome uniforms, and helped by selling war bonds. Tyrone Power was in Kedar's OCS class, and we met him a couple of times at the Blue Moon Café.

As the male population went off to war, women took their places in factories and offices, and those who stayed home knitted socks and sweaters for our allies in England and Russia. We removed the ends of cans, smashed them flat, and took them to the scrap collection point. We bought war bonds and prayed a lot.

Everything, everything was in one way or another affected by the war, but worst of all was the deep loneliness at being separated from Kedar. The day was bright and beautiful when a letter came from him. How he could write! He couldn't say where he was or what he was doing, but he relived on paper our good times, things he thought were sweet or funny, and his dreams about life together after the war.

Later he filled me in a little on what he did. He was on Guadacanal for the final mopping up operations and went ashore at Bougainville and Emereau with the first wave of assault troops and established radio contact with offshore ships, calling in air strikes and naval bombardment against enemy positions. A number of times he broke all records for digging a foxhole, but his close calls were few. One time, however, he was ordered to go back to supply to pick up another radio unit. Lt. Bob James took his place in an LSD. On the way in they had a direct hit from an enemy shell, and all aboard were killed. Kedar grieved for Bob and his family.

Kedar never drank when we were first married. To celebrate his acceptance in the Marine Corps OCS, we shared a glass of wine. I didn't care for it. For years he never had so much as a beer. His beverage of choice was coffee with cream and sugar.

During the fourteen months he was in the South Pacific he sold his monthly whisky ration for a hundred dollars a bottle and sent the money home for our nest egg. Those fellows must have had a mighty thirst to pay so much!

One commodity after another went on the ration list. Cards were issued for the meat, canned goods, gas, and even shoes. Just as soon as anything was in short supply, black markets were born to accommodate those with "special needs."

Adjusting to life as it came, I was able to share with Kedar the interesting events that accompanied my first pregnancy and getting ready for the baby. Most manufacturing was directed to the war effort, so there was precious little to buy in the baby department. I found sturdy second-hand furniture, cleaned it up, painted it, and it was as good as new. With Mother's guidance I bought patterns and material to make maternity clothes and a layette.

Some have written of the great sense of peace God gave them during times of crisis, but I didn't feel it. In the first few days after Kedar left I wondered why I felt only a terrible, crushing agony. As days turned into weeks, though, I was determined to make the first few verses of Isaiah 43, the rock on which I'd stand:

"But now, thus says the Lord, your Creator, O Jacob, and He who formed you, O Israel, Do not fear, for I have redeemed you. I have called you by name, you are Mine! When you pass through the waters, I will be with you; And through the rivers, they will not overflow you. When you walk through the fire, you will not be scorched, nor will the flame burn you. For I am the Lord your God, the Holy One of Israel, your Savior."

I'm well aware of my failings, but one thing I could count on–God is faithful, and He has promised never to let me be alone even in the worst of times. You can "take that to the bank."

Little flags with blue stars on them began to appear in windows, one star for each family member in the service. When one was replaced with a gold star, we knew they had received that terrible telegram, "We regret to inform you."

Mother claimed seven stars, which included two sons-in-law, so we pitched in and bought her a gold bar pin with seven blue stars on a white background.

Heydon went into the Navy Chaplain Corps, had several duty stations in the States and aboard the USS *Bougainville*, an escort carrier. After the war he returned to a civilian pastorate, decided he preferred the navy, and rejoined. He saw action in Korea, was stationed in Hawaii (tough duty) aboard USS *President Adams*; the USS

Greench Bay in the Persian Gulf; the USS *Wisconsin* and USS *Pocono* in the Lebanon crisis.

Willard joined the Army Chaplain Corps and was assigned to General MacArthur's troops in the South Pacific. He irreverently called his unit "Dugout Doug's Dauntless Dismounted Cavalry." His analysis of the war was that we won with mass troops, mass material, and mass confusion. He spent his longest time in the First Presbyterian Church in Beatrice, Nebraska.

Hunkey was a nurse in the Army Air Corps, posted to several military hospitals. Her favorite was Lawson General in Atlanta that received most of the amputees from the European theater. For a time she was on a ward for men who'd lost a leg and were being prepared for artificial limbs. In the meantime they were encouraged to do as much as possible for themselves. She urged them to make their own beds instead of waiting for her to do it.

"But Miss Lampe," they complained, "it's too hard with just one leg."

"Come on," she retorted, "you're strong enough to hop to the Coke and candy bar machines. Surely you can make your own beds."

"You don't understand. It's hard."

"Okay," she challenged, "I'll show you." With that she let them tie up one leg and in twenty minutes made every bed on the ward military tight (so you could bounce a quarter on the cover). After that there were no more complaints. She was just glad her supervisor didn't catch her.

Nathan was in the field artillery of the Third Division. He took part in Paton's drive across North Africa and saw action in Italy, where he landed on the Anzio beachhead. When that terrible slaughter began Nathan was walking up the beach. A low-flying plane appeared over a hill, strafing guns blazing. "Hit the deck," someone yelled, and he fell face down. A row of bullets spattered in the sand six inches from him, running the whole length of his body! The Germans gave them time to come ashore before opening fire, pinning them down.

He, Jim, and I all suffered from malaria as children, and in stressful situations it flared up. For three days he suffered racking fever and chills while he lay in his foxhole until help arrived.

Making their way through the mountains in central Italy on a dark, rainy night, he and another man wearing white shirts guided a convoy moving without lights. Twice they unknowingly stepped over land mines that blew up the trucks just behind them. He came home after three years of combat without a scratch.

Here's how it went for the rest of us: Betty held down a defense job in a laboratory and married Arlan McClurkin, a captain in the Army Quartermaster Corps. Fran married Kedar, who was in the marines in the South Pacific. Jim was a Navy pilot. Molly married Harwood Sturtevant, an Air Force doctor, but not until after the war.

Molly, Fran, Betty, Hunkey and Margaret (Nathan's wife)

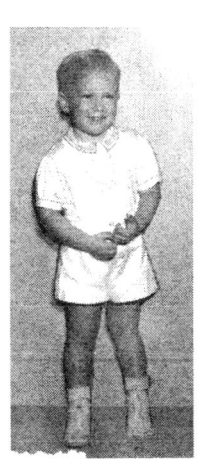

Edwin is ringbearer

"How in the world do you keep your sanity in days like these?" people often asked when they saw Mother's pin.

"It wouldn't be possible if I couldn't pray," she always answered.

My baby was due August 18th, but they say first babies are a little hard to shake loose, and he certainly was. On the 24th at 12:30 p.m. our first son, Edwin Kedar Bryan, made his noisy entrance into the world. At the time Hunkey was stationed at nearby Scott AFB and had advance permission to come be with me.

Maternity patients were managed quite differently then. I was kept flat on my back for a week, and nobody but clergy, Daddy, and Uncle Bill Lampe, were permitted to visit, not even Mother. Kedar could have if he'd been in country. After ten days I took my precious little guy home and learned all about mothering from the expert. It was sad that Kedar had to miss these early days, but that was just another of the sacrifices we made to try to bring sanity back to the world. Kedar had his first glimpse of his son when he was fourteen months old.

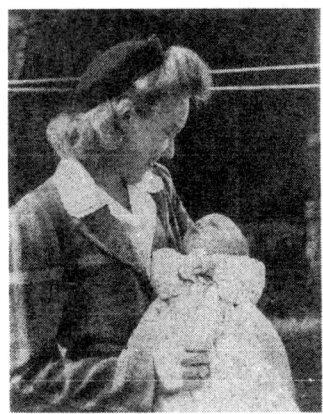

Fran and Edwin

Edwin was the smallest of our three, weighing in at six

and a half pounds. When I first looked him over I thought, Mother will be pleased with this one. He had pretty little pink-and-coral ears that lay close to his head, one of the characteristics she deemed the mark of a beautiful baby. I loved to look at his perfect little body, let his fingers wrap around my pinkie, and wonder what those hands would do when he was grown. He was a by-the-book baby and gave me no surprises. When he was about three weeks old I noticed a change in his eyes, and sure enough they were turning from blue to brown–Kedar's eyes. What a handsome little boy, and just like his dad.

"Yes, speaking." From the somber look on Daddy's face we knew it was no ordinary call. He took several deep breaths and offered only a few short comments as the conversation continued. "Yes, I understand. What's that number? We'll talk it over and get back to you. Thanks for getting in touch."

"What is it dear?" Mother asked in alarm.

"It's Jim."

"Has he had an accident?"

"He's very ill." Daddy reached for his handkerchief as he moved across the room to Mother. "The doctors think he won't live more than a few days at most."

"Not our Jim!" Mother gasped. "What is it? He's so young and strong."

"He has cerebral meningitis, and there's no cure." They clung together, sharing their shock and grief, each drawing strength from the other.

"We have to talk," Daddy said, wiping his eyes. "The officer who called asked where he's to be buried."

"I can't believe it," Mother sobbed. "But if it is true, of course we want him here at home where we can tend his grave. I can't think of life without our precious boy. Henry," she announced. "I'm going down to Corpus Christi to nurse him myself. I'll not let him go without a fight."

During WW II air travel for civilians was impossible.

They could be bumped by servicemen without notice, so Mother elected to take the train and was on board early the next morning.

Jim, a handsome ensign, loved every moment of flight training. The smart uniform, the discipline and drill suited his personality, but mostly he thrived on the sense of exhilaration and freedom characteristic of the natural-born flyer. He was at the top of his class.

One day he noticed a small swelling on his left eyelid. Within a few days, what had begun as a minor irritation became an enlarged lump. His whole eye was inflamed, and his head ached, but what the heck, it was only a sty and would pass. The end of the two-week "blind-flight" training session was just three days off, and there was no way he'd miss out by going to the hospital. He wore dark glasses to hide the redness and swelling and put in extra hours carefully memorizing every landing and take-off pattern until he could fly them in his sleep.

A little rocky but confident, he closed the hood of the Link trainer for the final exam and removed his glasses. His head throbbed and his eye was swollen shut, but when he gently pushed up the lid it stayed. He could see the instrument panel.

"Congratulations, Lampe," the instructor said, "It's the best exam I've ever given. Now go and have some fun over the weekend. Say, that's a nasty looking eye. Better get it checked out."

"I'll do that," he answered as he stepped from the trainer and shook hands.

By now the eye was on fire, and he knew he was running a fever because his pounding heart shook him with every beat. The corpsmen took his vitals–chills, temperature 104°, elevated blood pressure, nausea–and immediately rushed him to the main base hospital and called in the experts. That's when they contacted Mother and Daddy.

With every train stop Mother half expected a porter to

hand her a telegram saying Jim had died. Friends met her at the station and rushed her to the hospital, where Jim was in a coma but hanging on. A new drug for fighting acute infection was receiving rave notices in the world medical community, though not yet approved by the FDA. They had been waiting to try it on someone who was critically ill with absolutely no hope of recovery–Jim. Doctors flew in from all over the country to witness what happened to their guinea pig.

"Several times I came to," Jim recalled, "and when I looked up there was a ring of faces staring down at me. It certainly made me feel strange."

Exactly one week after Mother arrived he walked her to the main gate to kiss her good-bye! A miracle? Yes, you could say so. Starting with a small dose and increasing it to massive amounts, they administered their wonder drug to Jim, the first person in America to receive penicillin.

Mother was born on Christmas Day, so all festivities were in celebration of her birthday as well as Jesus'. One year we four girls decided we needed to do something special for her. She was in great demand by churches to talk about foreign missions. She was as popular with the Methodists and Baptists as she was with the Presbyterians. She had a fine wardrobe for speaking engagements, and she always looked wonderful except for her hair. She parted it on the side and pulled it back into a bun, but it was getting gray and a bit thin. We decided she needed a new hair style, a facial, and manicure. A whole day's pampering would be our Christmas gift.

I arranged for a stylist in the beauty shop of a major department store to take her in the morning with the rest to follow a luncheon break. I asked her three weeks ahead to hold the twenty-third of December open because she had a special date that was a surprise. I took her downtown and as we entered the salon told her what it was all about. She was thrilled, but when I announced that she was to have a haircut and styling she looked nervous.

"But what will Henry say?" she asked.

"Don't worry about Daddy. He'll love it." So she relaxed during the shampoo, the locks fell to the floor, and a permanent came next. The comb-out was fantastic. The facial and manicure sent her off to seventh heaven, the lunch was superb, and by 4:00 p.m. she was a new woman who looked refreshed and years younger. It was worth every dime and more. She seemed a little anxious as we walked up the stairs to the apartment, but when Daddy opened the door, he was beside himself with pleasure at the way she looked. My goodness, he strutted around like a young rooster. It was a very Merry Christmas.

Kedar's parents, grandparents, and Uncle Alvin Parker were interned by the Japanese in Shapei camp near Shanghai. Quite a few Japanese nationals were in the country, so an exchange of prisoners was arranged. The *Asama Maru* and the *Conte Verde* transported the Americans to Lorenzo Marcus, East Africa; the Japanese arrived on the *Gripsholm*. The transfer was carried out simultaneously. The ships were moored bow-to-stern on opposite sides of the dock. The Americans exited at the bows with the few bits and pieces they'd taken to camp and boarded the *Gripsholm* at the stern. The Japanese completed the circle, taking all kinds of baggage and household goods such as cameras, refrigerators, washing machines, metal filing cabinets, and furniture. The first meal served on the *Gripsholm* when they sailed on July 28 was a huge feast for the long-denied Americans, and not a few regretted overindulging.

On August 29, two months and 18,000 miles after leaving Shanghai, they entered New York harbor, singing, "The Star Spangled Banner." There was not a dry eye in the crowd.

The Japanese authorities permitted most to depart, but a few were held including Dad Bryan. He was released and returned to the States at the end of the war, none the worse for his experience and ready to go back to Shanghai as soon as possible.

Alvin Parker, Kedar's maternal uncle, worked for Standard Oil in China for many years. His wife, Reva, returned to the States when their two daughters were ready for school. After repatriation and checking in with headquarters in New York City, he went to Virginia to see his family but after a couple of weeks was ready to go back to work. He agreed to go to India by freighter, even though the war was raging in the Pacific, and enemy submarines were everywhere. His ship was torpedoed and sank, but he, the wife of the Hershey executive in India, and a Filipino cabin boy survived and were taken aboard the sub.

The Japanese must have thought that Alvin Parker was Filo Parker or a close relative because he received "special treatment." Filo was a top executive with Standard Oil, and evidently there was bad blood between him and the Japanese. Alvin and the cabin boy were taken on deck, their hands tied behind their backs and bayoneted before the ship submerged. The only reason we know this is that the cabin boy survived and was picked up by one of our vessels. The Hershey Company did everything possible to find the missing wife, but she vanished without a trace.

I was thrilled to receive Kedar's announcement that he'd soon be home. Every month in the South Pacific he filled out a fitness report, and at the bottom of the page was the question, "Are you willing to go to flight training?" He hadn't the slightest interest in flying, but if it got him back home, why not? He signed and within a week had orders to catch the next transport back to the States.

After a month's leave, he was to check in at Ottumwa, Iowa.

What joy! That stint was good for at least eighteen months, so life could begin again. God is good.

Uncle Bill was moderator of the General Assembly one year during the war and was very well known in Presbyterian circles. When he learned we were to go to Ottomwa, he got busy arranging for us to have a place to live. It's not a large city, and housing could have been a problem. Not to worry. A good friend was the Presbyterian pastor who would surely have helpful contacts, and he did. A wealthy parishioner was going on an extended holiday and would be glad to have us occupy her very nice home. God bless Uncle Bill!

Iowa winters were challenging, but being together as a family was all that mattered. Flight school students had classes when it was too cold or too snowy to fly, which was often. Navigation wasn't Kedar's favorite subject, and after a test he was sure he'd failed he'd come home saying, "Fleet Marine Force, here I come." But he did pass, and before long we were on our way to Corpus Christi, Texas, for the next phase.

We found a good two-door car, loaded it up, and headed south with a stopover in St. Louis to see Mother and Daddy. Long trips are tough on an active little boy, so we filled up the floor of the back seat with baggage and laid his crib mattress on top, giving him space to play and nap.

The day we arrived in Corpus Christi was hot and humid. Edwin was tired and cranky, so I broke my own rules and let him sit up in front with me. Because there was no air conditioning all the windows were down, and as I was searching for street names and a motel with a vacancy sign, he sat next to the door pushing and pulling buttons and levers. As we took a curve the door swung open with Edwin clinging to it! Holding on to him, I pulled the door in smoothly so as not to frighten him. Then clutching him tight I burst into tears.

"I'll pull off the road until you get your breath," Kedar said. He slowed and turned into the parking lot of an ice cream shop. I can highly recommend something sweet and cold as a remedy for jangled nerves and hot little boys.

Corpus was good. We found a nice house with a fenced-in back yard. The city was kind to service people, and Kedar got on with his flight training.

Out of the blue came a letter from my brother, Jim, who was assigned to San Diego, saying he and Kedar's younger sister, Peggy, were engaged! Several years earlier Peggy had married Roland Bowman and produced a son, Butch, born the same day as Edwin. She was living with her in-laws while Roland was overseas. When our boys were a few months old she and Butch came to St. Louis where we shared an apartment with my sister, Betty, and Gladys, one of her friends from work. Roland was the navigator on a B-17 that was shot down. Most of the crew landed safely, but not Roland. He was buried in France.

It was a terrible thing to see the shock waves hit Peggy, a slender little thing just barely twenty. She had no particular skills with which to support herself and the child. She was made of strong stuff, though, and got a typing job in one of the government offices. I kept house and took care of the boys. When news came that Kedar was coming home, she returned to Roland's family in San Diego. Before Jim left for California I gave him Peg's address and told him to look her up and take her out for some fun. Being a widow with a small child, she probably wasn't having a lot of that. We had no idea it would turn to romance but were so happy when it did. In a few months they were married with the Boman's blessing. Now our children would be double first cousins.

Kedar's grandparents settled in San Antonio after their return from Shanghai, and as soon as we had a long weekend we went to see them. Kedar was anxious to show off his wife and the next generation Bryan. Granddaddy was ninety years old and a dedicated Baptist missionary. He knew I was of the Presbyterian persuasion, so when we met, he held my hand and looked at me through the lower part of his bifocals.

"I know you are a good Christian girl, Frances, even though you're not a Baptist," he announced.

He was frail and suffered from spru, the irritation of the alimentary canal. He gulped bottle after bottle of Pepto-Bismo, but got little relief. After two more years of failing health he was confined to a hospital bed set up on the sun porch that looked out on their beautiful rose garden. One morning Grandmother Mamie was on her way to empty a basin after cleaning him up when he called out.

"Mamie, Mamie, come quickly." She rushed in to see him sitting up in bed, pointing to the window.

"Just look out there. The yard is filled with angels," he said. "They've come to take me home." With that he lay back and was gone.

When the war in Europe ended and full attention was given to the Pacific Theater, it was evident that the conflict would soon be over. At the least excuse flight schedules for the day were canceled. A program that should have taken Kedar six weeks to get his wings stretched into six months. He didn't give a hoot about flying anyway. By the time the surrender was signed in Japan, he had more than enough points to be discharged. He checked out, and we were on our way.

An interesting note: A Japanese official, Mr. Shigumitsu, was one of the signatories to Japan's unconditional surrender aboard the battleship *Missouri*. During Japan's occupation of Shanghai in 1939, he and Dad Bryan sat next to each other on a platform in some sort of ceremony. Dad left as soon as his duties as municipal advocate had been fulfilled. Fifteen minutes later a bomb went off under the platform, and Mr. Shigumitsu lost a leg.

Chapter 3

China

Once again Kedar took me to Mother and Daddy's home in St. Louis to stay until he found a job. There was just one place for him to go–New York City, where all the oil companies had their corporate headquarters. Standard Oil and Texaco were two big ones with which the Bryan family was well connected in Shanghai. Kedar talked about our future with Standard Oil, so when he called I was surprised to hear him say he'd signed on the dotted line with the Caltex Oil Company. After the war, Texaco joined with Standard Oil of California to form a new company that soon became larger than either of its parents. It would operate worldwide except in the continental United States and get its oil from Bahrain, Saudi Arabia.

From that moment on our lives changed. Our future was secure, Caltex would take care of all our needs, pay a good salary, and offer unlimited opportunities. Different from today, one joined a company presumably for life. After the uncertainties of the war years it was wonderfully freeing. All the gloom and worry of not knowing what would happen next vanished.

Following orientation in New York, Kedar went to Buffalo for on-the-job training in the regional office, which included pumping gas and changing license plates in sub-freezing weather. Edwin and I joined him there and were put up in a hotel efficiency apartment. It was a small, one-room unit with a kitchenette. A drop-down table seated me in the kitchen with the two of them in the main room. A Murphy bed swung out of the closet and filled the living room with just space enough to walk around it. For Edwin, the hotel provided a crib that fit snugly in one corner. Just six weeks made it okay, and it certainly constituted a learning experience.

Brother Jim got out of the navy when the war ended. He, Peggy, and Butch moved to Rolla, Missouri, where he entered engineering school. While they were there Peggy came down with double pneumonia and was too sick to care for Butch, so Mother brought him to us in Buffalo. She then returned to St. Louis and nursed Peggy back to health.

It was tight–Butch slept on the sofa–but great fun for the boys who played well together. Buffalo in the winter isn't fit for outdoor activities, but I had a lot of shopping to do in preparation for life in China, and the little guys accompanied me everywhere. In department stores we spent some time riding the escalators before I settled them quietly under a yard-goods table while I chose patterns and materials. More rides preceded visits to the linens and housewares departments. We took the city buses, but in those good old days stores delivered your purchases, praise the Lord.

One of Willard's assistants in the South Pacific was a man who came from Buffalo. When he heard we'd be there for a time, he suggested I give him a call. The young man was still in the service, but his mother most generously offered to take the boys and me to see Niagara Falls. What a treat! She picked us up in a prewar Buick, a luxury almost beyond measure, and we had a wonderful time. Returning to the city, she invited us to lunch too, and naturally I agreed. We went to a swanky restaurant complete with white tablecloths, live Hammond organ music, and waiters in swallow-tailed coats! I prayed that Edwin and Butch would behave.

I removed the boys' hats, mittens, and snow jackets before getting them into highchairs. Butch had a loud voice for a two-and-a-half-year-old, and anything he said could be heard for a mile around. "Mommy, Mommy, I want to pee," he suddenly announced. There was nothing to do but take care of his emergency, so I hustled him to the ladies' room. It was tiny, but we managed to squeeze in and shut the door. Then came the undressing process. Off came the snow pants, down went the trousers and underpants, and twisting around, I got him on the commode. He let out a little gas then proclaimed he was all done. I was in such a sweat that I was ready to flush him down the john. Everything went on again, and we made it back to the table. Fortunately Edwin behaved himself. Our hostess was most gracious.

On a beautiful spring day we had word that we were booked to sail from New York to Shanghai on the *Rattler*, a freighter with passenger accommodations for twelve. It was time to get our shots and passports and finish packing. Peg was well recovered, so we all returned to St. Louis for a visit before starting out on our great adventure.

A short stay in New York City allowed time for shopping at John Wanamaker's for furniture and appliances to be shipped as soon as possible. We then boarded the *Rattler* with nine others headed for the same destination. Among them was the Hess family, new members of the China Inland Mission. Their little Cathy, a godsend, was Edwin's age. They spent countless hours playing, listening to stories, and "swimming" in a big washtub provided for their entertainment.

The thirty-one-day trip took us down the east coast, through the Panama Canal, up the west coast, past the

Aleutian Islands, across to Japan, and finally up the Whang Pu River to Shanghai.

The river's muddy water stained the Pacific Ocean miles from shore, and as we entered it Kedar's juices began to flow. He was coming home! All day long we snaked upstream between low banks and rice paddies until we tied up to a buoy in midstream several miles below the city. Shanghai was jammed with river traffic, and we had to wait our turn. For three days we swung on the hook, and Kedar was getting impatient; but he was happy. It smelled right; it felt right. Vendors came alongside in little bumboats. I bought a beautifully carved camphor chest the size of a small trunk for five dollars. Kedar was sure it would warp and fall apart, but it didn't. Seamen were more interested in Red and Black Label Scotch Whisky at ten dollars a bottle. They carefully examined every one before shelling out the cash, but when they opened them they found they had purchased strong tea instead of booze. Were they mad!

When the engines began to throb we knew it was our turn. We packed up and were ready to go. On deck Kedar pointed out places he remembered. There were no docks, so again we tied up to a buoy, and lighters came to take us ashore. Several Caltex officials turned out to greet us, took us to the Cathay Hotel, and handed us a long schedule of hosts and hostesses who'd invited us to lunches, dinners, and cocktail parties. Things were looking up.

Within a week we moved to an apartment on the fourth floor of Hamilton House in the midst of downtown Shanghai. A few doors down the hall were Frances and Jim Voss, a new man in the legal department. Both apartments were small–one bedroom with bath, a large room for everything else, and a kitchen with a closet-size room for the servant. They assured us it was only until the company could find appropriate housing in a residential area.

Almost immediately we were involved in the social whirl that included several cocktail and dinner parties a week. Being the youngest and newest on the block, we weren't expected to reciprocate with the lavish entertaining for which the senior staff had an allowances. Kedar decided his favorite drink was the martini. It didn't bother me at first. He never got drunk or unsteady on his feet, but when he announced he'd had twelve in one evening, a little bell went off somewhere in the back of my head; I felt uneasy in the pit of my stomach. In the Bryan home there had always been liquor available, enjoyed while entertaining but never a daily routine. I wondered why he was drinking so much.

Kedar never drank when we were first married. Everything changed when we went to China in 1946.

We kept a variety of liquors on hand to serve when we returned dinner invitations. At first Kedar imbibed only when there were guests, but it wasn't long until he was having a couple before and after dinner, ending with a nightcap before bed.

At first I told myself he was just doing what all the others did, and it was nothing to worry about. He was always up and bright-eyed in the morning. He loved his work and could hardly wait to get to the office. He was never abusive, always affectionate and kind, so what was the big deal? Nevertheless, no amount of telling myself how unfounded my fears were could stem my growing apprehension. There was very little written about alcoholism in those days, so I had no solid information to help me understand what was going on. That warning bell kept getting louder, and the knot in my stomach was a constant presence.

Although I grew increasingly uncomfortable with Kedar's drinking, we didn't talk about it. Instead we played little games. He developed routines for getting an additional drink or two without my notice–he thought!

Being extra solicitous and talkative was a sure sign of what he was up to. I'd quickly fix something to eat, hoping it would slow him down.

While we were still living in the Hamilton House, one morning after an evening of heavy drinking I was so angry at him I didn't say a word as we ate breakfast. Edwin, who was four, looked from one of us to the other and finally said, "Daddy's been a bad boy." He was obviously upset by our discord, and my heart ached to think how this precious little fellow could be hurt by something I was unable to control.

Kedar's family home was out on Columbia Circle. Dad Bryan was stationed in Nanking, serving as a special advisor to Gen. George C. Marshall. Soon after our arrival he suggested we move into their house, at least until Mother Bryan came in four months. We were more than happy to get Edwin out of that dark, dreary hotel and into a spacious house with a yard and faithful old servants.

We took over the two bedrooms and bath on the third floor, and I began learning all about living with customs and servants totally different from anything I'd known before.

In Korea the servants didn't live in; here they did. We spoke their language in Korea, but in Shanghai all the servants spoke pidgin English, which you could pick up easily. In a few days it became second nature.

"Kumshaw" was a tip for services rendered, but "squeeze" was about 10 percent added by servants when they shopped for you, buying food and household needs. It was expected and accepted unless the servant got greedy.

Most good housing was bought up during the war and held by citizens of neutral countries such as Switzerland. They were available for key money, depending on size and location. The flat Caltex found for us had two bedrooms with bath, living-dining room, a small kitchen, and servant's quarters for $10,000 in U.S. currency. That was just for the key. Thereafter we had the privilege of paying $500 a month rent, which was at the lower end of the scale. Larger places for senior members cost $25,000 and up.

Fortunately the company paid all housing, transportation, medical, and schooling expenses. Even so, Kedar's salary of $250 a month that would have been fine in the States was scarcely enough to survive on in Shanghai. Prices were crazy. Anything imported was as high as an angry cat's back (coffee was four dollars a pound), and local goods were scarce. Years of war and Japanese occupation left the country stripped of everyday essentials.

Dad Bryan came down from Nanking for a visit soon after we arrived, and again a couple of months later. I was in the early stages of pregnancy with Anne, so he was surprised to see I'd lost weight. I wasn't trying to diet, but food was so expensive that we ate quite a bit less than we might have. Because he was with the Department of State he had access to the commissary. He handed me a list of what was available and asked me to check off the things we needed most. What a boon. We dined like royalty.

The cocktail party provided another means of survival. Every week we attended several, and I made good use of the bounty of small chow trays as waiters circulated with all sorts of treats. At first it was hard to be the only nondrinker at the party. I drank gallons of V8 juice and once in a while ginger ale, which looked like whisky-soda.

One of several things I loved about Shanghai was that fresh flowers were dirt cheap. Every weekend I filled the apartment with them.

After a few months enough people complained about prices that the company heard our cries and gave us a $450 high-cost-of-living (HCL) allowance and made it retroactive. What a relief!

One day Mother called to tell me about her next-door

neighbor's great misfortune. Tom Cummings was the manager of an American bank and was responsible for entertaining a visiting VIP who was on a Far Eastern inspection trip. The bank staff, too, complained bitterly about the high cost of living and asked that their HCL be raised to the level of other American companies. One of the major purposes of the executive's trip was to look into the problem.

Tom wanted to make a good impression, so he asked all bank employees to donate food from their precious stash for one big cocktail and dinner party. The guest was royally wined and dined. On his departure bank officials congratulated themselves on their fine hospitality, hoping the gentleman would remember their kindness when he returned home and grant their request. They probably should have fed him rice and tea. The low blow came the following month when his report was published. He recommended a cut in their HCL; it was quite obvious they were living very much better in Shanghai than were the hard-working stiffs back home!

Edwin was a bright little boy and a picture with his blond hair and dark brown eyes. He was slow to speak, but when he did he skipped baby talk. Pidgin English rolled off his tongue after we went to Woosee for a weekend and left him with the Vosses. Jim had him chattering a mile a minute saying things like, "How fashion? This side have got; other side no have got." When we moved into Grosvener Gardens, the amah regularly took him to the private park that was completely surrounded by three-story buildings. Other amahs were there with their charges, and his vocabulary increased.

In postwar Shanghai there were no maternity clothes. When word got out that I was expecting, I became the recipient of "loaners" from other Caltex wives all over the country who'd just had babies. Thus I had some of my own dresses and quite a few from others. Since the hospital had nothing for newborns, I provided everything needed–nightgowns, diapers, caps, and blankets. There was almost no heat in the hospital, and in January it was cold; so it wasn't until I got her home that I was able to unwrap Anne and made sure she had all her fingers and toes! As soon as she arrived I returned with thanks the dresses I'd borrowed and let it be known that I had some to share. They made several trips before I needed them again. It made me feel like some sort of pioneer.

For O.B. care, Caltex suggested I go to Dr. Litton, a German Jew who'd been in Japanese-occupied China during the war. It was good that I liked him because there weren't many choices. The only thing I questioned was his opinion that if cows had their young without anesthetic, why should women need it? He was concerned that our car was a jeep, and Shanghai's rough paving made for a bumpy ride. Toward the end he refused to be responsible if I went into premature labor if I didn't stop riding it, but I didn't.

Pregnancy with Anne was a joyful experience. I felt well, life was an exciting adventure, Kedar loved his work, and Edwin was a special pleasure. I had a healthy appetite and got as big as a barn. With Edwin the doctor made sure I kept my weight down, but Dr. Litton didn't seem to mind–you know, cows and women.

Two weeks before my due date I was restless and couldn't sit still. For relief I got down on my hands and knees and scrubbed two nine-by-twelve rugs. That evening my back ached like a boil, so Kedar took me out for a little ride. It felt wonderful when I pressed against the seat back. When we finally got to bed the first light contractions began. At eleven o'clock, Dr. Litton checked me into the Country Hospital, but things were not moving rapidly. He, Kedar, and I all had a good night's sleep. The next morning they went off to their offices, and I was left in the hands of Miss Chun, the OB nurse.

She was a precious little person. You couldn't put the tip of your finger between the pock marks on her face; it was a solid mass of scars. I remembered mother's conversation with a young woman in Korea before the vaccine was available. "We don't count our children until they have lived through the smallpox," she had said. It was such a deadly scourge that most infected infants died. Miss Chun's face was so disfigured that a marriage broker would probably be hard-pressed to find a family willing to accept her as a daughter-in-law.

Early in the afternoon I was tired of sitting around and had read every article in my *Reader's Digest*, and went down the hall to see a friend who was recovering from surgery. On the way back everything suddenly moved into high gear. Gasping for breath, I held up the walls as I staggered back to my room and rang for Miss Chun.

I was given "twilight sleep" with Edwin, which kept me semi-conscious. I really didn't know much of what was going on. Being wide-awake this time was a whole new ball game, and I found it both startling and amazing. Miss Chun checked me over and took me straight into the delivery room. She called Dr. Litton then did her best to slow things down.

"Breathe through your mouth," she kept telling me. "Don't push." I couldn't help it. It wasn't as if I had a choice–I clamped my teeth and pushed. It hurt like sin– but it was also irresistible and fascinating. Just as I thought I'd burst I looked up to see the doctor walk toward us in his three-piece, brown-tweed suit. The nurse slipped surgical gloves on his outstretched hands just before he reached down and took Anne as she made her headlong entry into the world. What a relief! What a wonderful sense of accomplishment! I watched as he cleaned out her mouth and gave her a sharp smack on her little bottom. Oh, my goodness but she was in good voice. I was proud of us. We had the sweetest little boy in the world and now a healthy daughter. Could life be any better?

Surely God is good. I began to feel very sleepy.

Kedar was waiting in the hall. What a pity that in those days they didn't allow any but hospital staff in the delivery room. He could hardly wait to hold his baby daughter, but was more than a little surprised to see her with a squashed-over nose, pointed head, and very red face.

"Don't worry," I assured him. "In a few days everything will be in place. She's just had a very rough journey, and newborns are usually a sad looking lot." Her nose straightened up; the top of her head rounded out and was adorned with soft brown hair with a hint of red. We watched as her blue eyes changed to dark brown, just like his. Our little Frances Anne Bryan was a beauty.

During the week I was in Country Hospital, Edwin spent most of his days at the Bryans house in Columbia Circle. Mother said she heard Edwin talking to Ah Ling and was much amused at his trying to correct the No.1 boy's English. Finding it difficult to pronounce the "w" sound, he called Edwin "Oven."

"Must call me Edwin," he said. "My name no belong Oven. Belong Edwin. Must call me Edwin. Must!"

"Yes, yes, little master. I try," Ah Ling answered, patting him on the shoulder.

They chuckled over the way he picked up names under discussion at mealtimes. The Hon. Monette B. Davis was the U.S. consul general in Shanghai. The Davises were regular guests in the Bryan home. Although Edwin was just four years old, he seemed to know which names were important. One morning Mother saw Edwin walking up and down the hall, hands clasped behind his back, as he said over and over in a very serious voice, "Monette, Monette B., Monette, Monette B.," with a strong emphasis on the "B."

With Anne's arrival Mother Bryan, Anne, and I were referred to as Old Missy *(lao-tai-tai)*, Young Missy *(tai-tai)*, and Small Missy *(shaw-goon-yang)*.

Edwin was much pleased with his little sister and wanted to "help" her. He patted her often, and put his face up close to hers to tell her secrets. Several times I found him trying to feed her things he thought were special, such as bits of nut from almond roaca candy!

I wanted to breast-feed her but didn't have enough milk for a sparrow. The amah said I could use a Chinese remedy which was sure to produce a lot of milk–pig's feet and peanut soup! I thanked her for the suggestion, but no, I didn't think I'd try that one. Now I wish I had; I'm told by Asian friends it really does work.

When Anne was about eight months old and cutting upper teeth, her gums were red and swollen. Kedar and I got home at about eleven o'clock one evening after a dinner party and were met by the amah, who said she couldn't quiet Anne down. I found bloody saliva on her sheet because she'd been grinding her sore gums with her lower teeth. Poor little thing! I rocked her, talked and sang to her; but she was having a hard time of it. I decided to try something I'd heard about that might help and gave her a bit of brandy. What a face she made, but with a little warm water from a bottle she dozed off and we all got to sleep.

The next day I called Dr. Milford, our family physician, and told him what I'd done.

"Not a bad idea," he said. "How much did you give her?"

"About a tablespoon, I think."

"Well, okay, but probably a half-teaspoon would have been enough."

"Thanks. The next time I'll know!"

It was fun being Kedar Bryan's wife in Shanghai. How he loved his hometown–the smells, sounds, hustle and bustle. Being Bob Bryan's daughter-in-law wasn't too shabby either.

Before World War II, Dad Bryan was municipal advocate of the International Settlement of Shanghai, which was the equivalent of attorney general. Each of the participating nations–among them the United States, England, France, and Germany–had its own court where citizens were tried and justice administered. Dad Bryan was the only one who knew Chinese well enough to argue cases in both American and Chinese courts.

Kedar didn't mind being introduced as Bob Bryan's son, but later when we were in Korea (my territory), he strongly objected to being identified as Fran Lampe's husband!

The city hadn't changed much since he left for college in 1940 except that it was rather shabby and worn-looking after years of wartime neglect. He took me everywhere, showing me places he remembered and enjoyed. Often we'd stop for a meal on the street.

"The best food in Shanghai's right here," he claimed. Pushcarts were everywhere selling rice, soup, and tea. His favorite was a heaping bowl of fried rice topped with a fried egg and generously doused with soy sauce. I wondered about the community chopsticks in a tin nailed to one of the uprights.

"You mean to tell me you use those things?" I asked, pointing to the dusty, fly-blown utensils.

"They're not all that sanitary, I know, so this is what you do," he said as he swished his around in the pot of boiling soup. I did the same, and somehow we managed to survive.

One evening on the way back to Hamilton House we passed a high, curving garden wall topped with tile. The street wasn't well lighted, but we could see a dozen or more women standing around in pairs.

"What are they doing there," I asked. "Is this a bus stop? I don't see any signs."

"No," he answered, "Those are ladies of the evening. The young one is the girl for hire, and the older one is there to bargain for her and receive the money before she departs with the customer." Every time we passed that way there were at least a few waiting for business.

Late in 1946 Mother Bryan arrived from the States after a stopover in Japan. Wherever she went she created quite a stir because she was a dead ringer for Mrs. Douglas McArthur!

Dad Bryan was able to retrieve a few pieces of furniture taken from the house after they were imprisoned by the Japanese. He found the large mirror that hung above the dining room buffet in a Japanese bath, and other pieces turned up in nearby houses. The most amazing thing of all was that a Japanese family took their beautiful Persian carpets, kept them cleaned and mildew-free all during the war, and when the house was once again claimed by Dad Bryan, returned them to him!

Ah Ling, a playmate of Dad's when he was growing up in the Baptist compound, became his number-one boy when he arrived back in Shanghai after university and law school. When the war ended he was there to take up his duties as soon as Dad returned. A good servant is a treasure beyond price, and Ah Ling was the best. Others came and went, but he was as much part of the family as any of us. What Mother couldn't bring from the States she was able to find or have made in Shanghai, and soon the place was humming with activity.

A luxury easily afforded by most American women was the weekly visit of Mary, the nail amah. Her time with Mother was a sacred appointment that would not be changed. Right on time she showed up on her bicycle to spend at least an hour giving her a manicure, pedicure, massage, and scalp rub.

Anyone who ever had servants knows that nothing is secret for long. No matter how well you think you're hiding something, they have a way of finding out, and it's in their nature to share interesting tidbits. Mary always had her cup of tea in the kitchen before plying her trade, so by the time she arrived in Mother's boudoir she was well armed with all the week's gossip–who was fighting with whom; who was sleeping around; who was drinking too much; who got a raise in pay, and who didn't. It was well to remember that the walls had eyes and ears.

Neighborhood servants pitched in and helped each other when there was a big party. The good china moved from place to place as did the silver and crystal. It was not unusual to be entertained by a friend and find yourself eating with your own cutlery. The number-one servant was entirely responsible for the family property. One day Mother was checking the flatware and found a salad fork that looked a little strange. She called Ah Ling to ask why it was different from the others.

"I so solly, Missie," he said. "One day fliend have one big party and I take silver, but when come home I savvy no have got twelve piece salad fork, so I catche one man can makie this thing."

He lost much face and probably spent a month's pay to replace the missing fork, perfect testimony to his honesty and loyalty.

Caltex hired a mix of married men and bachelors. In pre-World War days and for several years after, single men were forbidden to marry native women. Foreign society was strictly separated from local citizens, so marriage between them caused endless problems. Chinese weren't permitted to join clubs, where most of the social life took place. Getting U.S. citizenship for them presented huge problems, so it became a hard-and-fast rule that if you married a local woman, you were finished–packed up and sent home. One of the more promising young men who went to the Philippines broke the rule and was gone.

In Shanghai we had several bachelors who seemed to lead a high old life, but eventually they married young women from the States and settled down. One of them was the still-single John Van Tyle. Every now and then he'd entice one of our husbands to go bar-hopping with him after work on Friday. He then felt guilty about keeping them out late and rewarded the wives with pearls.

Postwar China abounded with treasures left by the Japanese. Pearls of all grades were available for a song. Van bought up a lot of "signet" pearls of high quality that were pierced on one side for setting. After a late night of drinking he presented me with one, and it almost made me forget how mad I was.

In his second year he finally talked Marjorie into coming out to be his wife, and from then on he was very much a married man.

Bill Connell was a good-looking blond, a real heartbreaker. His girl back home was a Pan Am flight attendant, who finally agreed to meet him in Hawaii for their wedding. In the days before jet planes, the trip was long and tedious with several refuelings along the way. At every stop the guys in Shanghai made sure he received a telegram wishing him well but reminding him that it wasn't too late; he could still change his mind and not go through with it. Several more messages reached him in Honolulu urging him to reconsider taking such a serious step, but he got in the last word with his answer: "Sacrifice made at the altar at high noon today. Bill"

Sunday tiffin at Mother and Dad's was always a treat. Several times a year they invited friends from their Shapei prison camp days for tsaw-mee, a soft-fried Chinese-noodle dish that was second to none. Ah Ling made it perfectly with the noodles just a little crisp, generously dressed with bits of pork, chopped cabbage, onions, mushrooms, and other things I didn't recognize but thought I shouldn't ask about, and dressed with lots of walnuts. That was it, just a huge platter piled high and loaded to the rim passed around and around until we couldn't eat another bite. The cups of Chinese tea and beer glasses were never empty, and the meal was topped off with fresh fruit.

The food was only secondary to the guests and conversation. During World War II they'd spent many months crowded together in Shapei Camp under the watchful eye of Japanese guards, yet to hear their talk laced with gales of laughter, you'd think they were the best years of their lives. And indeed one couple claimed they were. They met in camp, were married, and had their first child before repatriation on the *Gripsholm*. Although they had almost no privacy, the food was poor, and the future uncertain, they both looked back on those days as a special gift.

Most stories began with "Remember when?" One told of the wonderful care by Chinese friends on the outside. They noted the schedule of guards walking the fence, and when it was safe, passed many things through. Usually they got away with it, but not always.

One day a Trappist monk had just received a basket of eggs when he saw a guard approaching. Trying to hide the treasure, he moved to a laundry line nearby and took down lady's bras and panties, laying them over his arm to hide the basket. But it didn't work, and the guard arrested him. As punishment he was put in solitary confinement for thirty days! He didn't let on to the authorities, but nothing could have pleased him more than to be able to keep his vow of silence for a whole month.

All adults were required to do cooking, cleaning, and grounds maintenance. Mother told of endless hours going over the rice, grain by grain, to get rid of worms and sand. All eggshells were carefully hoarded and crushed to powder to feed the little ones. It was their only source of calcium.

Some who were teachers undertook classes for schoolage children. Others formed an orchestra and organized Bible study groups and a lecture series. Doctors took care of their health, performed minor surgeries, and delivered babies.

One very important part of the day was the beginning of the evening meal. Any special news was announced at that time. Some came through the fence, and the rest was from two forbidden short-wave radios hidden in camp that kept the inmates informed on the progress of the war.

One June night they were all asked to be quiet as the news was extra special. Keeping as normal a voice as possible, the spokesman announced, "Allied troops have made a successful landing on the coast of France." The words were no more than out of his mouth than everybody broke forth in cheers and shouts of joy. Hearing the noise, the Japanese guards rushed up to the open windows and pointed their riffles with fixed bayonets at them.

"What's all the noise about? Calm down or we'll shoot," they said.

"No, no, don't be worried," a man answered. "The food is so outstanding tonight that we are all cheering." It was just the same old wormy rice and clear cabbage soup, but that was enough to satisfy the guards, and they went away.

After Dad Bryan returned to the States at the end of the war, he was healthy though a little thin. His teeth needed attention, but on checking the results of his physical exam, a State Department officer remarked, "Bryan, the only way we can get rid of you is stand up against a wall and shoot you!"

With his job with the municipal council gone, Dad was looking for employment and accepted a position with the Department of State to go to Nanking as a special advisor to the U.S. ambassador, Gen. George C. Marshall. He was one of twelve on the team.

The mandate from President Truman was, "Find a way to bring peace and accommodation between the Chinese Nationalists and Communists." All sorts of talks were arranged and proposals taken to each side, but there was no way either would cooperate. Knowing China's history, Dad Bryan was convinced it wasn't possible to satisfy the mandate. "Oh yes," said all the others, "There must be a way." He felt it was a waste of his time and the U.S. government's money, so he resigned, moved back to Shanghai, to enter a partnership with Cornell Franklin to practice law.

One morning soon after it was announced that Ambassador Marshall was going back to the States, Dad got a call from Nanking asking if he could come for lunch. General Marshall's plane was there to pick him up and would return him later in the day. Naturally Dad accepted.

The general and all his original advisors were there. When they were seated around the table, Marshall thanked them for their hard work and dedication to the task, but it had failed. Raising his glass to Dad Bryan he said, "Bob, you were the only one who truly understood. You were right, and the rest of us were wrong."

We were happy in Shanghai but were delighted when in the spring of 1947 Caltex decided to move us to Peking, where Kedar would be the station manager.

We were moving again, but this time was easy–it was on the company. I took care of our clothes and personal things, and the packers did the rest. After the living-room furniture was shipped to the warehouse, they brought in a huge pile of straw and dumped it in the middle of the room. Anything breakable was set aside by one of the eight packers who worked sitting on the floor. He placed a big handful of straw between each of several stacked plates, for example, and taped them together. He then made a rope of straw and wound it around and around them to make a large ball.

They worked quickly. As I watched one of the men finish up a bundle, with a big smile he bounced it on the floor. I gasped to see him do that to my good china, but it all came through without so much as a crack or chip.

They were good, and they knew it. Because everything was to be shipped, it was a trick to figure out how to keep out just enough of the essentials to use before we moved to a hotel for the last few days. After several more moves I could do it in my sleep.

Kedar thought it would be a great adventure to take the coastal steamer to Tintsin, but I wasn't so sure. Cabins were cramped and without private baths. The small ships were notoriously overloaded, and if we got into a storm it would be ghastly, particularly with little children. As many doubts as I had, he prevailed, and we set sail for points north.

Jim and Frances Voss came to see us off. When we found our tiny cabin with four bunks so close together that only one person at a time could stand, they offered to take four-month-old Anne and bring or send her to us after we got settled. I didn't have to think twice about it, and handed her and her bag over to them, blessing them all the way to Taku Bar, the point of transit into Tintsin.

Praise the Lord, it was only a twenty-four-hour voyage because it was miserable. There was no air conditioning. Fresh air should have come from a porthole but we couldn't open it. The throbbing engine and strong smell of diesel oil along with a constant rolling from one side to the other did bad things to many stomachs, attested to by bathroom floors awash with vomit. The dining room was filthy, but at least it was on the upper deck, had fresh air, and served lots of hot tea. All during the trip I blessed the Vosses for their kindness.

We had a day's visit in Tintsin then with all our worldly goods took the train to Peking. Love that city. It wasn't much changed from when I visited in 1940 before leaving for college. Our house was at 7 Nan Ho Yen.

We wanted the transition to be as easy as possible for Edwin by making sure his and Anne's bedroom was settled first. When he saw their own beds and all their toys were there, he felt right at home and was ready to explore the neighborhood.

It was one of the nicest places we ever lived. Several years earlier the well-known Shoemakers bought up a cluster of houses and renovated them to satisfy foreign tastes. They kept the striking Chinese decor but added large closets and modernized the bathrooms and the kitchens. Opening between the living room and dining room was a moon door framed in black terrazzo made to look like marble and the same was true of the fireplace. The whole side of the long living room was made of glass doors covered with wooden latticework. I was mighty glad I didn't have to do the dusting! The doors opened onto to a full length flagstone patio, two steps above the postage-stamp-size garden. A moon-door barbecue in the back wall was sheltered by a tile-roofed tinge-za (small pavilion) supported by red lacquer posts. Our bedrooms and bath were off one end of the living room. The dining room and kitchen were at the opposite end of the house, and a guest suite adjoined the dining room. The children's and the guest rooms extended beyond the living room wall by twelve feet, giving the house the shape of a shallow U. There were black terrazzo floors throughout that were heated in the winter by warm-water pipes. The garden was completely surrounded by a high, gray-brick wall topped with tile. The other side formed the back wall of the house next door. Our barbecue and their fireplace shared the same chimney.

Two weeks after our arrival a friend coming to Peking for a visit brought our Anne to us, a pink-and-white, sweet-smelling bundle of little girl. It was such a joy to have her in my arms again, our precious daughter!

We weren't even settled when we saw we'd made a big mistake in bringing the amah with us. We didn't realize the language barrier she'd face and lack of community. It wasn't fair to her, so we bought a ticket and sent her home. Through friends we found an excellent replacement. We took over our predecessor's wonderful cook, wash amah, and gardener.

Anyone who has had to learn a foreign language to survive will appreciate my predicament. In Shanghai it was easy. Oh, there were adjustments and new customs to learn, but you can always get along if you can communicate. Kedar, born and raised in Shanghai, was fluent in the dialect, but even that wasn't necessary. The educated Chinese spoke better English than I did, and pidgin English or just pidgin was acceptable and understood by all. In a couple of weeks you can learn the lingo. If you forget how something was said, you'd wing it.

In Peking, the land of the Mandarins, it was a different story. Hardly anyone spoke English, and Pidgin was unthinkable. In Shanghai I could call up my in-laws when I had a question. Here I was left to my own devices, and Kedar was absolutely no help. Here they didn't even try to understand that down-river Shanghai talk!

I had a cook, baby amah, gardener, and wash amah. I couldn't talk to any of them. I had a husband, two little children, and a beautiful house to manage; but I couldn't make myself understood. Frustration! Fortunately the servants had worked for foreigners and were well trained. Things muddled along for a while, and I was not without my own resources. If I couldn't find a picture, I made gestures, drew sketches, or acted out what I wanted to communicate. Chinese seemed an impossible language, but all the other foreigners were learning it, so I took the plunge. On the recommendation of a friend I contracted with a scholarly gentleman to teach me. I had no interest in learning to read or write, only to speak well enough to get along with the servants and shopkeepers.

His name was Mr. Woo. He spoke English flawlessly, but he wouldn't say a word. Three days a week he came in the morning for an hour. He sat at one end of the sofa and I at the other. He started with *woh*, touching the end of his nose, *nee,* pointing to me, and *tah*, indicating another person. I understood, "I, you, he," I repeated after him until I had the tones just right. Next he said *wohmen, neemen, tahmen*, indicating we, you, they. Again I repeated after him until he was satisfied that my tones were correct. Add a *dee* to any of the above, and you have the possessive case.

It was great fun. At every lesson I had lists of words I needed to learn and discovered a very important tool. *Jugga shur shumma*, What is this? I'd point to an object or picture; he'd pronounce the word. As I learned phrases and sentences the grammar came naturally. In three months I could chatter along comfortably in the bazaar, bargaining for the best price. Talking with the servants became second nature. What a great sense of satisfaction to understand and to be understood!

Necessity helped me to listen and pick up important words. One warm day at the club pool, a woman sunning next to the children and me needed another towel. As one of the stewards passed she called out to him, holding up her towel, *"Boy, hyo-ee-gah."* He nodded and soon returned with her request. Good, I thought, *hyo* means "again," and must also mean "another." I added that to my vocabulary and it stuck.

Still there were words I simply couldn't retain. One such was the verb "to go," *(tso-ba)*. It was a strong command, more like "get out of here," or "scram."

One bitterly cold day I was walking of the Dung An Market when I noticed a woman making the final arrangement to a pile of tangerines on her pushcart. She had them stacked attractively in a perfect pyramid. As I approached I saw her toddler on the opposite side of the cart reach for one of them. He got his little fingers around it and pulled. It anchored the whole stack. Down they came, rolling and scattering all over the street.

The woman and I rushed to gather them up before they were squashed by cars and trucks. All the while she was shouting things at her child that were not in my vocabulary. When the last one was rescued she grabbed him by one arm and administered several good whacks to his padded bottom, scolding, *"Tso-ba, tso-ba, tso-ba"*.

For lack of use, I have forgotten most of my Chinese, but *tso-ba* will be mine forever.

In contrast to Shanghai, Peking had an air of elegance yet felt like a small, friendly town. The old city walls were huge, and the massive gates impressive. The major thoroughfares were wide and tree-shaded. Legations and consulates of most countries were in one section, complete with guards at the gates. Our U.S. Marines looked splendid in their handsome uniforms. Several Western-run hotels brought a touch of class, but most of the life of the city was in the *hootungs*, narrow streets and alleyways.

Our residence at #7 Nan Ho Yen was about a half-mile from the U.S. Consulate. A number of families with children Edwin's age lived on their compound, and he was frequently invited to come over for the morning or afternoon to play. We had just the one car that was kept at the office for business during the day, but that was no problem. Two doors down from us was an Italian restaurant, near which rickshaws could almost always be found. A servant called one, bargained for a price, paid the fare, and sent Edwin off. There was never a worry about anything happening to him. It was perfectly safe, but just for my peace of mind, the hostess at the other end called when he arrived. He was either sent back the same way or delivered by a consulate car.

Ever since Edwin was two years old he'd had regular bouts of tonsillitis and enlarged adenoids, but we were advised to wait until he was at least five before having them removed. One such episode occurred in Buffalo before we left for Shanghai. His temperature reached 106° F. That was scary, so we finally got it done in Peking after his fifth birthday. From then on he was completely free of sore throats and earaches.

It was interesting that the Catholic hospital was careful to observe local customs so as not to offend anyone. There is a belief that one must be complete with all body parts at the time of death, or the soul would be barred from entering heaven. As I waited to see Edwin after surgery, an attendant brought me his tonsils on a piece of gauze. I wondered what a Chinese mother would do with them.

I enjoyed all of the servants, but I cherished Dah-sa-foo, the cook. He loved his work and his food, to look at the size of him. Nothing made him happier than to be told to prepare for a dinner party for twelve or a buffet for forty or fifty.

In north China noodles were the staple rather than rice, and he preferred the ones he made to those coming from the market.

Our kitchen had a gas stove but also two of the traditional large iron Chinese cooking pots built into a brick-and-mud platform at one end of the room. Some sort of soup was always bubbling in one, and usually water in the other. Every few days Dah-sa-foo made noodles, and he put on quite a show. The table where he rolled out the dough was a good six feet away from the cook pot. After getting it just the right thickness he sliced it with his chopper, grabbed up the ends, rolled the dough in the flour on the board, whacked it once before giving it a quick stretch, put the ends together, and pulled them off. With one motion he then tossed the noodles into the pot of boiling soup without ever leaving his place, and he never missed! He loved to show off.

Shopping in Peking was extraordinary. The Japanese who had occupied the coastal cities of China from 1937 to the end of the war were all shipped back home after the surrender. They left behind huge quantities of their treasures, which soon showed up in shops and markets.

A Tale of Two Bamboos

There were pearls of all grades for a song, silk kimonos, obis, and paintings galore. Add all that to the treasures already there, and you had a shopper's paradise.

After WWII everybody was starved for quality merchandise, and we had it in Peking. Many of the company people our age had few choices for vacation spots, but we had a guestroom suite and were soon receiving friends from Shanghai. It was like a glorious feast, one couple after another.

Big-ticket items were hand-knotted rugs, furniture, and furs. You purchased those in reputable establishments, but most of the rest was found down the little *hootungs*. There was one for each type of merchandise, Flower Street, Jewelry Street, Silver Street, Silk Street, and on and on. The shops had much same choices, so I asked around and found one really good one in each category.

When I took friends out I told them, "You can shop anywhere you want to, but I've checked them out and recommend the ones on this list. If you want to save yourselves a lot of time, try them first. You'll get a fair price, but you certainly should bargain."

One of my favorites was #10 Jade Street. Kedar gave me a beautiful jade ring set with diamonds when Anne was born, and at this shop I found a filigree bracelet set with five pieces of jade about the size of the one in my ring. I thought they'd be wonderful together, but the price was way out of range, so I just enjoyed looking at it. There were prize pieces such as the jade hair ornament carved in the shape of a dragon for a mere eight thousand dollars and a perfectly matched strand of nine-millimeter jade beads for thirty-five thousand dollars. Mr. Chen supplied Asian artifacts to Gump's of San Francisco, so they probably ended up there. Because I brought him so many customers he gave them very good prices.

The exchange rate was going crazy, but we had an answer for that too. We guaranteed all checks written by our friends on U.S. banks. Mr. Chen could send them to his own account in the States or cash them with Kedar at the street rate, (we didn't call it the black market rate) when he needed Chinese dollars. You never kept cash around or it might be worth half the amount the next day!

Our big purchase was *whang wha lee* (rosewood) furniture. For years blackwood was preferred, but when an American woman discovered rosewood tucked away in obscure places and was able to get it out and market it to lucky people like us, it became a whole new industry. It is the color of natural mahogany and so hard that it had to be put together with dowels and glue. Like ironwood, it was too heavy to float. It was very old, had beautiful flowing lines, and minimal carving. I melted when I saw it. We bought an artist's display table, just the length of a scroll. It was made of a single log split in half so the knots on one side were mirrored on the other. It could accommodate only ten, so we also purchased eighteen-inch-wide small tables to add at each end to seat twelve. Two altar tables served as buffets and twelve Chinese chairs filled out the set. Additionally we bought a *whang wha lee* coffee table, a real treasure that nothing could damage.

Silver was dirt-cheap. For Christmas Kedar bought me a set of twelve goblets engraved with the family crest and a complete tea service–a huge tray, pots for tea, coffee, and hot water, a waste bowl, cream and sugar, all engraved with the crest. Stone marten furs were so cheap that I had to have a set of them, and four nine-by-twelve Nichols rugs. It was a shopping frenzy, and we could afford it.

Most of our purchases were made in shops, yet I liked one little man at the entrance to the Dung An Market. He had a square of green cloth spread on the side of the road on which were displayed all sorts of "jewels" such as jade, which looked more like green bottle glass, and bits of coral. I was fascinated with an eleven mm pearl. The color was very good, but it had a flaw on one side. The initial asking price was twenty dollars!

Edwin, Anne and Kedar

Kedar and I thought our family was complete with the birth of Anne, but in September we found that we were going to have a "Peking surprise." We were very happy at the prospect, but it meant that Anne and the baby would be just sixteen months apart. That pleased me, too, because they'd be good company for each other.

With regular trips to the market I frequently stopped to talk with the little man with the pearl. Sometimes he'd offer me a small stool and a cup of tea. He was interested in my growing abdomen, a very honorable estate. He told me about his family, and each time we talked about a better price for the pearl.

Just before the moon festival he must have been desperate for money for the traditional moon cakes and offered the pearl for two dollars in U.S. currency. It was done, and we were both satisfied.

An important part of any visit to Peking was sightseeing. The Forbidden City was right in town, and the Summer Palace was a short drive into the country. We picked up an English-speaking guide at the gate because there was so much to see at every turn. I never tired of the excursions, and frequently Edwin went along. After half a dozen visits he began repeating verbatim the spiel the guides used. It was amazing that he'd learned it so quickly because he wasn't very talkative; but he certainly had it down pat.

We were advised against going to the Great Wall and the Ming Tombs. The Communists were more aggressive, and skirmishes with the Nationalist soldiers were becoming an everyday occurrence. The railroad tracks between Peking and Tintsin were blown up almost every night, often in several places. It was a worry.

Guests usually wanted to have Peking Duck, so we took them to No.5 Chen Mun Wy-Toh (outside East Gate), which had the best reputation. Ducks were selected according to the size of the party. After our number was painted on the birds in some sort of black ink, we went up to our room to drink tea or something stronger and eat pumpkin seeds. The birds were delivered, done to a crisp over an open charcoal pit. The number was confirmed before they were carved up. Skin sliced off, they were presented with thin pan-cakes, spring onions, and sauce. It was a treat second to none. If we wanted to have a quick Chinese dinner with neighbors, we'd choose a restaurant within walking distance that served everyday food.

Our favorite was one that had a large room filled with tables and an open staircase to the second floor. A balcony ran around the four sides, giving access to private rooms. We took one of the rooms because the first floor was noisy. On our first visit we learned the rules. After

A Tale of Two Bamboos

paying our bill, the waiter stood on the balcony and shouted the amount of the tip at the top of his lungs. If it was too small you were ignored as you left the restaurant, but if it was generous there were many smiles and *chin-chin* (closed fists together and shaken).

Often we were entertained at the consul general's residence. One such was a buffet dinner where we served ourselves and at random chose a place at a card table. We happened to be seated with Matt Jameson (not his real name) the young vice-consul who was a Chinese language officer. He told of a recent trip through the country north of Peking during which he was taken with an appendicitis attack late one evening. His Chinese co-worker knew of a small mission hospital and took him there. It was the middle of the night when they arrived, but the doctor examined him right away and operated. The next morning the doctor stopped by to see how he was doing.

"How is the young mother who was having a difficult delivery last night? Are she and the baby okay?" Matt asked.

"How do you know about her?" The doctor seemed surprised at the question.

"While you were working on me I clearly heard the midwife ask you to come and help; she was having problems, but you told her you couldn't. She had to do her best. So how's the mother?"

"I'm absolutely dumfounded," the doctor answered. "It happened just as you said, but the reason I couldn't leave you was I was fighting for your life. You had no respiration, no blood pressure, and no heartbeat!"

"Hey, thanks, doctor. Thanks a whole bunch," Matt said. Within a few days he was back on the road, none the worse for wear. Missionaries brought a faith to live by and established schools and little hospitals all over China like the one that saved Matt's life.

The English-speaking Community Church was within

a block of our house in one of the buildings renovated by the Shoemakers. Sunday services were at four o'clock because the Chinese church used it in the morning.

One Sunday Kedar told me he was going to see a friend right after lunch. I was all ready for church on time, but he didn't show. I went ahead, expecting him to come in late. The service ended and he hadn't arrived. When I got home I was alarmed to see he wasn't there either and began to worry. The consulate sent out warnings that we should be careful not to go exploring, particularly at night. Communist activities were increasingly bolder, and some kidnappings had taken place.

I had my dinner, and when he still hadn't come by 8:00 I told the cook to put everything away. I could get something for him when he got home.

I waited another hour before calling friends to see if he might be with one of them. Nothing. At 10:00 I called the hospitals to see if a foreigner had been brought in from an accident or something. Nothing. I didn't want to do it, but at 12:00 I called the consulate general to report that he might be in trouble.

They went to work immediately to trace him down, and at 2:00 a.m. found him with a young bachelor who had an interest in cameras matching his. With a few drinks and snacks, they had lost track of the time. Boy, was the consul general steamed! They had visions of all kinds of horrible things happening to one of their citizens. To find he'd just forgotten the time left them relieved but mad. So was I. Kedar was drinking a whole lot more than was good for him, and I became fearful. I tried talking with him about it, but he just tossed it off as my imagination. The next day he was bright-eyed and bushy-tailed, giving the lie to my concerns. I was all too ready to accept it with a big sigh of relief–until it happened again.

As Communist activity increased and got closer to Peking, all of us began to feel the effects. The power plant couldn't get the coal it required for twenty-four hour service, so at around 7:00 it was turned off, to be restored in ten hours. Each evening we were given a five-minute warning by the lights blinking off and on. Anticipating the outage, Dah-sa-foo lit little oil lamps and put them on the windowsill in the dining room with the wicks turned low. At the warning he turned them up and distributed them throughout the house. It was delightful to dine by candlelight, but it was a poor substitute for good reading light. Likewise it made the streets very dark, a cloak for evildoers.

Caltex decided we should return to Shanghai for our safety. Replacing us was a couple without children who could be more easily evacuated on short notice.

I was not going to miss the dust storms that came in the spring. Every effort was made to keep the inside of the house clean, but nothing really worked. Windows were sealed shut and all cracks covered with strips of rice paper glued in place. The house was so airtight that it was almost suffocating, yet at the end of a storm, every windowsill had its telltale pile of sand. It got into everything–carpets and clothing, beds and closets. If we had to go out of doors we wore face masks, and women used veils as well, yet it got in our hair and ears and under our fingernails. Our nostrils were ringed with dust, and it settled in the corners of our eyes and mouths. It took at least a week to bring everything back to normal. That season we had three.

The Gobi Desert dust storms reached all the way into northern Korea and India. I can remember Mother protesting that many years she'd just get the spring housecleaning finished with sparkling windows, when a storm would come and rain mud. In New Delhi I remember hanging up the laundry one May morning when great swirls of yellow wind came down on me followed by a blessed shower that cleared the air. The laundry and I had to be rewashed.

After the date for our departure was set I went to see my Chinese OB for a final check-up at the Peking Union Medical College (PUMC). "I'm so sorry to be leaving Peking," I told her. "We love this city, and I wanted to have our baby here."

"Yes, yes," she answered, "I will be sorry not to deliver your third child, but it is better you go now–two babies outside, one baby inside."

With packing well under way, Kedar contacted Mr. Chen, the owner of #10 Jade street. With all their money exchanges, he owed Kedar about forty dollars, so it was suggested he take it out in trade. According to custom, when Kedar arrived at the shop, Mr. Chen offered him a cup of tea, and they indulged in the usual polite talk for a few minutes before he asked the clerk to bring the piece he'd selected for Kedar. He couldn't believe his eyes when inside the package he found the five-piece jade bracelet I'd been talking about for months.

"Thank you, Mr. Chen," Kedar said, "but I can't accept this. It's worth many times the amount you owe. Isn't there some other little thing my wife admires?"

"You must accept this little token of my gratitude for the great service you have been to me and your wife's kindness in bringing many good customers. Please, I insist."

"But how can I," he protested. "You are the one who has honored us by giving us and our friends the opportunity to buy the best jewelry in Peking. The debt is all on our side."

And so the debate went back and forth with neither giving an inch until finally Kedar realized that if he didn't accept the bracelet he'd be insulting Mr. Chen. As graciously as possible he gave in. Kedar figured that if he refused it, more than likely a little package would be delivered to the door just as we were departing for the airport. That was one time I was very glad he lost an argument.

A Tale of Two Bamboos

The railroad between Peking and Tintsin was under constant attack by the Communists, so they decided to fly us and our household goods to Shanghai. We boarded a DC-3 early in the morning. All the seats had been removed, and our lift vans took up most of the space in the middle of the craft, lashed in place with steel cables. We took our places in bucket seats all around the edge.

The other passengers were Chinese Roman Catholic nuns, also on the run from the Communist advance. After we'd reached about a thousand feet the plane took a sudden plunge of a hundred feet or more, and immediately the air was filled with the sound of a beehive as the women prayed aloud with their rosaries.

We no more than got under way when Edwin had to "do the needful," but the only facility was behind a curtain at the opposite corner of the plane. There was no way to get there because the lift vans came right up to our knees, so he was handed back from person to person. Fortunately he could take care of himself. The captain lowered the cabin pressure just a tad and both children slept the four hours to Shanghai. It was good to be reunited with friends and family, but my heart was still in Peking.

We settled back into 229-D Ave. Joffe, but it was tight and going to be more so when our third baby arrived, so Caltex gave us a choice of several houses. The one I fell in love with right away was "The Limit" at the end of Hung Jao Road. It was literally the end of Shanghai. Ours was the last house on a paved road that ended in four hundred yards and became a dirt track. The owners were Billy and Gladys Hawkins, who lived next door. A high, gray-brick wall separated us, and all around were fields. Gen. Clare Chanault's Flying Tigers airfield was about a mile beyond the end of the pavement. I mean, we were really out in the country.

Typical of the way houses used to be constructed, it

was all chopped up. The rooms were connected by a hallway that wrapped around the living room and den. It was dark; everything was closed up, and in my view, depressing. Fortunately the Hawkinses were pleased to let us make any changes we wished so long as Caltex paid for it, and they said, "Go for it." What a challenge and what fun!

First of all, the partition between the small living room and smaller den was removed, transforming them into one generous-sized room. The wall separating the three bedrooms from the living room on the west side of the house was left in place, but the one on the south side came out, thus enlarging the living room by another four feet and providing cross ventilation, north and south. The section of the hall on the east next to the kitchen was closed off at the south end, and a door was installed at the north, opening next to the dinning room. Shelves were installed, making it a wonderful pantry and storeroom. The master bedroom and dining rooms were at opposite ends of the "U" with a tiled patio between. Two sets of French doors from the living room, and one set each from the bedroom and dining room joined the whole house together. It was beautiful, spacious and airy and in the days before air conditioning, a tremendous boon.

The huge double-door gate was under a tiled roof and had a room at each side for the gardener/gate man and the other for storage. The driveway turned right to the front door and around the corner to the kitchen. To the left a path led through a moon gate, past a kitchen garden at the side of the house, and into a large front yard that sloped down to a stream bordered with willow trees at the end of the property. It was a picture.

It was our first time to be up close and personal with Britishers, and we liked them. The Gommersols lived across the road in a huge brick house on a hill. They had a little girl Edwin's age, and they frequently played together. If he was over there in the afternoon, he rarely ate anything for supper because they celebrated tea big-time. They always had little meat pies, fruits and cheese, scones dripping with butter and jam and more. Dinner for them was served much later, never at our customary hour of six-thirty. We were entertained there and at the Hawkins's where we sat down at eleven. While I was pregnant that was a little hard to take.

When we first arrived in China in June of 1946, the exchange rate between Chinese and U.S. dollars was $2,030 to $1. It rose slowly at first and then increased by leaps and bounds. The Nationalist government couldn't collect taxes because the Communists were taking over more and more of the country. The problem was solved by printing more money.

U.S. bills in good condition brought a better price than tattered old ones. On my way home from shopping one day, I stopped by the house to see Mother and found her washing a batch of twenty-dollar bills.

"I learned this morning at coffee that the going price for new-looking bills is 50 percent more than old ones, so I'm cleaning up those we have on hand. See these," she said, offering several for inspection. "They look like new, don't they? All I did was wash them off, and after they dried I ironed them between two pieces of wax paper." They did look like new, maybe not quite as crisp, but much better than before.

The poor Chinese were caught in the middle with nowhere to go. Over night their money became worthless, so the minute anyone had cash, it was spent. It's the custom for the elderly to purchase coffins before there is an immediate need and stock them with funeral garments, and according to their beliefs, things that would be needed in the next life. All coffin shops were empty and as fast as new ones came in, they sold.

It was the law that merchants had to charge at official rate, though it lagged far behind the street rate. As a result most merchandise disappeared from the shelves except for a few token items that were seldom purchased. It became a barter society.

The cook went to the market daily with enough money for fresh produce and meat. Everything else came from a compradore's shop, but their shelves were empty too. We learned how go get around that one. At about 10:00 p.m. Kedar drove down an alley to the back door of the shop where we traded, gave the owner my list of staples, and swapped them for five-gallon tins of Kerosene.

The last time we paid the servants their two-week wages in cash, Kedar brought home several packages of $100,000-notes from the U.S. Bank Note Company. The huge, red-wax seals were unbroken. We counted the bills by checking the serial numbers at each end of a wrapped bundle. From then on we paid them in tins of Kerosene, sacks of rice, and eggs that the company bought in the country.

Our house had huge windows in most of the rooms that needed curtains and drapes. Kedar asked me to make a list, and when he knew a big exchange break was coming, he sent the car and driver to take me to town. When I found what I wanted, I asked the merchant if he'd accept my husband's calling card. If he would, we were in business. I was never turned down when they saw the Caltex logo. I selected yards and yards of sheer and raw silk for the living room, dining room, and our bedroom. I picked bright chintz for the other bedrooms. It was a mountain of material. When he told me the final amount I wrote on the back of Kedar's card, "Darling, please pay this nice man $millions," and signed my name. There was much bowing and scraping as my purchases were loaded into the car. The next morning the calling card was presented at the office. Kedar exchanged dollars for twice what he would have received the day before. We felt so sorry for those who had only local Mickey Mouse money. For them it was a daily struggle for survival.

My OB physician for our third child was Dr. Charles Milford, one of several Americans in a medical practice. Just about the time the baby was expected he was booked to fly back to the States on personal business. On the due date I went into the hospital, and the nurse gave me a mixture of caster oil and quinine that was supposed to get things moving. Kedar and I walked the halls all morning; nothing happened. He had lunch. I had water. We kept walking, while he read aloud from the latest Reader's Digest. I distinctly remember several articles, one of which was "The Two-Fisted Wisdom the Ching," about a very savvy labor negotiator.

At about four Kedar and the good doctor had tea, then he announced, "Well, let's get the show on the road." As I sat on the edge of the bed he gave me a shot, and immediately my world began to spin. I watched the ceiling go by as they wheeled me into the labor room, where precious little Miss Chun took over. Dr. Milford left to scrub up, but he never had the chance. Our third child was on the way and there was no stopping it. Somebody gave me another shot to put me out, and the next thing I knew I was back in my room with a beaming husband telling me we had another son. Jimmy was slow in getting started, but when it was time he popped out like a greased sausage.

Looking back, I was glad to have been fully awake when Anne was born so I could experience giving birth, a woman's greatest privilege.

When Anne was born on January 14, 1947, the exchange rate stood at $8,900 Chinese dollars to U.S.$1. Our hospital bill of $1,068,000 was a bargain at just $120. When Jimmy arrived it reached $12 million to $1, yet the official rate which the hospital had to use was $1 million to $1. Our total bill was $140 million, but the cost to us was a ridiculous $11.20. Early in 1949 the exchange rate peaked at $15 million to $1 when all currency was withdrawn and a new one issued. It held at $12 to $1 for a few weeks before it, too, fell apart.

Jim Voss, the new man in the Caltex legal department, and his wife, Frances, arrived in Shanghai about the same time we did. She and I were both pregnant.

"First the flower, then the fruit," the Chinese office staff congratulated Jim when Susan was born. What they meant was, "We know how disappointed you are that the baby isn't a boy, but never mind, better luck next time!" We were in good shape when Anne arrived because we already had a son.

During 1946 and 1947 Communist activities in Shanghai increased dramatically. At every opportunity they made a big show of going to bat for anyone they considered an underdog. If a wealthy person or big company, particularly a foreign one, was involved in an accident, it was a monumental opportunity.

One rainy day a student from Chaotung University, the school that was known to have pro-Communist leanings, was hit and killed by a Caltex tanker truck. In the middle of the block, dodging between cars, he slipped and fell in front of the fast-moving vehicle. Customarily the party causing the death sent apologies and made restitution, such as paying for the funeral, whether he was at fault or not. Somehow the Caltex office was slow in doing what was expected, so a Communist cell group decided to act on behalf of the student's family.

After the exchange of several letters, it was decided that Jim would go and talk with the complaining students to settle the matter. Thinking it would be taken care of in a half hour or so, he told Frances he'd return to the office then send the car for her to take Susan to the doctor.

When he drove through the university gates he was immediately surrounded by thirty or forty angry students. They told him where to park, let the air out of his tires, yanked his door open, then pushed and shoved him into one of the classrooms, and locked the doors! It was evident that they were in no mood to talk, so Jim let them vent their rage. Chinese have a very soft spot in their hearts for children, so he decided to use that in getting a message out that he was in trouble.

"Please," he said, "I had hoped to send my car to my wife this morning to take our baby to see the doctor. May I call her and let her know that I'll not be able to do so?" They agreed, and took him to a phone in one of the professor's offices.

"Don't make any mistake," they warned. "You are to just tell your wife you can't come. That's all. Nothing else. Do you understand?"

"Yes, I understand," he answered then dialed her number. She answered, and in order to give the message he began with, "Frances, just listen, please. I can't come to take Susan to the doctor. Call the office and tell them that I can't come. Call the consul general and tell him I can't come, and also call Bob Bryan and tell him I can't come. Do you understand? See you tonight."

"Sure do," she answered. "I'll get right on it. Careful, dear."

There were a few minutes when the students seemed to quiet down and Jim hoped they could start talking, but then one of the leaders began to whip up the fury again, screaming at him in Chinese and English, until they were all shouting and making threatening gestures. He took out a cigarette and was lighting it when one of them snatched it out of his mouth. He asked for a glass of water, but they just laughed at him.

At about an hour into the ordeal after the pattern was clear, he realized that if just one of them actually did hit him, the rest would probably pile on, and his life could be in jeopardy. Little by little he backed up to a corner so at least one side was protected. Lunch time came and went, no food, no water, and no relief in sight. They left a few at a time for meals and refreshment, then came back to harass him some more. Several had flushed faces, showing they'd been drinking. As the day wore on they got meaner and moved in closer, blew smoke in his face, spat on the floor near his feet, and made obscene gestures.

Jim was a big man, well built and 6'-3", but he was no match for so many. He was sure that Frances understood he was in trouble because they'd discussed it at breakfast, and his uncertainty about being able to solve anything. When he'd been held prisoner eight hours he knew somebody had slipped up or he would have been rescued by then. The Chinese are great on face. He wondered if they would gain or loose face if they beat him up or killed him.

Frances's message to the Caltex office was taken by a clerk who didn't understand its urgency and just put it in a basket of messages for somebody to take care of eventually; the U.S. Consulate General didn't want to get involved, and the one to Dad's office sat on his desk until he returned from meetings that kept him out all day. He called Frances and learned that Jim had not been seen or heard from and in his haste went to the wrong university then had to cross town to where Jim was being held.

At six o'clock, ten hours after the ordeal began, Jim heard the sweetest music in his whole life–Dad Bryan's voice in the hall as he shouted demands and threats of reprisal and punishment to anybody who held an American against his will.

"What are your names," he bellowed. He had a paper and pen and took them down. Dad was only 5'-7," but he spoke better Chinese than most of them and with such authority that they backed up and didn't resist. Jim heard him going up and down the halls until finally a student pointed to the room where he was being held.

"Open that door," he commanded, "or I'll see you rot in prison the rest of your worthless lives." A key was produced, the door flung open, and Dad strode in. By this time they seemed to have had a change of heart and didn't say a word when he remarked, "What a bunch of cowards," and to Jim, "Come on, son, let's go home."

They drove away in Dad's car, leaving Jim's to be picked up the next day.

It was a good ending to a long hard day!

"How does it feel to be the hero of the hour?" Kedar asked Jim the next morning.

"Hey," he answered, "I was just one scared American."

The spring and summer of 1948 were glorious. The threat of Communism seemed far, far away and the family was thriving. We were thinking about where we'd take our first six-month home leave due the next year.

I was experiencing some problems related to two close pregnancies and Jim's very fast delivery. The doctor decided I needed a general repair to get things back where they should be, but that could wait until Mother and Daddy's visit from Korea the end of September. On the twenty-eighth he'd be seventy years old, the mandatory retirement age for Presbyterian missionaries. They would come to us for six weeks then fly on to India to visit Betty and Arlan in Allahabad.

When they arrived we were shocked. Daddy was terribly thin. The collar of his shirt hung loose, and his trousers were bunched up with his belt. His clothes were three sizes too large.

"What in the world has happened to you?" I demanded. "Are you feeling okay?"

"About six months ago your father began to shed pounds like Old Man Scatter Good," Mother said. "His appetite is fine, but it's probably the emotional stress of leaving Korea after forty years in the land we love."

It was true. He ate like a horse, and his energy was up; but even with a lot of TLC he kept loosing weight. Bananas, a favorite of his, weren't available in Korea but plentiful in Shanghai, and he ate mounds of them. One of our doctors checked him over and could find nothing startling. Because they'd been in Korea where intestinal parasites abound, it was decided to have him take *christoids of hexal resorsonal,* a drug formulated by Dr. Berkowitz, a former Korea missionary. It was guaranteed to clean out every critter that wasn't supposed to be there. Within a week Daddy quit loosing and began putting it back on. Apparently he had picked up whipworms that attach themselves to the small intestine and eat up all the good stuff from your food and let you starve.

After the war they couldn't return to Syenchun in the north with the country divided at the 38th parallel. They were assigned to Chungju, where the Presbyterian Church was well established; and they didn't have to break new ground so late in the game. Daddy was an evangelist and teacher who fit right in with programs already underway. It was a whole new thing for Mother. All eight of us were out of the nest, and with the drastic changes accompanying Korea's independence, all sorts of new challenges presented themselves.

Before the war there were perhaps five or six hundred Americans in the whole country. Now there were thousands of every sort and description–U.S. troops and advisors, government officials, a large embassy, businessmen by the score, and every church mission under the sun came in to share the Gospel. It was mind-boggling.

There was the huge task of sorting and distributing relief goods *(koo-ja-poom)* that came by the shipload. A large share of the job was put in the hands of missionaries. Speaking the language, they were well suited for it. Good clothing was in great demand. In five years when those from the north could move south without too much difficulty, five million came, leaving everything behind. For years Korea's natural resources were shipped to Japan to support the war, so you could hardly name a thing that wasn't needed.

Trustworthy helpers were rounded up and went to work in huge warehouses. A few things like lady's high-heeled shoes and fancy hats were of little value, but all the rest could be put to good use. Naturally a black market developed, nobody made a big deal out of it. One way or another clothing was getting to people who were in need. As one of them said, "If a man is given a good winter coat that doesn't fit, at the market he can exchange it for one that does."

In Asia the "bamboo wireless" is most effective. When friends in the north heard that Mother and Daddy were in the south, it was the catalyst for their departure. Many tried to make a go of it under the Communists but soon found it didn't work. Anyone owning a business or land was considered a capitalist, "a running dog of Wall Street". Impoverished with Japanese taxes, very few were wealthy. Those like Paik See Weerum (The Third Daughter) were imprisoned or killed. Many Christian pastors were executed.

Those who made it to South Korea sought out Mother and Daddy's home, where there was always a great reunion celebration, but the stories they told were enough to break your heart.

One is about a woman, her daughter-in-law, and infant grandson. Their husbands were dead. They saw no hope for the future so decided to leave, walking at night and hiding during the day. They were spotted by an army patrol looking for those trying to flee. They grabbed the young woman, but before they reached her she handed off the baby to its grandmother, who scurried away into the woods. Content with their prize, the soldiers dragged her into the back of their truck and continued down the road. She was placed with others next to the tailgate. After riding for an hour or more she saw her opportunity to escape when the vehicle slowed for a rough place in the road. There was heavy underbrush nearby so she slipped over the side and made a dash for it. They didn't miss her immediately, giving her time to get well hidden. She wasn't enough of a prize to merit a thorough search, and they went on.

Four days later she found her mother-in-law coming down from a high hill, alone. They embraced and wept for the precious son who had died for lack of food and water.

"I gave him to the Lord," the woman said, "as I placed him in his grave under a beautiful big pine tree. My heart aches that I'm old and my breasts are dry, not full as yours." Late in the night they neared a village and heard dogs barking. They crept up to a house to look for any discarded food. A dog with her litter was in the yard. Squatting and moving ever so carefully, she picked up one of the pups and held it to her aching breast. When it tasted the milk it drank hungrily. She got another for the other breast, and was much relieved. Braving the mine fields on both sides of the DMZ, they at last reached freedom and headed for Chungju.

Mother knew a family of eighteen–a young couple, their parents, sisters and brothers, and children, including an infant. They had a rubber-shoe factory and did their best to stay and make it work, but their ownership put them into the hated capitalist category, and the harassment never ceased. When they could take it no longer they, too, fled, leaving everything behind. When they reached the jumping-off place where they had to decide how to cross the border, they were faced with two alternatives–walking through the mine fields or going by sea in a sampan. Trying to get so many safely overland seemed an impossible task, so they opted for the boat.

They waited for the dark of the moon then paid a huge sum to a man with a boat large enough to take all of them. They boarded it several miles north of the border and headed out far enough to make a safe passage, beyond the high-powered speed boats with search lights and machine guns that did their dirty work and littered the beaches with the bodies of those who were too close to land. The adults lay in the bottom and held the children

A Tale of Two Bamboos

on top of them covered with blankets and straw. The silent fish-tail oar moved quickly with the rhythm of the man standing at the stern working it back and forth.

All went well until they reached the critical point where the patrol boats searched for their prey. In the still of the night sounds carry a long way on the water, and the baby began to cry! They did everything they could to quiet him but it was useless. The father reached down and took him from his mother's arms and quietly slipped him into the water.

"How could you do such a thing!" Mother gasped. "I know how much that baby must have meant to you. I just don't understand."

"It was the saddest thing that could happen," the father answered, "but it was better that he die than that seventeen should perish." Freedom at such a price!

When she was able to get beyond the shock of such a story, Mother asked about the rest of the family and how they were doing.

"We are having a little difficulty finding a place to live and some of the necessities of daily living," the father answered. "We have shelter under the big bridge, but we need a better place and some clothing."

"It's warm today," Mother remarked. "Aren't you hot in that overcoat?"

"Yes," he said with a smile, "but it's all I have to wear except for my underpants, so I'll keep it on if you don't mind."

"Henry," Mother said to Daddy. "Please take this young man to our bedroom and give him a pair of trousers and a shirt. And young lady," she said to his wife, "come with me into the storeroom, and we'll find something for you and the others."

That sort of encounter repeated itself over and over, and Mother and Daddy were so glad to have the means to help those who had given up so much to live in freedom.

In the 1960s I met young people who remarked, "I

don't understand all this fuss about Communism. If that's the kind of government they want, what's it to us?"

"Well just look at the traffic pattern when a barrier is put up as in Berlin, Vietnam, and Korea. It all flows toward freedom. Nobody's risking life and limb to get into those countries. Doesn't that tell you something?"

It was a whole new thing for my parents to live in close community with nonmissionary Americans. They made good use of the NCO and Officer Clubs, at which they were welcome. One of the jobs Mother undertook was distributing milk powder to families with babies. It involved measuring out a week's supply according to a doctor's orders. At first they made cones of glossy magazine paper, but soon it all was sacrificed to the cause. One day she saw at the back of the NCO club a mountain of empty beer cans. Light dawned. She found the manager and asked what they did with the empties. Might she have a few?

"Take all you want, lady," he answered, "and if you need any help getting them to your house, just let me know and I'll have a couple GIs give you a hand."

"I hope you know what you've offered," she said with a twinkle in her eye, "because I want every one in that pile, and probably more next week." He was astounded but good as his word, and a pickup truck delivered them to her back yard.

"I'll wager I took the tops off more beer cans than any GI in the U.S. Army," she remarked, "and they made dandy reusable containers for the powdered milk."

Several of the houses in and around the compound were occupied by army families, and the wives frequently asked Mother to help them out with the language and unfamiliar Korean customs. She was happy to take the young women under her wing and ease their adjustment to a strange culture.

Connie was Mother's favorite. Usually missionaries were rather formal with each other, and it tickled Mother

A Tale of Two Bamboos

and Daddy that she was so casual and familiar. Without being asked, she called them Ruth and Hank (Daddy had never been called anything but Henry) and breezed in and out of their house at any time of the day or night. She was just a very friendly type. They loved it. They were amused and not all startled when she came to tell them good-bye the day they left.

"You know, Hank and Ruth," she said, giving them each a big hug (another thing very strange for Daddy) "you're the best damned religious people I've ever met!"

My scheduled surgery would lay me up for a couple of weeks, so I was glad for Mother and Daddy to be there to make sure the kids were well cared for and the house run properly. They were ready for a little pampering too.

A couple of days after the operation I was completely free of anesthesia and sitting up when Dr. Milford came in for a visit. He seemed a little nervous.

"We began with a D&C," he said, "and found a three-month placenta. The baby was gone, but you have been pregnant since Jimmy's birth. Did you know ?" he asked.

"How could I have been?" I exclaimed. "You folks did a vasectomy on Kedar, so we took no precautions. How could it happen?"

"That's what the other doctors asked," he said. "They wanted to know how well I knew you and if you might have been playing around." His fears seemed to vanish when I laughed.

"You've got to be kidding. You know Kedar and me. He's my whole life, and there certainly is nobody else."

"Well, I thought I should let you know," he said. Now we'll have to check up on the old boy."

As soon as he left I called Kedar at the office and told him the news.

"You'd better explain yourself, young lady," he said.

"I've nothing to explain," I retorted. "The doctors want you to make an appointment to check you out."

And so he did—and they did—and guess what? He had a full sperm count! Their fault, not mine, so they did a follow-up without charge.

While we were in Peking we attended a charity ball and raffle, the big social event of the year. The prizes were outstanding. Caltex donated twenty five-gallon tins of Kerosene. Another company, a ton of coal. There were several hand-knotted Nichols rugs and antiques galore. Raffles are not kind to me, but this was my lucky day. I won a beautiful six-foot by four-foot by two-foot black-lacquer cabinet with antique black-and-gold paintings mounted in the doors. I was stunned and thrilled. It was the prize of the evening. When we set up our house at Hung Jao Road, it went perfectly at one end of the living room opposite the fireplace. It was ideal for keeping the liquor supply and bar paraphernalia.

When we were getting ready for Mother and Daddy's visit Kedar asked, "What do you think? Should I take all this stuff and put it back in the store-room while they're here?"

"Why would you do that? It's your house. If you think you shouldn't drink, why not get rid of all of it? It's up to you." He left it where it was.

Daddy is a curious sort, and after glancing at the cabinet for several days he went up and opened it. After looking it over he remarked, "My, look at all the 'oh be joyful.' " He closed it, and everybody relaxed and had a good laugh.

A Tale of Two Bamboos

Family portrait, Shanghai, 1949

Shortly after Mother and Daddy left for India, Jimmy came down with his first cold and cough. What a surprise! He sounded terrible, as if he were about to give up his toenails. I couldn't believe a six-month-old could cough like that, but it never quit. He didn't seem to be suffering, and in time it didn't trouble me.

When I took him for his regular check-up and shots the startled doctor heard it for the first time.

"How long has he been coughing like that," he asked.

"It's the only way he coughs," I answered. "This kid doesn't have a baby's little hack, but he seems to be okay."

"Well, we'll keep an eye on him," the doctor answered, "and if he develops anything strange or different, let me know right away, okay?"

To all appearances Jimmy was fine. He was eating well, had gained weight according to the book, was a good-natured little fellow with a sunny disposition. After his cold cleared up the cough persisted.

The childrens' amah slept in Anne's room, but I kept Jimmy's crib at the foot of our bed. Another cold brought on more coughing that racked his little body. Although his rosy cheeks gave the appearance of health, I began to fear there was something terribly wrong with him. He was restless and fretful even with medicated cough syrup. We elevated the head of his bed, but that resulted in his ending up in a bundle of sheets at the foot.

I awakened when he was having a prolonged coughing spell, but it didn't resolve itself in the usual way. It stopped right in the middle. I jumped out of bed and picked him up. He was unconscious! I shook him and gave him several hard whacks on the back. He began to cry, the sweetest sound in the world. After giving him some water I held him in the rocking chair the rest of the night. He seemed more comfortable, though he coughed periodically.

In the morning I called Dr. Milford and asked him what the next step was. For the first time I was concerned about our location. At the end of Hung Jao Road we were a long way from the hospital, and with the dusk-to-dawn curfew we might not be able to get him there at night.

"Bring him to the hospital this morning," he said, "I'll meet you there at 10:00, and I think we'll need to keep him for a couple of days until we can find out what's going on." I hated the idea of leaving him, but it was a relief to know something was going to be done.

"We'll begin with a TB skin test," the doctor said. "The city is full of it, and as sheltered as he's been, he could have been exposed. I doubt we'll find anything, but we'll do it anyway. If a baby this young gets the disease there is no way he can survive. It takes all his resources to grow." I heard what he said but was absolutely certain it had nothing to do with us.

A huge percentage of Shanghai's population had the disease. To get a job one of the requirements was a clear chest, so those who were well had multiple X-rays taken and sold them to those looking for work!

Jim's TB test came back positive, which was almost

expected, but just to be sure, chest X-rays were ordered. The next morning when I went to see our little guy, thinking to bring him home, I met a grim-faced doctor. He'd already called Kedar at the office, and the three of us went into a private room for consultation.

"I hardly know where to begin," he started, "but the X-rays of Jim's lungs are a disaster. They show lesions on both lungs. We'll formulate a diet that will give him every chance to fight it off. We'd send you back to the States right away, but we can't let him fly in today's poorly pressurized planes. You'll have to wait for a ship. Unfortunately Harry Bridges has all West Coast shipping tied up in a strike. We hope it won't last too much longer."

The two men kept talking, but I didn't hear any of it. My precious little Jimmy-boy was terribly sick, and our hands were tied. We couldn't get him back to the States where surely help was available. I was scared, angry, and felt cornered by that terrible disease.

I went into the nursery and found his crib isolated from the others. His long lashes brushed his pink cheeks as he slept, his ever-present blue blanket clutched in his right hand, his thumb ready to pop into his mouth when he awakened. I sat down beside him, drinking in every detail of his sweet little snub-nosed face.

"How can it be, Lord," I prayed, "that you gave us this little son and will take him away from us so soon? We called him our Peking Surprise, and every moment of his life has been a gift. Please, Lord, let us keep him. No matter what the price, we're willing to pay it. Please give us your peace, and thank you, for I know you will."

At home that afternoon Anne and Edwin sensed that something was wrong and stayed close to me. When I sat down in the living room Anne came, and reached up her arms to me. So we rocked, sang, and read stories until they felt comforted.

Much sooner than any of us expected, the steam-rolling Communist army gathered momentum and was projected to sweep over Shanghai before many months. The American ambassador ordered all nonessential personnel to leave. Women and children were to depart as fast as planes could get them out. We were stuck! Between Thanksgiving and Christmas they left by the planeload–babies, bottles, diaper bags–the lot, and the poor, forlorn-looking husbands stood on the tarmac waving good-bye. Club holiday parties were canceled, as were most other social events. We had but one thought–how soon could we get out of here?

Mother and Dad Bryan had no intention of going. His practice was still thriving, and many of the major American companies and banks were clients. His newest one was the Bank of America, for which he'd just secured a license to operate in China. His partner, Cornell Franklin, was staying too. The British attitude was that the Communists needed to have a thriving economy, so why wouldn't they work with those who knew the ropes? They all hoped so, anyway.

So at least we had Mother and Dad Bryan, and we made a big thing of including as many as we could for Thanksgiving dinner. At Christmas, Caltex men whose families were gone came to see our children open their presents. They wanted only one thing–to be with their own wives and kids instead of drinking too much and celebrating with a bunch of worried old men.

The New Year came, and the strike was still on. We weren't going anywhere. Jimmy wasn't better, nor was he any worse. There was talk of sending us to Hong Kong, but in the last week of January the strike was over and the American President Line's (APL) *President Cleveland* was on its way.

Caltex booked us into two adjoining first-class staterooms. What a relief. We preferred a ship to a plane any day. Just before sailing we heard of another who'd be aboard–the son of Mary the nail amah. Bless her heart, she scrimped and saved all those years of giving foreign women manicures, shampoos, and messages to send him to college. Now he was going to the States to medical school. There was such a rush to get out of Shanghai that every berth was sold. Very likely she got passage for him through her many contacts and called in all her chips to give her son his big chance. He was in third class, and normally there is no movement between the classes; but when we heard he was aboard we contacted him and got permission for him to come up to our room and paid him to watch the kids, particularly Jimmy, so I could have a little free time in the evenings. What a boon.

The day we sailed it was dark, cold, and miserable. All three children had bronchitis, which was particularly bad for Jimmy. Edwin and Anne ran low fevers, but in a day were up and around again. Jimmy began to take on a sallow look and coughed almost continuously, a worn-out exhausted sound. It was frightening. Our first stop was Yokohama. Caltex friends came to see us and took Kedar, Edwin, and Anne ashore for the day.

It was open-house aboard the *Cleveland* with all public rooms open to invited guests who they hoped would choose one of the APL ships when returning to the States rather than flying. The passageways were filled with U.S. service personnel. That morning I washed out some silk stockings and left my diamond ring on the edge of the basin.

Jimmy was worse than ever, and I began to wonder if we'd make it home in time. There was a knock at the door. A young American soldier was there and asked if he could use our bathroom. I should have told him there was a public facility down the hall but I allowed him in. When he left, my ring went with him. What a disappointment, but I was so concerned with my sick baby that it hardly registered.

In past episodes Jimmy recovered from his colds, but he wasn't doing so this time. I asked the ship's doctor to look at him and tell me what to do. He was coughing almost continuously and was exhausted.

"Let's take him to the ship's hospital," he offered. "You can spend as much time with him as you wish, but at night you need your rest too. We'll give him a very small amount of rectal ether so he can sleep."

"Sounds like a good idea," I agreed, so while Kedar looked after Edwin and Anne I spent most of my time with Jim.

Two days out of Hawaii the doctor suggested Jim and I leave the ship and fly the rest of the way to St.Louis where my sister, Hunkey (Cordelia), was head nurse at Bethsesda Hospital.

"Jimmy would probably be okay if you stayed on the ship," he said, "but flying will save several days. If it can be arranged I think you should go."

Kedar sent cables and made calls, and before we landed our tickets were ready for a flight straight through after a night in Honolulu. What's more, brother Jim, a navy pilot who was flying the Mars between Alameda and Hawaii, was in town. He would meet us and take us to the plane. It couldn't get any better than that.

After a day ashore with the family, Jim, Jimmy, and I watched the *Cleveland* sail in the evening. We flew out early the next morning. What a relief. Help was in sight.

Hunkey was there to meet us, and after giving me a big hug she looked at Jimmy.

"But he's beautiful, Fran," she exclaimed. "I can't believe he's so sick."

"Please, Hunkey, you just take him for a few hours," I said, handing him over to her and bursting into tears. "I'm exhausted and at the end of my rope."

She checked us both into the hospital. Very painful varicose veins in my right leg screamed for attention, and Jimmy needed somebody to save his life. I handed over the X-rays taken in Shanghai so the doctor would have something to start with. She called Dr. Bower, the man who took care of Edwin as an infant seven years earlier.

A Tale of Two Bamboos

"What's the matter with Jimmy," Hunkey asked. "He's been bathed and fed but he won't settle down and is crying his head off."

"Does he have his blue blanket?" I asked. "He always wants it when he goes to sleep."

"No he doesn't, but I'll find it right away," and she did. It was covered up with the bedspread. She showed it to him, put it in his hand, and immediately he brought it up to his face and popped his thumb into his mouth. Oh, bliss.

Even better news awaited us. They took another set of X-rays and found perfectly clear lungs! Apparently the ones taken in Shanghai were with damaged prewar plates. They found the cause of his coughing. His thymus glands that should have atrophied at birth didn't, and he was in danger of choking to death! That was scary, but the treatment of choice was a couple of shots of X-ray, and they did that right away. Another big puzzle was that he had rickets. Great balls of fire! I thought that was reserved for starving babies in Africa and India. We'd spent a fortune on all American baby food and tinned milk, not trusting local brands. What went wrong?

"You may have given Jimmy the best there was," Dr. Bower said, "but sometimes the child is unable to absorb it. I think that's what happened here. I'll ask the dietitian to write out a schedule of what he needs, and I'm sure he'll be over this in no time."

I could hardly believe the concoction that was prescribed. It was a mixture of yogurt, crumbled up brewer's yeast, black strap molasses, a little honey, and wheat germ. It smelled to high heaven, but Jimmy just lapped it up. I could hardly spoon it in fast enough, and he blossomed. Praise the Lord!

All this good news was almost too much to take in. This cute little guy was going to be ours after all, and in short order a surgeon took care of my leg. Kedar and the kids arrived just as we were ready to leave the hospital.

We moved into a hotel apartment for a week then with a new car headed for Texas and a few weeks of vacation.

Kedar called his grandmother, Mamie, to ask if we could use her house in San Antonio, Texas, for a few weeks until Caltex decided what to do with us. It was wonderful visiting members of the family, but with three little children a day or two was enough. As it has been said, "After the third day guests, like fish, begin to smell."

Granddaddy Bryan had died, and she was more than happy to visit her sisters to make the house available to us. They called it "a miracle house," as everything in it was a gift. They were on the first *Gripsholm* exchange of civilian prisoners in China and Japan. After forty years in Shanghai, they had no home in the States. Hundreds of Baptist supporters were eager to contribute to their retirement, and even during the war years when there was a shortage of all materials and manpower, they built a very nice little cottage just two blocks from their Baptist Church. "The biggest joy of all," Grandmother said, "was the wrought-iron railing around the front porch. That was something Granddaddy felt was absolutely necessary, but we were told all iron went into building ships, and we'd never be able to get it until the war was over. Well, they just didn't know that Granddaddy was praying for it, and what do you know? One day it was delivered to the construction site! Who knows where it came from," she said with a smile. "Heaven, I guess."

We visited them one weekend during the war when Kedar was in flight training at Corpus Christi. I remembered a very nice solarium with windows on three sides that looked out over the back yard that was lined with rose bushes, Grandmother's pride and joy.

It was a lazy, happy time–sightseeing, shopping, and trying out Mexican restaurants (we prefer Chinese). The Vosses came by one day for a visit as they would soon be headed for Hong Kong. During their vacation in Killgore (Frances's hometown) they hired someone to look after the children while they did some visiting. One day she found that the pearls Jim gave her were missing, but the woman swore she'd not seen them.

"You know how it is," Frances said. "She has so little and we have so much that she was just 'equalizing the situation a little.' What the heck, there are more where those came from, right, Jim?"

"Right."

On March 17, 1949, after the dinner dishes were cleared away, we listened to the evening news on the radio. The lead international story was the announcement that in Seoul, South Korea, Mrs. Horace Underwood had been shot to death. I was stunned. If ever there was a person who was full of life it was she. Short and well rounded with hair pulled straight back into a bun, she had a broad smile and a twinkle in her eye. I remember how she encouraged me when I was a teenager competing for a Nature Cup at Sorai Beach, once for pressed flowers and greenery, and another time for seashells. I won both years. Dr. Underwood challenged me to improve my time and form in swimming and diving. The whole family was very special, and now she was gone. It left me with a huge empty feeling inside. In time we learned how it happened.

Dr. Underwood's father was the first Presbyterian missionary in Korea and founder and president of Chosun Christian College, which is now Yonsei University. Mrs. Underwood organized a faculty wives' club. She invited them to a meeting at their house the afternoon of March 17 to hear a talk by a famous Korean poet, Miss Mo Yun Sok, who had recently come back from the United Nations, where she was part of the official delegation.

The meeting was held in the library, a beautiful room that occupied one whole end of the house, front to back, about thirty by fifteen feet. There was a huge stone fireplace, a large desk at one end, comfortable chairs, and bookshelves from ceiling to floor. Sliding doors connected it to the music room next to the front entrance. After the meeting began, she sat by the nearly closed doors to welcome latecomers.

She got up when she saw a stranger come in. She didn't know that others had entered the kitchen at the back of the house and scared the servants into silence. When she saw the man had a gun, she gave him a tongue-lashing and was backing him out the door when one of the gang came from the kitchen and shot her. The five intruders ran through the house shouting at the terrified guests, "Stay down! Don't move!" as they ran away.

Mrs. Paik was the first to come to Mrs. Underwood and heard her say, *"Keng-ge--hun-ta."* 'It's all right'."

They put her in the Paik's Jeep station wagon and rushed to Severance Hospital in downtown Seoul opposite the station, but she was dead on arrival.

The rest of the family was at Seomunan Church where Dr. Underwood was teaching a language-school course. When they reached the hospital she was already gone.

The young men were caught and confessed that they were after Miss Mo rather than Mrs. Underwood. I suppose they hoped to diminish their crime that way, or perhaps the police just said so, trying to soothe Dr. Underwood. We don't know. There was a lot of political unrest in the fledgling democracy. Two of the five were executed. Two escaped during the Korean War, and it was reported that one of them was a North Korean general at Panmunjom in the 1970s.

March 17 is a day of celebration for the wearers of the green, but for me a day of remembrance of a magnificent lady.

After six weeks Kedar was antsy and ready to go, but we had no idea where that might be. With the close-down of China, the Hong Kong office had taken as many as it could use; there were still other countries where we might be assigned, or even the New York office, heaven forbid.

We headed for the West Coast, stopping along the way to visit family and friends and ended up in Oakland, where we rented a small house in a nice neighborhood. Still no decision from headquarters, but they asked Kedar to return to New York for a maximum of six weeks, leaving the children and me in Oakland. Six weeks stretched into three months, and finally they decided on Korea. The assignment was conditional–if I could find a place to live!

After WWII housing was all but impossible. The country was bursting with every sort of American government and civilian agency. For thirty years under Japanese occupation the Koreans had no army or government, and all of a sudden they had to start from scratch with no experience or preparation. Koreans who fled for their lives because of Japanese oppression returned to have a hand in giving their county a new start. Syngman Rhee, the first president of South Korea was Presbyterian-educated, ambitious for his country, and got out before the Japanese put him in prison or worse.

Knowing we could go to Korea if I could find a place to call home gave me no qualms. I called Dr. Underwood. I had not the slightest doubt he could help us.

I booked a long-distance call, not knowing that to receive it, he had to make a trip into town in the middle of the night! When he picked up the phone I identified myself and told him what I needed.

"Why the hell are you calling me at this time of the night?" he bellowed. "You need a place to hang your hat? Of course you can stay with us until we can get one of the faculty residences ready for you at the university. Sure, sure. Come right along. We'll be expecting you, but next time call me at a civilized hour."

I could jump for joy. It was so wonderful to hear his

voice again, feel the welcome, and know that soon we'd be heading to the land of my birth. On the strength of his word that we'd be able to find housing, Caltex gave their blessing, and we were on our way again.

Chapter 4

Korea

Once again lists were made, resources checked, and off we went on a shopping spree. We'd need a three-year supply of underwear for the family, shoes in graduated sizes for growing feet, swim suits, yard goods to be made up as time and need dictates, and a hundred and one other things. It was such fun but mind-boggling. Korea was stripped clean by the Japanese during WWII and we were not eligible to shop at the PX or commissary, so having some of the basics was a good idea.

A family doctor gave us physicals and the necessary shots, and we were on our way. On a beautiful October day we boarded the *President Wilson,* sister ship to the *Cleveland.* This time we were all healthy, and Jim's illness of a few months before was just a bad dream.

My only regret was that we were missing Molly and Harwood Sturtevant's wedding in St. Louis. Before we left Shanghai, we sent her brocaded white silk for her wedding dress and as a personal gift a beautiful blue silk wedding nightgown. The other two sisters were in the wedding party.

Molly and Harwood Sturtevant

Marjorie and John Van Tuyle met us in Yokohama.

"Here comes the well-dressed Bryan family," Marjorie remarked with a laugh, "but Jimmy still has his blue blanket that he's dragged over several miles of floors." That did it! As soon as we reached their house, where we stayed for the day, I borrowed her sewing shears and cut the blanket up in four pieces and hemmed them. Jim got the cleanest piece and the rest I washed for future use. He got a clean one every day.

He was a funny little guy. When he was sleepy he curled up with his "hooga". If he was angry he threw it on the floor and stomped on it, but mostly he made sure it was someplace nearby, just in case. A vivid memory of that stopover was that Jim all of a sudden was potty trained. With Edwin it seemed to take him ages, and I wasn't too patient with him.

"Fran, when you come to think about it," Mother said to me one day, "the process of elimination is one of the most pleasurable experiences we have, so it shouldn't be a stressful time. Boys are not as easy to train as girls, so take it easy with him!" She very seldom gave advice on raising the children, but she certainly was right on that score. Edwin got it eventually, Anne was a snap, and I was taking my time with Jim.

When we returned to our hotel after being out all day, I put Jim down to change his diaper, presuming he would be soaked; but he was bone dry. What an opportunity! I raised the toilet seat, stood him on the rim, and urged him to go for it. He did and was enormously pleased with the noise it made. He could hardly wait for the next time. Kedar and Edwin encouraged him to "cross swords" with them. The new activity was exciting, and thereafter we had few accidents.

A coastal freighter took us to Pusan, and a few hours later we arrived in Seoul by train. The old station was as I remembered it, but nothing else was the same.

After Ethel Underwood was murdered, their son, Horace Grant, and his wife, Joan, moved from a faculty house into the Underwood home to keep things running for his dad. It was a big establishment, yet there was still plenty of room to accommodate us for a few weeks. Kedar and I had one room and the children another.

Growing up in Korea, we spent our summers at Sorai Beach and lived next door to the Underwoods. James and John were twins just younger than Horace Grant. I had a real thing for John but worshipped him from afar.

He was now a missionary in Korea, living in Kwangju. At dinner the night of our arrival John was late, held up at a meeting. He came in while we were eating and was introduced to Kedar. He said hello to me and sat down.

"Well, I'm disappointed," Kedar said after a moment or two of silence. Everybody looked startled.

"Why, what's the matter?"

"I expected John to come in and sweep Fran off her feet," Kedar answered. "She's been telling me for years that John was her secret passion when she was a girl. All he does when he sees her is to say hello."

Laughing, John looked at me across the table. "Why in the world did you keep it such a secret?"

The house designated for the president of Yonsei University was on the hill overlooking the campus. Formerly it was known as the E. H. Miller house. It was one of several that were built for Presbyterian and Methodist missionaries who were professors. Horace Grant and Joan occupied it for a time until they moved into the big house, but now it stood empty because Mrs. George Paik, wife of the president, refused to live out there for fear of thieves and robbers.

It was an ideal house for us, and when it was offered we were thrilled. Immediately an order was sent to ship our household goods from Shanghai, and as soon as they arrived we moved in.

My Korean left much to be desired. I spoke with a northern accent, but there were no serious problems. We hired a Western-trained cook, a baby amah from the village, an outside man, and a part-time laundry woman.

Electricity was a very uncertain commodity, so the company installed a generator in the basement, but we didn't use it more than necessary. It made a loud noise and gobbled up the gasoline. The stove that came with the house was an old-fashioned one that burned wood and coal. We had a Servelle refrigerator, so we managed the rest of the time to get by with kerosene lamps and candles. I found an old Singer treadle stand and set my Necci machine into it. Foot-power still works, and that's how I learned to sew in the first place. Adaptability is one of the key elements of living happily overseas.

Right away I discovered dozens of Korea mishkids of my generation who were in country as missionaries, in business, and in government. I felt right at home, and with so many friends the job of finding a new doctor, dentist, and the best places to shop was made easy. It was like living in a new frontier town. We didn't have U.S. Government privileges, but as you'd expect, it wasn't long before nearly everything from that source was available to us. A hillside at the edge of town was a maze of little paths and alleys for pedestrian traffic only. Anything you needed could be found there, right out the back door of the commissary and PX!

On my first exploratory venture I carried a big basket for purchases. A shop owner at my first stop immediately recognized my northern accent.

"Where did you learn to talk like that," he asked.

"I came from the North," I answered, and a big grin lit up his face.

"Where, which city," he insisted.

"Syenchun."

"My town too," he said, shaking my hand.

"My parents were Presbyterian missionaries, and we lived in the gray brick house with the big pine-nut tree out front. Do you know it?"

"No, I never saw the compound, but everybody knows of the missionaries, the good schools, and the In His Name Hospital."

From then on Mr. Uyn insisted on carrying the basket. He took me to stalls and shops to get what I needed and bargained for the best price. What a godsend. On subsequent trips he always spotted me, took the basket, and off we went, negotiating the muddy, rutted ways.

It wasn't long until we understood why Mrs. Paik refused to live at the university. On a hillside all by itself and surrounded by trees, it was an ideal target for thieves.

The first few losses were minor. Young Methodist missionaries, Don and Adra Payne, lived across the road. Once thieves got into our basement, but finding better pickings over there, they left our things and took theirs. As time went on they got bolder, and we suffered two major robberies.

We had only occasional electric power, so at night I turned a lantern down low and kept it on the stairs, three steps from the top. If I heard the children, it was a simple matter to get it, turn up the wick, and take it into their room.

The house was old enough to have developed the usual creaks and groans when the wind was blowing, and I was used to them; but one night I heard a steady creak-creak-creak on the stairs. Sitting up in bed, I looked down just as a man was reaching out to take the lantern!

"Noog-goo-yoh?" (Who is it?) I demanded. Like a flash he was gone. "Kedar, Kedar," I shouted, shaking him. "Get up. I just saw a man on the stairs."

"Calm down dear," he coaxed. Several times I had nightmares and woke up screaming. He presumed it was another one of those.

"No, no, really," I insisted. "I saw a man, and when I asked him who he was he ran away. Come on. Get up and let's see if anything's been taken." Grabbing our bathrobes we went down, and what a mess we found! Vases of forced forsythia lay spilled on the floor. Drawers were pulled out and contents scattered everywhere. Cabinet doors stood open, and silver and other valuables were gone. Things they didn't want were strewn around. We felt sick but glad they didn't get upstairs.

They worked in teams. They cut out glass from the storm windows, unlocked them, took them off their hinges, cut out the big panes of glass to give them easy entry. A ladder rested against the house where one or two came in. The others stayed outside to received the loot. They were quiet. We never heard a thing until that one man came up the creaky stairs.

We straightened things up so the children wouldn't see the mess and said nothing about it except to the servants. The windows were replaced and new locks installed, but we knew they would probably try again. And they did.

The thieves were notorious, but if anything good could be said about them it was that they never hurt anyone. That gave some comfort to those suffering the loss.

We had a total of seven "visitations," but the next big one was the worst. We were in town for a formal dinner dance and didn't get home until after 1:00 a.m. Kedar took Kang-see down to the village. We were about ready to turn in but we both wanted something to eat. I went down to the butler's pantry to see what there was, made a couple of sandwiches, poured two glasses of milk, and went back upstairs.

The next day was a holiday so we slept in–or tried to until the kids stood by our bed with big eyes and shook us.

"Wake up, Mommy, wake up," Edwin urged. "You must come downstairs and see what's happened. Mommy and Daddy, come right away." One look at his face was enough, and we hurried down. Somebody must have been taking orders. Most of the Lenox was gone, but four dinner plates were still on the windowsill ready to go, as were four crystal water glasses. At least they had good taste. The Desert Rose dishes were there and the silver plate. The sterling was gone.

Apparently the work was in process when I went into the butler's pantry, a swinging door away from the thieves. They were gone like the wind and didn't come back to finish the job.

Things began disappearing off the laundry line too, so one of the servants kept watch while they were drying. In particular demand were good sheets and towels, and I can understand why. They'd be hard to trace.

Shortly before the evacuation we arranged for two

men to come at night and *tangie* (walk around) all night. A resting place was set up under the first-floor sun porch. They didn't want to confront anybody so asked that a bell in our bedroom be attached to a string going down to their shelter. They could pull it if they feared trouble. A yank or two would be enough to arouse us. Oh, my!

The severe water shortage we faced was another challenge. In the attic were four connected fifty-five-gallon water-storage barrels. A hand pump on the ground floor delivered water to them, and it flowed by gravity to the kitchen and bathrooms. Water was hauled from the well a hundred yards down the hill, and there were times when it was almost dry. Finally it gave out completely, so water was delivered from the city by a tank on a bull cart. The kitchen and bathrooms had water storage *tokes* (large earthenware jugs) with dippers, and every drop was hoarded. Drinking water was boiled and put in a filtration jug, where it passed through a chalk-like candle.

Bath water was heated on the kitchen stove and carried upstairs to the tub, where all three children used one load. Dirty water was saved to flush the toilet. The motto was, "If it's yellow, let it mellow. If it's brown, flush it down."

Kedar and I used a washtub, and it wasn't half-bad. First I sat in the tub and put my feet on the floor. I washed down to my knees then sat on the john and scrubbed from my knees on. Anyway, it worked.

We sold our master bedroom suite before we left Shanghai and brought a new mattress, springs, and adjustable bed frame from the States with the idea of getting the rest of the set made in Korea. "Just show them a picture, and they can make anything," we were told. Fine. We selected a design and chose a very pretty birch. It was guaranteed seasoned wood, and if it turned out to be anything near our expectations, it would be a bargain.

A Tale of Two Bamboos

In a couple of weeks it arrived by bull cart and was carried up to our room. We tested the drawers; everything worked, and the price was right. I was thrilled.

Surprise! For the first time, it was in a heated house and began to shrink. Snap! Bang, like a pistol shot next to our heads; more popping and banging on the other side of the room. We jumped out of bed. It sounded like the Fourth of July. With the lantern turned high and flashlights we found huge cracks had opened up. Every drawer was stuck shut, and the vanity mirror was broken. Seasoned wood, my foot. We sat on the bed and laughed at the way we'd been taken.

"Oh, well," Kedar said, "if they are anything like the Chinese they will have it patched and fixed up like new, and they'll be so sorry about the mistake."

Pong-see-bang, the outside man, hurried down to the shop the next morning, returning with the owner, who was amazed that such fine, seasoned wood could shrink so much so quickly; but not to worry–it would be fixed like new; and it was.

Edwin was in the first grade and went to the Seoul Foreign School. Kang-see and I kept Anne and Jimmy busy at home. She spoke only Korean, so the children began to pick it up quickly. I was delighted at the way got their tongues around difficult words with ease.

Anne, a typical little girl, loved to play with small things and was especially fond of opening and closing the eight little drawers to my Chinese jewelry chest, clumping around in my shoes, and investigating all the wonders of our walk-in closet.

One morning as I worked at my desk she came to stand beside me and pointed at a tablet of paper she wanted. She didn't say anything because she was rolling something around in her mouth. I had no idea what it might be so I put my hand up and said, "Spit it out, please." Out popped the beautiful "peace offering" Signet pearl John

Van Tuyle gave me after he'd taken Kedar out for a night on the town while we were in Shanghai. I was thankful she hadn't swallowed it or it would have been lost forever. After that I put out of reach all edible pieces.

There wasn't much to be had in the way of breakfast cereal except for Quaker Oats (from the hillside black market), so except for pancakes on Saturday we had it every day. Mother gave each of her twenty-three grandchildren a silver porringer for their first birthdays. Its design was perfect for the young child with sides that curved inward at the top so food was pushed onto the spoon instead of spilling over the side.

Jimmy was beginning to feed himself, and he loved oatmeal. The cook brought a bowl for each of us and gave Jimmy's to me to add milk and sugar and let it cool. As I got it ready, he sat there with a bent-handled spoon in each fist, shaking with anticipation. As soon as it was in front of him he went at it with both spoons and shoveled away until every scrap was gone. Jimmy's breakfast was a daily source of amusement for the whole family.

I loved our cook, a small man with white hair and a neatly trimmed mustache. He was a genius with the wood stove and an oven door that didn't stay tightly shut. He made wonderful bread, and each Tuesday he baked enough for the week. One morning I was in the kitchen when he opened the door and put his fist in. Satisfied with the temperature, he loaded the six loaves, closed the door, propped a stick under the handle, gave it a kick to make it tight, and set the timer. When he called in about forty minutes, I knew I was in for a treat. The loaves had been tipped out of the pans to cool. A couple of thick slices were steaming on a plate, and he handed me a knife and the butter. Just heavenly!

Friends who'd returned to Korea after WWII finally felt safe enough to do more than "camp out." They sent for their silver, good china, and precious things they didn't want to loose. A beach resort was established at Tae Chon, which was much like Sorai Beach of my youth, just four miles north of the DMZ and out of reach. I booked rooms in the beach-operated inn for two weeks in the middle of the summer, and began collecting things to take along.

One day early in the spring, Edwin, Anne, and Jimmy were invited to a birthday party. The custom was that the mothers came too and enjoyed a social hour while the little ones played games, opened presents, and had refreshments. We had arrived in Seoul the previous fall, and since I was much involved in settling our house at Yonsei University, there were many in the foreign community I didn't know.

It was my first meeting with Helen Hopkinson and her son George Gray, nicknamed GG. Helen was in her midfifties and GG could not have been more than two.

"When people meet us for the first time they're not sure if I'm his mother or grandmother," she said with a laugh.

Others old me that Helen was a very busy person, and most efficient. If you wanted something done well, you asked her to manage it, and it was sure to be a success. She taught English in a couple of Korean girls' schools, and was president of the American Women's Club.

She was a jolly person, short, well rounded, sometimes serious, but mostly wearing a look of anticipation on her face. She wasn't beautiful, but you remembered her because she was so interested in everything. As we kept an eye on the children she told me her story.

"My husband, George, is an advisor to the Bank of Korea. When he first came out I wasn't permitted to accompany him because housing was in short supply, but after several months I was able to join him.

"I'd been there for about a year when we vacationed in Japan. We rode airway trams, climbed mountains, and packed all kinds of experiences into two weeks. On our return we had a wheels-up landing at Kimpo, and passengers were helped to jump down onto stacked-up oil drums to deplane. The following night we attended a formal dinner at the Seoul Club, and while dancing, I felt a little dizzy.

"It might be a good idea," I said to George, "if I see our Seventh Day Adventist doctor and ask him to put me on a diet. I've gained about twenty pounds, though nobody would know the difference–I'm already so big. I've not been feeling too well, and perhaps the extra pounds are the cause."

"Good idea," he agreed, so I made an appointment and in due course, went to see the doctor. As he was writing a few notes in my file, I tried to hurry him up because I had an English class and was pressed for time.

"Now Dr. Lee," I said, glancing at my watch, "if you'll just tell me what I should eat or not eat and if there are any exercises I should start, I'll be on my way." But Dr. Lee was not to be rushed.

"Please sit down for a moment," he said. "I won't take much time, but I do have some things to discuss with you. Have you ever had any children?"

"No," I replied. "George and I have been married for twenty-five years, and gave up the idea of a family long ago, but really, I have to go or I'll miss my class, and I'd hate to do that. Dr. Lee's next remarked stopped me cold and got my attention off school."

"Mrs. Hopkinson," he said. "During the examination I heard two heartbeats, and only one of them is yours!"

"When may I expect this baby?" I asked after a pause.

"Oh, I'd guess in ten days or two weeks."

I was hard-pressed to believe it because I'd never felt movement, and being over fifty I wasn't concerned about the end of my periods. It was truly life altering news.

"Thank you, Dr. Lee–I think. I'll call you tomorrow, but now I need to go tell George and make some radical adjustments to my schedule." Somehow I got home and sent a cable to my sister, which read, "Airmail a complete layette. Baby arriving unexpectedly."

"Request on the way," came the reply. "You're the worst procrastinator in the world, but I don't know how a baby could arrive unexpectedly."

"The package arrived just before I went to the hospital and was delivered of our beautiful baby boy."

June 15, 1950 was a quiet Sunday. I played a violin solo, "Meditation by Thais", for the special music at worship in the afternoon. We went home for a quiet supper in the side yard under the wisteria arbor. It was loaded with blossoms and filled the air with fragrance. We followed our Sunday evening routine of stories and games until bedtime, and after the children were tucked into bed, talked about plans for the coming week. We turned the radio on to get the world news at ten o'clock before calling it a day. We heard a very off-handed report of a little scuffle at the border, but that happened regularly, so we thought nothing of it and went to bed.

At two-fifteen in the morning we were awakened by a pounding on the front door. John McClearie, the Caltex manager, was there to tell us we had to evacuate.

"Serious fighting has broken out on the border, and Ambassador Mucho has ordered all women and children to assemble in the KMAG (Korea Military Advisory Group) compound at three, that's in just forty-five minutes. Fran may take only what she can carry."

"Can't we just sit this one out?" Kedar asked. "We're a little tired of running away from the Communists."

"No way, man," he answered. "You'll be staying, but the families must go. It might be nothing, and they'll be back in a few days; but nobody knows. I hope we'll all be together again in a week and have a big celebration."

"Okay, I'll drive them into town and check this whole thing out."

"Good," John said, "and they want you to bring any firearms you own. We might be called upon to do guard duty while the families get down to Inchon."

We were stunned, but when an emergency arises it's amazing how easy it is to obey orders. Kedar got out the largest suitcase we owned, and I began to select a change of clothes for each of us. I found a soft-sided purse, opened the drawers of the jewelry chest and dumped everything into it. A toothbrush for each of us, soap, one towel and washcloth (times like this you share), toiletries, and basic medications. Most important were Jim's diapers and extra underpants. The enormity of what we were leaving behind was so great that I couldn't even think about it. Kedar wasn't going yet anyway, and that gave me some comfort.

"It's funny what you do sometimes when under pressure," a friend said as we waited for the bus. "I thought that somebody, sometime would probably need a needle and thread, so I chose a spool of black and one of white and one needle out of the packet. It would have been just as easy to take the whole thing."

The children were sleepy, but the idea of a great adventure in the middle of the night was exciting. They didn't object too strenuously. The streets were quiet as we drove into town, and I began to wonder if this was some sort of exercise or drill. At dawn we were asked to line up for transport to Ascom City, a military base near the port.

Even in the worst of circumstances things turn out to the advantage of some. Just ahead of us was Esther Scott and the Korean baby they were trying to adopt. A very young-looking corporal stood at the door and took down our names as we boarded.

"Esther Scott and daughter Susan," she announced. She turned around and winked at me, and I had a hard time containing my joy.

Esther and Denny were battling U.S. bureaucracy in trying to adopt Susan. The law on the books was that you couldn't adopt an Asian baby unless you could prove at least 51 percent caucasian blood. Now how in the world can you make a claim like that of an infant found in the steps of the police station? Their congressman back home was going to introduce a private bill to allow them to have her, but he wasn't too hopeful. As we boarded the bus nobody was asking questions. We didn't even have our passports, so off we went with a very happy young woman and her baby!

The military base had only Quonset huts. We were free to move around as long as no planes were sighted, and none were. It was the middle of the afternoon before we had any food and water, and the kids were getting mighty cranky.

Helen Hopkinson and GG were there.

"I don't know which to be more concerned about, a possible war or George."

"Why? What's the matter with him?"

"He's not been well, so I took him to the hospital yesterday. The two American doctors couldn't agree on a diagnosis. The young man thought it was just the flu, but Dr. Lee feared polio. There has not been time to get a report on blood specimens. They advised me to evacuate with GG and promised that one of them would be with George at all times."

"I think you can trust them to do so," I consoled, "but I can see why you're worried. It's a rotten spot to be in."

Kedar joined us an hour before we were loaded into sampans and towed out to the *MS Rienholt*, a Norwegian freighter that had just unloaded a cargo of fertilizer.

"Nothing has happened so far," he remarked. "I was asked to stand watch at a crossroads on the way down here but was told to forget it when all was quiet. What could I do with just a hunting rifle anyway. It's all sort of silly."

"Well, what will you do when we've left?"

"John and I will burn a few papers at the office then go home. There are all kinds of rumors floating around, but I've no idea whom to believe."

Kedar took pictures as we were helped into the boat and waved until we were out of sight. There was no place to sit, but it wasn't long before we faced the huge, vertical climb up a rickety ladder to the deck. Edwin went first, showing Anne how brave he was. She was right behind him, and I carried Jimmy, who clung to me like a baby monkey. A seaman hooked our bags onto a rope and hauled them up several at a time.

It never fails that funny things happen even in the worst of circumstances. Just ahead of us was a woman with two energetic little boys, the older one of whom was excited about the adventure and chatted a mile a minute. She was beautifully dressed in a silk suit with matching high-heeled pumps. As they reached the deck, one of her shoes slipped off, and quick as a flash he picked it up and tossed it overboard. It didn't bob around a moment so those below could retrieve it, and was she furious. The air was blue with the scolding he got, but what to do?

The captain and crew of seven surrendered their quarters to the passengers. Women with infants and those expecting birth momentarily were assigned according to their need, and the rest of the 750 of us were divided between the forward and stern holds. Each family was issued a thin cotton pad, and it was up to us to find a place. I chose a spot next to the hull opposite the hatch. If it rained we were far enough away not to get wet but would benefit from the light. The hold was at least sixty feet deep and there were only a few dim lights in the ceiling, leaving us in a perpetual gloom.

Parking the suitcase in the middle of our "claim," we climbed the steep steps to the deck to check out the facilities. The ship boasted two toilets and showers, and that was it. Immediately we got in the shortest line and waited, and waited, and waited. When we were three away from our turn, it was "out of order"! Somebody got it stopped up, and there was no unstopping it. We went to the back of the other line and waited some more. Finally, when all three kids were dancing on one foot and the other in their anxiety we finally made it, and oh what a relief!

An army captain was in charge, and immediately she organized the galley for feeding the "five thousand". Somebody raided the commissary in Seoul and brought large tins of Dinty Moore Beef Stew, #2 tins of Dole Pineapple Chunks, and boxes of Lipton tea bags, paper plates, cups, and napkins and plastic spoons and forks. Nobody went hungry, but we were a little tired of the menu by the end of the third day.

When the children dozed off I went on deck to stretch my legs and found the kitchen crew getting ready for the next meal.

"What do you do with those large tins when they're empty?" I asked.

"Oh, we just toss them overboard, why?"

"Because I'd like to have several if I may, and if you have any paper bags that can fit over the top, I'd like them too." No problem, so I took all they had and carried my treasure back to the hold, kept several for ourselves and gave the rest away. Voila–covered potties for anxious little kids, not exactly comfortable to sit on, but they worked! The word spread quickly, and no more # ten tins hit the briny deep until they had served a second use.

The *Reinholt* sailed south in the Yellow Sea, around the southern tip of Korea, and over to Fuokoka, Japan, home of a large U.S. Army base. Nobody knew what North Korean plans were, so Mac Arthur sent P-38s to escort us to safety. They passed overhead every fifteen minutes, which was reassuring. There was speculation that the enemy might send U-boats to sink us, but I suspect that was the last thing on their minds.

Word came the second day that the Communist army had taken Seoul and all foreigners had been evacuated. For all we knew the whole country was lost. If they could take the capital so easily, what would stop them from going all the way to Pusan? The enormity of the suffering that was soon to be was too much to contemplate. I thought of those who worked for us and the problems they'd face for having accepted employment from "those running dogs of Wall Street". The joyful sense of freedom from the Japanese the country enjoyed for just five years was lost, and now they were faced with a worse oppressor.

And I thought of our home and all the beautiful things we carefully purchased in China–rugs, lacquer, silver, old Chinese furniture, and the special things such as pictures, mementos and treasures of the children, especially their silver porringers. I reasoned that after all they were just "things", but I hated to see it all disappear in a moment. I was thankful that nothing such as the silver and good china was put away for special times. We enjoyed them every day.

The quiet times in the bowels of the ship were good for contemplation and prayer. "What now, Lord?"

After we left, Kedar went to the U.S. Embassy, but there was no clear word on what was planned. He went home, found that the servants had everything cleaned up and dinner was ready. The Armed Forces Radio had no news except that people would be well advised to keep off the streets, so he went to bed around ten o'clock.

Once more he was awakened in the middle of the night and told to go into town. Thinking he'd be home again in a few hours, he dressed in casual clothes and drove in with John McCleary instead of taking our car. The place was a madhouse. Koreans were rushing every which way. Panic was written on their faces as they loaded everything they could move into cars and onto carts and headed south. Word at the embassy was that the Korean army had not been able to stop the Communist invasion, but it was trying to take a stand. Hour by hour the delaying action turned into a retreat then a rout.

All Americans were ordered to go to Kimpo, where they'd be picked up by planes from Japan. Kedar wanted to go back to the house first to get his passport, five hundred dollars in cash he'd left on the dresser, a few papers, and some clothing. Nobody wanted to take him, but finally John agreed. They got to the pass that leads out of town toward the north when they saw gun flashes, so that was it. They could go no farther, turned around, and joined the stream of cars headed for the airport.

One plane after another came in, loaded up, and left. One suitcase per person was permitted, no more. Koreans accompanying them stood off to the side. As they boarded, men turned around, and tossing their car keys in the air called out, "Whoever catches these can have the car."

Early in the morning of the third day we heard the *Reinholt's* engines slow and knew we were entering the harbor. One more meal of beef stew, pineapple chunks, and tea. They'd run out of paper plates and were serving it in pineapple tins.

"You know, Fran," a friend said to me as we stood in line, "I don't think I could eat it if it came in a #10 tin!"

We cleaned up our little spot then climbed the stairs to be on deck for the nose-count and landing. Gen. Walton Walker was walking up and down on the wharf while lines were made fast and the gangplank lowered. His men were standing in formation at parade rest, waiting for orders. It was quite a scene. Off to the side I noticed a familiar figure–Kedar! All of a sudden I was overcome with a sense of gratitude. The children and I were safe, we were together again, and nothing else mattered! The thought came to me, this is the way we go to heaven. We take nothing with us. It's just us and none of our baggage. The three precious little ones stood close and were as thrilled when I pointed Kedar out to them.

"Daddy, Daddy!" they yelled, jumping up and down, but there was too much noise and confusion for him to hear us. He did see us wave, and that was enough for the moment.

Responding to shouted commands, the troops peeled off into a line and quickly came up the gangplank. Two women expecting babies any minute were carried off on stretchers, as was an elderly man who'd taken a tumble and cut his head. Women with infants came next. At about the middle of the pack we were told it was our turn. Each was assigned a soldier. Edwin, Anne, and Jimmy were picked up and carried; I was taken by the arm to disembark. We were led into a warehouse set up to receive us.

You've seen newsreels of refugees going through a line to be handed toilet articles, towels, and washcloths, ending with a Hershey bar. I wanted to laugh when I was doing the same, receiving gifts for our immediate needs, and movie cameras were turning. I hoped we didn't look too bedraggled.

Next came the tables where we sat down to answer questions, fill out forms, and send messages. We were allowed a free cable to one address with the set message that we'd arrived safely and were okay. I sent mine to Mother and Daddy, knowing they'd tell the rest of the family. The children were still under the care of their assigned soldier, so I was free to tend to business. The great big fellow who was taking care of Jim sat down and held him when he got sleepy. A Stars and Stripes photographer snapped pictures, and the next day a shot of Jimmy, sound asleep in the soldier's arms, appeared on their front page. In the States it appeared in the *New York Times,* the *Chicago Sun Times,* and other major papers!

Sleepy little boy   Jimmy, Fran, and Kedar

Kedar was allowed in to join us once he convinced the guards he was also a refugee. The moment he landed in Japan he found out our port of arrival and got on the next train to join us. Most of the others waited for their families to be brought to Tokyo. I was so glad he'd come. I needed all the hugs I could get, and it was a comfort to the children as well.

Because sorting everything out took time, we were bussed to a big U.S. army hospital, women and small children on one floor and men and boys on another. Edwin felt mighty grown up at being considered old enough to stay with his dad.

The P.A. speaker announced that the Red Cross needed to contact Helen Hopkinson and asked her to go to the main desk. I hoped it would be good news, telling her where her husband was so she could join him. Soon we got the word, and it was not what we'd hoped. George indeed did have bulbar polio, and shortly after we departed, he died. Even in the midst of all the confusion he was buried before the hospital staff fled to Pusan.

After supper in the cafeteria I saw her in the hall helping someone find a lost piece of luggage. That was Helen, always thinking first of others needs. I lost track of her when we scattered to the four corners of the earth. One thing I'm sure of is that GG has the strongest, best mother in the world.

Toward the end of the first day a harried corporal came into our ward.

"Do any of you have small children?" he asked. "If you do, please take a yellow tag for each and write your name on it and attach it where it can't be torn off. We need to know where they belong if they get separated from you." I took one each for Edwin and Anne, secured them with some pins and told them not to take them off. I soon found out the reason. One of the little boys got into an old self-service elevator that was operated by a lever that was moved around a half-circle to send it up and down. Turn it to the right and you go up; to the left, and you go down. He closed the folding gate and off he went–up and down a mile a minute, laughing all the way.

"What's your name," people shouted at him as he went sailing by. "Where's your mother? Please stop the elevator and open the door," to no avail. He was having the time of his life and wasn't about to comply. There was nothing for it but to turn off the power. The elevator bandit was captured. Couldn't help laughing. Was it the same little fellow who'd pitched his mother's shoe overboard?

In the meantime Kedar was on the phone with Caltex in Tokyo. They advised him to bring us to the city, and they'd sort things out.

We arrived in Tokyo by train Saturday evening and checked into a suite of rooms on the second floor of a downtown hotel. Clothes we'd lived in for a week went to an overnight laundry, and we took stock of our situation. First on the agenda was increasing our wardrobes to keep us decent, then we'd see.

The previous week had been stressful, so we planed to sleep in Sunday morning. Around eight the next day a car on the street below backfired several times.

A Tale of Two Bamboos

"Get up, Anne, quickly, get up," Edwin urged his sister in the next room. "Hurry, I hear them shooting, and we'll have to escape."

"It's okay," Kedar said, going into their room. "We're okay, really. It was just a car making that noise," he assured them, "We're in Japan, and nobody's shooting here. Now that you're awake, how about some breakfast? Want to go to the dining room on the roof, or shall we order room service?" He was wonderful with the kids, and they'd missed him terribly when we were separated, leaving him behind. Being together again comforted them.

"Let's get room service." Edwin brightened. "That will be neat, and can I have bacon and eggs the way you like them, Daddy?"

"Sure, anything you please," he answered, giving them all a hug, "and we'll get oatmeal with brown sugar for Jimmy."

"Yeah," they chorused, "Jimmy and his oatmeal." We watched carefully for signs of anxiety over the evacuation, but that was the only time any of them expressed it.

Earlier in the month Mr. Lefevre, Caltex general manager, suffered a heart attack while in the States on business, and his wife, Nell, flew home to be with him. In Karizawa, a beautiful mountain resort, they had rented a summerhouse at that was standing empty. Guess what? It was a dandy place for the Bryan family for a while, anyway. Bravo! Within the week we were on our way after we'd had a gratuitous shopping trip to the PX for clothing and necessities, including a Singer Featherweight sewing machine, some patterns, and a few notions.

The house couldn't have been nicer. It was big enough for us all with rooms to spare for guests. It was completely furnished, and had Sho, the cook, on staff. Where Tokyo was noisy, dirty, and sweltering, we were cool, clean, and quiet. Kedar stayed a few days until we were settled in and knew our way round then went back to Tokyo. Every weekend he came from Friday night to early Monday morning.

The Caltex manager asked us to make a list of everything we'd lost, and if possible, give a dollar value. Wow, what a task! We pictured our house room by room trying, to remember everything. After writing it down, we went over it again. How in the world do you estimate the value of a three-year supply of underwear, shoes and socks for the children and ourselves; yards and yards of fabric, patterns, and notions, sheets and pillow cases, towels, wash cloths. We did what we could, and for months afterwards one or the other of us remembered something left out. All told our estimated loss came to around twenty-five thousand dollars.

Our only transportation was a bike, but with a bit of arranging, we all fit. I got a child-carrying basket that perched over the front fender for Jimmy, and Edwin and Anne shared the baggage carrier on the back, well padded with bath towels. It was a gradual down-hill ride to a recreation area on a lake two miles away, so that part of the trip was easy. Going back up was the challenge.

Transportation

On our first venture out I reminded the children to keep their feet away from the back wheel because it would really hurt if they were caught in the spokes. I guess Anne had to test that bit of information, because just as we got up to a good speed, wham, we stopped dead in our tracks, and she let out a piercing scream. That's right, her foot was jammed! Edwin slipped off the back and steadied the bike while I lifted Jimmy down. I needed both hands to free Anne's foot and get her off of the seat. There was no help in sight. It was a residential area with tall trees and hedges on both sides of the street and an occasional gate to private property. I called and called, but no one answered. About a block away a gentleman dressed in a kimono and smoking a cigarette in a long holder strolled out his gate. He gave no sign of seeing or hearing us. He turned and went back in, closing the gate. I was so frustrated and angry that I was crying, too, which didn't help Anne in the least.

I was frightened because her ankle was twisted and I was certain something was broken. It seemed impossible to free her without assistance. Edwin helped hold her while we laid the bike down. I was at last able to move the wheel and ease her foot out. What a relief to find that when her partly pulled-off shoe fell, her ankle wasn't twisted. The wheel was in good shape, too. After rubbing the bruises, wiping tears away, and blowing noses, we were on our way again. I didn't need to give a second warning about keeping little feet away from the spokes!

The recreation area was commandeered by the U.S. Army for a military and government R&R center. A snack bar and small PX provided the usual things was well attended by women and children. On weekends husbands joined them. It was the focus of social life on the mountain.

There was a lake with a roped-off shallow area for small children. We women sat around tables under umbrellas to visit and keep an eye on them.

We were the new ones on the block, and when they learned we were the recently arrived refugees from Korea, they wanted to know all about it. A woman named Sally had a story to top anything that happened to us. She had two daughters of about thirteen and eight.

"At the beginning of the war when it looked as if the

Japanese were coming, we were leaving the Philippines on a troop transport," she said. "My husband stayed behind with his men, but they needed to get us out.

"Late in the afternoon of the first day our ship took a torpedo and began to sink. The captain told those of us who made it up on deck to get off as quickly as possible and swim away from the ship. Lifeboats were being lowered and would pick us up, but we had to jump. To those of us who had little children, he said, "Toss them overboard first; they'll pop up like corks, and then you jump. If you try to hold on to them, you'll carry them down too far and hurt their lungs.' It was the hardest thing I ever did, but I picked up five-year-old Jane. We hugged and kissed, and I told her to jump, that I'd be right next to her in a minute. She was a good girl, and with my help she landed several yards from the hull. She surfaced immediately and somebody got her into a lifeboat. The captain was right, but even so it was almost impossible to let little Ellen go, just an infant, but I flung her out as far as I could.

"You know how it is in the tropics, dusk comes very quickly, and when I jumped it was nearly dark. I looked everywhere, but I couldn't find Ellen. I swam around, refusing to get into a boat until they told me they had to pull away from the ship or get sucked under. I was devastated. Jane and I clung together and cried. In thirty minutes the ship sank with some women climbing the stack, trying to save themselves; but they all disappeared in a final swoosh. It was terrible.

"It was cold, a night I thought we'd never survive, but finally the dawn came. I didn't know how I'd face another day without my sweet little baby.

"There was only one canteen of water, and we were rationed two ounces each. As I gave Jane her sip I noticed a big hulking seaman sitting in the forepeak. He was hunched over with his forearms on his knees, and it looked to me that he had something under his shirt."

A Tale of Two Bamboos

"What do you have there," I asked. He looked up.

"I found this little baby in the water and nobody seemed to know who she belonged to, so I've just been keeping her warm," he said. He sat up straight, pulled his shirt back, and there was our little Ellen!

"I was overcome with joy, once again holding my precious baby in my arms. Life has not been the same since. My milk was gone, but that didn't matter; she was alive! We were picked up that day by another ship and taken to the States. My husband got out, too, before the Philippines fell and is now serving in Japan."

I felt humbled by her experience and forever thankful for our safe departure from Korea.

One week before the evacuation we celebrated Father's Day big-time. I gave Kedar portraits of the three children painted by Rosemary Muldoon, a fabulous artist and wife of the Shell manager. I hated to leave them on the living room wall, but there was no choice.

We had one glimmer of hope, however. Sean and Rosemary were staying in Tokyo. I wrote and asked if they'd like a weekend in the mountains, and if she could possibly do the portraits again. The most she'd be able to do was make sketches then finish them up at home. Oh, the joy when she yes. One treasure at least was not to be lost.

Edwin and Anne had spent many hours at their house in Seoul and knew that when she said they needed to sit just so for a little time they complied. She was really good, keeping them happy with soft music and biscuits (cookies) if they got tired.

Redoing Edwin and Anne wasn't too difficult a task, but Jimmy was another matter.

Sunday morning the light was just right. I sat and held him, reading stories and playing games. He was thirsty and wanted a Coke. Normally that was off limits, but this was a special occasion. I relented, and he drank a whole bottle. In time he got sleepy and leaned his head against me. I sat up very straight to get in the right position for Rosemary.

I was sitting on a cane-bottomed chair. Soon I felt warmth in my lap as he wet, but that was okay, the light was good and time was of the essence. Soon there was more and more. It ran through the chair and made a little puddle on the floor. It became a stream running toward the door. The others came quietly into the room to see the progress, saw my predicament, put their hands over their mouths and left the room before hooting with mirth. The sacrifices one makes for the love of art!

Three weeks later Kedar came for the weekend, bringing the finished and framed portraits, a prize beyond measure. Every time I look at them I remember Rosemary and her tremendous kindness to us.

Caltex had a place for Kedar in Okinawa, but there was no family housing. They said he'd have to go alone, and the children and I would stay in Japan for at least another six months to a year. He could visit us every month.

He turned it down. There seemed to be no compromise, so he resigned. I knew it was a hard decision because he loved the company and the oil business.

"I had to be away from you eighteen months during the war, but that was a different situation. I refuse to be separated again," he said.

He gave me the news on his next weekend visit. Soon we were packing up and making yet another life-changing move. We boarded the *MS President Cleveland* in Yokohama harbor, bound for San Francisco.

Chapter 5

USA

After a delightful crossing we flew to Iowa City, where Kedar left the children and me with Mother and Daddy and proceeded on to Caltex headquarters in New York City.

During his separation processing, he submitted the claim of twenty-five thousand dollars for our losses in Korea. In the chain of command it went to the desk of a man who'd been in the Philippines at the start of WWII, and he was furious. Apparently at the time his claim against the company was not well received, and they gave him only a third.

"Look, Bryan," he stormed, "twenty-five thousand-that's ridiculous. It's way out of line. You'll be lucky to get half that."

"So far as I'm concerned," Kedar answered calmly, "you don't owe me a dime. There is nothing in my contract that states Caltex will be responsible for my losses, but I was asked to submit an honest estimate, and here it is, okay?"

Word about the altercation traveled quickly to top management, and the senior vice-president asked to see it. Kedar saw the document later that he'd signed and had written, "Pay in full." Wow, that was good news!

Kedar bought a car and headed to Washington. He checked the employment opportunities in the Departments of State and Commerce and found an opening that suited him perfectly—the Petroleum Division in the Department of Commerce. He applied, and after a background check, signed on. He found a little house in Falls Church on Westmoreland Street (how Virginian can you get) then drove to Iowa to bring us to our new home.

In the meantime I was taking care of family separations paperwork. We were asked to have thorough physical exams so if we'd acquired an illness in Korea or China, the company would be responsible for medical bills related to treatment and cure.

As a child in Korea myself, I remembered without much joy the semiannual deworming that went along with spring and fall housecleaning. Right on schedule Mother heard us grinding our teeth in our sleep and knew it was time to order Santnan from the hospital. It was horrible tasting stuff Mother tried to make tolerable by covering it with jelly, but it was still awful. The next night came a big dose of Epsom Salts, not so bad if you held your breath while drinking it, but it was still one of the worst things we had to face twice a year. It did, however, clear up the problem.

This time the children's lab work came back negative. I couldn't believe it, but the doctor humored me by prescribing *christoids of hexsol resorcinal.*

The dosage was four little pills to be swallowed, not chewed, or they'd burn the mouth and stomach. They were made to dissolve in the gut and kill the critters.

I was worried about getting the children to swallow them until Hunkey offered to help. She was a nurse, and they'd do anything she asked. They did exactly what she told them, and down they went without a whimper. I was so relieved.

A Tale of Two Bamboos

The next day all elimination was carefully examined, and sure enough they had them. Jimmy still needed help cleaning up, so when he was ready he called out, "Mommy, come wipe my tail-fedders." He bent over with his little bottom in the air, and there hung several inches of a round worm! Oh, my. I eased it out gently, and Hunkey put it in a bottle of saline solution and tied a ribbon around it. The next day she took it to the University Hospital and suggested the lab look at what they'd missed.

Hunkey was living with Mother and Daddy while she studied for her master's degree to qualify for the position of director of nursing services, a new offering in large hospitals. Their house had just two bedrooms but a nice big, warm basement that took care of us very nicely. There was plenty of room for the kids to play and for me to sew without cluttering up the rest of the house.

After years in Korea facing a shortage of ordinary things, Daddy was in the habit of saving string. He carefully removed it from packages, knotted lengths together, and wound them into a ball. Before the days of Scotch tape, good, strong string was a valuable commodity.

Another item in short supply in Korea was good paper. He and Mother both always had note paper at hand; he cut out the backs of envelopes for that purpose. One day he came to me with a puzzled look on his face.

"Fran," he said, "I can't find my string and the stack of note paper that we keep in the closet. I don't know what could have happened to them except that perhaps the children found them interesting and took them."

"I'll find out, Daddy," I answered and went to where the children were playing. I sat on the floor and helped them with their building blocks, and when they seemed ready to try something else I asked, "You know, Grandaddy is wondering what could have happened to his ball of string and stack of paper in his closet. Do you have any idea where they could be?" They merely looked down at their hands, so I continued.

"Maybe you thought they were something special, but he needs them now," I said, "If you know where they are, he'd really like to have them back. Do you suppose you could help me find them?" Without hesitation they went to the closet under the stairs, going deep into the far corner for their treasures.

"Good kids," I praised. "Now you can take them to him, and I know he'll be happy. Thank you so much for helping."

"We were just trying to keep them safe," Edwin said as they marched upstairs. This was the only other evidence we saw of their reaction to being suddenly deprived of things they valued; they were trying to save something they thought precious. That afternoon Mother and I went shopping for a few toys and games to replace theirs lost in the evacuation.

Mother and Daddy listened regularly to a radio program that was broadcast from a nearby farmhouse. A farmer had a breakfast program on which he gave the latest news, weather forecast, grain and hog prices, and frequently an interview. Soon after our arrival he called, asking if I'd be his guest. I felt honored, and we set a date.

A huge round table was set for all of us and a microphone hung from the ceiling in front of the host. The program proceeded with a background noise of murmured conversation and the clatter of silver on plates. Jimmy sat next to me and thoroughly enjoyed his pancakes. When the interview took place I gave as informative answers as possible. The subject, of course, was the start of the Korean War and our escape.

Hunkey wasn't able to be with us because of a class, but she listened to it on her radio. She thought it went well.

"I had to laugh, Fran, because when you were answering questions, I heard Jimmy's little voice in the background saying, 'Mommy, mommy, mo budda. Mommy, mommy, mo budda'." Poor child, I don't know if he got it or not.

As soon as Kedar could get away for a few days, he drove to get us. In such a short time we'd accumulated more stuff than would fit into the trunk, so we bought a little one-wheeled trailer that had two attachments to the car. It was by no means a heavy-duty carrier but suited our purposes. We got a tarp to cover it and were on our way.

It didn't take long for us to find that the little house Kedar bought wasn't big enough, so we put money down on a new one on a another street in Falls Church. The builder was just finishing it, so we got to choose the paint and wallpaper. What a bonus.

We were no more than settled when the house across the street all of a sudden showed lights, too, and the John Jarman family moved in. It had to be the best thing in the world for me. John was the freshman congressman from Oklahoma's fifth district. He came first, followed a week later by his wife, Ruth, and two children, Jay and Susie, who were the ages of Edwin and Anne. We hit it off immediately. We were both transplants, and our backgrounds could not have been more different, but right away Ruth and I were sisters. She was one of the most devout Christians I ever knew, yet she had only a nodding acquaintance with the organized church. They were Presbyterians, which gave her an edge, but going to worship every Sunday was not one of her priorities. She soaked up everything that brought her into a closer relationship with God and loved to share it with me.

All I ever know about politics was learned from Ruth. John was a Democrat, but it didn't bother her that we were Republicans. What I knew about American politics you could put in your eye, so she set her mind to educating me.

"When John was running for the House seat, his hardest fight was to gain the Democratic nomination. Once that was behind him the election was a cakewalk.

"We like our politics hot and heavy," she told me, "but when we first got into it I had no idea it could get so rough. I worked right along with John, and his press began to pick up. We went often into neighborhoods where John was not doing well. He took one side of the street and I took the other. We knocked on every door for blocks and blocks and asked everybody we met to vote for John.

"We visited chicken-processing companies and shook hands with people who were cutting up the birds. Do you have any idea how it smells and how yucky it is to shake those slimy hands? Anyway, I did it, and John's numbers were going up.

"The opposition decided I was making a big difference, and I guess I was, so they did their best to get me to quit. I wasn't surprised when it came, but when it did I was ready for it, and what a blast I had.

"One morning a woman with a very nice voice asked to speak to me. When I picked up the phone she said, 'Mrs. Jarman, I just thought I should tell you that I'm expecting a baby, and your husband is its father.'

" 'Lady,' I answered, 'if I were you I'd get a good lawyer and sue!' On top of that all sorts of rumors were circulated that a very good-looking black woman who'd gotten a scholarship to a prestigious private college did so because John had put in a good word for her, and that was after she'd slept with him."

"And you hung in there through all this," I said with disbelief.

"You bet. The worse it got, the tougher I got, and John won with room to spare."

Often she called in the middle of the morning with, "Fran, some important things are scheduled to be debated on the floor this afternoon. We'll take the kids and leave them with the secretary in John's office. Come on, get your hat and let's go." Those were the days when you wore hats and gloves downtown and to church. So off we went, and Ruth's enthusiasm was such that you couldn't help being infected by it.

As we approached the capitol I kept an eye out for parking places and pointed them out to her.

"No," she answer, "I'm sure there's something closer," and she kept going. Without fail when she pulled up right in front of the Capitol steps there was an empty space, and she'd say, "You see, the Lord knew we needed this place and saved it for us." How could you argue with that?

I'm sure the Lord put us together for another reason, too. Her brother, Hamilton, had a drinking problem, and she told how the whole family tried to save him. If he wasn't in by a certain hour, one or more of them checked the clubs and his favorite watering holes to find him and bring him home.

"We did our best to save him," she said, "but there's really nothing you can do but pray and hope he hits bottom sooner rather than later, because until then he won't be serious about it and get help. He's been in AA for the last five years, and now we know that when he disappears for several days it's not because he's drinking but that he's helping another person tough it out. I can't tell you how many people have come up to me and said, 'Ruth, your brother saved not only my life but my soul'."

I began to be very concerned about Kedar's drinking. It wasn't only what he drank but that he was hiding it from me. He always had a beer or two before and after dinner, but one day while putting away clean clothes I found several empty gin bottles at the back of his drawer. I put them on top of his dresser, and when he came home that afternoon I asked him why he put them there, why not in the kitchen?

"Oh, no reason," he answered in an off-hand way. "Just didn't think about it I guess." I didn't believe him, and it made me feel awful. I loved this man with all my heart, but where was he headed with his escalating drinking and no apparent concern about it? Even so, life settled into a comfortable pattern. Kedar kept having his martinis though rarely to excess. I didn't like it, but who's perfect? I was sure there were things about me he would dearly love to change. Denial took over big-time.

We were invited to a cocktail party in Georgetown. The place was packed, and several tables offered "small chow," and the booze was flowing freely. The glasses were extra large, and I noticed he had one martini after another. In Shanghai that wasn't a good sign, so as soon as it was reasonable, I suggested we go home and relieve the baby-sitter. He tossed back a couple more, thanked the host, and we left.

His driving was okay and his speech clear, though he was showing telltale signs of trying to cover up by being overly solicitous about my day and the children. I wanted to take the sitter home, but he'd have none of it. He left and I cleaned up the kitchen. She lived just two miles away, so I expected him back in twenty to thirty minutes at least. It was late, and there was little traffic. Two and a half-hours later he came in looking just awful.

"What happened? Why did it take you so long?" I asked.

"I've been shot," he said, "but it's okay. Let's just go to bed."

"What do you mean you've been shot. Where? How did it happen?"

"I'll tell you about it in the morning," he said as he gingerly pulled his left arm out of his jacket. "See, there's nothing to it," he said, pointing to his arm. I could see where the skin was broken just above the elbow at the back of his arm. If a bullet had entered, there was no place where it had exited. I knew it needed attention, and sooner was better than later. It had to be reported to the police. I looked outside, but there was no car.

"Before I do anything," I demanded, "tell me what happened, and we'll know what to do next." From the tone of my voice and look in my eye he knew I meant business, and he'd better tell me.

"It was just one of those crazy things," he began. "I let the sitter off and started home when I had to relieve myself. I should have done it before we left the party–but I didn't, and I was about to pop. You know how it is over in that area–no trees or bushes to go behind, but a house nearby had a shadowed side, so I went there and began to pee. The owner thought I was a peeping tom. He shouted at me and threatened to shoot me. I took off. I was out of his yard and running up the street when he fired. My left arm took the bullet; but it wasn't enough to stop me, and he didn't try again. I didn't want to go back to the car and walked home."

I was flabbergasted. Things like that happened to other people, but not to us. His arm was beginning to swell, but he still just wanted to go to bed and snuggle. From the looks of it I knew it would be awfully painful. He needed immediate medical attention.

He didn't object when I called an ambulance and rode with him to Arlington Hospital. While there, they called the police and he made his statement. I felt sick to my stomach. I had to go home. The children couldn't be left alone any longer. I called a cab and told Kedar I'd be back first thing in the morning.

After Edwin was off to school the next day, I called Ruth and asked her what to do. I had no idea what would come next or how to prepare for it. I needed to know what would be done for Kedar. Somehow I felt disoriented and didn't know where to focus. I felt torn apart. John is a lawyer, and Ruth knew the basics of how to manage a problem like this. She talked with him briefly.

"I'll drive you over to get the car," she said, "then we will look after the children while you go see Kedar." It was such a relief to have somebody else tell me what to do. It made me feel confident that this business could be managed after all.

John made a few calls and found that the shooter also reported the incident and that he was bringing suit against Kedar for trespassing. I was horrified. What now?

"Don't worry, Fran," he said. "I have the name of a good lawyer right here in Falls Church, and he'll see you later today. Ruth will go with you, and don't worry about the cost. You'll probably have to pay no more than fifty dollars."

"Thanks, John," I said. "For you I'd almost become a Democrat."

The car was parked right where Kedar said he'd left it, another great relief, and after leaving the kids with Ruth, I drove back to the hospital. X-rays had already been taken that showed the bullet had entered the humerus just above the elbow and disintegrated, splintering the bone. It was still in his arm and would have to be removed. What a mess, and by that time Kedar was hurting a lot. Phone calls and consultations followed, and with a lot of in-put from John, Kedar was transferred to the VA hospital in the District, where the best surgeon was called in to make the repair. Praise the Lord for good government health and accident insurance.

The next step was the lawyer, and I had absolutely no idea what to expect. I trusted Ruth to make it work and had no anxiety about it. In the meantime he'd made some calls to get the lie of the land and offered his solution, which suited perfectly. Because the man had filed a suit against Kedar, we'd file a countersuit for his shooting Kedar outside of his property, both would be dropped. How in the world does anyone manage without good friends like the Jarmans?

A Tale of Two Bamboos

I had heard and read about depression, but had no appreciation for its debilitating effects. My attitude toward it was, come on, get a life, get up, get to work, and it will go away. How wrong I was! The second day after Kedar was hurt it took me all morning to comb my hair and do the breakfast dishes. Lead weights hung on my hands and feet. Nothing connected. Nothing worked. I was undone. I tried to pray, but there was no relief.

Ruth recognized what was going on and commiserated with me in my helplessness, saying that God was the one who would heal me. She prayed with me. She assured me that it would pass, that I shouldn't fight it. I must make sure to eat well and rest, and she'd look after the children. Knowing Ruth was there to see me through it made all the difference. In a few days the fog began to clear away and I stepped out of a long dark tunnel into the light. Depression? I came face to face with it and pray to God it will never happen again. Likewise I know how to empathize with others who are suffering with it.

During surgery they opened up Kedar's arm, both front and back, and picked out all the fragments. They put the splintered bone back together and applied a big cast. The first time I saw him he looked pitiful with his arm elevated and in traction. For a few days it was uncertain whether or not they could save the arm because of an infection, but the latest wonder drugs took care of it, and in a week he was home again.

The lesson is, "If you've got to go, go; and for goodness sake, do it on the far side of the car."

Now that we had no household help I spent more time with the three children. It was interesting to see how they were developing. Edwin was the quiet, thoughtful one. He enjoyed being with adults and listened. A day or two later he'd make very insightful comments on the people and the conversation.

If we had a dinner party with four or more guests, I

usually fed the children separately and put them to bed before we sat down. One night Edwin insisted he wanted to be included with the adults.

"Okay, son," I challenged, "you may eat with us but there's to be no getting up and down and running around. Do you understand?"

"Sure, I can do that," he agreed. We set a place for him. He was as good as his word, but toward the end of the meal I felt about two feet tall when I saw him sitting up straight in his chair with his head a little tipped to one side, fast asleep!

He, Jay Jarman and Jeffrey Blasom, a boy next door to the Jarmans, were the same age and played together doing boy-type things and often huddled together, whispering.

"I'd give my eye-teeth to know what those boys were talking about," Ruth confided one day. They were building a fort with blocks in the middle of the living-room floor and talking quietly when all of a sudden Edwin piped up saying, "Well, my father kisses my mother any time of the day or night!"

Anne attended a preschool in the neighborhood where mothers helped the teacher for a half-day every other week. She played well with others but showed a strong stubborn streak. I didn't object to it in the least. Nobody was going to push our Anne around. She was a pretty little thing with her curly golden hair and dark brown eyes. She and Susie Jarman were soulmates and never tired of playing with their dolls.

Jimmy was a bundle of energy and in constant motion. He stayed close to Ruth or me most of the time and was seldom quiet. Soon after we were settled he walked into the kitchen where I was working, holding my sewing shears.

"You know what, Mommy," he said, *you know what* prefaced everything he said, "I wouldn't think of cutting the curtains." He had the sweetest, most innocent look on his face.

"Do you want to show me something?" I asked as I offered my hand. He took it and led me to where he'd made a big cut in one of the dining-room sheers. We had a little conversation about it to establish that he was not allowed to get into my sewing things. There were tears and promises never to cut anything again without permission. It lasted for a little while anyway.

When the kids saw the car turn into our driveway at five o'clock they were out the door and all over Kedar because he always had a treat. After I got a kiss, too, he opened a beer, hit his recliner and tipped back for a few minutes to unwind. Jimmy had to have a conversation with his dad.

Falls Church, Virginia, 1952

During our second year on Linden Lane the Hess family moved in next door. Johnny was Jimmy's age. There were conflicts from time to time, and when Kedar came home we usually learned all about them.

"I hate Johnny Hess," Jimmy announced, sitting astride Kedar's lap.

"No, Jimmy. He's your friend, and you don't hate your friend."

"Yes, I do. I hate Johnny Hess."

"Can you tell me about what happened today," Kedar coaxed. "Did something make you feel that way?" Jimmy thought a little. Not being able to keep it in any longer said, "Well, we both had to pee, and since we were playing 'cowboys and Indians' out doors and didn't want to take the time to go in the house, I showed him how much fun it was to pee in the window-well. He went and told his mom," he said. "Boy, was she mad and made him go to his room. She didn't let us play the rest of the day. I really hate Johnny Hess."

I was in the kitchen fixing dinner and could hardly keep from laughing out loud. I knew by Kedar's voice he was having a hard time being serious, but he did his best to impress on the young man what a stinky mess we'd have if we did that. Really, she was right to be upset. With a little help Jim was able to see the logic and that he should apologize. Reluctantly he took his father's hand and they went next door to make it right. Oh, youth!

During the war, my sister, Betty, met and married army Lt. Arlan McClurkin, a veterinarian from Clay Center, Kansas. In 1946 they were appointed by the Board for Foreign Missions, Presbyterian Church (USA), to serve at the Allahabad Agricultural Institute in India.

In quick succession they had two little boys, John and Mike. When they were seventeen and four months old they contracted polio. The mission doctor was on furlough, so Dr. Carl Taylor came down from Futegahr and stayed with them for a week teaching them how to use the Sister Kenny treatment on John, whose left side was paralyzed. On his way down by train he stopped at every station to locate an iron lung for Mike because from the symptoms he was pretty sure he had bulbar polio. There were none. Before starting out, though, he asked all missionaries to drop everything and pray for Mike. He expected to find a dead baby, but the prayers were answered, and miraculously Mike survived.

John's left side was paralyzed, as was the left side of Mike's face. Mike's problem was most noticeable when that side of his mouth didn't smile. Also, he couldn't shut his left eye, but it did close when he relaxed in sleep. His paralysis gradually disappeared.

John's left deltoid muscle was destroyed, but he learned to compensate beautifully after three months of treatment. They lasted an hour at a time, during which the ayah sat and told him stories and sang to him. He learned Hindustani so well that Institute students loved to come and talk with him.

In 1951 they returned home on a leave of absence from the mission so Arlan could use the GI bill to get his P.h.D. in virology at the University of Wisconsin. The family stopped off for a visit in Falls Church. Their children and ours enjoyed each other, though there was very little communication. They spoke only Hindustani!

I was so thankful for Ruth's friendship in another area of my life–money. Kedar and I were brought up quite differently. He was the only son in the family and very little was denied to him. One of eight children, I grew up in the mission field. We always had enough, but very few extras. We had what we needed and most of what we wanted, but our wants were very different. If what we had worked, we kept it; but Kedar usually wanted something a little better, and therein lay the rub.

I paid the bills and managed the household finances. Often I was extra careful in order to get ahead when we were saving for something special. Just when we began to show a decent balance, without a word, he'd spend it. For example, we had a Buick that was just two years old and ran perfectly. When he saw the new Roadmaster Reviera he had to have it. Saying nothing to me, he traded in our car and paid off the balance from our account. He had the world on a string, and I was ready to chew nails I was so mad. Seeing him so happy I soon got over it, and we coasted along until he did something like that again. He also loved good cameras and watches. His toys were the expensive kind.

"Hey, Fran," Ruth said to me one day when I was terribly frustrated with the merry-go-round, "you're acting like a martyr, and on you it doesn't look good."

"What do you suggest I do about it?" I shot back. "I simply don't know."

"Easy," she said. "Kedar loves you, you know that; but he needs to learn about money management. I suggest you let him do it. The next time bills come in, stack them on his dresser along with the checkbook and tell him you've resigned as banker. Don't pay another one; don't ask about money or even how much he makes. You know he'll take care of you."

"That sounds pretty radical," I said, "but if you think it will bring some peace of mind, I'm willing to give it a try." And I did. It was the best advice I ever had. Kedar began to plan for our financial future and made sound choices on spending and investing, something we'd never done before. Oh, the Lord is good!

In the early 1950s most clothing was made of material that needed ironing. Wash-and-wear was usually nylon and very hot in the warm weather. Several in the family invested in an Iron-Rite open-ended ironer. With my weekly load it sounded like a good idea, but at $245 it was fearfully expensive. I spent at least one full day a week ironing, so Kedar decided it was a good investment. It really was a wonder. No more aching back and legs from standing hours on end; no heat and steam in my face during the summer. Ironing sitting down was a restful task to do at the end of the day. I could finish one of Kedar's shirts perfectly in two-and-a-half minutes!

"One of the problems about birthdays," Kedar teased, "is that you ask me for money and buy something I might not even like." I'll fix his trolley, I thought, and decided on a way to earn the money myself. Most of my neighbors ironed their husband's shirts, so I made the rounds and asked if they'd like to pay me ten cents apiece to do them. They brought them to the house washed and starched the way they liked them, rolled up and with hangers to put them on. They each had a day of the week, and most important, they were to say nothing to Kedar. When I got them done, Edwin made the delivery and collected the money. The kids thought it was exciting and managed not to tell. As May 11 drew near we talked about how his gift was growing and had him thoroughly convinced we'd bought a plant of some sort.

When the big day arrived, along with his cake we gave him an envelope containing a crisp, new fifty-dollar bill. Kedar always had a wish list, and a bonus of that size was fantastic. The next day we paid a visit to Heckinger's, where he bought a drill set he'd coveted for months.

"Ten cents a shirt!" he exclaimed, "That's a bunch, and I deeply appreciate it," he said, giving me a big hug. "But what about something that was growing?"

"The fund, silly," I said with a smile. "The fund was growing."

My neighbors were not about to let me off the hook. I kept ironing their shirts and other things like embroidered and cutwork tablecloths that were easy for me but backbreaking with the flat iron. Before we moved I'd made more than the cost of the machine, but Kedar did complain that the electric bill was a bit high. Tough beans!

Television was still so new that not every family owned one. We did. Sunday afternoon and evening became TV time, starting with "Victory at Sea" (showing how the navy won the war), the news, and a couple of shows like "Lassie Come Home" and "Bonanza."

Huntley-Brinkley was a must for weeknight viewing,

and sports events became very popular. One night a boxing match was scheduled at ten o'clock that John was aching to see, but they didn't have a set. He called to see if they could come over to watch it, and of course we said yes. Ruth was held up with one of the kids. In his pajamas and bathrobe John walked alone across the street and up to our door just as a car passed, going very slowly.

"Well, Fran," he said, "one of our neighbors down the street looked me over very carefully and probably thinks that either you or Ruth is being compromised. What a hoot."

Ruth didn't make it on time; it was one of the shortest bouts in recorded history. The winner knocked out his challenger in the first two minutes.

After Hunkey received her master's, degree, she accepted an appointment with the Holston Valley Community Hospital in Kingsport, Tennessee, as director of nursing services. Her responsibilities covered everything from managing candy stripers to the most sophisticated surgical and intensive-care nursing. Her job was to make sure the work assigned fit the skill level of each employee. She relished every moment.

She met Jim Dennis, one of the eligible bachelors in town, and before long they were an item.

A wall in Mother and Daddy's dining room featured the Rogues' Gallery, portraits of their eight children on the top row. Below each was a picture of the spouse, but it was never straight. Hunkey wasn't married, so the second row didn't exactly match the top one.

"Sit down," she said to Mother and Daddy when she called one evening. "I have some special news for you, and I don't want you to fall over in a dead faint."

"Okay," they answered, "we're sitting, and now what have you been up to?"

"I did something today so Daddy can straighten up the Rogue's Gallery," she said. "Jim and I got married. Because he's Roman Catholic we compromised, and an Episcopal priest married us in a private ceremony, just the two of us and a couple friends as witnesses. How about that?"

"That's wonderful, Cordelia," they chorused. "Now we'll have to drive to Tennessee and meet our new son-in-law. We are delighted; you know how to pick a winner." And she did. She moved into his apartment and continued her work at the hospital.

Rogues' Gallery

Eastman Kodak is one of the big industries in Kingsport. One of their plants manufactured dangerously unstable chemicals for processing colored film. The building was protected with double walls to contain the blast if there was an explosion.

One day just after Hunkey came off duty and was easing her sore back onto the bed, she heard a hoo-umph and knew immediately what it was–the plant had blown. Her back never quite hit the mattress. She raced to put on a fresh uniform, and before she got to the front door the ambulance sirens were wailing as they rushed to the disaster.

She knew it would be a mob scene as soon as the injured began to arrive and half the town wanting to know if a family member had been hurt.

"The first thing I did," she said, "was to find four men who seemed to be calm and dependable and put one at each of the doors. "Don't let anybody in who doesn't need treatment," she ordered. "Tell everyone else to wait outside. As soon as we have any information we'll notify them."

It was a pleasant, cool evening. The crowd gathered, circling the hospital and after a while began to sing hymns. As patients were identified, family members were called in. There was an orderly chaos amid which the greatest number of the injured and dying received appropriate care. Hunkey later learned that the men she'd assigned to guard the doors were pastors!

One of the nurses noticed a woman sitting in the hall. "I just got a pain in the belly," she said. The poor little thing saw so much trauma all around that she didn't press her needs.

"By any chance are you in labor?" a nurse asked after she'd heard the answer several times.

"Yes'm," she replied. They got her to the delivery room just in the nick of time.

I don't recall the number of dead and injured, but one of the city's most beloved citizens was at the center of the blast. All they found of him was one hand and his left jawbone.

After the city quieted down and normalcy was restored, Hunkey received a letter from the president of Kodak.

"It was brought to my attention," he wrote, "that after the explosion our people received the very best of care in an expeditious manner and that you were largely responsible for managing the crowds and patient care so that the greatest number were helped in a timely manner.

We wish to express our heart-felt gratitude in a tangible way. At your convenience, please come to our gifts room and make a selection."

She had no idea what to expect, but on the agreed date she went to select her prize. The room was full of every sort of treasure–a set of Spode for twelve; twelve place settings of sterling silver; fabulous linens from China; cameras and home-developing equipment–on and on. Typically, she chose a solid gold Omega watch for Jim.

After the Communists took over Shanghai, all was calm for a time. The troops entered quietly, walking on each side of the main street. When they rested, they sat on the curb, minding their own business. Shopkeepers hesitantly greeted them, offering tea.

Soon potholes in the streets were filled. People queued up in an orderly way to board city busses. Things were looking pretty good. Dad went to his office every day, but there was little to do. He still represented a dozen or more foreign interests, even though all business had ground to a halt. There was no hint of problems ahead, yet a quiet unease rested on the expatriate community. The American-run Columbia Country Club closed its doors; the French Club continued with its Sunday tea dances and dinner parties. People drank too much, worried about the future, and kept a watch over their shoulders.

Once the Communists were well entrenched, they closed the vise and terror began. Businesses were taxed to the point of bankruptcy. One large Chinese establishment saw no future so settled its affairs in a unique manner. The head of the family gave a huge feast for his family and the officials who were ruining him. The food was good and plentiful and laced with a deadly poison that killed them all!

Cars were garaged for lack of gas, and even the wealthiest learned not to wear their best clothes in public. One story tells of a merchant in a padded silk gown riding a rickshaw to work. He was pulled over to the side of the road by a soldier. Moments before, a pull-cart bumped a farmer carrying baskets of fresh eggs on either end of a shoulder pole. Two hundred eggs were broken.

"This poor farmer can't afford to lose the cost of his eggs, and the man who bumped him is also poor; so you pay," the soldier said.

"But I had nothing to do with the accident. I wasn't even here," the merchant protested. "Why should I pay?"

"Because you are rich and they are not," was the answer.

"I don't have any money with me," the man said, getting angry, "and I have an important meeting to attend."

"No," the soldier said, "you will stay here and send the rickshaw back to your house to collect the money from your wife. We will wait until he returns." He waited and he paid and learned an important lesson about how to dress in public.

There was also a flip side. A young British bachelor was out to dinner with friends and bargained for a rickshaw ride back to his apartment. As the operator pedaled, he sang out all manners of complaints against foreigners.

"They are all worthless, rich bastards and don't care about poor Chinese like me," he chanted. "Just a bunch of running dogs of Wall Street, as the good Comrades call them, and that's so. Mao is the hope of China and the sooner these foreign devils leave, the better." The passenger was amused until on a deserted road, half way to his home the man stopped.

"The price was not enough," he said. "I want twice as much, or I'll not go another inch."

"You can't do that," the young man shouted. "We agreed, and that has always been enough. Now come on, let's get going. It's late, and you're the slowest, laziest man in Shanghai."

A Tale of Two Bamboos

The argument continued with voices raised until a soldier rounded the corner and asked what the trouble was. With much shouting and gesticulating with loud curses, the rickshaw owner poured out his complaint.

"How much did you agree on?" the soldier asked. He berated the poor fellow, telling him to be honest and do the right thing. "The amount of the fare is half my monthly wages, so get on with you and be thankful you're not in the army."

He remounted the cycle and pushed on, mumbling all manner of invectives against the Communists.

"How in the world is a man supposed to live with these turtle-egg soldiers running things?" he cursed. "Oh, that the foreign devils would come back. They are much more generous," he moaned. "The gods are angry and we must suffer."

The compassionate passenger gave the man a large tip.

Huge sweeps in the middle of the night took place regularly, during which people disappeared. In a small village near Columbia Circle where the Bryans lived, five hundred were taken. There was no defense against unlawful arrest. Large sheets of paper pasted on walls listed the names of those found guilty of crimes against the people. Their sentence was given. Usually they were shot.

People stopped their ears at the sound of shrieking police sirens that swept a path before truck convoys racing through the city with their cargo of victims. Riding in the back, crammed in like cord wood, they stood with baskets over their heads and hands tied behind their backs. Their destination was vacant land near the airport, where they were off-loaded, lined up next to a ditch, shot in the back of the head, and covered with dirt. People trembled at the sound, knowing what it meant.

On January 17, 1953, the Saturday Evening Post published the first of four articles about Dad Bryan's ordeal as a prisoner of the Communists in Shanghai.

He was in his morning shower when there was a loud pounding on the front door. Al Ling, their faithful servant of many years answered; the police pushed him aside and went to the second floor.

They hauled Dad out of the bathroom, told him to dress and not to bother to collect anything as he was just being taken for questioning and would be back before dinner.

When Mother realized what was happening, she called out to him, "Be sure to dress warmly, Robert." They grabbed her and hustled her to the third floor, locked her in a bedroom, and told her to shut up!

Dad Bryan built the Ward Road Jail when he served as municipal advocate in the International Settlement of Shanghai. He was alarmed when they took him there and shoved him into the death cell with its cork-lined walls. He didn't go home that night or ever.

Mother tried repeatedly to find out about him, taking packages of food and vitamins. At first the guards accepted them kindly and promised they'd be delivered, but before long they cursed her and threw the packages back in her face saying, "Go away and stay away. Bo Liang (the nearest they could come to Bryan) will soon be put to death." All alone in their big house at 87 Amhurst Ave, she was terrified and felt utterly helpless.

Even in the worst of circumstances funny things do happen. One of their good friends was Ms. Barbara Littleton, a British Salvation Army officer. She did a lot of rehabilitation work and was respected by all. Women who'd served time in prison were often released to Barbara's custody. One day she called Mother.

"Gertrude," she said, "come to tea on Wednesday and bring a picture of Robert. I've just received a Russian woman who was released from Ward Road Jail. She did time for being an accomplice to a murder with a Korean woman who owned a brothel. Perhaps we can find out if she's seen him. She was put to scrubbing floors, and maybe she'll recognize him." Mother was more than happy to do anything to find out if he was still there.

"Yes, yes," the woman said when she saw Dad's picture. "He's on the fifth floor in the death cell, and he's getting very thin. Aside from that I don't know anything. I just saw him as I washed the hall floors."

"Is there any way you can get back in to find out about him?" Barbara asked.

"Well, maybe," she considered. "Since the brothel where I worked is closed, the wardresses tried to rehabilitate me by teaching me to sew and knit. When I left they said I could come back to take orders from them if I needed the work, so I could do that," she said with a smile.

"Splendid," Barbara exclaimed. "How soon do you think you could go?"

"Any time," she answered. "Perhaps tomorrow, and I'll see what I can find out about Mr. Bryan."

The wardresses were pleased to see her and know that their work with her was paying off. When all the business was negotiated as casually as possible she asked, "And what about that foreign devil on the fifth floor?" What is to become of him?" The words were no more than out of her mouth when the atmosphere changed from friendly to boiling anger.

"Why are you asking about that man, anyway?" With that they started shoving her toward the door, hitting and punching her. "He's a dangerous American spy, and he'll soon be shot along with all the other scum of the earth. Out, out of here, and don't ever come back again, do you hear?" they shouted as they gave her one final shove out the door.

"I don't know," she protested. "It's just that before I was arrested he was one of my regular customers, and he always treated me very well."

Miss Littleton and Mother were sorry that she didn't get a glimpse of Dad, but at least they knew he was still alive, and that was a comfort.

When Mother realized there was nothing she could to help Dad, she got an exit permit and left. Amazingly she was able to ship out all their household things, and in due course they arrived in good condition.

She came to stay with us in Falls Church for a few months until she could decide what to do next. She phoned, wrote letters, and pestered everybody in Washington she thought might be able to help, but China was not open to any diplomatic overtures, and it all seemed hopeless. She took a job at the National Cathedral School for Girls and moved to staff quarters on campus. The Department of State kept her informed of all they knew, which was precious little.

One other interesting thing happened that could not be explained until Dad returned to the States.

His older sister, Catherine, lived in Atlanta with a Chinese companion who looked after her. One afternoon as she napped, Catherine had a strange dream. "I kept seeing Robert's face," she said. "He came and went and kept saying to me, 'Catherine, I can't come just now. I can't come.' I don't know what that meant, but his presence was very real. I pray he's all right."

Catherine told Dad about the dream and when she'd had it. Thinking back on his experience in prison, he was able to relate her dream to the time he was being questioned and refused to admit that he was a spy. They tied his hands behind his back and beat him into unconsciousness with a rubber hose and left him on the floor for eighteen hours. After he came to and they returned him to his cell, his hands were numb and useless for days.

When he absolutely refused to admit he was a spy, they took him to the prison clinic, jerked his pants down, threw him across the operating table, jammed a needle into his spine, and injected him with sodium pentathol and questioned him. They found that indeed he'd been telling the truth, so they couldn't execute him after all.

They devised a plan to show him a way out that would let them save face. Face is everything. A captured Kuomingtang officer was put in his cell, and after a few days he explained that there were two ways Dad could effect his release. The first was to implicate someone else. Dad rejected that out of hand.

The second was possible, and he attacked it with relish. They wanted him to write a criticism of the U.S. Government, and after having served under Ambassador George C. Marshall, he was more than happy to do so. You will recall that he was an advisor to Marshall, who was mandated to negotiate a peaceful settlement between the Nationalists and Communists. Dad was the only one who said that the way they were told to do it would never work, and he was right.

For weeks as he wrote he also went through their re-education program. He pretended to agreed to all they said and parroted it back on command. He also had to confess and ask for forgiveness of all the crimes he'd committed, such as bringing Mao's second wife to trial because she tossed hand grenades into restaurants. Altogether he tried 11,000 cases; there were 10,000 convictions and 3,000 extraditions.

When they finally decided he was ready to leave, they put him on a train to Canton. The windows of the compartment were covered, and he never saw daylight until the train reached the Hong Kong border. All during the trip, his guard was Mr. Doo, a violent little Communist with a one-track mind.

"Boo Liang, promise me one thing," he said as he shook Dad's hand. "When you get to the States, you tell the truth about China."

"Yes," he answered. "I promise that when I get to the

States I'll tell the truth about China!"

On June 29, 1952, after sixteen months, seventeen days, and six hours of imprisonment by the Communists, Dad walked over the bridge to freedom!

In 1953 the U.S. Government launched another reduction in force (RIF), and Kedar got his pink slip. The rule was "last in, first out;" he was out. More than anything, he loved the oil business and living overseas. Hat in hand, he went to New York. Caltex let him sweat for a couple of weeks before asking him to come for some serious talks.

He was so happy to be back with them again. They wanted to keep us in the States for at least a year, and that was fine. He found a furnished rental house in Leonia, New Jersey, belonging to the Fitches (YMCA people from Shanghai and friends of the Bryans). We made the down payment and once again contacted a transfer company to move us. Leaving wasn't so hard because the Jarmans bought a larger house several miles away and were spending more time in Oklahoma City, but it's never easy to say good-bye to friends and start all over again finding doctors, dentists, and making all the adjustments to a new location.

Leonia is a delightful small town, one square mile, and you know when you're entering and leaving by the signs at the side of the road. It's west of Fort Lee, south of Engelwood, north of Bogota, and east of Hackensack. The Meadowlands were just a big swamp. They called themselves "high-minded, low-income" because a good percentage were professors in Columbia and New York Universities and City College. The police knew everybody, and if you didn't look as if you belonged, they kept you moving along. There were no bars. One could buy booze, but they didn't want you to sit down and drink in their town!

We immediately found a welcome in the Presbyterian

A Tale of Two Bamboos

Church, and I joined several support groups in the school and community. The kids walked to school and the police on duty at the crossing knew them all by name.

After several months in the Fitch house one that suited our family perfectly came on the market; and with a loan at 2.5 percent, we jumped at the offer. There was no need to carpool, for Kedar was able to catch the bus to New York a block away, which connected with the subway to the office.

Slowly we were becoming domesticated Americans. When we were in Falls Church, Kedar had his first experience with gardening. Our house was new and needed a few more shrubs and trees, so we sent an order to a nursery in New Jersey. It all came one morning the next fall-balls of dirt in sacking, a stick coming out of the top with a tag saying what it was and planting instructions. That meant digging a lot of holes, deep ones, and more than I wanted to do. I bought a shovel and a bag of fertilizer and was ready for the old boy when he came home.

He suggested I might want to undertake the task, but I told him it was a man's job, and I'd do the watering. Once he got to it he enjoyed the exercise and that evening put them all in.

A wonderful thing happened to Kedar the next spring. Before he came into the house at the end of the day, he checked on his "babies", holding up the new shoots to see how much they'd grown in twenty-four hours. He was so proud.

When he was a child in Shanghai, the gardener took care of the yard, and if he needed anything indoors, all he had to do was find the nearest bell (each room had one) and ring for Ah Ling.

In Leonia the garden was beautiful, but we wanted to do a little interior decorating and decided to tackle it ourselves. The small dining room, separated from the kitchen by an arch, had a loud "Johnny Appleseed" wallpaper with big red apples and branches of green leaves. We wanted something more neutral and decided to paint it. The owner of the hardware store suggested we strip the walls. We bought a sprayer and scrapers for the job. Little did we know the previous owner had protected it with a plastic spray so steam didn't soften the paper! Every square inch had to be scraped off bit by bit. It took days. Kedar did the upper half and I the lower; I also stripped a dozen or so layers of paint off the baseboard, the door to the sun porch, and window frames. At last the day came to paint. We got the very best and carefully followed instructions. It was a thing of beauty and a joy forever, and we were terribly pleased with our handiwork. What an accomplishment, and we did it! When it's the first time, it's wonderful.

All three of the kids seemed to have to put their hands on the walls and particularly the doorframes. Somehow they couldn't walk from one room to the other without touching them.

As we finished a leisurely dinner and were lingering over a second cup of coffee after the children had excused themselves, Jimmy stood in the doorway a moment until there was a break in our conversation to ask something, and naturally he had both of his hands on the newly painted woodwork.

"Get your hands off the walls," Kedar shouted so loudly that the poor child was traumatized. "Can't you see they've just been painted?" he thundered.

"Gee, Dad," he stammered, "but it's dry, isn't it? What's the big deal?"

"Sorry, son," he relented. "We just got through painting this room, so don't go and get it dirty right away, okay?" Before then he was totally oblivious to finger marks, but now that he'd put his own sweat into the job, he saw every little one.

After we'd lived there a year Kedar asked the company about their plans for him.

"Nothing at the moment," they said, so that was fine.

Accordingly, we bought a new set of tires for the car and added some kitchen cabinets.

Chapter 6

India

"Guess what the vice-president told me today?" Kedar asked with a big grin.

"I haven't a clue. Come on, tell me," I coaxed, knowing he could hardly wait.

"How would you like to live in India?" he asked. "How about going next month?"

"Wonderful," I answered, "but they just said we'd be here for another two years. Talk about women changing their minds."

"The family that was scheduled to go can't, so we're it. I'm excited about the opportunity."

In a moment everything changed. We had to terminate involvement in local activities; collect family medical, dental, and school records; schedule shots and physical exams; and update passports. We added stocking up on a three-year supply of underclothing and socks for the whole family and dozens more tasks to the to-do list.

Soon after Kedar received his official assignment to Madras, we were invited to a dinner for Bob Marshall, an Australian accountant who worked at the company's headquarters in Bombay. Seated next to him, I pumped him all evening about what to expect.

"Bob," I said, "does Madras have the cool season?"

"My deah," he answered, looking at me over the top of his bifocals, "Madras doesn't boast a cool season. It's either hot or a hell of a hot."

I began to feel the tiniest bit apprehensive after calling several friends who had lived in India. Initially their response to my announcement was the same–dead silence followed by half-hearted congratulation. The first I spoke to was a near neighbor. "Barbara," I said, "you were born and raised in Cochin, so I'm counting on you to fill me in on details they don't put in guidebooks."

"Sure," she said. "Fran, we need to talk. How about lunch tomorrow. Twelve-thirty?"

"It's a date," I said, wondering at her slight hesitation instead of the hearty enthusiasm I expected.

"How old is Anne?" she asked as we began to eat.

"She's eight; Edwin's twelve, and Jim is six."

"The boys will be fine, but you'll have to take special care with your daughter."

"We're always careful with her. What are you talking about? What's the difference between here and India? Tell me," I insisted.

"You're probably aware," she continued, "that I have periods of 'down time.' Things build up slowly until they're just too much for me. Then I go under the care of a psychiatrist, sometimes in the hospital for a month or so. It saves my life," she said with composure, though I noticed a slight tremor in her hand. She didn't look me in the eye as she spoke.

"It all began when I was six. You have to understand that we lived quite differently in India. The houses were big and open because of the heat–wide verandahs all around, high ceilings, and fans. The caste system required different servants for everything–they beat unions a mile. Each had a specific job and didn't do anything else. Much of what we go to shops for here was taken care of at home. For instance, a barber came around every Saturday. Mother made sure he used our instruments so we wouldn't catch other people's head lice and skin diseases! Another regular was the *durzie* (tailor) who sewed for us. All he needed was a picture, and he'd make a perfect copy of anything. It was a good thing, too, because there weren't any ready-made clothes in the market but plenty of good cloth.

"As you know Dad was a professor and founder of the Cochin University."

"Wasn't he given special recognition for his work?"

"That's right, and Mother worked right along with him. We children were left pretty much to the care of the servants. All of them were professed Christians, so our parents felt we were safe," she said with a sigh, "but I wasn't." Barbara looked sad as she stared out of the window, remembering.

"The *durzie* sat on the floor out on the balcony, working with his hand-turned sewing machine. One day he was cutting out a pair of shorts for me. As he took my measurements he ran his hands over my bottom, and when he took the inside seam on the legs, he pressed up with his fingers. I pulled away.

" 'Be a good girl and stand still,' " he said. He was a trusted person, so I obeyed." I noticed her hands were trembling and winced at the expression of rage on her face.

"Barbara," I said, "I get the picture. You don't have to go on. I know it's terribly painful for you."

"No, I must tell you," she said, regaining her composure. "I owe it to you and Anne. As you might guess, it didn't stop there. For six years he fondled me and eventually raped me several times. He finally quit when I began having my periods."

"Why didn't you tell your parents?" I asked in horror.

"He said he'd kill me if I did, and I believed him. 'It is easy to bring in a cobra to bite you or put poison in your food you'll never taste,' he said. Since he was a professing Christian, I was sure my parents wouldn't believe me, so I just kept quiet. I'm still paying a terrible price."

"Oh, my precious friend," I said putting my arms around her, "I'm so sorry. You've had a rotten time of it, but I'm glad you told me. I'll be super careful with Anne."

"Just make it a rule never to be broken that she won't ever be alone with a man. Having an ayah in the house is good insurance, so hire one."

I felt sick at heart for my friend, but that was just the beginning of such tales. Another told of a missionary family that believed the best way to minister to the people was to live among them. Instead of residing in a compound they chose to have a house just like others in a small town, and it was open to all. The community was friendly and accepting, and they were encouraged.

Each year during the heat of summer, missionaries take their long vacation in the mountains, where the children's schools are located–Woodstock in the Himalayas in the north and Kodaikanal in the Nilgiris Hills in the south. Extreme temperatures on the plains are hard on the young, so they are sent off to boarding school at the tender age of six. The three months of vacation are a reprieve for those who must endure premature separation from their little ones. It's also a time for dental check-ups, annual physicals, and booster shots.

It was during such a time that two young girls in one family were found to have syphilis. Questioned, they said one of the neighbors invited them in, and to be polite and friendly they went. They were sexually molested. They said nothing because they were told that was what you did in India!

Forewarned is forearmed. As soon as we were settled into 13F Cenotaph Road, I called the servants together. After laying out the daily schedule and what we expected of each, I addressed the ayah.

"Your most important job is to make sure Anne is always safe. She's never to be alone with a man. Do you understand?"

"Yes, memsahib," she answered, "I understand." To the men I made it very clear that if anyone ever bothered her, he'd answer for it. They got the picture, and I moved on to other matters.

"If we are to stay healthy and strong it's important to wash your hands frequently. Please use the soap and nail brushes I've provided, and the towels are to be changed daily. Everything connected with food is to be done with clean hands." That was by no means the end of it. I watched them like a hawk, concluding that having servants is a mixed blessing; but when in Rome.

Once again parties became an important activity. At the time, India had prohibition except in clubs and hotels. In order to get all the booze they wanted, foreigners only had to sign a statement that they were alcoholics, which allowed them to buy four fifths of spirits a month. What strange psychology! Instead of drinking less, those attending parties seemed to feel duty-bound to finish up any open bottles; thus more alcohol was consumed than ever.

Late one Friday afternoon we were getting ready to leave the Gymkana Club when one of South India's violent storms hit. Almost without warning clouds gathered, lightning split the sky, and thunder crashed. The heavens opened. Kedar had just arrived from the office to pick us up, and since such storms were usually of short duration, we dashed to the main building to wait it out. Children under the age of eighteen were not welcome in the lounge. The only alternative was for us to stay out of doors under shelter. We encouraged the kids to be quiet and not draw anyone's attention. We sat talking about the day when Eric Sopher, Kedar's immediate boss, stopped by to say hello. Kedar stood with him, briefly discussing business while the rest of us waited.

One of the children's routines in the States was watching Saturday morning cartoons. Getting started on a fast departure, a character spun his wheels, then clouds of dust billowed as he whizzed away. Surprise was shown as eyeballs shooting out and back. Everything was greatly exaggerated.

Mr. Sopher's eyes were slightly protruding, which Jimmy found very interesting. I should have been alert to his careful scrutiny of the man.

"Mr. Sopher," Jimmy piped up during a lull in the conversation, "you must have seen a lot of exciting things, because your eyes are popping out."

Oh, that the earth would open up and swallow me! Immediately I saw the connection Jim made, but no amount of explanation was going to fix that one. I don't remember what happened next, except that the rain stopped as suddenly as it began; we said our good-byes and departed.

"While living in India," the district manager said to us soon after we arrived in Madras, "we ask you not to discuss politics or religion. We're here to sell oil, and it's inappropriate to involve ourselves in those areas."

"Understood," Kedar said, "but that will be hard for Fran–she finds them the best of all topics. We'll honor the request, though, won't we dear," he said, looking at me. Naturally I agreed. There was one stipulation I liked, however. If we were asked about what we thought or believed, it was all right to have our say.

Indian politics was interesting; but as long as Nehru was prime minister, there was really no contest on the national level.

One of the principal subjects of debate was a common language. Hindi was declared official in the north, but those were "fight'n words" in Madras, where they spoke Tamil. There are a half-dozen major and hundreds of minor dialects. Only English was spoken throughout the land, thanks to the two hundred years of British rule when it was taught in school. With independence in 1947 it was dropped as a required subject.

When Kedar traveled the countryside to visit dealers and distributors, one or two Indian salesmen accompanied him. They'd often cover territory with as many as three different dialects, so business was conducted in English.

In Bangalore we were invited to many official functions because Kedar was the station manager. We were there when Nehru gave the major address at the opening of the Integral Coach Factory. After the traditional prayers and offerings to the gods, he was presented with garlands before addressing a huge crowd of several thousand. Kanerese is the local dialect, but he used English with no interpreter, even though most couldn't understand him.

He spoke of how the factory would create many jobs and fill a need for well-built train coaches for all of India. Then he launched into one of his favorite subjects–education. No matter what he said, every time there was a pause, the crowd roared its approval. That man could do no wrong. Near the end of his talk we were much amused when he bellowed over the loudspeaker, "This is a cow-dung society with a cow-dung mentality!" and they shouted his name louder than ever.

Religion, however, was another matter. Because my faith is very precious to me, it's hard not to talk about it; but I found a way. The saying goes, "Scratch an Indian, and he'll talk about his faith." That's true, so I did a lot of scratching. When I accompanied Kedar on business trips, we spent long hours in car or train that were excellent opportunities for conversation. My tactic was to ask our traveling companions question after question about their beliefs until at last they'd ask about mine. I was ready.

A good Hindu is constantly giving money to the temple or doing something for charity to gain salvation. That phrase is frequently used–it's something never far from their minds. Karma ordains that they are born into one of the many castes, depending on how good or bad they had been in a former incarnation. If they were very good and lived exemplary lives, there was a chance their next one would be at a higher level. If not, they'd find themselves reduced to a lower caste or even to being dogs. Only the gods could tell.

If a person lived a blameless life and was generous at the temple, his soul would go to Nirvana, oneness with god. After hearing a lengthy explanation of the process one day, I asked a friend about it.

"Do you know of anyone who has met that standard?"

"One or two very good, holy people I've known may have attained salvation, but I'm not sure."

"And how about you? Do you think you can make it this time?"

"I doubt it," she answered with a laugh, "but perhaps I'll gain salvation next time." What a hopeless future. I felt sad for her. On a trip during the monsoon, Kedar, two sales reps, and I got into a long discussion about what we believed. The Indians were astonished to learn that Christians don't earn their way to heaven, that the price was paid for our sins when Jesus died on the cross, and salvation is free to all who accept him as savior and turn away from their sins.

Near the end of the day we came to a rickety bridge crossing a rain-swollen river. The brown water boiled just under the planks, whose supports looked none too sturdy. We sat there wondering if we should try to cross or wait a few hours for the flood to subside.

"I suggest," said one of them, "that Mrs. Bryan cross first; then if it's safe the rest of us can follow. If she falls into the river and drowns, it doesn't matter since she has already gained salvation!" We all laughed, but I was pleased that he'd heard the Good News, even in a backhanded sort of way.

We took an overnight train trip to the Sirohi, north of Ahmadabad, to present a plaque to an outstanding distributor. The town was in the territory of the Jains, a very strict Hindu sect to whom all life was sacred. Holy men wore gauze face masks to avoid breathing in microscopic life and walked along sweeping the path ahead so they wouldn't run the risk of stepping on insects. All cooking was done during daylight hours so no bugs would be attracted to the fire and killed. Considered destructive of plant life, eating vegetables and fruit with many seeds was forbidden.

We went to view a huge granite statue on top of a hill overlooking the city and in the evening were entertained at a golf club. As we sat on the patio for drinks before dinner, I got to talking with the son of the day's honoree. I asked about his family, his business, and of course his adherence to Jainism. The religion is very specific in the number of incarnations one must pass through–a quarter of a million–beginning as a single-celled life form and working up to a human being. The ultimate goal is to attain such perfection that all attachment to things in this life is broken, and one becomes completely centered on god. In due course the young man asked me what I believed.

"I'm a Christian," I answered, "and our relationship to God is explained in the Bible as that of a father to his children. You have two precious little ones, and I'm sure you love them with all your heart. There is no way they can understand your love just yet, but as they grow and mature they will appreciate all you've done for them, the sacrifices you've made, and the joy it was for you to do so. It would break your heart if they didn't return your love.

"It's the same with us and our Heavenly Father. He sent his only Son to make the ultimate sacrifice for our sins in his death on the cross. And by accepting his forgiveness, he's made a place for us with him in heaven. Our salvation is secure. In the meantime he fills our life with every good thing, and it makes his heart glad when we're appreciative." The young man nodded but looked perplexed. "For example," I continued, "if you went to the market and bought a bright red toy car for your little son, wouldn't it be a great pleasure to see his eyes light up with joy, to have him thank you and give you a big hug?"

"Of course," he said. "He's a smart little fellow, and I love to spoil him and his baby sister."

"What would you think," I pressed, "if he said he didn't want any more gifts and turned them away?"

"But he wouldn't do that. I know what he likes."

"My point exactly. Our Father in heaven delights in providing us with good things, and it gives him joy when we thank him." During the conversation the sun set, and the sky was ablaze with color. Rays of light shot up between gathering clouds. It was breathtaking. "Just look at that," I said. "God has painted a beautiful picture for us to enjoy. Every day he shows us his love and care in so many different ways. All he wants in return is our obedience, love, and thanks."

"Thank you, Mrs. Bryan," he said as the bearer called us to dinner. "I would like to give you a copy of our holy book, the Bhagavad-Gita."

"I appreciate your kindness," I said as I accepted it, carefully using my right hand. "And may I give you a copy of the book of John from our scriptures?"

"Yes, certainly," he said, taking it with a slight bow.

I never saw him again, but I've often wondered if his heart was ready to receive John's message. Perhaps a seed was sown, another will water it, and in time it will take root and grow.

Privacy. Everybody wants it, but if you have household servants, forget it. As circumspect as you might be, they still know everything you do, think, or say and love to share choice tidbits. Because the British ruled India for two hundred years, even the poorly educated speak some English, which makes life a lot easier for foreigners.

Robert was our bearer, the number-one boy who managed the rest of the staff. Although I spoke to all of them, he saw to it that my orders were carried out. His principal tasks were to dust and clean, set the table, and serve. He greeted guests, took messages, and mixed drinks. His uniform was a starched white cotton Nehru outfit and cap.

Because we had so much more of this world's goods than they, it was generally accepted that they'd equalize the situation without taking more than their share. It's a fine line. When something was missing I was sure I hadn't lost, a friend suggested a method for retrieving it. In 1955 ballpoint pens were still a luxury and quite expensive. I had a three-year supply but used only a couple at a time. Occasionally one disappeared.

"Robert, while you're cleaning today, please see if you can find my pen. I'm so careless these days. I keep putting it down and forgetting where. Perhaps it's fallen between the sofa pillows–I don't know," I said, all the while looking bewildered. More than likely he'd hidden it to see if it was missed, and if not, after a few days out the door it went. The lost was often found and returned with great ceremony. Oh, the games we played!

The cook had the greatest opportunity for "squeeze" because having the necessary contacts, he did almost all the grocery shopping. I particularly liked the crayfish man who sometimes showed up at our back door with what he had left over after making the rounds of hotels and restaurants.

"Good and fresh, memsahib," he'd say. "Only two rupees one piece (about fifty cents). You can try?"

"Well, let's see," I answered. "Empty the sack on the back porch. Any that are still crawling around I'll take." It pleased him, when only a couple had given up the ghost. Good for us, too, as we had an eighteen-cubic-foot freezer with lots of room! I love lobster salad for lunch.

The ayah did the laundry in a wringer-type washing machine, took care of my clothes and the children's, (Robert was responsible for Kedar's), did odd jobs around the house while keeping an eagle eye on Anne. The chokidar cleaned the floors, swept the walks, washed and waxed the car, and tended the garden. He was a skinny little fellow and worth every annah of his pay.

From noon to four o'clock was rest time when the whole community seemed to put up a "Don't Disturb" sign. You didn't ever call or expect to be called. It was too hot to move. Days started early while it was cool and went until late when it was tolerable once again. I used the time to write letters and read.

One afternoon there was a terrible fight in a bamboo hut right next to the fence, ten feet from our house. I could hear the blows falling on somebody's back accompanied by wild screams. After a moment or two of silence it started again, so I rang for the bearer.

"Robert, find out what's going on. I'm afraid that woman's being severely injured."

"Yes, memsahib." He shook his head and left. Within five minutes all was quiet.

"What did you do, call the police?" I asked him at teatime.

"No, I just went over there and told the man he had to quit beating his wife because it was disturbing memsahib's sleep."

Robert was willing to go with us to Bangalore for our second year in India. There we acquired Sam, the cook, from the Caltex family we were replacing. He was a delight–large, jolly, and eager to show off his talents. Nothing pleased him more than for us to have a luncheon, dinner, or cocktail party–the bigger the better and as often as the budget would allow. He was wonderful and could make anything, but he was also light-fingered with our stores; so I locked up all that didn't need to be refrigerated. As we went through a recipe for say, muffins, I reminded him what the yield should be, and we always got exactly that many–but they were very small! He did have a wife and seven children, so how else was he to feed them?

When we left Bangalore, Rita Van Warmelo hired him. She'd had many a meal at our house and recognized a good cook. A month or two later I had a letter from her. "Fran," she complained, "Wybe and I each have just a little sugar in our tea, yet Sam says we're using ten pounds a week, and all our staples seem to disappear like magic. Did he do this to you?"

"Hey, you've got 'Stealin' Sam', " I wrote back. "If you want to survive his services you'll have to keep the keys to the larder in your possession. Sorry, I should have warned you." She kept him but was a lot wiser.

Probably the best we had was Basimba in New Delhi. After several disappointments, he came to us as a gift from heaven. He was a cook/boy, which gave him high status and better pay. A proud man, he refused the use of the servant's quarters on the property. He lived in a large made-over moving van and dared not leave it for fear it would be stolen or invaded by strangers. He was well trained and required little guidance. Even the best of them, though, needed correction from time to time, and applying it was almost my undoing. He stood in front of me, head down, hands clasped behind him. As I enumerated his shortcomings he repeated over and over, "Yes, memsahib, thank you, memsahib," until I could stand it no longer. Fortunately, he rarely needed scolding.

One of the funniest stories I ever heard about domestic help came from friends while they were escaping the Madras heat. Arthur Conway worked for one of the British banks. At the time, he and Betty had two small children, so she took a hotel cottage in Bangalore and he spent weekends with them.

Arthur and Betty were accustomed to having a drink before dinner. Each had noticed that the booze was going down rather fast and thought the other was drinking alone.

"Betty, do you sometimes have a drink before I come home?" Arthur asked one night.

"Heavens no!" she responded indignantly, "but I thought perhaps you might be."

"Well, if you're not and I'm not, then that leaves the bearer. If he's helping himself to our liquor, he'll have to go. I'm sorry about that, but we simply can't have him drinking up our supply." They expected him to deny it; then they'd sack him. After dinner Arthur took the plunge.

"Yes, sahib," he admitted, looking Arthur in the eye, "quite often when it is very hot and dinner is late, I take a little nip. It helps me to keep going." They were so taken aback by his honesty that they decided not to fire him but laid down the law about no more drinking.

Many households employed sweepers whose exclusive job was to clean toilets. Every bathroom had an outside entrance, so they needn't go into any other part of the house. They were hired and fired by the bearers who regulated their pay. Of the untouchable caste, they were filthy, and went from house to house with brush and bucket, doing their lowly job.

After several changes Betty was confronted by one who had been replaced several months earlier. She was obviously pregnant and wanted to inform Betty that her bearer was responsible.

"When family go off to Bangalore for summer, your number-one man do this to me on the memsahib's bed," she reported.

"I tell you," Betty said, "I was fit to be tied and could hardly wait for Arthur to get home. It made my flesh crawl to think of that filthy creature in my bed!" After dinner the culprit was once again called to account for his behavior. He looked thoughtful, nodding from time to time as he listened.

"And this sordid business took place on the memsahib's bed!" Arthur concluded.

The man drew himself up with a look of indignation. "Not on the memsahib's bed; on the nursery-room floor!"

India boasts two fine boarding schools; Woodstock in the Himalayan Mountains in the north and Kodaikanal in the Nilgiris Hills in the south. Both were organized and run by American Protestant missions to keep their children in country through high school rather than sending them abroad.

For the British it's a given that their young will be packed up and sent to boarding in England at the tender age of seven. They return in droves for summer vacations, looking terribly white. They immediately shed their uniforms for comfortable clothes and kick up their heels. There is much joy and celebration of their homecoming, but they also seem a bit like strangers. Two months is not really enough time to become a family again.

The custom of sending children away for school started when England first occupied India. Caucasian youngsters did not do well in the intense heat, and diseases for which there were no cures wiped out whole families. Rupert Main, a Caltex gentleman in Bombay, asked us to check records and cemeteries in Bangalore for traces of his family that had served there more than a hundred years. We didn't locate his name, but it was terribly sad to see one small grave after another bearing dates just days apart when the little ones died in cholera epidemics.

Edwin was the first to go to Kodai, and he adjusted quickly. I had no qualms about sending him because my boarding school experience in Korea was so good that I cherished the same for our three. Anne and Jimmy attended Bishop Cotton's boys and girls schools, first in Madras and then in Bangalore. Jimmy tolerated it pretty well but not Anne. She couldn't wait to go to Kodai as soon as there was an opening. She was admitted after we moved to Bangalore, and Jim went the following year.

Kodai is 7° north of the equator, and at an elevation of

eight thousand feet the climate is near perfect. Located on a plateau on top of a mountain, it is cool and lush with pure, uncontaminated air. The classrooms, gym, chapel, dining room, and kitchen are in the center. The boys' dorm is down a slope on one side and the girls' on the other. A small lake within view of the school gives the campus a picture-perfect alpine appearance.

All three of the children suffered some degree of homesickness. Anne expressed it the most strongly with her tear-stained letters that arrived weekly her first term, even though she had been anxious to go there. When friendships developed and she got into more extracurricular activities, the splotched writing paper gave way to cleaner sheets as she told of the regular Sunday afternoon three-mile walks around the lake. She loved hikes out in the hills to gather flowers for the church, particularly at Easter when they covered the big chapel cross with lilies. Edwin loved to hunt for wild orchids and found beautiful blossoms for a girl he was taking to the school party one Saturday night. Jim's letters were full of the fun little boys have, and he especially liked rowing on the lake.

Once when I was kissing them good-bye, I noticed the tissues I normally had in my sweater pockets were missing. Anne fessed up that she and Jimmy had taken them because after I'd gone, they tucked them under their pillows and took them out at night to hold to their faces because they smelled like me. Precious babies–how I wanted to hug them. It reminded me of when I was young and loved to hug my mother, breathing in her fragrance.

Bangalore was not on a direct route to Kodai, but I usually managed to bum a ride once or twice a semester with other parents going up. JT and Ruth Seamands, Methodist missionaries, were good friends whose four daughters were there. They offered to take me, and I jumped at the chance. We were at their house at five in the morning for a cup of coffee before leaving. Then, tucked in with loads of gifts and treats for seven children, it was time to go.

"First let's pray," JT said. Kedar and I held hands through the open window and bowed our heads. "Lord," he shouted, "protect us from drunks and fools, Amen." JT turned the key in the ignition, flipped on the lights, and we roared out the gate. We left Kedar standing there with a look of surprise on his face at such an abrupt prayer.

When the polio vaccine became available in the States, Caltex sent enough for all company children in all foreign countries. The assignment for India was packed in ice in a cooler and hand-delivered to a staff member in the Bombay airport. There it was re-packed in coolers for several destinations. The one for those in Kodai arrived at the Bangalore airport that evening. Early the next morning we were on our way with the precious cargo. We were so thankful that Caltex took so much care for our kids' protection.

The student body at Kodai is not large, but a full curriculum is offered from grades four through twelve with college preparation and Christian education as its principle goals. A number of small village inns are within a block or two of the school as well as guest rooms in private homes that welcome visiting parents. Our favorite was Allie Stool's cottage right on the western bluff. She ran a perfect Scottish establishment complete with three meals a day, chota-hazri, little breakfast, served in your room consisting of a banana each and a pot of tea, milk and sugar and high tea at four o'clock. Tea was serious business with scones, butter and jam, meat pies, mixed fruit with cream, cheese balls, sandwiches, cake and cookies, and a few other goodies thrown in. Once during a stay the children were invited to tea without charge. After that you paid, but the price was small.

We always booked a room with Allie well in advance of our visit. We couldn't get enough of the stout, jolly woman with her thick accent and generous heart. She loved to share stories of the ghosts she'd seen, and the greatest gift we could give her was anything having to do with Queen Elizabeth. Her admiration was little short of worship. On one occasion she wept, holding to her generous bosom a copy of Life magazine we'd brought her featuring the royal family.

The public golf course a few minutes away by car was a challenge. Its clubhouse was right on the edge of a thousand-foot drop-off. At the end of the day if there were balls full of "smiles", it was fun to make a spectacular drive as the ball sailed off into the thin air and dropped out of sight.

The weather was so unpredictable that we carried rain wear in our golf bags. Once Lou Berdine and I crested a hill to see a huge black cloud coming right at us. Within minutes we'd be soaked if we didn't don our gear in a hurry. Both of us wore our hair in a chignon, and I was always envious of how perfectly she did hers.

"Lou Berdine, you cheat," I said as I watched her remove a few bobby pins and tuck her hairpiece into a pocket of her golf bag! All there was left was a little stump of hair a couple of inches long and held together with a rubber band.

"Sure beats doing what you go through every day," she said with a smile. "How long's yours?"

"Down to my waist. I'm so used to putting it up I can do it in the dark," I answered. "But I'm envious of your arrangement. I can't cut my hair, though. Kedar likes to lie in bed at night and watch me take it down and give it a hundred strokes–he's a sentimental guy."

When we moved to New Delhi after home leave, we decided to send Edwin, who was in high school and floundering academically, to McCallie School in Chattanooga, Tenn., where Kedar said he'd spent the best years of his life. Anne and Jim in grade school were doing well, and we relished the idea of having them at home with us again while they attended the New Delhi American School.

Soon after arriving in Madras, Edwin developed a persistent cough. He was a healthy twelve-year-old, so I assumed it would run its course and go away. It didn't. He was what the clothing industry called "husky," but when he began to shed pounds and became listless, I made an appointment with a doctor recommended by Caltex. After what seemed to be a thorough examination the doctor prescribed a tonic. "You know, Mrs. Bryan," Dr. Gupta said, "you are new to this country. The tropics are hard on youngsters from temperate climates, but I think this will build him up quickly." Edwin took it, but it didn't help.

After several more trips to the doctor he was no better, and my new friend, Patty Evans from Australia, laid down the law. "Fran," she said, "you must tell the doctor to take a chest X-ray and run blood tests. He hasn't done that yet, has he?"

"No he hasn't, but he's the doctor. I can't tell him what to do."

"Oh, yes you can, and you must," she scolded. "I've been here for ten years, and believe me, you've got to take control."

"Okay, I'll call today," I answered. "I don't like the way Edwin looks, but I don't like telling the doctor his business, either."

"It is your business when it's your son's health. Now call." I did and made another trip into town.

"Dr. Gupta," I said after seeing him go through the same routine as before, "Edwin's been sick too long. Will you please order chest X-rays and blood tests to find out what's going on?"

"Good idea, very good idea," he said as he reached for his prescription pad. "Tell your driver to take you to the hospital, and be sure to give this chit to the person at the desk. He will take you to the right departments and make sure the tests are completed today."

I took the paper and put my arm around Edwin as we

left. Patty was right, but it felt strange. All my life I was told not to question the wisdom of a medical doctor. He went to school for years and knew how to treat what ailed us. If he said "jump," we asked "how high?"

The next day Edwin was worse and was running a fever. By noon it was 102°F. "Have the results from the tests come in?" I asked Dr. Gupta's nurse.

"Just a moment, please," she answered. "I'll let you speak to the doctor."

"Yes, Mrs. Bryan," he said when he picked up the phone. "I'd like you to bring your son in again this afternoon. He has a serious lung infection and pneumonia. How soon can you get here?"

"I'm not taking him out of this house," I said, anger showing in my voice. "His fever is going up steadily, and I'll be most grateful if you'd come to begin whatever treatment is indicated."

"Yes, yes, I'll be out straight away," he said and hung up.

By the time he arrived Edwin's temperature was 104°F, and he was too quiet. A week after several penicillin shots he was back to normal; the cough was gone, and he was raring to go.

I now understood what Patty meant about taking control, but it still didn't feel right. It was a whole new world, and I needed to learn survival skills from those who'd been here for many years.

Edwin was no sooner back on his feet than Jim came down with a bad sore throat plus huge tonsils and adenoids. After the acute infection was gone the tonsils were still very large; we consulted a surgeon. Edwin's had come out in Peking, Anne's in the States, and now it was Jim's turn.

"You may stay with Jim until he's asleep if you'd care to," Dr. Rao said. Being able to remain until the little guy was completely out was awfully nice I thought, so I stood by the operating table holding his hand. Not a good idea at all! After a couple of breaths of ether he was out; but fighting for air, he thrashed around so hard it took four attendants to hold him down. When he was completely under, he was quiet, but his struggle left me shaken. The surgery went well, with hardly any aftereffects.

Jim, in the sixth grade, joined Edwin and Anne at Kodaikanal boarding school in the Nilgiris. His roommate was Pat Berdine. The boys thought it was neat to have the same initials, J. P. B. Mike, his older brother, was in junior high. Their parents, Denny and Lou, were with Caltex, building a refinery at Vishagahaputnam (Visag for short) on the east coast of India. It was a good-sized town with a university, small industries, and a hospital. The Berdines had just moved into their new house when Mike and Pat went home for the two-month Christmas break. Lou used potted plants everywhere to soften the still unlandscaped lot. One morning Mike jumped over a croton, slipped, and fell from the second-floor balcony. Unfazed, he got up and went back up the stairs to his bedroom.

"Oh, boy, Mike," Pat yelled, "Mom's going to be mad at you for breaking her pot."

"What happened," she asked. "Are you all right, Mike?

"It's nothing," he said. "Sorry about the pot. My leg hurts a little. I think I'll lie down for a while." Being a nurse, Lou checked him over and decided an X-ray was in order. Sure enough, his leg was fractured through the femur.

"What a rotten time for this to happen!" she said to Denny as they waited for Mike to come out of surgery. "Only two days until the opening ceremonies for the refinery with Nehru and the U.S. and Indian big shots. What a mess."

"The good news, though, is that the chief of staff is an orthopedic surgeon," Denny answered. "Could we ask for anything more?"

"Yeah–that it didn't happen," Lou answered, "but we're lucky Mike will have good care. We can party and do all the ceremonial stuff without worrying." Mike's leg was set with a pin, and he stayed in the hospital during the festivities. After the dignitaries departed, Lou was shocked to see how ill her son looked. His color was bad; he was lethargic and complaining of terrible pain.

"I think he's just missing his home," Dr. Sandi said. "Why not take him back with you, give him food he likes, and he'll come around quickly." That's what they did, but Mike kept getting worse. Several times Lou asked to see the X-rays taken after the surgery, but they were never forthcoming.

"I demand to see those films," Lou stormed, "and I'm not leaving until you show them to me."

"Yes, of course," the technician answered. "Here they are," he said as he clipped them to the light box. Lou was stunned. The pin was improperly placed, and the femur was thirty degrees out of position. Left unattended, it would slough away, and the child would be crippled!

"Dr. Sandi, how in the world could you say Mike was fine after you saw these X-rays?" she demanded.

"I'm sorry," he answered. "I did my best. Perhaps it's the Lord's will." Not trusting herself to open her mouth, she took the films and left.

Markers were called in and wires pulled. With four seats removed to make room for a stretcher, they were on a Pan Am flight direct from Calcutta to New York, landing the day before Christmas. A skilled orthopedist performed corrective surgery in the nick of time; the femur had already started to deteriorate. A body cast for six months then crutches didn't slow Mike down much, but it was too close for comfort.

While living in Bangalore, both Kedar and I had physical problems that needed attention, but there wasn't a local doctor worthy of the name. We made appointments for thorough checkups at Velore.

The hospital there was founded in the 1920s by Dr. Scudder, a missionary with the Church of the Brethren. He chose to locate it in the middle of a huge area of south India that had no modern medicine whatsoever. But there was a problem in treating women. Custom didn't allow a man to examine them, and thousands went home to die for lack of adequate care. His daughter, Ida, longing to help, went to medical school and returned to open an OB/GYN department along with nursing and medical schools for women. Women doctors? The idea was revolutionary!

Under British occupation the Velore Medical School was not accredited, but as soon as Dr. Ida was ready to graduate her first class, she asked permission for her students to take the exams along with the men from the other colleges. They were seated reluctantly, and much to the dismay of all, their performance exceeded that of their male colleagues. With accreditation granted, a medical school exclusively for women became a reality. Now only 50 percent of the students must be women.

After World War II the institution grew huge and ungainly. The Rockefeller Foundation responded to an appeal for streamlining patient management. When we went in we first met with Dr. Graham, a general practitioner, who gave us a once over lightly, and wrote out orders for tests. The next stop was the cashier, where we paid before beginning the rounds. After labs and X-rays, Kedar went his way and I went mine. We met for lunch then had a couple more appointments. At four o'clock we were scheduled to see our doctor, who would have all test results.

I was fine until my GYN appointment. In a long row of examining booths, the doctor went from one patient to the next, dictating her findings to a secretary at her elbow. Her questions about any complaints were routine, but when she began the exam, I could hardly get my breath.

"The patient's uterus is soft and greatly enlarged," she began. "It is probably cancer, and I'd suggest surgery and appropriate after-treatment as soon as possible. Good-bye, Mrs. Bryan. Take care, and God bless you."

Stunned, I let the young nurse help me up to dress. I found Kedar at the tea room waiting to see Dr. Graham.

"I don't know how to take this, but the doctor I just saw said I probably have cancer," I told him. "How could that be? I feel strong, have a lot of energy, and I just can't believe I'm that sick."

"I'm sure it's not true," he said as he put his arms around me. I was doing my best not to cry, but with his gesture of tenderness, the floodgates opened and I lost it. At the appointed hour we met Dr. Graham, who was surprised to see me in such distress.

"Just have a look at the GYN report," I suggested, "and tell us what you think." He spread out my documents, and typical of physicians, rubbed his chin as he made m-m-m noises.

"Looks like you'll need a D&C to find out what's going on," he said, "but I'm certain you don't have cancer. All of your other tests are fine–nothing indicates a big problem, so we'll just have to forgive Dr. Pani. I'm afraid she sometimes uses scare tactics inappropriately. Most Indian women are so terrified of surgery that they'll refuse it unless you frighten them into it. In your case it wasn't necessary, and I'm sorry she upset you."

"Well, that's good news," I said. What a relief. In two weeks we were back for the procedure, and it turned out to be fibroid tumors. Home free? Not quite. Within six weeks they were back as big and bad as ever.

Just forty miles from Bangalore is a small Methodist Mission hospital at Kolar run by Dr. Mary Shoemaker. We went to see her, and as good fortune would have it, an Indian doctor arrived the day before. She had just completed two years of advanced study at Women's Hospital in Philadelphia. After discussing our options, we mutually agreed that surgery was indicated, and the sooner the better because we were due to leave for the States in two months.

"When would you like to do it?" Dr. Shoemaker asked.

"How about tomorrow," Kedar said. "Might as well get it over with, don't you think?"

"Let's go ahead," I agreed. "I don't want to sit around and think about it." So we were back at six the next morning. I was given a spinal. When all was ready, the doctors on either side of the table looking like spacemen in hoods and masks, folded their hands and prayed out loud for my safety and skill for themselves. I was utterly at peace, knowing I was in God's hands.

Kedar had never observed major surgery and asked if he could watch. "I thought you might be interested," Dr. Shoemaker said. "We'll see that you are properly gowned, and I'll let you know when to come in." She intended for him to enter after the incision was made and the area draped, but he came in as she was making it, and he turned deathly white. Kedar sat by my head, and when I looked up at him I asked, "Doctor, how's my husband doing?"

"Looks like he could use some hemoglobin, doesn't it? Want some water, Mr. Bryan?"

"No, thanks," he answered. "I'll be fine, really." They talked back and forth as the operation progressed.

"Now look at these, they are your wife's ovaries," Dr. Shoemaker said, holding them in her hand, "and see this place that looks like a blister? She's about to ovulate."

"I know more about you, Fran, than you know about yourself," Kedar remarked, feeling proud of himself. Everything went well and they were starting to close when the anesthetic wore off.

"Doctor," I gasped, "it feels as if you've poured boiling oil into my gut."

"Morphine," she instructed the operating room attendant. He wandered over to a cabinet, and when I again looked up at Kedar, rage was written all over his face. He was ready to kill the guy for taking so long.

"Jeldi, jeldi!" (quickly, quickly) Dr. Shoemaker commanded. Oh, the bliss of instant relief! I didn't care what they did–I was floating.

Recovery was quick and pleasant. After the first day they moved me into a beautiful room with two beds so Kedar could come for dinner and spend the night. He had breakfast with me before going back to Bangalore.

Several times Dr. Shoemaker stopped by to check me out and stayed for tea and conversation. Curiosity prompted me to ask her about the nursing profession in India.

"We have a unique situation because of the caste system," she said. "As you know, the Harrijans, such as barbers, are the lowest of all because they perform personal services. Christians are outcasts who don't rate even at the bottom of the heap. Since everything a nurse does is a personal service, almost all are Christians. Isn't that wonderful?" she said with a sparkle in her eye.

"One of the ways our nursing program has a profound effect on the community is that participants are required to take an extra year of midwifery. In the villages the midwife is usually married to the barber. She has no medical training and follows traditions handed down in her caste. The worst part is that she often uses a scythe or the barber's razor to cut the umbilical cord, and all too often the baby gets tetanus and dies.

"When village women come to us for care, one of our midwives is assigned to follow the entire pregnancy. If problems arise, she makes sure the mother comes into the hospital for delivery; otherwise, the birth is at home. The mother gets instruction in nutrition, the importance of good health habits, and having everything clean and ready for the baby. The nurse stays until mother and child are well settled and the infant is nursing.

"The barber's wife's routine is brutal by comparison. Once the baby is breathing, she executes the branding which they believe wards off evil spirits. Laying needles on the fire until they are red-hot, she places four or five in a row on the newborn's abdomen. Instead of relying on the mother's first milk to cleanse the baby's system, mineral oil is poured down its throat. Poor little things," Dr. Shoemaker said. "It's a wonder any of them survive. Thousands of mothers and babies have Christian nurses to thank for a better start in life."

After a week of TLC I was dismissed. Within three weeks I was up and at 'em, packing and getting ready for a six-month home leave and our move to New Delhi.

"This one last piece, memsahib," said Robert, serving Jimmy and me each with half a papaya.

"But Mommy," Jimmy protested, "if there aren't any more, what will we have for breakfast?"

"It's all right, honey," I told him, seeing the serious look in the big brown eyes of my precious little eight-year-old with his turned-up nose and curly blond hair. "I'll get some in the market while our trees rest for a few weeks. It won't be long before the new ones will be ripe. As soon as the showers come they'll grow big and sweet."

We had three papaya trees in the side yard of our house at 6 Cunningham Road in Bangalore. Anne, age nine, and Edwin, twelve, were away at boarding school. Kedar didn't care for papaya, so in season Jimmy and I shared one about the size of a large acorn squash. They were seedless and so sweet that just a little salt and a squeeze of fresh lime made them a treat.

Jimmy was quiet during the rest of the meal until I reminded him it was time to get ready for school. He said, "You know what? I think I can get us some good ripe papaya free!"

"How would you do that," I asked, wondering what was cooking in his fertile young mind.

"You know Mr. Rama Rao who lives just down the street in the White House with a high wall all around it and the big iron gates? Well, I'll go to see him. He has trees just like ours. We'll get to be friends because I'll tell him how much we like the Indian people. I'll say that sometimes Americans aren't really as smart as they think they are, and we'll have a good time talking, and then I'll look up at his papaya tree. (He rolled his eyes.) "I'll say, 'My, you really do have some nice papayas.' I bet he'll give me some!"

I never met Mr. Cardell, but when we moved to Bangalore in 1957 we began hearing stories about him. A typical tale concerns a little village in Mysore.

Hans served with the USAID program in rural development and sanitation. A hard-and-fast rule for the agency was that change was undertaken only at the request of the villagers. Outsiders were not welcome to come in and impose "good works" on people steeped in traditions from their parents, grandparents, and great-grandparents.

Hans was a tall, well-built blond of Danish ancestry with a good sense of humor and a love of people, particularly children. He and his Indian interpreter, Mr. Chandra, roamed the countryside in a jeep, looking for ways to improve the lot of India's greatest population group, small villagers. Frequently there was no electricity or seweage disposal, and the only water supply was a poorly constructed well.

One day they found such a well way off the beaten path not far from Bangalore. At the center of the village stood a huge banyan tree. Close to its base was a row of stone tablets dedicated to the snake god carved with the image of a cobra, hood fully extended, as it stared with sightless eyes. In front of several of them burned little oil lamps. The well was nearby, with thirty to forty thatched huts scattered around it. The dirt path connecting them was edged by a ditch that carried human waste and household water past the well and out to the fields.

Not a soul was in sight. The only sign of life was a few chickens scratching in the dirt and a couple of pigs that scavenged for food. Hans and Mr. Chandra peered down into the well. It was about twenty feet to the water, and it looked clean. But in several places the fieldstone wall was crumbling, and seepage left a slimy green trail.

"I sure would love to help these people fix it up," Hans remarked, "but I wonder if we can persuade them to ask us. Let's just sit down a while and see who shows up." Before long, a few children's curious faces peeked around the nearest hut. The two men appeared not to have seen them as they continued to talk. By twos and threes kids inched forward to see the strange pair. Smiling, they greeted the youngsters, and when they came near enough, Hans did his favorite slight-of-hand trick. He produced a silver rupee from behind one little boy's ear and gave it to him. Another and another stepped up for a chance to see where the coin came from, and all were dumbfounded and delighted with their prizes.

At the happy sound of children laughing, women were emboldened to come out. There was quite a crowd when finally the men and older boys made their appearance.

"Looks like they're all here," Mr. Chandra said. "Want to talk to them about the well?"

"Let's do it," Hans answered. "That man in the middle of the group, the tall one with the young boy in front of him is probably the village chief, don't you think?"

"I agree. You talk and I'll interpret," he said as they both stood, dusting off the seat of their pants.

"Namasthe," Hans began, joining the palms of his hands together and making a slight bow. "You have a very nice village here," he then said in English. "My friend and I've been looking at your well and wonder if we might help you make it better and safer." As Mr. Chandra spoke in Kaneres there was little change of expression on the chief's face.

"You know," Hans continued, "it doesn't matter all that much if you or I should get sick and die. We've had full, happy lives, and we are old men now, but I can see that you have a great love for your son. He's a handsome young man and will do great things some day. It would be tragic if he got sick and died because of dirty water. Wouldn't that just break your heart?" As his friend spoke, murmurs of assent began, and children moved closer to their parents.

"It wouldn't be hard to make your well perfectly safe and will relieve your mind of a lot of worry, particularly about your little ones." They nodded and shuffled their feet in the dust. A woman tugged on the end of her sari and squatted to put her arm around her toddler. "We're from the USAID, and our work is to help people such as you have better water in your villages. But we'll come only if you ask us to. If my friend and I bring the cement and other materials next week, how many are willing to help us fix your well?"

The men surged forward with their thanks and enthusiasm. And so it was done; another village had a safe well.

One day Hans discovered a lump on the under side of his right arm. It was sore to the touch. He was sent immediately to NIH in Washington, D.C., but the cancer was well advanced. He died six weeks later. When the sad news reached Indian villages, they lighted thousands of little oil lamps and prayed for the man who'd brought them so much good.

From the time I was a little girl I wanted to dance. Growing up in Korea there was no opportunity beyond acting out native nursery rhymes taught by the amah: "The beautiful baby boy was born from a full-blown peony," and "The good carpenter who did everything well." In our teen years at boarding school it wasn't allowed because in the local culture dancing was practiced only by professional prostitutes.

As an adult I enjoyed ballroom dancing, but it wasn't until our second year in India when we moved to Bangalore that I entertained the notion of learning bharata natyam, one of the four main classical styles in India.

It developed from ritualistic dances performed in the past as offerings to the deities in Hindu temples and in a more sophisticated form in courts by solo female dancers. The traditionally conservative South maintained a style closely related to the type of dancing mirrored in temple sculpture during more than two thousand years of movement recorded in stone. The great wonder of Indian dance is that it can be at the same time an act of religious devotion and a superb entertainment.

During the two hundred years of British rule, everything English was regarded as being the best, and local art expression was ignored or considered second rate. At a dinner party we were introduced to Mr. U.S. Krishna Rao and his wife, Chandam. He was a chemistry professor at Mysor University, but his avocation was teaching and performing the dance. It was okay with Kedar for me to try it, so we called on the Raos to talk it over.

"We'll begin with the *alalipoo*, the innovational dance," Krishna said. "If you can master it reasonably well, we'll continue, otherwise we'll go no further. My schedule is very full, so if you're not up to it, there is no reason to waste my time and your money."

"Sounds fair enough to me," I answered, and vowed to myself I'd do so well he'd beg me not to quit. We began with two lessons a week, and I loved every minute of it.

It was tough. Thai dancing, which derives from the bharata natyam has soft, gently flowing movements; but not this one. Lines of the body are straight and clean. Head, eye movements, hands, and feet are coordinated with the music as the dancer performs in a slightly squatting position. Bare feet slap the floor beating out the rhythmic pattern. Krishna sat on the floor with his feet pulled up and crossed in front of him and set the pace by tapping a stick on a block of wood. After beginning with a measure or two, it was time to start. *"Tah-lang-goó-taka-di-me-gee-na-tohm,"* he said. He sang out the measures with, *"Sah-nee-da-ah-pa-ga-ma-ah-pa-ga-pa, sa-nee-da-ah-pa-ga-ma-pa-da-nee,* repeating it for each new movement. Soon I was singing it in my sleep. I found that my front thigh muscles were not well developed. Ouch. A thirty-minute lesson left me soaking wet and breathless but so challenged I could hardly wait to zip home on my Lambretta for a shower and an hour's practice.

As time passed Krishna and Chandam became fast friends. They shared their Hindu faith and we our Christian beliefs.

I wondered about the propriety of my involvement in a dance that is closely connected with Hindu worship, so I talked it over with JT and Ruth Seamands.

"Sure, why not, JT said, "as long as you aren't worshipping. There are many ways to strengthen friendships and cultural ties. We say go for it."

A story from Hindu mythology accompanied every number. In many ways they were similar to those of the Roman gods who shared human emotions and frailties. There was the goddess Sita who was kidnapped and carried off to Ceylon. Trying to rescue her, Krishna asked the good winged monkeys to bring huge boulders to build a crossing from India to Ceylon. They were too heavy, and the monkeys dropped them along the way. I don't remember how Krishna succeeded in getting Sita back, but the stone bridge didn't work.

When we took the children to boarding school in Kodai, we drove through the area where they say the stones were discarded. For mile after mile mountains of rounded boulders supported nothing but an occasional tree–all the fault of the monkeys! If the kids were restless and needed a break, we let them get out to explore, warning them to watch out for snakes. A short distance from the highway there was a huge bolder resting on another that looked as if it could be easily toppled. Edwin wanted to see if he could shove it over. No luck.

When word got out that I was taking lessons, several Caltex salesmen came to Kedar. They held the outdated notion that there was something not quite proper about a Westerner performing classical Indian dance and were worried about my reputation. It had been declared a "fine art" by the government, but old notions die-hard.

A Dance Move

"Thank you for your concern," Kedar said, "but perhaps it's best if we just let her do it. All three of our children have gone off to boarding school and she misses them. It gives her something new that she enjoys." They agreed. The first dance went well, so the lessons continued.

Krishna and Chandam thought it quite a feather in their caps that I, age thirty-seven, could master the dance that was usually taught starting at five or six. Before long they asked me to do some of the simpler numbers at public performances, which were covered by the press. Pictures and flattering write-ups appeared in the local papers, and without fail the salesmen brought them to us. It gave them much face that the sahib's wife honored their culture.

In recent years interest in the reality and presence of angels has exploded. Monthly magazines give graphic stories of visitations. They are unashamedly discussed on the air and TV programs; Billy Graham and others have written books about them.

I believed there must be such as they are spoken of in the Bible, but the first time it came close to home was when Granddaddy Bryan saw them in the garden outside his window as he was dying.

During our second year in Bangalore, we drove the three children to their boarding school. It's a long, hot, ten-hour drive on a poorly paved highway, most of the time trying to get around bull carts and herds of goats. Frequent showers were welcome, but made dust coat the windshield. We neglected to clean it off before leaving the hot plains behind for the last thirty-mile drive on hairpin curves to eight thousand feet and blessed coolness.

The road was narrow with very few guardrails or protecting walls. While we were on the outside of the road, all of a sudden the sun shone on the dusty windshield in such a way that seeing through it was impossible. It was as if a yellow blanket had been thrown over us. Kedar pulled hard to the right, just missing a two-hundred-foot plunge, but at that moment I saw an angel standing there in bright white robes with outstretched arms. I was so surprised it took my breath away. I looked at the others, but they said nothing. Peering over the edge, we were glad we'd missed the drop-off. I was so touched to see God's protection but had no desire to share it at that time.

Several years later we took our summer vacation from New Delhi in Kashmir. Anne and I took the overnight train to Pathankot where we met Kedar and Jim, who had driven ahead and spent the night in a hotel. We were taking a small five-passenger Fiat to a dealer in Kashmir and picking up a Jeep station wagon to return to New Delhi. The pass over the mountains was strictly controlled by the Indian Army. Because of the limited capacity of the highway, traffic moved in one direction for four hours, then changed to the other direction.

We were near the top of the pass when our time ran out. Fortunately we were on the side hugging the mountain when a long convoy of enormous military trucks came whizzing around the bend. Kedar pulled over as far as possible when a monster missed us by a whisker.

"Wow," he said, "Thanks for two inches." That tiny car would have offered little protection if we'd been hit, but once again I saw the beautiful angel with his arms outstretched between us and disaster! Why I was permitted to see him I don't know, but I was thankful.

"Be sure to take your clubs," friends admonished. "Golf's one of the things you'll enjoy no matter where you're posted." Neither Kedar nor I had ever played, but we bought second-hand sets in case we wanted to learn.

The Gymkhana Club had a driving range, putting green, and a pro. We signed up for lessons. Early on, Kedar decided it wasn't for him and dropped out, but I loved it. The magic of the game is that you can spend hours making one rotten shot after another, but when the day's over you remember just the one or two good ones, so easy that your whole body said yes!

In Madras women had a weekly tournament, and as soon as I rated a thirty-six handicap I joined. I never was any good, but the exercise (no riding carts), camaraderie, and a few lucky strokes kept me going back for more. In the South we played on browns, not greens. They were flat and covered with two inches of coarse sand. Putting was easy. I lined up the ball and cup with a bright-colored grain of sand a few inches in front of me, and if I could remember to keep my head down, it went straight to the flag. A broom lay on the ground near each brown to sweep away footprints and ball marks.

Mrs. London always amazed me. She was short and frail but won most of the big tournaments because she never got off line. Others had long, spectacular shots but not always on target. Hers stayed in the middle of the fairway, she one-or two-putted, and took the prize.

Snakes were a constant presence, though rarely seen. One brown was near a huge clump of bushes that housed a pair of large cobras. How did we know? If you were the first in the morning, you'd see the distinctive zig-zag markings in the sand where they'd crossed. One morning our foursome was going up a long, sloping fairway when my partner stopped to get a club from her caddie. Checking her lie she said, "Say, look at this." She nudged a baby snake wrapped around her ball. It reared up in a striking position, and immediately we knew what it was. The caddie snatched the club from her hands and commanded, "Step back, memsahib. Quickly! I kill it." Others came running and there wasn't much left of the little thing when they'd finished. If you've found one, more than likely there are others around because there are as many as eighteen to a clutch. We walked carefully the rest of the day.

Other creatures were in evidence too. One afternoon while the whole family was knocking the ball around the course, Jim was the first to come to a hole beside a huge banyan tree that housed a gang of monkeys. "Hey Daddy," he called, "look at that nice monkey. Can I pet him?"

"No, no, no!" yelled the caddie as he ran forward brandishing a club. "Don't touch him. He bite you. Very bad. No want to touch him." The intruder scampered into the lower branches of the tree, where he perched to watch us. Jim made the mistake of taking a closer look, and the monkey peed on him!

"The caddie told you to stay away, didn't he?" Kedar scolded. "Now come on over here with us." The poor child had to endure a stinky shirt until we got home.

The flag stick was wrapped with barbed wire to discourage the little beasts who loved to climb up and rock back and forth until it broke the cup out of the hole!

In Bangalore there was a different problem. Crows stole balls and took them off to their nests, which necessitated a fore caddie, usually a child of nine or ten. He went ahead the distance he thought you'd hit and as soon as the ball came to rest covered it with his hat or a cigarette tin. My best game was in Bangalore because I never seemed to have a poor lie. The youngsters with their frisky toes managed to get the ball up on a nice clump of grass or mound of sand before covering it—unless you were known to be a poor tipper; then it found every rut or divot!

In New Delhi we lived at 44 Golf Links Road, just across from the eleventh green. It was prime property, right in the middle of the city, but that didn't keep animals from roaming freely to feed on the lush grass. Several patrons were high-ranking Indian army engineers who conducted a training exercise for their troops that consisted of erecting a steel-slatted fence all the way around the course. Fabulous! Wonderful grass and no cows or goats to eat it up and trample the greens! Not far from our front door, two slats were slightly bent apart so a body could squeeze between them. If I wanted to play but didn't have the car

A Tale of Two Bamboos

to go the mile to the gate, I slipped through, and within a few yards a *chokidar* (worker) appeared, offering to carry my clubs.

I continued to take lessons and enter tournaments, but my handicap remained high. We were at a cocktail party just before the Captain's Cup Challenge, in which partners took alternate strokes on one ball, and handicaps were averaged. Good golfers tried to find somebody with a high handicap thinking they could make up for the other and with a few extra strokes have a chance for the cup.

"Mrs. Bryan, I understand you need a partner for the tournament Saturday," Billu (P.G.) Sethi said. "How about it, shall we be a team?"

"I'd be honored, but you know my game isn't the greatest. Are you sure you want to put up with me?"

"Of course. It's only a game, so if you're willing I'd be delighted. Is it a deal?"

"Sure," I said as we touched drinks glasses. "See you on the first tee."

Captain Sethi of the Indian Air Force was a scratch player, so we were placed in the last foursome. Kedar would be at the clubhouse to join me for the dinner following the match.

On the appointed day I played pretty well. Billu drove off on the long holes, and put me in a bunker several times. I was encouraged to know that even the best of them blunder, so I relaxed and enjoyed it.

I knew we were doing well but had no idea how our score compared with others. It was dark by the time we reached the eighteenth green, and the floodlights were on. It was my putt, and I was in the lower left side of a two-tier surface with the cup in the upper right-hand corner.

"If you sink this putt, Fran, you and Billu will win," a friend said. "Two-putt it, and you share first place, three putts and the folks ahead of you take the prize."

"Don't worry about it, Fran," Billu said as I lined it up, praying for a miracle. "It's is just for fun, so give it a bash." I did, and it went in! He gave a whoop of joy, picked me up and whirled me around and around. Spectators began to cheer as Kedar joined them, shading his eyes against the bright lights.

"What's going on out there?" he said in amazement when he saw us.

"Fran just sank an impossible putt, so she and Billu won the tournament. How about that?" So ended my only claim to fame, and I have proof of it with our names engraved on a beautiful silver beer mug.

"Oh, my goodness, Tom, would you just look at that? There's a monkey in the car, and he has my new banner. What will we do?" moaned Mr. Pat Taylor.

A consummate Rotarian, Mr. Pat (as he preferred to be called) never missed a Tuesday noon meeting in his hometown of Wadesboro, North Carolina. He arranged his trip to India to visit his daughter, Caroline Craig, with stopovers in London and Paris on the way out and another in Rome on the way home.

Carrying a dozen or more banners from his home chapter, he exchanged one with each club. He vowed never to miss a meeting during those two months, visiting a different chapter each time. His son-in-law, Tom, helped him make contact with the groups in and around New Delhi.

Mr. Pat took a great interest in the Indian people—the graceful women in bright saris and handsome men, particularly the Sikhs, distinguished by their colorful turbans and stainless-steel bracelets on their right wrists. He was fascinated by their customs and the Hindu faith, which claims over three thousand gods and believes in multiple reincarnations of the soul.

Near the end of his stay, Tom drove Mr. Pat to Jaipur for their weekly luncheon and exchange of banners. Before starting back to New Delhi, they drove up a hill where they could have a good view of the city with its distinctive pink sandstone buildings, particularly the ornate structures making up the palace of the maharaja.

It was a hot day, and the car was not air-conditioned. They left the windows open while they climbed a little farther on foot to get the best view. When they returned to the car they found a monkey inside, examining Mr. Pat's new banner. As they approached, the monkey, banner in hand, jumped out and shot up a tall tree. They couldn't go up after him, but a small Indian boy offered to retrieve the stolen banner. With the promise of a couple of rupees he scampered up after the thief.

Perched on one of the upper branches, the monkey unrolled the banner. He picked at the fringe, biting the fabric, tugging it this way and that, until he tore a number of holes, loosened the fringe, and added smears of saliva. Jumping up and down, screaming with delight, he waved the prize it over his head. The little boy went as high as it was safe. Several times the monkey lowered the banner to where the child could almost touch it, teasing him. As the little fellow reached for it, the monkey snatched it back, chattering, delighted with the game they were playing.

A crowd gathered below. Tom and a disappointed Mr. Pat were just about to give up and leave when the monkey rolled the banner up in its paper wrapping and handed it to the child. Astonished, Tom and Mr. Pat gasped. An Indian gentleman standing with them watching the little drama remarked in clipped, precise English,

"There is just one explanation for this. Definitely, that monkey possesses the soul of an American Rotarian!"

New Delhi, May 1960. We were in the midst of the hot weather, the three months from mid March to mid June when the temperature ranged from 110° F. to 120° during the day and rarely went below 100° at night. Frequently the sky turned yellow and heavy, so laden with dust that it was possible to look straight at the sun without damaging the eyes. Wind followed, bringing more dust in swirling waves. Then came a quick, blessed shower, leaving the air sparkling and clean.

The preceding winter we'd had a lot of trouble with rats. They stayed outside during the day when it was warm, but at night when the temperature dipped as low as 40° they sought warmer places. The house had uneven terrazzo floors, so the doors had wide gaps at the bottom to avoid sticking on high spots. It meant easy access for the rats, and there seemed no way to keep them out. We tried traps but never caught a single one. We couldn't use poison because of Snooker, our cocker spaniel.

Quite often we'd sit down to dinner with croquet mallets, mops, and brooms at the ready in case any vermin appeared, but it was a losing battle. One evening a huge fellow ran past us, hugging the wall. We jumped up, grabbing our instruments of warfare, and pursued him to the master bathroom. You have to understand the plumbing to appreciate what happened next.

Waste from the shower/tub was not connected to a pipe. It emptied onto the cement floor. The two sides of the tub away from the wall were tiled from its lip to the floor. At the back corner next to the wall was an opening that released the water to a three-inch channel that ran behind the toilet and along the wall to the far corner. There it passed through a hole in the outer wall and emptied into a drain in the ground. The waste pipe from the basin reached to within three inches of the floor. The water splashed into its retention area and was channeled to the same hole. A little door in the side of the tub gave access to the plumbing at its front, and a small opening at the back afforded ventilation.

The rat got under the tub. Kedar opened the little door and poked around with a broom handle to encourage him to escape through the vent hole. I waited with a croquet mallet, ready to do him in; but he was too quick. Every time he pulled back before I could get him. We starting laughing at our own version of the "Anvil Chorus," thrust-bang, thrust-bang! To solve the problem, I stood in the tub right above the hole, holding a big dust mop. The kids were armed with mallets, and Kedar worked through the little door. He poked; I let the rat come all the way out, and dropped the mop on him. The kids struck. We had one very big, very dead rat. It was an exhilarating exercise but not one we wished to perform every night.

Even if we didn't see the creatures, there was always evidence of their presence–droppings had to be swept up daily.

When we heard that a family leaving for the States wanted to find a home for their Siamese cat, our offer was accepted. Two days before he was due to arrive, Snooker ran into the road and was hit by a passing car. When I reached him he was lying with his head in a puddle. At my call he stumbled to his feet but began to cry and run around in circles.

"Hurry!" I called to Anne. "Bring me a towel." I wrapped it around my hand, and forced it into his mouth, allowing him to bite down without hurting me. My neighbor drove me to the nearest veterinary hospital, where they found his temperature had shot up to 108 degrees in a matter of fifteen minutes. They rubbed cakes of ice on his back to cool him down.

"You can go home now," said Dr. Gupta. "We'll do all we can to save your dog."

"He nearly died about midnight," the doctor said the next morning, "but I worked on him for several hours. I believe the worst is over."

"You are so kind. There's no way I can thank you enough, but please accept this small token of our appreciation," I said, handing him a basket of fresh-baked cookies.

"Oh, madam, there was no need," he protested. "When my children see them I'll probably be lucky to get a crumb or two!"

I went in to see the poor little guy. He couldn't raise

his head, but he did manage a few thumps of his tail. He showed steady improvement, and after the fifth day he was strong enough to come home.

Meanwhile Raja had come to live with us. He was a beautiful sealpoint of a somewhat rakish appearance. When he was a baby, some boiling oil got spilled on him, burning a bald spot about the size of a quarter on the top of his head. A part of his right ear had to be cut away.

When Snooker walked into the living room, there was Raja, whose back and tail went straight up. With his fur puffed out and his head pulled back, he stood his ground, emitting a warning growl. Snooker had neither the strength nor inclination for a fight and gave Raja a wide berth whenever they met. Thus it continued for about a week.

Our bedroom was air-conditioned, so we congregated there to wash up and talk until lunch was served. Snooker lay by the bed, exposing as much of his tummy to the cool floor as possible. We were just drying our hands when Raja came in, pushing through the swinging doors, entering as if he owned the place. His pace was deliberate, and his tail was straight up in the air. The scene struck us as so unusual that nobody spoke or moved. We sensed something important was about to happen. There wasn't a sound, and Snooker didn't stir, didn't even quiver. Beginning with his hind feet, Raja went all around him, touching every part of him with his nose. Snooker never moved his head, but his eyes and brows were doing a veritable dance as the examination progressed. When Raja had finished, he touched his nose to Snooker's, stepped away and romped out of the room with Snooker at his heels.

From that moment on they were the greatest of friends, racing and playing all over the house. Whenever Raja had enough he took a flying leap up onto a windowsill, wrapped his tail around his forepaws, narrowed his eyes to slits, and appeared to forget Snooker's existence. And sometimes when he was lying on a chair and Snooker walked by, he'd rake his claws along the dog's back.

Snooker became very protective, chasing off other cats that came into the yard. On cold winter nights, Snooker slept on a rug on the extra bed in Anne's room with Raja curled up against his tummy, embraced by his forepaws. The joy these pets found in each other was a delight to watch. And best of all, we never saw another rat!

The New Delhi American Women's Club needed an advertising manager for the *News Circle*. I was asked and accepted though I was totally clueless about the job. It represented a challenge I knew I could handle.

Within a few days the retiring officer brought me a carton of folders, loose papers, and general information.

"Here it is, Fran," she said with a big smile and a sigh of relief as she dumped it on the dining room table. "It's all there. Just take a little time to chew through it, and you'll get the picture." I'd expected "how-to" suggestions on where to go and what to do, but not so. On her way to an engagement, she wished me well and was gone. That was okay. I figured if she could do the job I certainly could, and maybe even better.

The *News Circle* was a six-by-eight-inch booklet on news print put out by the club nine times a year. It contained information about the community, items of local interest, culture, and a write-up of several advertisers, each highlighted once a year. It was a give-away to hotels, offices, and public buildings. The advertising revenue generated met all costs and provided several scholarships for deserving Indian college students.

At our first meeting I got permission to offer a 10 percent discount if payment was received before printing of the first issue. I made out like gangbusters and had most of the money in hand by the due date.

I loved the job. Former advertisers felt the cost was reasonable and boosted sales. I enjoyed the give-and-take of negotiation, talked several into taking a larger space, and found new merchants who wanted to give it a try. Before I knew it, so much space was sold that they had to increase the *Circle's* size by 50 percent. A rule of thumb said that no more than half the space could be in advertising.

Usually merchants gave me cash, but I did receive a few checks. In India you can't really be sure you've been paid when you accept a check. Several bounced, but when I made a second visit the cash was handed over with nothing more than a shrug and sly smile as if to say, Silly woman, didn't you know any better?

That was until I went to call on Ah Swani. He had the best brass shop in town, located in Sunder Nagar Market right next to an apartment complex where many foreigners lived. He took out a half-page ad that cost 750 rupees, at the time more than the month's wage for a middle-income family. Three times I returned his bad checks; he simply gave me another one. It was evident he had no intention of paying, so when the year was half over I brought it up at a staff meeting.

"How much did you say he owes," one of the women asked.

"R. 750"

"I have an account with him, and I think it's just about that amount. Why don't we go there after the meeting, and we'll take care of it."

"Sounds like a good plan," I said, and I began to have a happy feeling in my soul.

"Mr. Ah Swani," Helen said as we entered the store, "I have an outstanding bill with you that I'd like to pay today."

"Certainly, memsahib," he said, going to the office for the account book. While he was busy I handed her the bounced check and receipt.

"R.725 is what I owe; I'll pick up a few more things to make it an even 750," she said. She found what she wanted came back.

"Now is that the right amount, Mr. Ah Swani?"

"Yes, yes, memsahib," he answered, his hand out for payment.

"Here's what we'll do. Since that's what you owe the *News Circle* for your ad this year, I'll give the money to Mrs. Bryan, our advertising manager, and here's your check and receipt for that amount. Dismay was written all over his face, but he was a good sport.

"Oh, yes, Mrs. Bryan, I remember that I do owe you, and now I'm glad it's done. Thank you for coming." We departed with many good wishes for a long life and prosperity ringing in our ears. Outside we had a good laugh and a hug for our victory.

As we rounded the last bend at the top of the pass, the Vale of Kashmir spread out below. High, rugged mountains surrounded lush, terraced fields that stepped down to a wide valley. Since partition in 1947, the Indians and Pakistanis have been fighting over this little knob of territory that joins them in the north. Thousands of lives have been lost in a struggle that remains unresolved.

During our visit there was little evidence of the conflict. We drove to the tourist office in Srinagar for directions to our reserved houseboat on Naghene Lake. At twenty dollars a day, it was a wonder. A two-storied affair with a deck and chairs on top, it had three bedrooms, bathrooms with flush toilets, and polished teak walls and floors in the living room and dining room. Hand-knotted carpets covered the floors. There was a small kitchen, but it was mainly used as a bar. A cookboat was tethered to the stern where the servants lived and all food was prepared. It was hard to believe our good fortune.

Our Houseboat

We were anchored fifty yards off shore and had a small dingy to row to the land or out to the huge platform in the middle of the one hundred-acre lake. We rented sailboats several times, but since all sewage emptied into the water we were not much inclined to do a lot of swimming. Every morning, slender little craft accommodating one person made the rounds to houseboats. You could tell when the post office boat was in the neighborhood by the ringing handbell. He sold post cards and postage and picked up outgoing mail. The flower boat was a sight to behold, filled to overflowing with all manner of cut and potted flowers and greenery. The vegetable and fruit, and meat boats came, too, making trips to the market unnecessary.

One lazy afternoon while we were sleeping or reading, a merchant who sold local artifacts arrived at our door. We'd been in town to shop that morning. I purchased a ring-wool scarf so fine and soft that one measuring a square meter can be drawn easily through a wedding ring, thus the name. The salesman's arrival was not welcome.

"No," I said as he began hauling huge bundles of goods into our boat, "No thank you. We don't need any today. Please don't bring your things in here because we really don't want any." It was futile. He kept talking a mile a minute as he untied bundles and with lightning speed set up his wares all over the living room. The chatter continued as he held up each item, telling of its good quality and low price. He tossed a scarf toward me saying it was a gift. I couldn't stop him or shut him up, so I went up stairs to get Kedar.

When we returned, Kedar sat in a big overstuffed chair and never made eye contact with the merchant, nor did he say anything. After a minute or two he began to twitch, first a shoulder, then his head jerked this way and that and his eyes rolled around. He made funny faces and loud biting noises. The poor guy was terrified, and with greater speed than I thought possible, he had everything back in bundles, including the scarf, and over the side into his boat. Without looking back he paddled furiously until he was well away from us. I felt a little sorry for the man, but it was evidently the only way to get him to leave. When he was well away, we all roared with laughter.

"Daddy," Anne said, "I didn't know you could do all that stuff. Where did you learn it?"

"I thought if he was afraid of a crazy man he might go, and he did," Kedar answered. "Now why don't we all drive into town for some good Mongolian barbecue?"

One week on the lake was all we'd hoped for, but more adventure was planned for the second week. In town we exchanged the Fiat for the dealer's Jeep station wagon, rented everything for camping up in the mountains–tent, lanterns, folding cots, chairs, stove, pots and pans, plates, cups, cutlery–the works, bought some groceries and staples, all for about fifty dollars, loaded it into the Jeep and headed for the hills. We made arrangements for ponies and guides to come to our camp site at eight thousand feet a couple of days later for a trip to Tullian, an alpine meadow at twelve thousand feet.

We camped through Europe on earlier vacations, so the kids knew the routine. It was so quiet, and at that elevation I was inclined to sleep a lot. The gentle wind singing through the pine trees, the rushing water in a nearby stream were so soothing. Anne and Jim filled a large gunny sack with big pine cones for Christmas decorations, we read, wandered in the hills, and enjoyed being alone our little piece of the world. We needed sweaters and light jackets in the evening, and how delicious to snuggle into down sleeping bags at night!

Early in the morning on the appointed day, four men with ponies arrived for our trip up the mountain. The light saddles felt fine at first, but before long we knew we were in for trouble. We hardly noticed the discomfort when we began the climb. It scared me half to death, and my stomach still does weird things when I recall the scene. It was a steep, narrow path cut into the side of the mountain. In places one side went straight up and the other dropped away for hundreds of feet. Many loose stones spelled potential disaster. One slip and you were gone! I wanted to lean toward the mountain, but that would upset the pony's balance, so I kept my eyes straight ahead and prayed that our guardian angel would watch over us. Anne and Jim thought it was an exciting adventure. I noticed that Kedar had little to say until we reached the top.

The meadow looked very much like the one pictured in *The Sound of Music*. It was wide and covered with tender grass and wild flowers. At the upper end water gushed right out of a rock. We scooped it up with our hands to drink and splash on our faces. It was so cold that at first it was hard to swallow. The agony of the ride seemed to melt away in the glorious setting.

We shared our lunch with the drivers after exploring the valley. I got out the skin cream, for at that elevation our faces and hands were turning red.

A Tale of Two Bamboos

Trip to Tullian

After filling our canteens with fresh water, we began the return trip. This time I chose to walk, and although my feet slipped several times, I preferred it to riding, partly because saddle sores were making themselves felt. Before turning in for the night I treated the family bottoms with soothing cream on broken blisters!

At the end of our two weeks we packed up and headed for Patoncote, where we expected to spend the night before driving the last twelve hours to New Delhi the next day. We reached our destination at noon, much earlier than we had thought and decided to go ahead and drive straight through, getting home at about midnight for hot showers and our air-conditioned bedroom.

The Jeep station wagon was one of early vintage–a boxy vehicle with minimum insulation and fitted with hard, army-type seats. The temperature was 117°, and the dust was so thick the sun looked like a big orange ball. Since the car wasn't air-conditioned, we bought a metal tub to fit between the front seats to accommodate a sixty-four-pound block of ice. We also picked up two twenty-four-bottle cases of a soft drink that tasted like Sprite and filled up the water canteens. I got hand towels and wash cloths out of the suitcase, and we were ready to go.

We rolled up the windows to keep out the dust but

opened a vent at the dashboard to let the wind blow on the ice. No matter what we did, it was hot. We had to keep drinking water and soda. As the ice melted we wet towels to put on our heads and washcloths to wiped our necks, arms, and legs. When there was enough water I scooped it up and poured it down Kedar's back. Determined to press on and get home as soon as possible, we ate our sandwiches and fruit as we drove. The greatest wonder of all was that there was not a single call for a rest stop. Whatever we drank we sweated out.

We cheered the first familiar places in the outskirts of the city, counting the minutes until relief was ours. When at last we reached 44 Golf Links Road we were surprised to find the gate standing open. The *choki-dar* (gardener) must have thought we'd be home that night. The sound of our fumbling with the keys woke Snooker, who came barking to the door. As soon as he recognized us his alarm turned to yelps of delight.

The living room was cool and sweet with the desert cooler going full blast. What a surprise, though, and crushing disappointment to find our bedroom occupied! Out-of-town friends asked to use our apartment for a week during our vacation, and naturally we agreed. They were to have left two days earlier so the servants could change the beds and clean up. When we arrived home they were out at a party, but their ayah and two little children were asleep on the floor. There was nothing for it but to shower and sleep in Anne's and Jim's rooms. It didn't really matter. We were so exhausted from the twelve-hour ordeal that we collapsed on whatever was in a horizontal plane and slept the clock around.

In 1962 we were near the end of our second three-year term in India. We'd lived one year in Madras, two in Bangalore, and three in New Delhi. But the Indian government mandated that local personnel were to take over management positions as soon as possible, and reduction of foreign staff was the order of the day. When we arrived in 1955 there were sixty-five expatriates. The new target number was six! Kedar's name was on the to-go list.

Although he'd had an exemplary track record with Caltex, Kedar had committed the unthinkable sin of leaving the company for five years after our evacuation from Korea in 1950.

Kedar was deeply disappointed because he loved the oil business. Daily he welcomed each new challenge. Now at the age of forty-one and with three teenagers to educate, he was losing his employment in a declining job market. He was sad more than frightened, but ever the optimist, he could see nothing but bigger and better things ahead.

We were sorry to be leaving India but happy that Edwin, who was in a military prep school in the States, could come home, and our family would be together again.

Edwin in his school uniform

Once more it was time to pack up, but I'd done it so many times it held no terror for me. We were able to sell quite a few bulky things such as our eighteen-cubic-foot freezer and the porch furniture. Packers measured everything, gave an estimate, and went off to build the lift vans. I made sure Kedar would be fully occupied elsewhere and not around to "help" me! He had involved himself with the move when we left Madras for Bangalore. Soon enough I found that two bosses on the job were one too many. I knew the order and the way in which I wanted things done. We had several pieces of furniture that came apart for easy packing. To facilitate reassembly I bagged all nuts, bolts, and fittings and strapped them to the particular piece to which they belonged. That made sense to me, but Kedar wanted to put them all together in one box.

"What if it's mislaid or lost," I protested. "In this land where it takes an act of Congress to replace such things, I think keeping the connecting parts with the furniture is safest." Kedar saw some merit in the idea and gave in, but he still insisted his way was best.

Our little variable step-down transformer also became an item of contention. It was very handy in view of the uncertain electric current, which most of the time was 220–but not always. On one side, 110 was a given for our appliances. On the other side there were several options to correspond to the local voltage. Without the screws to make the connection, the transformer was useless. My idea was to make sure they were secure, and then wrap the whole thing up. Kedar had a better one.

"Since they're so important, I'll put them in..." When we unpacked in Bangalore neither of us could remember where! We searched high and low, but they were not to be found. Fortunately our cook, Sam, was handy with a lot of things and got a pair made for us in the market. Two years later when we were packing for home leave, I found them in the pocket of a suit coat. Oh, well.

Wrapping and boxing started two days before the lift vans arrived on the back of a truck. I set apart things like lampshades that needed special protection and added pillows and other soft items to pack with them. We had a

A Tale of Two Bamboos

large native rain hat made of palm leaves that served as a shade on a bottle lamp in the den. They could have put it in any number of places but they kept shoving it aside. The first van was filled and bolted shut. Several times I reminded the boss to be sure the shade was packed carefully.

"True, true, memsahib, not to worry," he kept saying. They loaded the last box and removed the handlebars of the kids' bikes so they'd fit into the tightly packed space. We went back into the house, and there in a corner on the living room floor sat the rain hat.

"Mr. Kumar," I called out. "Will you please look at this?" Mopping his brow with a towel, he came, and I pointed to the lampshade.

"Oh, Mrs. Bryan, you don't really want to take that, do you," he asked in bewilderment.

"What do you think I've been talking about these past three days," I demanded. "Now what are you going to do about it?"

"If you really want it, I must make an additional box," he said. "It will be ready tomorrow to accompany the two vans. I'm truly sorry. It was my mistake, and I'll bear the cost."

"I appreciate it," I answered. Having won that battle, I felt a bit sorry for the man, but it was typical of the way women were treated. Never in a million years would he have tried to pull such a stunt on Kedar.

For much that happened during our six years in India we were thankful. The children matured and came to appreciate another culture. It was easy for them to fall into a pattern of looking down on the Indians and calling them stupid just because they did things differently.

"Enough of that!" Kedar warned when one of them made a derogatory comment. "You're not to forget for a moment that we are guests here. How do we treat our guests? With respect and kindness, and that's what we're enjoying every day. We may not agree on everything or even a lot of things, but we'll have no disrespect for others in this house. Do you understand?" They did, and with a positive mindset we counted our blessings daily.

Opportunities were endless. We had the privilege of shaking hands with Prime Minister Nehru and President Eisenhower. We heard symphony orchestras from Berlin, Moscow, London, and Tokyo, and vacationed in Kashmir, going on horseback up to Tullian at twelve thousand feet in the Himalayan Mountains. In every city we met wonderful people who enriched our days. We had the chance of a lifetime to travel, to attend a Dassara in Mysore. We visited villages and towns from the primitive to the cosmopolitan. We spent a whole day at the Taj Mahal. After touring the building, we settled in the shade of some nearby trees, had a picnic lunch and supper, and watched its appearance change with every hour. Nothing can compare with its mystical beauty in the moonlight.

We often ordered coffee at a roadside stall, enjoying the merchant's showmanship as he mixed a strong decoction with boiling water and sweetened condensed milk. Pouring from one large mug to another, holding them farther and farther apart, he asked, "How many yards do you want?" If we ran out of drinking water, we made a quick stop by the roadside to purchase a tender young coconut. The seller cut an opening in one end from which we drank the cool sweet milk.

I came to love and appreciate Krishna and Chandam Rao, who taught me to dance, and the caddies who encouraged me with cries of *"Shabash!"* every time I made a good shot. I gained confidence in my ability to manage my advertising job with the *News Circle.*

In every place we found a Christian community that nourished and challenged us. The Lord is good, and I knew for a certainty that if one season of our lives was ending, what lay ahead would be even better. We were healthy, happy, and could hardly wait to see what was just around the corner.

It was the month of May with its deadly heat that made it unsafe for planes to take off during the day. We left at midnight on the 4th when the temperature had dropped to a permissible 100°. With vacation ahead, we were bound for a few weeks of camping in Europe before boarding the Italian liner, *Christiforo Colombo,* for New York.

Chapter 7

Hong Kong

Teenagers are a challenge anywhere, and living in Hong Kong added an interesting dimension. At fifteen, Anne was a good student and had no difficulty qualifying for King George the Fifth School (KG Five). Jim, a year and a half-younger, was a different kettle of fish. His idea of success was how well he could work his teacher, not his books. The many switches between the American and British systems left him bewildered and disinterested; however, he was accepted at the British Army School.

The finest thing in the colony for parents was school uniforms. Hallelujah! No more arguments about "What shall I wear today, Mom?" Each school had a distinctive outfit, easily identifying which one the students were attending.

Entering the British system at the sophomore level was difficult. Anne loved history and English but not math. Students there carried eleven subjects from the first form (grade), through high school, advancing a little each year, so on graduation they're well informed on all. Following three years in an American school in India and a year in the States, where she took algebra, she was ahead of most of her classmates except for geometry, which she hadn't had.

Her biggest adjustment was to teacher-student relationships. If she dared speak to or smile at her teacher while passing in the hallway, she was reprimanded for being "cheeky." There was no such thing as getting help for a difficult subject. If required, it was up to the parents to seek outside tutoring.

"Please, sir," Anne asked her teacher when she realized she was way over her head in geometry, "may I come to you after school? I must catch up with the rest of the class."

"Absolutely not," he answered. "If you're behind, ask one of your friends for help."

"In British schools," remarked Bill Rodd, one of our American friends, "the teacher teaches the subject. In the American system, the teacher teaches the child." Anne wanted to like her instructors, to feel they liked her, but there was no interaction whatsoever. Her grades plummeted from straight A's to just barely squeaking by.

Jim was doing no better in the B.A.S. and was failing French. On the advice of the staff we arranged for him to go to Madame Popp for extra lessons three times a week. She didn't take any guff and quickly brought up his grades.

"It might have been cheaper to buy him a French wife," Kedar remarked when he looked over the bills, "but if this is what it takes, we'll go for it."

I paced the floor one Wednesday night waiting for Jim to come in. House rules required him to be home by 10:00 p.m. We'd had several go-rounds on the subject, so when he left that evening I reminded him of the deadline–not even 10:01 p.m., and if he didn't make it he'd be grounded the following weekend. "Sure, Mom," he tossed off, breezing out the door. At 10:45 he was surprised to find me still up as he pocketed his house key.

"Son," I asked, "what time is it, and what was your understanding about the hour you were to be in?"

"What's the big deal," he asked, frowning. "I would have been on time, but my buddy was so drunk I had to take him home, way over in Kowloon, and pour him under his door. I couldn't just leave him out on his own. You wouldn't want me to do that, would you?"

"No I wouldn't, but you could have called to ask permission to come in later. There are phones all over town, so there's no excuse. Before you left I warned you about the penalty." If looks could kill, I would have been very dead! He turned on his heel, went to his room, and slammed the door.

The next morning he was still seething. He didn't utter a word at breakfast and ate almost nothing. Picking up his books, he left for school earlier than usual, and without a good-bye kiss. I knew the next weekend was going to be a long one. That afternoon while I was teaching Ah Pong how to make a soufflé, the phone rang.

"Madame Bryan," said Madame Popp, "where is Jim? He is already fifteen minutes late. Sometimes that boy is a silly ass."

"I'm so sorry," I answered. "If I hear from him I'll tell him to hurry. He should be with you any moment." I went back to my cooking, wondering what he was up to. He enjoyed his French lessons, so why was he late? A few minutes later the phone rang again.

"My next student is here, Madame Bryan. What shall I do about Jim–have him wait, or do you want me to send him home?"

"Please ask him to come home," I answered. "I apologize again that he's upset your schedule." There was just time to get the soufflé in the oven and have the potatoes baked for dinner. Now what, I wondered as I picked up the phone again.

"Are you Mrs. Bryan?" a man asked, "and is Jim Bryan your son?"

A Tale of Two Bamboos

"Yes, he is."

"Kedar, Edwin, come quickly!" I shouted. That call was from Queen Mary Hospital. Jim was brought in unconscious. "They want us out there right away." I stood outside in the hall, stabbing futilely at the elevator button while they seemed to take forever to join me. Edwin came with a glass of water and two pills in an outstretched hand.

"What's that?"

"Take them, Mom," he coaxed. "They're mild tranquilizers, and I think you can probably use them. Go head." I did just as the elevator arrived. All the way to the hospital I kicked myself for not asking how Jim was, were bones broken, was he bleeding, and what happened to him. I also began to think about the grounded weekend ahead, and how that should be handled. In the emergency room we found him on a cot looking very pale and subdued.

"He's going to be fine," the doctor said. "He has a concussion and should stay quiet for the next several days. We've taken X-rays, and everything's in order." At that, I went to pieces, blubbering all over the place. As much as I wanted to wring his neck about once a week, I loved the little rascal, my baby, with all my heart.

"Mom," Jim said, big brown eyes pleading, "can't I go to the dance on Saturday night?"

"That isn't fair, and you know it," I said, regaining my composure; "and besides, the doctor said you need to stay quiet for the next few days. We'll do what he says, okay?"

"Sure," he said, sneaking a little grin. "I just thought I'd try."

As we questioned him, the story unfolded. After getting off the ferry on the island side, he went to a music store to listen to a new record he wanted to buy before going to his lesson. He took the demo into a small, stuffy booth. After several minutes he opened the door and passed out, giving his head a hard crack on the cement floor. Jim wore his shirt collars a little tight as was the style. Combine that with his boiling anger over being grounded, little food, and the enclosed booth, and he simply fainted. When he didn't come to right away, they called an ambulance.

"Fran," Hunkey said, "I'm sorry to have bad news. Mother died last night." The call came late one night soon after Kedar had left for a two-week trip through Southeast Asia.

"I guess we've been expecting it," I answered, feeling strangely alone, "but it's hard to think I'll not see her again this side of Glory. How's Daddy doing, and when's the funeral?"

"It'll be Saturday, here in Iowa City, but she'll be buried next week in Nebraska in her family's plot. Father's fine," Hunkey said. "He's busy making arrangements and calling everybody. Reality won't set in for a while. I'll stay with him as long as he needs me."

"I wish I could come. Kedar's off on a trip, and we aren't settled into the school routine enough for me to leave the kids just yet. Kaiser would pay my way; but I can't do it, and I'm so sorry."

"We understand. Father appreciates your situation," Hunkey consoled. "I'll send a tape of the service and write you."

It was the first break in the family circle. Mother wore a seven-star pin for family members in the service during World War II, and praise God, not one was lost.

Over the years I became Mother's personal Christmas shopper. We lived in interesting places abroad where I could find affordable gifts for them to give on their missionary's retirement income. I made several suggestions for her to chose from and bought something for each of my brothers and sisters. We were living in New

Delhi when the Dalai Lama and thousands of his followers fled from Tibet. Many of them survived by peddling their treasures from door to door. I was able to buy beautiful copper-and-silver tea pots for a song. In New York they'd cost a hundred dollars or more! Surface mail took months, so Mother's packages were always on their way by the end of August to make sure they'd arrive on time. As soon as we reached Hong Kong in July, she sent her Christmas list. Knowing it was on her mind, I took care of it right away. She was so pleased when the gifts were delivered.

Mother suffered numerous heart attacks and strokes over a ten-year period. Several times all the family in-country went home to see her one last time, but she kept bouncing back. As she became less and less able to do things for herself and around the house, Daddy took over. For a man who never so much as wiped a teacup for forty years, he pitched in without complaint or fanfare and did what she could not, and he did it with such grace. Mother had all sorts of medication to take at specific times, and he saw to it that she got them on schedule. Once while we were visiting, he came to the bedroom with the some pills. Instead of carrying them in one hand with a glass of water in the other, he brought them on a silver tray saying, "This is for my lady."

We arranged our trip to Hong Kong with a stopover in Iowa City as her health was deteriorating rapidly. I needed another hug, to hear her voice once more, look into her beautiful blue eyes and tell her how I loved her. She was not a perfectionist, which made life with eight children a lot easier, but she radiated a special sort of comfort and joy. She loved to laugh, have a party, and bask in the presence of her children. No wonder she was named the 1956 Iowa Mother of the Year.

The third floor of a downtown bank building housed the American Club, center of most social activities of our sizable community. Concerned that our teenagers learn rather than stumble into social graces, several mothers organized a cotillion for alternate Saturday afternoons during the fall and spring of our second year in Hong Kong. We engaged a couple of English teachers as dance instructors, and gave them full authority to do it right. Since it was they and not we laying down the rules, objections from the youngsters were few.

We watched in delight as they performed the fox-trot, waltz, quick-step, and cha-cha. All were required to dress properly in their Sunday-go-to-meetin' best, including white gloves for both boys and girls. I never thought I'd see it, but they liked it!

The instructors insisted that two formal dinner dances were essential to round out the course, so we held them at Christmas and Easter. Several weeks beforehand, the lesson demonstrated party etiquette for ladies and gentlemen, including mingling, managing drinks (Coke) and hors d'oeuvres, sitting and standing with grace and ease, signing dance cards, table manners, and much more.

By the end of the year, Anne and Jim were polished dancers and won first place in the waltz. As they gracefully twirled I thought. "Isn't it nice they're having such a good time together. They're actually smiling at each other." I hadn't known that one of the requirements was a pleasant expression.

"All during our routine," Anne told me later, "I had to smile through clenched teeth while reminding Jim to do the same. At least he didn't step on my feet once. It was wonderful."

Jim began to notice girls and dated several. Ellen, daughter of acting U.S. Consul General John Lacy, particularly took his fancy. They lived out of town, two miles from the Repulse Bay Hotel.

"What should I do, Anne?" he asked. "I have enough money for a one-way taxi ride. Should I use it to pick her up or to take her home? The other time we'll take the bus."

"When you go to get her," Anne advised, "she'll be all dressed up with her hair fixed, and it would be better not to have it get wind-blown at the start of the date. Take her home by bus. That's what I'd like."

Nevertheless, it was a long jaunt. They went to his school dance by taxi into town, the Star Ferry across the harbor, and bus to the far end of Kowloon. They didn't find the party interesting and retraced their steps to the Hilton Hotel on Victoria Island. I was always thankful for the all-night coffee shop where our children could get something to eat at a reasonable price; it was clean, safe, and well-lighted. Jim and Ellen didn't pay any attention to the time until it was past the hour she was supposed to be home. They rushed to catch a bus and forgot to let the Lacys know where they were.

"Say, Fran," John phoned. "Have you heard from the kids? We expected them home before now."

"No, I'm sorry, I haven't," I answered. "If I do I'll let you know."

When Jim and Ellen reached the bus station it was after 11:00 p.m., and the one stopping near her house wasn't running. The only bus remaining went to Repulse Bay, which meant they had to walk two miles along an unlighted coast road and up the hill to the Lacys house. It was 2:00 a.m. when they arrived at her front door, hand in hand, talking and laughing.

"Gee, I'm sorry we're late, Mr. Lacy," Jim said as he looked up to see an angry six-foot-two father standing behind the screen door in his shorts and undershirt.

"And so am I," he thundered. He hustled his daughter inside and confronted my son. Full of apology, Jim explained and begged forgiveness for his thoughtlessness.

"I'll go on back and catch the next bus to town," he said, doing his best to get away from the embarrassing situation.

"You'll do nothing of the kind," John stated firmly. "I'll call a taxi and let your mother know you're on the way." A chastened, broke young man crawled into bed in the wee hours.

The next day I suggested it would be appropriate to write a letter of apology to the Lacys, which he was glad to do.

"I guess this is one of the few places in the world where a couple of young people can walk on a dark, deserted road in the middle of the night and be perfectly safe," Mary remarked a few days later. "It gave us a scare when they were so late, but thank God they were okay. We appreciated Jim's note too." Instead of turning out to be an "incident," the affair helped our two families develop a closer bond.

It was easy to spot the kids as I pulled up to the curb where they waited for me at the Kowloon ferry landing. In the midst of thousands of Chinese who rushed on and off the boat, their blond heads easily caught my eye. As soon as I stopped they jumped in, lugging heavy school bags. Going to Kai Tak Airport to meet Kedar was a happy time. He was away so much that we celebrated every moment he was home. We took a table near the huge windows overlooking the runway, and I ordered afternoon tea with Cokes for the kids. They were both full of the day's events as we relaxed, waiting for Kedar's plane.

"Look over there," Anne whispered, nodding toward a table ten feet away. "Isn't that Marlon Brando?"

"Yes," I answered. "The paper said he was in town for a few days on his way back to the States. I guess the reporters are asking him about *The Ugly American.* He just finished filming it in Cambodia."

"I'm going to get his autograph," Jim said as he jumped up, paper and pen in hand. He went over but stood quietly until recognized. "Mr. Brando," he said, "may I please have your autograph? We're looking forward to seeing your movie when it comes to Hong Kong."

"Sure, glad to, and I hope you'll enjoy it." He smiled at Jim, shook his hand, and turned back to the reporters.

"Oh Jimmy, please get one for me too," Anne begged, handing him her paper and a pen, "Please?"

"No way," he answered as he sat down. "You want it, you go get it!"

"I'm too shy, you know that. I can't go over there with all those men, ple-e-e-se."

"No." Her brother was determined not to help, leaving her squirming in her chair until she could stand it no longer and slid out of her seat.

"Well, aren't you a pretty young thing," Brando said, looking her up and down and noticing her uniform, "Are you English?"

"No, sir. I'm American, and proud of it," she replied, blushing. "May I have your autograph too? You just gave one to my brother." He continued to look her over with approval, which made her blush even more.

"Sure," he said, "What's your name, young lady?"

"Anne Bryan," she said, trying to see what he was writing.

"There," he said as he stood. "Keep on being proud to be an American and as pretty as you are." He held her hand a moment longer than necessary, which thrilled her no end. She smiled her thanks and returned to us just as Kedar's plane was announced. I doubt she was aware of walking as she floated out the door and down the stairs. I shall always love that man. He made her day.

In the 1960s Hong Kong had the reputation of consuming more alcohol than any other city in the world. It was available everywhere without restriction, and that worried me. Anne and Jim were frequently invited to homes where we didn't know the parents. Tales abounded of wild parties, unlimited booze, and no supervising adults.

To protect the children from harm and embarrassment, it was time to set some boundaries with which all of us were comfortable.

"There are two no-nos, I said. "First, if a parent isn't present, excuse yourselves. Second, even if one is, leave if there's drinking. You can tell them your mother made the rules, and you don't dare break them. I'll be happy to take the blame. Just grab a cab and come home." Both children agreed.

The children were easy to manage next to Kedar who was now drinking beer almost exclusively. We kept other drinks on hand for guests, but I was encouraged by hearing someone say, "Oh, don't worry about a beer-drinker. It isn't strong enough to hurt anybody." The problem was that Kedar drank a 12 percent German beer, and lots of it. Having two quarts at lunch was usual, and another four to six quarts before the day's end. It's a wonder he retained a slender figure.

One day as I sat at my desk paying the monthly bills, realization that Kedar was a full-blown alcoholic hit me like a ton of bricks. As manager of the Far Eastern Division, he traveled at least 50 percent of the time. Most of my grocery shopping was done by phone, and I was sent a bill at the end of each month. The amount for beer and cigarettes seemed awfully high, so I checked it carefully. With three of us at home full time and Kedar part time, the cost of his indulgences was over half the tab for the whole month!

More was being written about alcoholism, its dangers and consequences, and I found it devastating. One thing seemed perfectly clear; the substance abuser will not stop for his wife or children no matter how much he loves them. He'll stop only when he's thoroughly convinced he will die if he continues. Kedar was healthy, was doing a fantastic job for Kaiser, was a loving husband and good father. But looking ahead to what was bound to come made me feel as if we were at the top of a mountain in a car with no brakes.

On the surface things seemed fine. Kedar was able to stop drinking for a few days whenever it was important to do so. If company executives were visiting, or if a business deal depended on his having a clear head, he stayed sober. I looked forward to those special times during which he was absolutely wonderful. I lived for them.

Every summer the midshipmen from the U.S. Naval Academy came to Hong Kong aboard an aircraft carrier. The naval attaché's daughter was in Anne's class and made sure she was invited to the tea dance on board. It was an exciting time for all the sweet young things. I delivered her at shipside and waited to see her safely up the gangplank.

"What a blast," Anne said as she twirled around in her new dress, all bubbly and excited. "The moment I was on board an officer paired me up with a cadet of the right height, and he was my date. Thanks for letting me go with him and the others for dinner and more dancing, but I was afraid I'd have to come home alone."

"How's that?"

"After the guys and some of the girls had a drink and were ordering another round, I told Tom that if he did, I'd have to go home. He drank Cokes with me the rest of the evening. Wasn't that neat, Mom?"

As good a kid as Anne was, we had our moments. We were never on the same wavelength when it came to buying clothes. She had only about half the wardrobe of some of her friends and felt deprived. Deciding we needed peace on the subject, I asked her to estimate what she required for a clothing allowance, and we'd try it for six months. She made lists, figured costs, and came up with an amount I was sure was too low. We went out for one last shopping trip, with me paying for most of the basics. From then on she could use her allowance any way she chose. It went well until I noticed her beginning to be uncomfortable with our arrangement, especially at Christmas when she wanted a new formal for the cotillion.

"I had no idea it cost so much, she sobbed. "I did my best, but what I told you wasn't near enough."

"I know, sweetheart," I said as I put my arms around her. "I knew it all along but you needed to learn an important lesson. What would you say to keeping the same arrangement, if I double your allowance and make it retroactive?" Happiness is! That ended that battle, leaving the door open to a much closer relationship.

When Anne was a junior we met Paula Brown, wife of the air attaché at the Consulate General. A former Powers model, she undertook to conduct charm classes for teenage girls followed by a modeling course. Once a week for six months she put fifteen gawky, gangly kids through their paces and turned out poised, polished young women.

"Fran," Paula said to me one day, "in all the years I've been teaching, there are only a half dozen who are natural models, and Anne is one of them. She has a sense of what to do with her hands, and when she turns it's as if she's always known how. I'm putting her and two others in the fashion show at the American Women's Club dinner dance this spring."

So Anne strutted her stuff, modeling two dresses and a swimsuit. She was a knockout. Too bad she wasn't five feet ten or eleven instead of five two and a hundred pounds soaking wet!

Getting summer work for our young people was a problem. Live-in amahs did the baby-sitting; there were no newspapers to deliver; local men who needed jobs to support their families did the yard work. The same was true for clerking in stores, flipping burgers, or washing cars. So what could they do?

Through the bamboo wireless Anne heard of a young English girl who needed a governess. Her father was head of the jewelry department at Lane Crawford's, Hong Kong's finest store. A few months earlier his wife had died in childbirth. Bridgett was too old for an amah and too young to be left on her own all day. A teenage governess/companion was the answer. The kid was a spoiled brat, but Anne understood why–not that she didn't find first-class seats at a live Beetles concert to be the highlight of the summer! The worst part of the job was the daily two hours of math tutoring. As far as Anne was concerned, it was the hardest money she ever earned. She was glad when the summer ended.

We put our heads together and came up with a Big Brother program for Jim. We knew of at least two dozen young boys from eight to twelve whose mothers would probably give their eyeteeth to have them out of the house for a few hours. We made up a flyer to circulate in the American community and were amazed at the response. They loved the idea. The rules:

1. No more than eight boys a day
2. Pickup in the lobby of the Hilton Hotel at 10:00 a.m.
3. Delivery at the same place at 4:00 p.m.
4. Bring sack lunch and one soft drink
5. Reserve space for one month, payment in advance, no refunds.
6. Operational five days a week; recommend M-W-F or T-Th

Within a week the first month was fully booked and more wanting to attend. I had to put my foot down on the numbers. Jim was a teenager himself, and I didn't want him to go beyond his ability to manage a bunch of young boys. If their imagination were half as lively as his, he'd have his hands full.

I called a friend in the insurance business and made an appointment for Jim, got him spiffed up in his best suit, and sent him down to talk about his business venture. He took out liability coverage for a nominal sum. Making progress.

Then came the tough part–planning three programs a week that would interest the boys, be doable within the available time, and deal with public transportation. Hong Kong is rich in all sorts of interesting things to do and see, so it was a matter of selecting the best. Once he took them to a factory in Kowloon where tons of plastic flowers were turned out daily. They watched hoppers feed a stream of granules into heated molds and move on to high-heat-and-pressure stamping equipment. A careless finger exploring the machinery could come off in a second, so before they went on the floor Jim instructed the boys to put their hands in their pockets and keep them there. After the tour he herded them into the owner's office (a friend of ours) to learn more about making plastic items and have a chance to ask questions. Another time he took them to the botanical gardens for a lesson in marching. That was followed by a bus ride to Turtle Cove, where they swam for the rest of the day.

The buddy system worked well, and he never lost a boy, though a couple of times it was close. Jim paid transportation and bought each child one soft drink per day.

At 4:00 p.m. eight happy, bedraggled little boys marched back into the Hilton.

"The worst I threaten them with is keeping them home instead of going out with Jim," Peg Bordwell told me. "It has made my summer!" And at the end of the season, Jim cleared two thousand dollars!

During Edwin's second year at Tulsa University, we began looking into the possibility of taking his junior year in Hong Kong. Chung Chi College offered enough courses in his major in English to make it worthwhile. At the same time Anne was accepted as a high school senior at Morrison Academy in Taiwan. It was wonderful having the family together again, if only briefly.

In September we took Anne to Taichung and settled her in the unapologetically Christian Morrison Academy. Nothing new for her as she'd gone to boarding school in India. We left with but a few extra hugs. She was happy to be back in an American school.

Evangelistic meetings were scheduled in October. Students were excused from evening study hall to attend, and a week later we received a letter: "This is hard to write," she began, "but two nights ago I gave my heart to the Lord. Mr. Green from South Africa was a wonderful speaker. I was convinced on the very first night that I needed something more than I had but was ashamed to say so. After all, I've been baptized. I'm a church member and read my Bible regularly, but somehow it hasn't felt genuine. What would my friends say, I wondered, if I went forward? I was torn all week long, but on that last night I could hardly wait for the invitation. I jumped up and ran down the aisle. It was the happiest, most wonderful thing that has ever happened to me, and I wanted you to know."

"Yeah, yeah," the boys sneered, rolling their eyes as I read her letter aloud." "We know. All this emotional stuff will wear off in a few weeks, and she'll be the same old Anne again." They had their opinion, but I was thrilled for her and for myself too. My daughter was a new creature in Christ, and our relationship would change to a deeper, stronger level. I was eager for her return at Christmas.

The three of them shared a bathroom, and before going away she used to keep them waiting for ages while she did her hair and got her makeup just right. Not any more. She was no longer tough to live with but smooth as silk. Her brothers were impressed.

"You know, Mom," she said to me one day as we wrapped Christmas presents, "now I understand those things you've been telling me for years. All at once everything's come together and makes sense. Isn't it wonderful?"

I hugged her. "It's the best of all things to be absolutely sure of your relationship with Jesus. There's nothing like it." It's been different for us ever since and it's all good.

Edwin thrived at Chung Chi College. A forty-five minute train ride took him from the station at the ferry to the school in the New Territories. Classes were small, and he particularly liked the one on Russian history. He and Tally Wilson, a sociology exchange student from California, became immediate friends, and before the end of the year they were hearing wedding bells.

"I have a present for Peppy" (our miniature French poodle), Edwin announced one day when he came home. He unzipped the Pan Am flight bag he used for his books, and out popped the head of a tiny kitten. The little thing was only a couple of weeks old and pathetically thin.

"The mother has a whole litter living in the station at Chung Chi," he said, "and I thought I'd rescue at least one. The place is crawling with rats that are a lot bigger than the kittens. Probably the rest will be dinner." We found a carton with high sides, lined it with clean rags, and began feeding the kitten with an eye dropper. The next day we added Pabulum and soon the little creature resembled a tight ball with skinny little legs and a head protruding from it. When he was big enough to leave the box, "George" became the focus of Peppy's attention. He endured being licked and knocked about just so long before disappearing behind the sofa where Peppy couldn't follow. Often he'd walk nonchalantly out the other end while Peppy waited for a half-hour or more for him to return.

When George was half grown I noticed a bald spot on his back the size of a dime, so we took him to a vet.

"I'm afraid I have bad news," the doctor said as he came to the waiting room. "Your pet has an extremely virulent spore infection that transfers to humans. It's almost impossible to get rid of it. It starts with itching around collar bands and cuffs. Twice I've had to shave my head and..." He didn't need to say anything more.

"So what do you suggest?" I asked. I could just see all of us shiny bald, and already I felt itchy.

"It was good of you to give the little waif a home," he answered, "but if you'll allow it, I'll put him to sleep. The cost is five dollars." I looked at Edwin. It was his choice, but given the alternatives, he nodded his consent. We were sad to leave without George but glad none of us had the disease.

For our last Easter in Hong Kong we decided to have our own private celebration on the *Duchess*. Edwin and Tally wanted some time alone; Anne was in Taiwan, so Kedar, Jim, and I went out for the weekend. Our destination was Double Haven, a small sheltered bay near the Communist border. With a full larder and gas tank, we took our time running up the coast. A medium-sized freighter that had gone aground in the last typhoon was still there, half submerged. Jim thought it would be neat to investigate, so we stood off a hundred yards while he explored the wreck with mask and snorkel. Late in the afternoon we anchored in a cove with a white sandy bottom and easy access up a hill that over looked Mainland China. We were completely alone. No footpaths, villages or boats. After supper, a gentle breeze rocked us to sleep.

Up before sunrise, we read the Easter passage in the Bible and prayed; then after a hearty breakfast we prepared to leave. The plan was to go down Tolo Channel to meet Edwin and Tally for dinner at a floating restaurant in Tolo Harbor. That is, until the engine wouldn't cooperate! When the electric starter quit, Kedar and Jim took turns with the rope but no luck. It was dead.

Because of Hong Kong's serious water shortage, the Plover Cove Scheme, largest reservoir in the world, was under construction not far from where we were stranded. The project involved several islands near the mainland that were to be joined together with a wall through which underground pipes leading to the city were to be laid. The dam and water distribution systems were only a part of the task. The rest involved numerous catchments to keep it filled. We took out our charts to locate the nearest engineering site, and Jim agreed to go for help. I packed a sandwich, and he swam ashore with clothes, food, and a Coke on his head. Dressed, he waved good-bye and set off.

We had no idea how long the exercise would take, so we settled down with some good books. With plenty of provisions, we were in no hurry. At 4:00 p.m. on that most beautiful sunny day, around the corner came a huge sea-going tug with all its bunting flying! What a glorious sight.

"I say there," a man addressed us with megaphone, "are you the Bryans? If you'll come alongside we'll see what we can do to help you."

"We're the Bryans, but sorry, we can't go anywhere," Kedar shouted back. They, too, did their best to start the engine, but it wouldn't kick over. They even hooked up a whole series of powerful batteries, but still there was no sign of life.

"Well, I guess there's nothing for it but to tow you into Tolo Harbor," the captain said. "You can tie up for the night at our dock and in the morning find a mechanic."

"Thanks, we appreciate your help," Kedar said. Lines were secured to the *Duchess* from the tug's stern, and away we went, trailing a sea anchor to keep us from fish-

A Tale of Two Bamboos

tailing. It was dark before we got there, and Kedar began to wonder what all this was going to cost. We counted the money we had aboard, and keeping out some for repairs, hoped we'd be able to pay for the rescue.

"You've been very kind," he said to the captain. "What do we owe you?"

"In Her Majesty's service," came the quick reply. "You don't owe us a thing. Glad to help!"

"That's most generous," Kedar answered. "Will you accept a gift for your Widows' and Orphans' Fund?" He handed him all our spare money, which was about fifty dollars.

"Glad to," he said as he stuffed the bills into his shirt pocket, "and cheery-o."

"Phew," Kedar said after the captain left, "what a relief." We phoned home to find out how the boys were and to thank Jim.

"No trouble," he boasted. "I found an engineering outpost about ten miles from Double Haven and asked to see their charts. They were a little surprised, but fortunately a couple of English employees were there. I don't know what I'd have done if they'd been out for the holiday. Anyway, I was able to give them your exact location, and asked them to radio the harbor police for assistance. A Land Rover was about to leave for town, so I hitched a ride."

"Thank you, son," Kedar answered. "We'll try to get fixed tomorrow and head for Tai Tam. See you later."

"Okay, Dad," Jim said, "I'll see you when I get home from school. Careful now. Love you."

The next morning we set out to find a mechanic. Within a block we came upon one sitting at the edge of the road beside a three-by-five ground cloth covered with tools and parts.

"You savvy engine?" Kedar asked in his finest pidgin English.

"I savvy. What side you boat?" he asked as he got to

his feet.

"This side." Kedar said, pointing.

"Okay, I look-see can fix-ee, no can fix-ee." Poking around for a minute, the man tapped the starter motor. "Think so maybe this thing. I take out, can do?"

"Sure, sure, can do," Kedar answered. "You can fix-ee, you number one." We settled down with our books again after looking around the village. Within in hour he was back, grinning from ear to ear.

"I think so okay. We try," he said after he'd reconnected the motor. With a turn of the key the engine roared to life.

"Yes, sir, you number one!" Kedar congratulated him and handed over double the negotiated price. We stopped and restarted the engine several times while maneuvering the channel just to make sure it wouldn't die when we entered the open sea. A brisk wind was whipping up some good-sized waves, and we didn't want the *Duchess* to share the fate of the freighter we'd seen two days before. It was a quick trip and so good to get home again.

Typhoon means "big wind" in Chinese. In the West we call it a hurricane. It was July 1962, the early part of the storm season, when we arrived in Hong Kong.

Within a couple of weeks, Kedar was summoned to Tokyo to attend a meeting between the presidents of Kaiser Jeep, International and Mitsubishi Industries. He left Anne, Jimmy, and me in the Repulse Bay Hotel as we still hadn't found a place to live. Almost at once Typhoon Wanda roared in and immediately became synonymous with death and destruction. The hotel hardly lost power, but elsewhere in the colony it was a different story. Huge mudslides wiped out hundreds of tarpaper squatter's shacks perched precariously, one above another, on the steep hillsides surrounding the airport. Fishing boats that didn't make it to shelter were tossed about like toys and dashed on the rocks. The loss of life was staggering. A number of merchant ships sank, and the twisted, broken trees on the mountains gave everything a sad, forlorn look.

We had been considering an apartment in a tall building with a spectacular view of the mountains and the ocean but didn't take it because it was small for our family and somewhat off the beaten path. We thanked God we hadn't signed for a unit when Wanda did a number on it, sucking out the flimsy aluminum window frames curtains and all. Some apartments lost furniture as well. The building was a mess and not habitable for weeks.

Within the month we found just what we wanted on the tenth floor of a building on Robinson Road, perched on a cliff halfway up the mountain. Huge ceiling-to-floor plate-glass windows in the living room and master bedroom overlooked the botanical gardens, the governor's mansion, and the harbor. A short trip by car, an easy walk through the gardens, or a cheap bus ride took us to the central district of Victoria Island. If "location, location, location" is what matters, we had it. It was by no means palatial, but it was comfortable and felt like home. For his office Kedar rented the other apartment on the same floor, half the size of ours. Although the storms were a disaster to some, they were a blessing in the rain they brought. In the early 1960s Hong Kong suffered a critical water shortage that required strict rationing. Our taps were dry except for three hours every fourth day from 6:00 to 9:00 a.m. On those days we were up and ready to go at 5:45. The moment the first gurgle sounded, we went into action. The washing machine, loaded the night before, was turned on; everybody showered and shampooed; the kitchen and bathrooms were scrubbed down. Before the flow stopped we filled the bathtubs and set planks across them to support the huge plastic containers we carefully topped off. Bottled drinking water was a necessity. Culligian's business was booming. We put buckets under the sinks and removed the traps to catch the water to use for flushing toilets.

Kedar traveled the whole of the Far East and was usually out of town when typhoons hit. One time, however, he was home. In the middle of the night when the storm was at its worst, I was awakened by the bed's violent jiggling. I thought Kedar was having a nightmare. But in the bathroom I saw the water in the tub sloshing back and forth. The whole building was swaying! I checked for cracks in the walls and ceiling and the windows for leaks, but there were none. I was again thankful for God's provision of a good, secure dwelling.

While Edwin was attending Chung Chi College one weekend, he and Jim decided to take our tent and climb the mountain on Lan Tao. A cluster of stone cottages up there served those wishing to escape Hong Kong's stifling summer heat, but the only way up was a narrow, steep footpath. I wasn't sure it was a good idea because the number one signal was flying, announcing a typhoon in the area. The boys were eager for adventure and promised to come straight home if the number five flag went up. Reluctantly I consented. A French boy Jim met in school wanted to go along and his parents gave their permission–so why not? They took along a walkie-talkie with a fifteen-mile reach, and we agreed to make contact at 8:00 p.m.

The trio caught the noon ferry to the island and had no more than left port gone when news came that the storm had changed direction. It was headed straight for us! Shortly thereafter the number seven flag appeared, meaning all public water transport was shut down. There was no way for them to return. I had to trust their good sense to take shelter in a secure building. I wanted them safe, and I didn't want to have the tent torn to shreds.

Line-of-sight transmission to Lan Tao meant I had to drive to the top of the pass on Mount Road. At 7:30 p.m. the wind was wild, driving the rain every which way. I hesitated about going, but I'd promised; so I set off in our

Jeep station wagon. Rain hitting the three-foot stone wall at the side of the road bounced straight up, and fell back in a reverse waterfall. As heavy as the car was, every time I passed an open place in the wall, I was blown sideways several feet. It was terrifying, but I kept going. I was thankful there were no others on the road. They had better sense.

Finally at the gap I pulled over and opened my window a crack to feed out the antenna, then punched on the instrument.

"May day, may day, may day, over," came Jim's voice, loud and clear in spite of the static.

"What do you mean 'may day'," I demanded. "Where in the world are you, and are you okay? Over."

"Sure, Mom," he answered, "we're fine. A very nice Englishman and his son in one of the stone houses have taken us in. He's teaching us to play gin rummy. Over."

"I could skin you alive for that may-day bit. You shouldn't scare your mother like that, but I'm glad to know you're all right; and thank the nice man for his hospitality, won't you? Over."

"Sure, we'll do that, and please don't worry. We'll be back late tomorrow afternoon. Love you, Mom. Sleep well. We will. Over and bye."

That little villain–I could wring his neck and love him to death at the same time! Knowing they were safe, I did sleep well.

The telephone was ringing when Anne and I returned from church the next noon.

"Please, madam," said a man with a thick English accent, "are you the owner of the *Duchess*?"

"Yes," I answered, "is there something I can do for you?"

"I'm sorry to inform you that your boat has sunk. I would suggest it might be a good idea to check on it this afternoon before the damage becomes too great."

"Thank you so much for telling me. I'll be right out," I managed to say, stunned and wondering how it could have happened.

When we first settled in Hong Kong we decided to buy a boat rather than join a sports club, thinking it would be the best value for the family. We could enjoy it together, and it was something we'd never done. The *Duchess* was a twenty-one-foot cabin cruiser with an inboard-outboard engine, a galley, a head with shower, and bunk space for four/six, in a pinch. Most weekends we went out exploring coves and bays until we found just the right one, to which we returned whenever we could.

We stocked the galley with basic foods, tinned goods, and utensils. Ah Pong, the house girl, and I worked out a list of staples to pack for every outing–water, soft drinks, fresh fruit, cookies, bread, and some kind of meat and salad. The kids invited their friends, and we had a royal time.

Mr. William Ostramoff, Repulse Bay Hotel manager and our good friend, offered advice based on his many years in the colony.

"It's best to keep it at Tai Tam," he said. "It's a small but well-sheltered harbor, and a man from the village will be happy to watch after it for you."

"I thought we'd take care of it ourselves," I answered. "With the girl to clean up and tend the flat, the kids are getting rather spoiled. What do you think?"

"Sorry, but that's not such a good idea," he responded.

"It costs a pittance, but if you don't have a boatman, strange things happen, and nobody has the slightest idea who's responsible! It's awfully cheap insurance, really." So we bought our little craft, rented a mooring, and dutifully hired a boatman; still it sank. How come?

At Tai Tam all was peaceful in the bright sun. I found our *Duchess* with just a foot of the forepeak showing and the rest under the murky water.

"Where's Mr. Kwan?" I asked a villager. "We have to

get the *Duchess* up. The tide's going out, and now is a good time to see what's needed."

"I call him," he answered. "Maybe he catch chow."

"Please," I said, "tell him to get two boats and lots of line so we can haul the boat now. He can eat later, savvy?" He returned with a shame-faced Mr. Kwan, but he'd brought several friends, two junks, and stout line. They knew what to do and in no time had her beached, whereupon they left us to the job of cleaning her up and finding out what made her sink.

Everything was covered with gasoline and particularly unpleasant mud smelling of human waste. I had to laugh when I saw an intact roll of Scott paper towels, still in its holder in the galley. I wished I could take a picture to send the manufacturers. What an ad that would make! We hauled out everything that wasn't fixed and put it on the bank to dry. Even when we washed down the bulkhead and rinsed out the bilges we couldn't find a reason for the disaster. We were sitting down to rest when a short, wiry Englishman came by with a curious expression on his face.

"I say," he exclaimed, "where are your men folk?"

"Well," I answered, "my husband's in California, and my two sons are on Lan Tao. I expect them back this afternoon."

"May I introduce myself," he continued. "I'm Geoffrey Brown, in Her Majesty's service. My occupation is the care of all small craft belonging to the Crown. May I be of service to you, madam?"

"You are so kind," I answered, "and I'd certainly appreciate your help. We can't find what made the boat go down. I don't know what to do." He careened her one way and then the other. As we held the line tilting her over, he went down on his knees and finally discovered a little hole just two inches in diameter near the keel.

"Here it is," he announced. "It's not much, but enough to sink her. Now we need to set a tingle so she won't be tidal." I gulped. This man was speaking English, but I hadn't the foggiest what he was saying.

"And how do we do that?" I asked. The ball was in his court.

"A tingle, madam, is a patch," he explained. "I need a piece of copper lined with fabric that can be fixed to the hull to keep the water out when the tide comes in."

"I'm afraid there's no place around here where we can get anything like that," I said. "Can we make a substitute that will work for the time being?"

"This will do," he said in triumph, holding up a piece of plywood.

"I can rip off a piece of the torn boat cover."

"Splendid," he said, "and now all we need is a screwdriver and four screws."

"We have them right here," I called as I retrieved the toolbox from the bank. We held the *Duchess* on her side while Mr. Brown performed the operation.

It wasn't long before he found out what had happened. The capstan on the forepeak was not molded as a unit. The pin was a separate piece that slipped into the base plate. With the jerking of the wind it came out, the mooring line fell off, and away she went on an unauthorized voyage. When she ran into whatever it was that punched the hole, water flooded in, and down she went.

"Now what do we do?" I asked.

"First thing in the morning I'll see if I can get you into a boatyard. They'll be jammed after the typhoon, but I have a lot of pull. I'll find something, I promise. We must get that engine taken apart and cleaned before rust takes over. I'll call you tomorrow if I may have your number." I could have kissed him. We loaded the stinking gear into the Jeep and were about to head home just as Edwin and Jim arrived to see what we were up to. Our men folk, ha!

"It's all arranged," Mr. Brown announced. "I've sent a tug around to haul the *Duchess*, and we'll take her to a very fine yard. They'll do the engine straight away then I'll have everything cleaned up for better inspection. Could you meet me tomorrow afternoon for a consultation?" he asked.

"I'll be there. And Mr. Brown, you're wonderful. I just can't thank you enough."

"You're welcome," he answered, "and think nothing of it. My pleasure." When Kedar got back from the States the boat was better than new, all fixed up and for a very small price, thanks to our new friend and guardian angel, Mr. Geoffrey Brown.

After Mother died Daddy found the big house too much of a burden. Betty and Hunkey helped him sort and dispose of its contents. He sold the house and moved into a small apartment in the heart of town. At first it seemed okay. His weekly letters told of getting into a schedule of cleaning, cooking, and laundry, but the one task he found difficult and frustrating was ironing his shirts. He began to miss yard work, and his view of a back alley didn't compare with the one on Otto Street with its wild cherry tree, flowers, and vegetable garden. Most of all he missed Mother. "For years," he told me one day, "I tried to bring comfort to those who'd lost a loved one and prayed to God what I said was helpful, but I had absolutely no idea of how terribly it hurts. Now I know."

A routine check-up with the family physician showed he had put on fifteen pounds, and the doctor scolded. Mother used to say, "Henry'll eat any old thing for dinner so long as he has a good dessert." I suspect he was getting more than his share of goodies when he shopped and ate alone.

He began looking around for other options. He made application at the Presbyterian Retirement Home in Duarte, California, and his name was put on the waiting list. It had every facility for a conformable retirement. That many of the residents were friends from Korea and other foreign mission fields was a strong drawing card.

"There are two problems," he confided. "It's too far away from any of you children, and people go there to die. I'm not ready for that yet. I want to be where folks are still interested in living."

Daddy packed up his things, put them in storage, and began making the rounds of his children. He stayed from a few days to several months with each of us. Being overseas, we were last on the list. He arrived on a clear and sparkling fall night. I turned off the lights in the living room as we entered the apartment and guided him to the ceiling-to-floor windows overlooking the city and harbor with U.S. Navy ships all decked out in their dress lights.

"Come look," I said. "Isn't that a spectacular sight? Have you ever seen anything more beautiful?"

"Yes, very nice," he answered, groping for something to hold on to. When I placed his hand on the waist-high typhoon bar, he felt comfortable about coming closer to what appeared to be a step out into space.

"I've found that I can live with any of you girls," Daddy said one day. "The woman of the house is the one to set the pattern, and all four of you are rather like your mother. It's comfortable for me." He stayed three months.

Daddy fit nicely into our family. Anne was at Morrison Academy in Taiwan, Edwin had come for the year, and there was plenty of room for him. He observed our routines for several days and then began establishing his own. For years he'd called at hospitals, making the rounds of all who wanted to talk with a minister. He got a list of four or five on the island, checked bus schedules, and took off three days a week. Not infrequently, people greeted him on the street while we were shopping.
"Hello Dr. Lampe. How nice to see you again!" He returned the greeting, but after they moved on he'd ask, "And who in the world was that?"

"Sorry, Daddy, I haven't the faintest idea, but it's probably somebody you called on in one of the hospitals."

Rain or shine he kept his schedule and was always pleased when he found a Presbyterian or two.

Daddy didn't need to be entertained. He read several books at a time and wrote letters by the score. At eighty he also enjoyed the challenge of learning something new.

"I've always wanted to know how to multiply and divide on an abacus, he announced one day, "so I'll buy one with instructions and see if I can learn how to use it." And he did. In no time he had it all worked out. It was almost too easy to be any fun.

For about two weeks near the end of his stay, he seemed restless and distracted. The mail arrived at our apartment by ten in the morning, and he was always at my elbow to see if there was anything for him. One morning he reached eagerly for a letter, and instead of waiting for the rest, rushed off to his room to read it in private. A short time later he returned with a huge grin on his face, pleased as punch about something.

"Well," he said, "I have good news. As you know, I have a place reserved for me in Duarte that I'll have to take within the next month or forfeit it. It's a good place, but I wasn't too happy about some of the regulations, so I wrote to Molly and Harwood. They're building a house soon, and I told them I'd be happy to contribute my little nest egg if they'd add a room and bath for me. I assured them I'd understand if they didn't think it a good idea, and it wouldn't hurt my feelings if they said no. Today's letter was all I could hope for and more. They wrote, 'Sure, Dad, we'll be thrilled to have you, but just to make sure it was okay with our five kids, we asked them at dinner. They jumped up and down yelling, "Yes, yes, we want Grampa, we want Grampa!"' Now that it's settled, I feel much better." So that was what was troubling him! He fairly floated through the next few days until he headed north to celebrate Easter in Korea.

With the apartment settled, Anne and Jim in school,

and Kedar in and out of town on business, I began to test the waters for things to do. Everything was out there, enough to fill a dozen calendars, but with only twenty-four hours a day and a modest budget, I had to choose carefully.

After joining the International Church on Kennedy Road and taking on the junior high Sunday school class came the American Women's Club. In the fall they went into high gear to prepare for the annual charity fund-raising sale the first of December for the Mary Anne Rykle Aid to Lepers.

The big kick-off was a cocktail party and sale put on by Katherine Kelsch, doyenne of the American commercial community. She and "the captain" had a fabulous house on the Peak. Husbands were warned to come with full wallets, and after imbibing a number of the house specials, they were ready to be generous.

All year long in home workshops we prepared things for that sale. Hong Kong's stores and markets sold most of what we needed. Many items were made by members meeting once a week for a morning of work and companionship, ending up with a bag lunch. It was a huge effort involving dozens of women and resulted in a profit of thousands of dollars.

At the January meeting I was asked if I'd take on the chairmanship of the project. I had seen just the tag end, what it took, and it seemed daunting. But in my girlish enthusiasm I said "yes," much to the relief of the president. Soon thereafter I received boxes of materials and folders of information about what was expected of me. Wow! I had a few doubts about my ability to pull it off, until I remembered the *News Circle* in New Delhi, and said to myself, Hey, I can do this too.

The first order of business was to find women who'd gather friends to work each week. A dozen or so in five groups had wonderful ideas and the know-how to realize them. We chose one or two projects at a time; then I asked Lynette Lee to buy the materials we needed. She was Chinese, married to a local businessman, and could buy what we required for half the price I'd pay. We turned out novelties–linen cocktail napkins with snap-on Christmas ornaments, baby quilts to be auctioned, taffeta toilet-seat covers decorated with clusters of plastic flowers, toddler's bibs with zippers to open and close, buttons with button holes, shoe laces to tie, a pocket with crayons and a pad of paper, and another for a packet of tissues; Christmas ornaments for the tree, hall, door, and gatepost, "one-size-fits-all" bed socks because Hong Kong in the winter is cold and damp, and dozens more.

Regularly I made the rounds and helped where I could. Soon the finished articles began to accumulate. Storing them for months until the sale was a problem.

I called Bob Moyer. "Since you're the manager of Du Pont, how about helping us with some plastic? Can your charity budget stand it?"

"Sure," he answered. "We can give you several widths of tubing from four-to-eighteen inches. Each item can be slipped into the plastic of the appropriate width, cut off and stapled shut. Will that be okay?"

"Fantastic," I said, "and thanks so much. You're a doll. And how much can you give us?"

"Whatever you need," he answered, "and I'm really not a doll, just 'Mr. Wonderful.' Jill's the doll! I'll send you some, and you can let me know if you need more, okay?" All such generous gifts helped to increase our profits.

At one workshop I spent the morning sewing and in another knitting bed socks. Early on there was no problem if a ball of yarn didn't finish a pair. There was plenty more, but as we were nearing the end of supply and time, one partially knit sock might have to be ripped out to complete a set.

Wendy Martinson, wife of a business tycoon, was a skillful knitter. Her stitches were so even you couldn't tell her work from a machine-made article. She came whenever she could, but frequently official duties kept her away. On one particular morning she arrived and rummaged through the supply box.

"Where's my sock?" she inquired. "I put it in here last time, but I don't see it."

"Oh, Fran ripped it out so Helen could finish her pair. That's the last of the pink yarn, I'm afraid," the hostess answered.

"Well," Wendy stormed, "what's the use of my coming if my work isn't appreciated? If there's nothing more, I'll be on my way. I have better things to do." With that, she was gone. Busy in another room, I had no idea of the uproar. When we sat down for lunch I asked were Wendy was. As tactfully as possible, the others let me know the business had really hit the fan. I didn't think too much about it until the next week's board meeting.

"I'm afraid your name is mud, Fran," one of the women said quietly. "Wendy's told everybody on the cocktail circuit that she didn't like having her work sacrificed!" While we heard reports from the various committees, I noticed Wendy wouldn't look at me. I had to nip this thing in the bud, so as soon as we broke for coffee I confronted her.

"Wendy," I said, taking her face between my hands, "I'm terribly sorry about the sock. Will you please forgive me?"

"Well of course!" she sputtered, giving me a big smile and a hug. The incident was history.

A great deal of entertaining was conducted at the company residence on Kowloon, and since I was free so much of the time, Wendy frequently asked if I would fill in at official luncheons. I was delighted to do so. She ran a tight ship with wives of the company staff, and when she required them to attend, they resented it.

During the water shortage everybody cut back on home

entertaining, giving families more time together. Wendy and Tom Martinson had two children in college, and ten-year-old Paul was their "fall crop." His pet ducks were housed on the flat roof, protected by an iron railing and accessed by stairs from the driveway at the back of the house. One evening Paul went to tell the ducks good night.

"Please sir," yelled the family's frightened driver, "come quickly. There's been an accident. Paul fell from the roof." They rushed out to find their young son unconscious, flat on his back on the pavement. The doctor broke all speed laws getting there, checked him over, and called an ambulance. X-rays showed nothing broken. For thirty-six hours Wendy never left his bedside. Moaning, he constantly moved his head, arms, and legs back and forth.

"I can tell you exactly what happened," he announced when he suddenly opened his eyes. "I was just starting down the stairs after kissing my ducks good night when the railing above broke off and hit me on the head. "See this bump," he said, feeling the knot on his forehead.

"That he was knocked out before he fell was a blessing," the doctor said as he checked him over. "He was totally relaxed when he hit the cement. That's why no bones were broken. The reason he moved so much while still unconscious was that he was in pain from his bruises. Look at them–on the back of his head, elbows, and heels, but he's young, and will mend quickly."

"I'm taking Paul home," Wendy said on the phone to Tom, "and he's perfectly fine. Praise God. I'm so thankful!" Paul was a less than an enthusiastic student and had been denied a TV until his grades came up, but when Tom heard the good news he went out an bought his son the biggest one in Hong Kong.

The event had a profound effect on Wendy. Her "top-sergeant" attitude disappeared and was replaced by a gentleness and compassion born of suffering.

A vague wanderlust began to evolve into definite plans for sailing the seven seas after we met the Parishes. Every weekend and holiday we cruised the bays and island around Hong Kong. Ours was just a small cabin cruiser, but the sense of freedom and adventure we experienced made us yearn for more.

We also discovered that there was a large population that lives aboard sail and power craft, traveling the world, sometimes solo but often in groups. Those we met were a breed apart–always helpful and friendly.

Homer, Julie, and teenage Cathy left California in the early sixties. His trade was creating special effects for the movies. They had no schedule or destination but went from place to place as the spirit moved them and work opportunities opened up. Before departing the States they practiced sailing their thirty-five-foot Tahiti ketch around Catalina Island, honing their skills at plotting courses and reading charts. With the larder stocked, home-schooling materials for Cathy in hand, and a degree of self confidence, they headed south to Australia. As we became better acquainted they shared the tales of their adventures at sea.

"The first thing that impresses you when you lose sight of land," Homer said, "is how vast the ocean is and how tiny you and your boat are. In a liner you're on the water but not in it as we were, riding just inches above the briny. On clear, moonless nights when I got up to check the automatic pilot and the set of the sails, I was amazed at how bright the phosphoresce was. Walking along the deck, I cast a shadow on the sails! Another astounding thing," he continued, "was the size of the waves in midocean. They were more like rounded hills as much as two hundred feet high. Riding up and over them was an awesome sensation."

"We ran into foul weather that lasted five days as we neared Australia. There were no sun, moon, or stars for a fix, but with current charts, wind, and dead reckoning, I was pretty sure where we were. At the end of a long, rough day, Julie and Cathy went below to get some sleep, and I stayed at the helm. They were no more than settled when wham, we smashed into a reef. A big wave had carried us over the first ridge and into the second. We were stuck between the two. The next wave picked us up and slammed us down on it again. The backwash sucked us away, and the next one hurled us forward to another battering!

"The moment we hit, Julie and Cathy ran for the cockpit. Waves came at us every which way, and we took on water fast. The cabin began to fill. 'Get a jerry can of fresh water and cut loose the dingy,' I screamed over the raging storm. Those were shark-filled waters, and it would be a miracle if any of us survived. Just before the final line holding the life boat was severed, a huge wave came from our port, and as if it were the hand of God, lifted us up and set us free."

The tone of Homer's voice and the look on his face as he spoke were expressions of wonder and worship. "Everything was awash," he continued, "but when I turned on the bilge pump it worked and emptied the cabin in a matter of minutes. I set a course around the reef and to the nearest harbor. We were sure that with the pounding we'd taken several of the teak planks in the hull had sprung, and we'd need a boatyard right away. In the morning we made port and before long had the boat hauled. The hull was as sound as the day it was built and had suffered only a few scratches! We were delighted and praised God that all she needed was a little touch-up of antifouling paint and a lot of fresh water to wash her down.

"We were glad that the long reach across the Pacific was behind us and headed north to Borneo. Whenever we ran low on fresh water, vegetables, and fruit, we put into a fishing village to resupply. One of them was particularly delightful and friendly to the point of not allowing us to pay for anything, even the plump chicken Julie picked out for dinner. During these stops we never stayed close in at night.

"After roaming the village, buying a few mementos, and having supper, we pulled a quarter mile out to sea to anchor for the night. Information about this part of the world stated that there were still a few cannibal tribes along the shores, and caution was advised. Julie and I have the forward cabin with a hatch opening over the bunk. I got out my .22 and put it in the little hammock beside me. It was an absolutely calm night without a whisper of a breeze. Around midnight Julie nudged me gently. 'Listen,' she whispered, 'do you hear something?' It was almost inaudible but unmistakable–the sound of water dripping from paddles! Those friendly villagers! I thought as I reached for my weapon. I fired one round skyward through the open hatch, and all hell broke loose. *'I-ee, iee, iee,'* a dozen voices screamed as they beat a hasty retreat. That was enough for us. We pulled anchor and motored ten miles farther down the coast to an unoccupied bay."

The Parishes spent two years in Singapore, where he worked with a movie studio before he was hired by Run-Run Shaw, a huge movie-making company in Hong Kong. They had to leave the boat and come by air because the winds weren't favorable. They soon made themselves at home in the foreign community. Anne met Kathy at school, and Julie was a regular at the weekly workshop on the Peak. I took every opportunity to ask how she managed living at sea weeks on end without having boring meals.

"Some of the best things to have are fresh onions," she said. "A can of stew tastes wonderful with a little sautéed onion added, and if you have an oven, hot quick bread makes an ordinary meal a feast. Margarine doesn't turn rancid, and fresh eggs keep indefinitely, even in heat if you dip them in melted paraffin, cool, and place them in cartons. Turn them over once a week, and you'd never know they weren't laid yesterday. Hey, laundry's a snap.

Trail it in a mesh beg, and in an hour or so rinse in fresh water and hang it to dry. I have several books with great tips," she said. "I'll lend them to you."

One morning Julie seemed worried because Homer was overdue, and she hadn't heard from him.

"He flew to Singapore to sail the *Sultana* up here and should have arrived last week," she said with a frown. "I'm scared. The winds we hoped for still haven't come up, and he may be in trouble."

"Have you notified the authorities?" someone asked.

"Yes, and they've alerted ships to look out for him. The boat's too small to be seen from the air," she said with a sigh.

A radio played soft background music as we worked. Suddenly the program was interrupted by an urgent announcement. Someone turned up the volume, and we stopped what we were doing to listen. "We are pleased to announce," the voice said, "that the sailing vessel *Sultana* has just been sighted entering Hong Kong waters. Congratulations, Mr. Parish!" There was a moment silence before we all erupted with shouts of joy as Julie dissolved in tears of relief.

We gave them a few days to recover before asking them to join us for dinner. "So what happened to delay you?" Kedar asked.

"A whole bunch of things," Homer replied, "not the least of which was that the two-way radio went out. Actually, the biggest disappointment was having such light winds that we had to use the engine. We can go a thousand miles on a tank of fuel, but my Lord, it's slow.

"A young Chinese actor I'd worked with wanted to come along. I was delighted to have his company because we had to follow shipping lanes, and they can be dangerous. Two sets of eyes are necessary if you want any sleep. After taking the first night watch, I instructed him what to look for. 'A tiny speck of light way off on the horizon can be a big ship that'll be right on top of you in fifteen minutes.' He was to give any he saw a wide birth.

"Sure, sure, sure," he said, so I went below. I was in a deep sleep when his frightened voice called, 'Uncle, I think you need to come now, quickly!'

"On deck, I looked up to see a huge freighter looming above us! I grabbed the flashlight, shone it on their bridge windows then on our sails. At the same time I turned hard to starboard. They got the picture and did likewise, avoiding disaster by inches. We were almost kindling wood! Fortunately that was the only near miss. It made a believer out of my young friend."

Most of their experiences were happy and rewarding, but the tough ones they shared with us were lessons we'd rather not learn the hard way. The last we heard from Homer and Julie thirty years ago, we were in Singapore and they were headed for the Middle East. It's my guess they're back in the States enjoying their grandchildren.

"Where did you get that?" asked a breakfast table mate, eyeing Maxine's purse. "And how much did you pay for it?" My friend was shocked by the questions. She was on an overnight trip on a President Line ship from Hong Kong to the Philippines to visit her children at Brent School up in Bagio.

"As a matter of fact I bought it last week in the Walled City of Kowloon," Maxine replied. "Why do you ask?"

"Because," the woman answered in a huff, "those are supposed to be available exclusively from Nieman Marcus in Dallas. What did you pay?"

"Four dollars at the factory. What do they cost in the States?"

"Not four dollars! The week I left they were being offered at the 'bargain price' of thirty-five! That really makes me mad." Maxine felt better than ever as she looked at hers, in natural straw lined with artificial leather and fitted with the top grade of bamboo-shaped brass handles and clasp.

Max was one of my best friends. A redheaded former model and fashion plate, she was completely down-to-earth. Her two older children were the ages of Anne and Jim, so before they went off to Brent, we'd been brought together by the kids' activities. She also hosted a weekly Bible study group for women.

One day she asked if I'd like to go along on her regular visit to a World Vision feeding station in the Walled City. I was curious and agreed to go. It's an eight-block area that housed two hundred thousand people. Gambling establishments abounded, prostitution, drugs, and crime were rampant. The area originally belonged to the Manchus, and its status was never established after the New Territories were ceded in 1898. As the city grew around it, the Walled City became a famous resort of villains. Never being absolutely sure what their rights were, the British generally let it be, hoping that it would wither away of its own accord. It very nearly did but revived after WW II when squatters by the thousands moved in. By the late 1960s its only real administration was provided by the Triads.

From the bus stop across from Kai Tack Airport, we approached a row of glass-fronted surgeries of unqualified dentists. Their windows were full of pickled abscesses, illustrations of impacted wisdom teeth, and grinning rows of dentures. In the background of each shop, a dentist's chair stood waiting, sometimes with the dentist himself reclining in it between customers while his ornamental goldfish (good for patients' nerves) circumnavigate their illuminated tank. We entered an alley between two buildings. Within a few feet we stepped from bright sunlight into deep gloom. The strong, sweet smell of opium made me choke and yearn for a lungful of fresh air. The clack of mahjong tiles echoed from a dozen gambling rooms, and drowsy drug users lounged in doorways.

It's a frightful slum. No vehicle can enter–there are no streets wide enough–and its buildings, rising sometimes to ten or twelve stories, are so inextricably packed together they seem to form one congealed mass of masonry joined by overlapping structures, ladders, walkways, pipes, and cables, and ventilated only by fetid air shafts.

"You come down here every week?" I asked as I held a tissue over my nose and mouth. "This is a place from hell!"

"Watch were you walk," Maxine cautioned. "The feeding station is just a few streets in–careful, you don't want to step in that." She indicated a pile of dung. The passageway was wide enough for two abreast, but I chose to follow. Open gutters on either side ran with raw sewage, there was only an occasional light, and overhanging stairways gave access to upper floors. Burlap sacks stitched together hung from the railings, giving a modest amount of privacy to whole families living behind them under the steps.

I hoped it would be a little better at our destination, but it wasn't. Located right across from a pig sty complete with smells and flies, it was worse. When Max unlocked the door and turned on the lights in the clean little room with white walls and cheerful posters, it seemed the most welcoming place on earth.

"Here's what we do, Fran," she said as she moved toward an old-fashioned wringer-type Maytag washing machine. "Eight gallons of Culligan water go into the machine; then we add milk powder." One at a time I hefted the bottles to the counter and emptied them. She got the milk from a cupboard, measured it out, and turned on the agitator. "You see," she said with a smile, "there's more than one way to skin a cat and mix a large supply of milk. I wonder what the Maytag repair man would think if he could see how we use this one!" After all the lumps disappeared, she showed me how to fill a quantity of large glass pitchers by turning on the motor to expel the milk through the hose.

As we worked, the light from the window was like a beacon to those who came, certificate in hand, to get a day's supply for their infants and children. At eleven o'clock we opened the window, pulled up a counter below it, and began taking orders. Card holders' children had been examined by a mission doctor who noted the amount each was to receive. We measured it into the containers they brought and gave them locally made protein wafers that tasted like graham crackers and were provided by the Church World Service.

Some who came were remarkably joyful, happy people. Others had sad, tired faces, were hunched over and sickly. Living in such a place, it's a wonder any survived. We tried to be cheerful in our greetings and generous with the measures. They usually responded in kind, though they faced yet another hard, dreary day. I couldn't help thinking, "There but for the grace of God. . . and giving thanks."

On arrival we put a huge bucket of water to boil on a gas hot plate. When the last customer had been served, we used it to flush out and wash the Maytag and pitchers for the next day's use. We swept the floors, cleaned the counters, and left.

"Want to go see a nice little factory I found?" Maxine asked, leading me farther into the city's depths.

"Sure, if you think it's safe," I answered. I'm not a fearful person, but that place really gave me the willies. However, two white women presented no threat to residents, and I was ready for adventure. I'll never understand how Max knew every twist and turn, but we ended up at another door through which we walked into a well-lighted, well-ventilated room. What a relief! A recent customer, she was greeted enthusiastically by the owner.

"Nee how mah?" (How are you?) she began.

"How-how-how," (fine-fine-fine) he answered with a bow, coming forward. That was the extent of her

Cantonese, so the conversation continued in broken English.

"I like the purse I buy last month, Mr. Ma and want more. My friend too, she also like see."

"Okay." He nodded vigorously. "Still have plenty. Next week all go to Texas. By and by no have. You want, you buy now."

"Look over here, Fran," Max said, moving to a huge pile. They were made in several colors, but the neutral and black bags were my choice. At such a bargain I splurged and got four.

I was hooked. Max and I went to the feeding station every week until we left the colony. It was one of the best, most rewarding experiences of my years in Hong Kong.

Mother and child

Children
with milk & crackers

Kedar finished packing, glad to be leaving Rangoon for the last time. It was 1965. The Communist government imposed all manner of regulations that would try the patience of a saint. One such allowed foreign tourists and businessmen to stay no more than twenty-four hours. Because you had to show you'd be going on to a destination other than the one from which you had come, Kedar routinely flew from Hong Kong via Bangkok, stayed his allotted time, continued on to Calcutta, turned around and went back to Rangoon for another day before returning home.

He made many trips to Rangoon while negotiations with the government dragged on over the sale of fifteen hundred Jeeps for their police force. As he read the paper at breakfast on the morning of his second visit, Mrs. Gill came from behind the hotel desk and introduced herself. She was small and slender with the light complexion and dark eyes typical of Eurasians. Her coal-black hair was pulled back into a French twist, that gave her a trim, business-like appearance in spite of the little wisps curling in front of her ears. Gray streaked her temples, and worry lines creased her forehead and around her mouth. She must have been a knockout in her youth, Kedar thought, the kind of exquisite, fragile beauty that one sees in children of Indo-Chinese and Europeans.

"Won't you join me in a cup of coffee?" Kedar asked as he stood and pulled out a chair for her. She nodded. He seated her then signaled the waiter.

On the first of several such meetings she was pleasant and impersonal. Mostly she inquired about his home and business with the Burmese government. Each time he returned to the Strand Hotel, the only one in Rangoon that catered to Westerners, she made a point of dropping by at breakfast. He was quite aware of being pumped.

"You must feel I've been doing a lot of prying," she said on their fourth encounter, and indeed I have, but one has to be careful these days. Not many people can be trusted since the Communists took over, and it is so difficult in my situation." She seemed comfortable with Kedar and pressed on with her story. "My husband and I owned this hotel. Mr. Gill's family built it before WW II while the British were in control. Those were glorious days, but then came the war, the Japanese, and the internment camp. I fared pretty well, but Thomas was forced to work on the Burma Road. The hard labor and poor food broke his health. He never was really strong again.

"After the war we returned to pick up our lives, and for a time it was good. Then the pro-Communist government came to power. That was the end for us. We were forced to sell the hotel to them at their price but were permitted to stay on to run it. We would have left right away but they wouldn't allow us to send any money out of country. We decided to stay until something could be arranged. As I said, Thomas was not strong. Three years ago he died in his sleep, heart failure perhaps, I don't know. I think he simply lost his will to carry on.

"Now they're forcing all foreigners to leave, even those who have been here for generations, like the Indians who claim Burmese citizenship. They are truly pitiful as they board the planes. All their lovely jewelry is taken from them. Their household goods and lands are confiscated. They're allowed to take just one small bundle each. Women can't even keep their wedding rings. It's shocking."

"Yes," Kedar agreed, "I've been on planes carrying them to Calcutta, and they're a sorry-looking lot."

"It's nice to have a chance to chat with a friendly person such as yourself, Mr. Bryan. Will you be coming again?"

"Yes," he said, rising as she pushed back her chair. He gestured to the waiter that he wanted the bill. "I hope to get the contract finalized within the month. I'll be back for the exchange of documents on a final trip."

"I see," she said. "One last visit within the month?"

"Yes," he responded. "The new man in government purchasing is eager to close the deal. It's a good one for them and us, and enough silver has crossed his palm to get him moving!" They laughed and shook hands. The waiter brought the chit. Kedar put his room number at the top, drew a line diagonally across the unused portion to avoid later additions, and signed at the bottom. The waiter, clad in a blue-and-gold cotton sarong that reached the floor, white shirt, colorful vest, and cockscomb headdress, accepted it with both hands. Noting the generous tip, he made a deep bow and hissed approval.

"Come in," Kedar called, in answer to a light tap on the door.
"Mr. Bryan, please take this to Hong Kong," Mrs. Gill said, dropping a small package into his open briefcase. "I'll write very soon. This represents everything I have in the world. I hope to be leaving for the U.K. before long, but as you know, I can't take anything with me."
"I'll do what I can," he answered. "I know your situation, but please remember, I do it at your risk."
"I understand," she said, "and I deeply appreciate the favor." He watched her turn and go as quietly as she had come.
Kedar was curious about what was in the box, twice the size of a package of cigarettes. He half wondered if he had been set up.
Big money was made smuggling opium, and a tip to the customs officials would get her 50 percent of its value. He'd go to jail for a long time. He didn't think she would do such a thing, but she was pretty desperate, and who could tell?
He filled out the forms before landing at Bangkok, and all went well. He breathed a sigh of relief at clearing customs and hailed a cab for the Iriwan Hotel.
After a quick shower and a cold beer, he broke the seal and lifted the lid to see an assortment of gold bracelets, pins, rings, and pendants set with stones. They looked like real gems, but he couldn't be certain, so slipped a sampling into his pocket and returned the rest to his briefcase. Before dinner he stopped by a jewelry shop in the lobby. The proprietor, a fat Chinese gentleman, waddled out from a back office, picking his teeth and belching

loudly. His broad smile displayed a mouthful of gold teeth.

"What can I do for you, sir?" he asked as he dusted the top of the counter with his sleeve. "We have very nice things for ladies and gentlemens."

"Not just now," Kedar said. He reached into his pocket. "Please tell me what these are worth. Are the stones real or fake?"

The merchant took a loupe from a drawer and adjusted it between his cheek and brow.

"I can't tell you exact value without taking out and weighing stones. Also, they not all same quality. This one have got thirty number-one Burmese rubies, and other one have thirty quartercarat diamonds. Take me two maybe three days to give price."

"No, thank you," Kedar said picking them up. "I just wanted to be sure they were genuine. Now perhaps you have something for my wife. I think she'd like that pearl ring in the center tray, the one with a sapphire on either side."

"Here's a little something for you," Kedar said, opening the little box when he unpacked at home two days later." And you can enjoy these for a few weeks," he added, tossing another package on the bed.

I couldn't believe my eyes as I laid it all out. There were two gold bracelets with quarter-carat diamonds all the way around, two more with rubies, and two with emeralds of the same size; a large square-cut emerald in a gold ring set with diamonds; a pendant with earrings to match; a diamond brooch and earrings; a locket; a wedding band; and a child's ring.

Kedar told me about Mrs. Gill, her life and problems in Burma. "So," he said, "now you have some beautiful jewelry to wear and enjoy until we hear from her."

"Oh, honey, I couldn't," I said. "This represents the cost of a hotel, all she has to live on for the rest of her life. I wouldn't want to risk any part of it. Tomorrow I'll rent a safety deposit box.

A Tale of Two Bamboos

At last a letter arrived, further telling of her troubles and ending with, "Please send the jewelry to my banker in London." I couldn't believe it; there was no name or address!

I felt so sorry for the poor soul. Obviously the pressure she had been under and the trauma of the past years were telling, and she was, as the Chinese say *oo-lee-oo-doo* (a little tetched in the head).

We were leaving within the week, so I wrote, giving her my brother's name and address in Frankfurt, Germany, and the time we expected to be there. I urged her to send specific instructions as to where the "merchandise" should be sent. The day before we departed Hong Kong I got the jewelry from the bank and closed the account.

"Want to check out a VW camper?" Kedar asked as he put down the phone. "The dealer has a new model with an attachable tent on the showroom floor. Let's see if we like it."

Our assignment in Hong Kong was nearly over, and after much figuring and planning, we decided to spend half of our three-month vacation traveling the continent. Kaiser's policy was to send us home by air first class or give us the equivalent amount of money. With three healthy, hungry teenagers it wasn't a matter of making a profit but of enjoying a vacation without going broke.

Edwin was enthusiastic about European history and wanted to include a trip through Russia. "Okay," Kedar agreed, "go to the InTourist office downtown and find out what it will cost. Pick up whatever suggested routes and travel packages they have to offer." We were delighted to find we could fly to Japan, take the overnight ferry to Nahadka, an eighteen-hour train ride from there to Khabovorsk, fly to Irkutz, stay two days to see Lake Bikal and the famous icons in the four-hundred-year-old city, fly to Moscow for four days and nights, and on to

Vienna–all of which included meals, transportation, and first-class hotels for just ten dollars apiece more than the five-hour tourist class flight, Hong Kong/Vienna! It was a deal. We were Tour # E-84.

In the 1960s Russia was not big on the tourist circuit, so prices were reasonable, but huge savings came in the eleven-hour flight across the country, $86 at domestic rates. In comparison, the two-hour flight from Moscow to Vienna at international rates was $285. In other words, for that $50 difference between the direct flight, Hong Kong to Vienna, and the package tour through the U.S.S.R. we could house, feed, and transport the whole family for a week!

You've heard advice that says, "Figure what clothes you'll need and cut it in half. Decide how much money you'll require and double it." It applied to us. Space in a VW is limited, so we had to pack smart for six weeks of very close living. I measured the baggage space inside and the rack on top. When we got home I marked it off on our bathroom floor. We stacked and arranged the suitcases to see what would fit and decided it would work. We paid for the camper and ordered it to be delivered at the Vienna airport the day of our arrival. We packed up the camping gear to go airfreight and arrive a day earlier.

During our last month in Hong Kong we stayed at the Hilton Hotel. Kedar had some trips to take, I supervised the final packing and shipping of our things to Singapore, and the three children looked forward to days of freedom at the end of school. Anne decided to try baby-sitting for hotel guests whose small children might be more comfortable with an American teenager than a Chinese amah. She let the desk know she was available.

One day as Jim went through the lobby he noticed a family with three small children. He introduced himself, and told them about Anne. "We're right here in the hotel if you'd like to call her," he said.

"Well, thanks," the husband said. "May I have her name and room number?"

"Sure," Jim answered. "I'll write it down for you." In his haste he misspelled her name writing Amne instead of Anne.

"That's an interesting name," the man said when he saw it.

"Oh, yes," Jim answered, always quick with his overgrown imagination, "My parents were crossing the Gobi Desert when she was born. The camel driver helped to deliver her, so she was named for him, Amne Bella-Sousa Frances Bryan." Odd, they never called her!

Edwin

Anne

Jim

First stop–Japan. Kedar had a meeting with Mitsubishi, so the kids decided to climb Mt. Fuji. A mere suggestion to the right people and arrangements were made for them to spend the night at a hotel at the foot of the mountain.

Kedar received periodic phone calls about their progress–they enjoyed the ride on the bullet train; they were settled in their rooms; they ate a hearty sukikaiki dinner; they breakfasted early and took the bus to the station from which they began the ascent. The kids were totally unaware that their every move was reported to us, but it was a comfort to know they were okay.

Kedar had his appointment while I shopped the Ginza,

and about eight that evening three bedraggled, happy kids trudged into our room. It had been a cold, rainy day for the climb (sleet at the top), but they were glad to have done it. They flourished walking sticks with the stamp of each station burned into the shaft. Upon reaching the summit they were entitled to buy ribbons with small bells at the end to tack on the top.

The boys dashed ahead, but Anne wondered if she'd ever make it. Those on the way down encouraged the climbers with, "Just a little more. You are almost there." To her it looked endless, yet she had to laugh at a sight she encountered along the way.

"I've heard," she said, "that for many Japanese it's their life's ambition to climb the sacred mountain at least once. I saw a couple that must be enjoying a double blessing. The husband was a skinny little man, but his wife was huge. Determined to get her to the top, he had a rope around her waist and was pulling her up every inch of the way. Standing on a step above her, he hauled, they both grunted, and up she came. I had no difficulty passing them. Going down a cinder slide with fifteen to twenty feet per step, the return took only minutes.

We took the overnight ferry to Nahadka, near Vladivostok. Martial music blared over loudspeakers everywhere, even in the cabins, and there was no way to shut it off. Thank heaven it stopped at 10:00 p.m., and didn't start again until 6:00 the next morning. Breakfast consisted of pickled fish, sliced cucumbers with sour cream, and tea. Much more of this, I thought, and I'll shed a few pounds!

Customs inspection was routine until they asked to see our jewelry. I'd declared mine plus Mrs. Gill's. Every piece was laid out, examined and noted.

Apparently they were interested only in the gold and that we take out of the USSR all we'd brought in. An official list was given to me, which they verified as we left

Moscow a week later.

A bus tour of the city occupied us for several hours. With a hundred or so Japanese, we were driven around what looked like a frontier town in the old West. The streets were wide but unpaved and heavily rutted from traffic in past rains. Buildings were few–new but crudely constructed except for the library that was their pride and joy. It seemed palatial. Again and again they urged us to take with us any volumes we wished, so I chose *Uncle Tom's Cabin Explained*–Communist propaganda at its best.

In the late afternoon we boarded the tourist train north for Khabarvosk. We weren't sure what our accommodations would be like because we chose "hard class" instead of "soft class." We figured the considerable difference in price would be worth it for just eighteen hours. A compartment held four, so at night Edwin shared one with three other men. Soft class had dark red velvet curtains at the windows–we had pull-down shades; they had hot and cold taps on their basins–we had only cold; they had a toilet–we used the one at the end of the car, but everything else was the same. What a bargain!

In Nahadka we were given food coupons for all meals and teas. The use of Russian money was discouraged, but if you chose to order something that was under the value of the coupon, the difference was given in currency. Jim, never wanting to be short of cash, saw great possibilities and ordered tea or coffee with dinner coupons. He always had money to spend.

When we went to the dining car, I noticed that Kedar was watching and listening intently to the headwaiter as he took orders at nearby tables. "He's from Shanghai," he whispered to me.

"How can you tell?"

"By the way he speaks English. He has the unmistakable accent unique to Russians refugee in China."

When it was our turn to be served, Kedar smiled at

the nice-looking man of about fifty. "When did you leave Shanghai," he asked.

"You too?" he responded in surprise.

"Born and raised there," Kedar said, standing to shake his hand. "Kedar Bryan," he said, "and this is my family."

"Nice to meet you," he answered with enthusiasm. "Yuri Constantionovich Goluvkin. Just call me Yuri." There was no time for conversation, so he agreed to come to our compartment when he was off duty.

"Told you so," Kedar said smugly. "I'd know that accent anywhere."

An hour later Yuri knocked on our door, and we heard all about his life. He was born in Shanghai of Russian refugee parents. They prospered. He and his sister enjoyed their youth in that city, but being stateless, they had no national identity. In the late 1940s the USSR offered citizenship to all who had fled during the Bolshevik Revolution and wanted to return. Yuri, his daughter, sister, and parents elected to do so. His wife divorced him, and she and her parents stayed. "It was important to have something of value to contribute to society when we arrived," he explained, "and because I was a professional boxer, I was sent to high schools to teach boxing."

"Where did you get your training?" Kedar asked.

"At the YMCA from an Australian named Billy Tingle."

"My teacher too," Kedar said. 'Isn't that something! I was an underweight, puny kid, and my father wanted to toughen me up. He sent me to Billy, and at the age of six I won the all-Shanghai 'skeeter-weight' title."

"Have you kept in touch with him?" I asked. "He's living in Hong Kong , so if you'd like to write him a letter, I'll send it to a friend who'll make sure he gets it."

"Thanks. I'll do it tonight."

"After a time," he continued, "the government decided I was too old for boxing; and since I have a good command of English, they put me on the tourist train because all foreigners speak it. Lucky for me. It's a good job and not as hard as teaching hundreds of kids!"

We came on the trip well supplied with small gifts and were happy to give Yuri a forty-five rpm record of Western music, nylon stockings for his daughter, and the greatest prize of all, a package of Chesterfields for his mother, who hadn't had an American cigarette in twenty years.

"She'll love you till her dying day. The local ones are terrible," he said, making a face.

For several years we kept in touch with Christmas cards and know he and Billy corresponded, but in recent times we've heard nothing from him. I wonder how he's doing.

The next day we passed through dozens of small towns and villages, and huge state-run farms. There were no lawns or flowerbeds around the houses. Their yards were given entirely to growing vegetables from the property fence right up to the door; not an inch of space wasted. Collective farming turned out to be a miserable failure, and homegrown produce actually provided 85 percent of the country's food.

We were in Khabarvosk for only a couple of hours before our flight. It was interesting but couldn't compare to four-hundred-year-old Irkutsk on the shore of Lake Baikal. Sidewalks joined the buildings to the streets. Again, there were no lawns or gardens but lots of flower boxes and trees spaced four to a block. The whole town appeared antiseptically clean and well swept. The hotel was ancient too. Our keys were kept by a dour-looking clerk at the end of the corridor. The rooms were dark, with deep windowsills, heavy draperies, dim lights, and badly worn carpets. Turn-of-the-century bathroom fixtures worked, though there was precious little hot water. The beds were okay, but the blankets were heavy and made me feel pressed into the mattress. Oh, for a Hilton!

Lake Baikal is wonderful, and the Russians are justifiably proud of it. A small museum provided vital statistics: It's the deepest lake in the world—one mile and holds more water than all our Great Lakes combined: Its two hundred species of aquatic life are found nowhere else in the world. In the winter it freezes deep enough to allow train tracks to cross it. Fresh-water seals warm the ice with their muzzles to make breathing holes at the surface.

Because the water on that June day was sixty-five degrees, the shore was well populated with jubilant citizens frolicking and splashing. We were happy to be wearing sweaters, thank you very much!

It was Sunday, so I asked our guide if there was any place we could worship. "Well," she answered hesitantly, "I think there's a church that has a service at 6:00 p.m. I'll find out." Soon she returned saying, "I was right, and I'll take you there; but may I ask you something?"

"Of course," I said.

"Do you believe in God?"

"Yes, I do. Don't you?"

"Oh, no," she was quick to respond. "We believe in the state."

"Well, one day you probably will," I said. "Your people are very interested in science, and that's good. Science is a search for truth, and when you look hard enough and long enough you will find that God is because He is. You may not choose to believe in Him, but you will know that there really is a God." She was very thoughtful for a few minutes, "Yes, maybe one day I will know," she said with a smile. "Thank you." I would have given my eye-teeth for a Bible to give her. Every one of our guides asked the same question, and each time I answered the same way. I have always wondered about their spiritual journey.

Anne and I went to the little Russian Orthodox Church that seemed to be a tourist attraction more than a place of worship. People wandered around examining ancient icons hung on the walls. Small shelves below them were adorned with vases of flowers and burning oil lamps. Several white marble caskets had fancy lace covers, and an oil lamp burned by a picture of each of the entombed. It all seemed sad, dusty, and poorly cared for. Young people wandered in and out, pointing and snickering with total disrespect for God's house.

At a quarter to six the faithful arrived–an elderly priest, his young assistant, and a handful of equally old worshippers. The women were mostly rotund, wearing head wrappings and clean white aprons over long dresses. The men were in plain dark suits. They followed the priests to stand in front of a large icon (there were no seats), and the service began with ritual prayers. We were surprised by two things. First, the priests never turned to face their small flock; and second, when they began chanting the scriptures the people responded to each phrase in high, clear voices. We were mesmerized with the beauty of their harmony and range.

The flight to Moscow was long and tedious in a DC-3 and required several refueling stops. Passengers, mostly peasants with bundles, bags, and even a crate of chickens, came and went. Our hotel was more modern than the last, but was still ruled by a warden on each corridor who eyed us carefully. We discovered that Red Square is only about a quarter the size it appears in newsreels; the famous GUM department store is just a fancy front covering a bazaar with small booths selling everything from wrist watches to salted fish; the Kremlin museum's treasure is mostly looted from the Church. Gorky Park is trashy and poorly maintained. Unique is the city's heated outdoor swimming pool, which is in use all year long.

"In the winter," our guide told us as we stood on the grounds of Moscow University overlooking the city, "a cloud hangs over the pool. It's mist that rises from the warm water."

"How in the world can you go swimming in subzero weather and not freeze to death?" Edwin asked.

"Naturally we can't swim as we would in the summer

because we must keep our arms under water. We enter a channel that connects the dressing rooms to the pool," she explained, "and walk in it to the out-of-doors. Let me tell you, there is nothing as delicious as being in the lovely warm water with the snow gently falling on your fur hat!"

On the way to the airport we gave the taxi driver the last of the gifts, for which he thanked us profusely. You'd have thought they were made of gold. After checking through customs and being shown to the transit lounge, we had the most expensive breakfast on the menu to spend as many food coupons as possible. There were still some left, but they could be used only for food.

"I'll be darned if we'll give them back to the USSR," Kedar said. "Let's see if there's something else we can buy." We were permitted to take out of country one bottle of Champagne apiece, so we took five and spent the balance on chocolate bars.

It was a dreary, gray day when we lifted off from Moscow, but we landed in Vienna's glorious sunshine that highlighted every begonia in the airport's overflowing flowerbeds. The air seemed lighter, the sun brighter in the joyful atmosphere that greeted us. What a striking difference from the Communist country we'd left behind. As we entered the terminal a loudspeaker announced, "Family Bryan, family Bryan, please come to the information counter."

"That's us," Jim piped up. "Dad, we're 'family Bryan,' aren't we?"

"Yes we are, son," Kedar answered. "I wonder if it's about our camper." And it was! The dealer was there as scheduled, and in a matter of minutes Kedar signed the papers and received the keys. We loaded our bags and picked up the camping gear that had arrived at the freight office the day before. With the help of Europa Camping Guide, we had already decided where to go that first day and traced on the map how to get there. However, trying to read the long names on street signs that were usually hidden behind telephone wires and trolley cables proved impossible. After getting thoroughly lost we pulled over and waved down a car, hoping to get help from a citizen who could direct us. The kind gentleman did his best to explain, but noting our puzzlement he threw up his hands and exclaimed, "Acht, follow me." Bless his heart, he went miles out of his way, patiently shepherding us to a beautiful campground on the edge of town. He waved and was off.

It took us several days to organize things for easy access. We divided up chores to share the housekeeping load, and laundry was Anne's. The dirty clothes were shifted several times, ending up in a box under one of the seats where we'd stored the Champagne.

"I can't find the laundry anywhere," I said in frustration." Does anybody remember where we put it?"

"Sure," Edwin answered, pointing. "It's down there. Champagne and panties."

"Hey," Anne chimed in, "That would make a swell title for your book, Mom. Bet you'd sell a million copies!"

Our first destination was Frankfort to visit Nathan, my Air Force brother, and his family. Thank God, a letter from Mrs. Gill awaited us, giving all the instructions we needed. Getting her jewelry safely on its way was a tremendous relief.

The tent that attached to the camper didn't have a floor, and the ground was cold and wet. Nathan took us to a construction supply house, where we bought a fifteen-by-fifteen-foot sheet of heavy plastic. The tent was ten-by-twelve, so when it was set up, we laid the plastic down and tied the corners to the inside tent posts, making a snug, dry area for the kids' sleeping bags regardless of the weather. Man alive, did we feel smart! Kedar and I slept in the camper.

We headed north to the Scandinavian countries and reveled in the northern cool. Having just left the humid heat of Hong Kong's summer, we found it a tremendous relief. All went well until we visited Oslo's Frognor Park to see its massive granite sculptures. We left the car at the front gate in a semicircular parking area complete with uniformed guard. We were inside a little over an hour and returned to a shocking discovery. Kedar's and my suitcases were missing from the top of the camper. I was stunned. My beautiful Hong Kong-made wardrobe was gone. All I had was the plaid skirt, twin sweater set, and loafers that I stood in! A great sense of relief washed over me as I realized Mrs. Gill's jewelry was safely in England. Would she ever have believed me if I told her it too had been lost? All my best jewelry was gone–the jade-and-diamond ring Kedar gave me when Anne was born, the carved coral rose pin and Quanyin head, the diamond brooch from the Bryan family, and several strands of pearls. But it didn't matter–Mrs. Gill's treasure was safe.

There wasn't time to report it because we had to rush to make the overnight ferry to Copenhagen. After checking into a camp ground the next day, we drove into town and found the Pan Am office. With Kedar's Clipper Club card in hand, I explained our predicament to the manager and asked if they had an English typewriter. He did, so I wrote a letter to the chief of police in Oslo and listed the contents of both suitcases. I gave our address in Oakland, California, but had little hope anything would be recovered.

Kedar needed to see the Kaiser manager in Rome, so we gave the kids money, told them to have a good time at the Tivoli Gardens, and kissed them good-bye at the airport. For two days Kedar went to the office, and I shopped for replacement clothes–several knit suits, handsome shoes, and stunning casual wear-it was almost worth the loss.

It wasn't always easy to make ourselves understood, particularly when asking about something out of the ordinary. Several times we ran low on fuel for the camp

A Tale of Two Bamboos

stove, and hunting for more took far too much time. In Germany we met some English-speaking students.

"How do I ask for it?"

"No problem," one of them answered. "Just say, *'Sports ka-shafee mit camping ar-TEE-kle.'* I repeated it several times, and sure enough it worked.

Our next assignment was Singapore. The International School began its fall term the middle of August, but we weren't due to arrive until October, so we made arrangements for Jim to fly ahead to spend a few days with his grandparents in Arlington, Virginia, then on to Singapore to stay with an American family for a couple of months. The rest of us were booked on the *Hanseatic* out of Hamburg.

It was an end-of-summer crossing with lots of young Americans returning home after a vacation of bumming around Europe. It was definitely not a fancy-dress voyage and with our limited wardrobes, made us feel very much at home. The four of us shared a stateroom.

One night Anne got up suddenly and left the dinner table. When I went down to the cabin to check on her I found her in tears.

"Mom," Anne said, "I need to tell you something that happened last fall in Taiwan."

"What is it, sweetheart?" I asked. With that the floodgates opened. Anne told me about a time Kedar had visited her in Taiwan.

"Daddy," she said, "wanted me to take the train from boarding school and visit him over the weekend while he was on a business trip to Taipei. I didn't feel comfortable about making the trip for some reason, but didn't feel like I could say 'no'."

"He bought me an expensive camera and took me out for a lavish Chinese meal. He ordered wine and suggested I was old enough to drink a little. When I said I didn't want to he got mad, so I took a few sips to please him. After the meal Daddy took me back to his room, an elegant suite at the Grand Hotel. When we got there...." The story of the molestation and her journey toward healing is Anne's to tell.

When I confronted Kedar with what Anne told me he was furious.

"Why did she have to tell you?" Nothing happened, really." Then he turned away, refusing to discuss it further.

The denial that had taken over a good share of my life in coping with Kedar's alcoholism quickly expanded to subsume his sexual abuse of our daughter. My unquestioning loyalty to my husband kept me from giving Anne the support she needed and deserved. Living with that knowledge still breaks my heart.

The day we landed in New York we were handed a cablegram from the Singapore office saying Jim had not arrived. Immediately I was in a panic! What could have happened to him? But not Kedar. "Don't worry about Jim," he consoled. "We could drop him into the jungles of New Guinea, and he'd get out by himself. He'll show up. I know he's okay."

"I'm not so sure," I agonized. "Darn, why did we let him go off alone?"

"Look," Kedar said, "I'll check his flight with Pan Am and see what he's up to. They'll have his trip record." Sure enough, the little rascal decided it would be fun to surf at Waikiki and took a twenty-four hour stopover without bothering to tell anybody. Love that boy, but he had an uncanny way of scaring the daylights out of me.

After arriving back in New York we visited family and dropped Anne and Edvin off at their colleges. It was hard saying good-bye to them, particularly Anne. But she'd been away at school before, and that made it easier. When we arrived in Oakland we advertised the camper and sold it the first night at cost plus the transportation across the Atlantic. We got our trip through Europe and the States for the price of the gas and oil! We were pretty proud of ourselves.

The best surprise of all was a letter from Oslo's chief of police. He enclosed several enlarged glossies of jewelry recovered from pawnshops that answered the description I'd given. All but one small pin was mine. Found were a strand of pearls, a gift from the president of Mitsubishi, the black pearls, the amber beads from Peking, and several other small pieces. Still missing were the jade ring, the two pieces of coral, and the diamond brooch. It didn't matter. I was so glad to get anything back. I wrote to thank him, giving our address in Singapore, where they were sent.

Chapter 8

Singapore

Kedar's separation from Kaiser Jeep, International, was unbelievable and extremely painful. He was the manager of the Far Eastern Division for three years in Hong Kong. His relationship with headquarters was flawless, and he frequently received commendation for the way his division performed.

After a six-month leave we moved to the new division offices in Singapore, and several men and their families arrived from the home office in Oakland, California. During our holiday David Marcus assumed management of Kaiser Jeep International at corporate headquarters.

Kedar swore he could get along with anyone, but Marcus presented a challenge. A young man, he seemed more interested in appearances than substance. Kaiser Jeep, U.S.A. was in the red, but the international divisions were doing well. Mr. Marcus was viewed a hotshot who could infuse an organization with such enthusiasm that they'd move out like gangbusters, sending sales figures off the charts. He was given a substantial sum to get the ball rolling.

The first thing he did was to stage a grandiose conference in the Paris Hilton. All the big dealers, manufacturers, and distributors worldwide were invited. The best rooms and suites were reserved, lavish banquets given, and new Jeep models displayed.

"At no time will I handle my briefcase," Marcus instructed the junior members of his staff. "One of you will be with me to pick it up and carry it, even across the lobby." After greetings as they met for the first time at the reception desk, he reached over and relocated Kedar's tie clip from the middle of his tie to the lower third saying, "It's the fashion. Be sure to wear it there from now on."

The Paris conference was impressive, and everybody enjoyed it, though it failed to result in better sales. Within six months the company was showing an additional twenty-five-million dollar loss. We were all wondering how long Marcus would be with us, and who would take his place. But he was well connected at the top. He stayed.

Business was good in the Far East. We settled into a nice house. Jim adjusted well as a junior in the International School, and I was enjoying life in that interesting city.

On our return from a weekend in the Cameroon Highlands, a cable awaited us asking Kedar to join Marcus in Karachi, West Pakistan. It named a hotel and set a meeting for 8:00 a.m. two days later. No big deal; he was used to picking up at a moment's notice and taking off. He made reservations, and I drove him to the airport.

"I'll let you know when I have a return schedule," he said as he kissed me good-bye.

I was surprised when he called the day of his meeting. Watching him as he stepped off the plane, I knew something was wrong. He looked upset, and there was heaviness about his walk.

"I can't believe what's happened!" he said as we got into the car. "I got to Karachi, had a good night's sleep, and was ready to go to work. David knocked on my door at exactly 8:00 a.m. and came in.

" 'Kedar, you're fired,' " he said. "He turned on his

heel, walked out, and slammed the door! If he was trying to be dramatic, he succeeded."

"I don't trust anyone who didn't come aboard with me, so I had to get rid of Kedar and promote someone I know," we later learned he said to one of his staff.

At first Kedar was tempted to fight it. He had friends at court, but David Marcus was in a powerful position and wanted him gone. It wasn't worth it.

Just weeks before, Kedar received high commendation from Duke Golden, the chief legal officer, for righting a wrong done by Mitsubishi, our Japanese partner.

Shortly after we arrived in Hong Kong, he was summoned to a meeting in Japan of Kaiser's President Gerrard, with several vice presidents and the president of Mitsubishi and his staff. Before they began Kedar asked that an item be put on the agenda dealing with Japan's manufacture of two-wheel-drive Jeeps when they were licensed to produce only four-wheel-drive vehicles. The company engineer reported seeing them in Malaysia, and there was no question as to their origin because they carried the Mitsubishi hood ornament.

"Do you manufacture two-wheel-drive Jeeps?" Gerrard asked.

"No we don't," came the quick reply. Kedar began to feel extremely uncomfortable. At the beginning of the meetings he'd been reminded that he was to observe only, not to participate in any of the discussions. Several times Gerrard repeated the question, using the same words and getting the identical answer. Kedar ached to ask him to preface the question with, have you ever, or do you on special order? believing the answer would have been much different, but he was the new man on the block and had been advised to keep his mouth shut. He felt like a fool.

On a routine trip to Malaysia, he visited the local dealer and noticed a field where three hundred Mitsubishi Jeeps were stored. From where he stood they looked like two-wheel-drives.

"Sure," the dealer said, "we get them from Japan on a special order. It's not their regular line." The tell-tale evidence was the gearbox. With permission he photographed a close-up, then the whole field. The pictures, along with the dealer's orders were sent to Duke Golden, who took it to the top and collected a half-million-dollar penalty from Mitsubishi for breaking the contract. Vindication at last!

Well, what next? Within a week Kedar had three offers and accepted the one from Lincoln Brownell of Brownell, Lane International, Ltd., a manufacturer's representative headquartered in Saigon and expanding into Thailand. It was an opportunity right down our alley, and we were excited about what lay ahead.

It meant another move, another school for Jim. He had already been in eleven different schools, in and out of the British and American systems twice, and was anything but a serious student, so Kedar felt it was time to send him to the McCallie School in Chattanooga, Tennessee.

Within a few days all arrangements were made and they departed together, Kedar for Saigon to see Lincoln, and Jim to travel to the States by himself.

Six weeks earlier our miniature French poodle, Peppy, arrived from Hong Kong. He'd been with friends during our vacation, and was quarantined upon coming to Singapore. The day Kedar and Jim left I was able to bring him home.

Kedar and I frequently took an evening stroll, about a mile's loop through the neighborhood. That night as Peppy and I walked, almost every residence produced a barking dog. I hadn't noticed them before, but we hadn't had a dog with us either. He stayed very close to me without any coaxing.

We were passing a house with a little foot bridge over a creek to the road when a big yellow chow and a mutt came toward us. I didn't pay any attention until Peppy went wild, trying to crawl right up my legs. I picked him up. I heard the dogs following but kept going until the chow lunged and bit me on the right calf.

"Go home," I commanded, and kept walking. He bit again!

It's the only time I've even known primal fear. The hair on the back of my neck stood up, and my heart pounded. The dogs weren't about to leave me alone, so I turned toward the house from which they had come.

"Help! Come help me," I yelled at the top of my voice. The dogs kept circling, so I kept yelling. Finally, a man came and whistled to his pets.

"Madam, do you live in these parts?" he asked in a thick British accent as he approached.

"Yes, at 34 Ridout Road, and your dog bit me," I answered. I was facing the streetlight so he couldn't see the blood running down my leg, filling my shoe.

"All right," he said, "you go along, and I'll hold the dogs." I would have expected some sort of apology or perhaps, "Do come in and let us fix you up and I'll drive you home." No such thing. I retreated as fast as I could with tears of rage and fear streaming down my face. When I got home blood was still gushing from the wound, but it was too late to call the doctor. I got into the shower, turned it on full force, and let the water hit the back of my leg until it ran clear.

I was glad of Singapore's reputation for having absolutely no rabies but thought it a good idea to check. The next morning I called our family physician.

"Is Singapore rabies-free?" I inquired.

"And why are you asking?" At my hesitation, he persisted.

"If you must know, a dog bit me twice last night."

"Well, I want you to come in immediately for a tetanus shot–no two ways about it. I'll see you in an hour."

Just weeks before I'd heard that the rabies virus can lie dormant for up to a year before it becomes active, so I had friends check on those two dogs for several months. They were only mean, not sick. Thank God!

My feelings about Singapore were mixed. I was sad to be leaving, but excited about new adventures that awaited us in Thailand, so once again we sorted, packed and shipped all we owned to a new destination.

Ever hear of a cerebral accident? I hadn't until Daddy had one in late 1965 while we were in Singapore and he was living with Molly and Harwood in Springfield, Missouri. On a Saturday morning they pulled up to their house after retrieving their run-away dog from the pound. Daddy was in the middle of the front bench seat. He slumped forward, and Molly caught his head just before it hit the dashboard. After a moment he sat up and looked around, confused. The kids and dog piled out the back of the station wagon, they out the front. As Daddy stood on the sidewalk he didn't know where he was or who all those people were, though he recognized Molly.

"Who are you?" he asked Harwood.

"I'm Doctor Sturtevant, Molly's husband," he answered.

"Oh ho, is that so," Daddy replied.

Harwood realized right away what had happened. A cerebral "accident" is caused by a small blood clot that lodges in the brain, in this case the area that controls memory. It completely wiped out fifteen years.

He ate little that night and went to bed early when shown his pajamas, bedroom, and bathroom. Harwood made an appointment with a doctor and warned Molly that her father needed to be watched. There was a good chance he'd wander off.

"Molly, where's your mother? Where's Ruth," he asked first thing in the morning.

"Daddy, Mother's dead," she answered. Several times he repeated the question but couldn't retain the information.

"Where's she buried?" he asked at last.

Memory returned in bits and pieces as he responded well to several medications. He spent hours pouring over his five-year diary and wondered at entries for days just past and those of previous years. As events came back to him, surrounding information returned as well. He wrote, "I read today that last year I was in Hong Kong with Fran and Kedar, but I don't remember any of it!" In time his memory was completely restored.

Early in his recovery Molly heard the screen door slam and rushed out to see if Daddy had escaped. He stood on the front porch, hands on his hips, looking at the lawn.

"Yes, seems to me I've cut this grass," he said.

Following Daddy's retirement he continued his work of pulpit supply and calling on Presbyterians in local hospitals. Every week he kept to his volunteer schedule.

Within a few months the physician stopped Daddy's medication. All tests indicated he was back to normal, but he began to have blackouts at regular intervals. Without warning he'd pass out, and it scared people half to death. Here was a nice-looking elderly man on the ground for no apparent reason. It happened while he was boarding a bus, in a jewelry store, and in other public places. To avoid problems, he carried a card in his breast pocket that gave his name, a request that he be taken to St. John's Hospital, and that Harwood be called. The episodes were becoming more and more frequent, leaving him unconscious for increasing periods of time. Harwood warned us that probably before long he'd have one and not recover.

The worst one happened when he was driving his little blue Volkswagen beetle. After a morning working on the garden at Molly and Harwood's new house being built in

Southern Hills, he was on his way home for lunch. It was his habit when he came to a red light to put in the clutch and shift into low, ready to go when it turned green. He stopped where the lights were on a post in the middle of the intersection. He blacked out, his foot slipped off the clutch, and the little bug shot forward plowing into the base of the concrete pylon.

Fortunately, Harwood was on his way out to the new house and was on the other side of the intersection. He saw it happen. A friend in another car was right behind him. Both of them pulled around next to Daddy's car. Harwood called an ambulance and got him to the hospital while the other man took care of the bug.

Thankfully, the injuries were minor–a clean fracture of a vertebra, a cut and broken nose, and two very black eyes. They were just finishing suturing his face when Daddy came to. Thinking he might be entering the pearly gates he asked, "Where am I?"

"You're in St. John's Hospital emergency room," Harwood told him.

"Oh well, I was coming here this afternoon anyway," he announced.

Giving up his car would be difficult, so several brothers and sisters decided to preempt Daddy's making the decision. The VW was fixed, and before he was out of the hospital ten days later, Hunkey drove it to her home in Kingsport, Tennessee. An ad in the paper brought a couple who wanted it for their daughter who was in a sociology program that required her to make calls on folk way back in the hills. The sale was "as is" but the couple was anxious that it serve their daughter well.

"There's something you can do to make sure this car behaves," Hunkey offered.

"What's that," they asked, at once attentive.

"It's used to special care. If your daughter continues to give it, there won't be any problems, I promise. It gets a bath every Saturday and goes to church every Sunday."

"It's a deal," they agreed.

The accident slowed the old man down a little but not for long. He studied the bus schedule and continued his rounds, rain or shine. On his ninetieth birthday he announced he was giving up preaching on a regular basis.

When his doctor took him off all medication and he began having blackouts, Daddy said he didn't feel right after one of the drugs was withdrawn. He asked if he could have that particular one again. The doctor refused, but Daddy persisted, and after ten more blackouts he relented, mostly to humor his patient. Daddy never had another episode!

Chapter 9

Thailand

Thailand was yet another country, a different culture for us to experience. And now there was a new company to serve. We had adjusted to life in China, Korea, Japan, India, Hong Kong, and Singapore. We figured we'd be able to take the next one in stride.

We bought a little MG 1100 and opted to drive to Bangkok. Because Jim had left for the States, there was no school schedule to meet; our time was our own. They said Malaysia was safe, but travel in rural Thailand was another matter. Thai police had the reputation of working two jobs–as cops during the day and bandits at night.

During six years in India we learned to live off the land. We always carried drinking water in a cooler and bags of fresh fruit. The rest was safe enough if the food came hot off the stove. Likewise, we had our own cups, plates, cutlery, sheets, pillows, and towels.

The highway in Malaysia was paved and well marked. We had the impression of going through a park as we passed rubber and palm-oil plantations, but on the Thai side of the border we immediately hit rough, unpaved roads. We made good time, however, and spent only two nights in native inns.

Every town had several hostelries that were cheap and quite clean. At each of our stops we had a second-floor room containing two single bed frames with cotton mattresses. A private, tiled bath boasted a basin with a cold water tap, a drain in the middle of the floor, and a squatty-potty. Upon request they delivered two pails of hot water and a dipper for a soap-up-and-rinse bucket bath, much better than using a tub of questionable cleanliness. On the ground floor were shops and individual garages, one of which we rented for the MG. The owner made sure we saw that the door was securely locked, and handed us the key. There were no guarantees for any vehicle left on the street.

Beautiful fruit was always available for breakfast as well as tea or coffee and strange-looking singed bread. Eggs were never in short supply, and their preparation was unique. The cook broke one into a bowl and poured boiling water over it. By the time it cooled, the egg was somewhat cooked. She poured off the water, adding salt and pepper. You pretended you just loved runny, parboiled eggs.

Lunch and dinner were better. The typical roadside stall was equipped with tables and benches. On a cooking cart were a huge pot of rice, covered to keep off road dust and flies, and a big caldron of hot soup, complete with bones. On the side, bowls contained a variety of raw meat such as chicken, fish, beef, and pork. They were cut in bite-sized hunks, with no way of telling what part of the beast they came from. You pointed to what you wanted and the shop owner piled it into a little wire basket and lowered it into the bubbling broth. When it was done to your satisfaction, he dished up a bowl of rice, dumped the meat on top, and added a ladle full of soup. Give it a splash of soy sauce, and you were in business. In time we ran out of drinking water, but there was always tea, coffee, beer, and coke. We survived very well.

The Rex Hotel on Sukumwitt was our home until we could find a place to rent and our household goods arrived from Singapore.

As soon as Kedar went to work, I began hunting. In the mid-1960s Thailand hosted thousands of U.S. military and civilian personnel involved in the Vietnam War as well as missionaries and a thriving foreign commercial community. There was plenty of housing available, but most of it was way out of our price range. Real estate brokers estimated what you could pay by finding out your military rank or civil service status and showed properties accordingly. After insisting we could pay only $150 a month, I saw every flea-bag and mosquito-infested dump in Bangkok. I was thoroughly discouraged until I learned that the sales girls were paid half a month's rent as commission. The next day I told the young woman who came to pick me up that I'd give her a full month's rent if she'd find us something good within our means. That very day she showed me three. We took Mr. Sun's guesthouse in his secure compound. Happily for us, it never flooded when everything else was knee-deep in water during the rainy season. What a relief, what a joy to be settled again. Thailand was beautiful and different, very different from other Asian countries as we soon found out.

"I have one round-trip ticket to the States," Kedar said, "our final connection with Kaiser. Do you want to use it, or shall I ask Anne if she'd like to come for the summer? It's good for another six months."

"Let's ask her." I had little doubt what she'd say.

"I'm dying to see you, and it sure beats the lousy job I had last year," came her quick reply. "I'll get my visa application in right away and check on immunizations. Can hardly believe it, and thanks a bunch."

Jobs were plentiful in the booming economy fueled by support for the Vietnam War. She found a clerk/typist position with an American mining engineer at ninety cents an hour. Without skills beyond typing she had little to offer. It would at least give her something to do, provide a little shopping money and lots of experience. The office was a block from mine with Utah-Martin-Day, which facilitated transportation.

Anne earned her pay and more. Bangkok's summers are hot and humid. Her office had no A/C, but fans made life almost tolerable. Her boss bid on contracts from several Asian governments which she typed with twelve carbon copies without error or correction, and this was in the days before computers and printers. A set of six was sent one week followed by another a week later; hopefully the recipient would get at least one. Valuable stamps tempted postal workers, so it was not uncommon for them to be stolen and the documents deposited in the "circular" file.

One bid was addressed to a junior member of the Lao royal family. Traditionally the name given to even minor princes is long and flowery. As Anne typed out the two-line prefix she added a few embellishments of her own, thinking to be humorous. She had it all ready when His Royal Highness arrived at the office. Anne handed the folder to her boss who looked at it, turned pale, excused himself, and asked Anne into the adjoining room. "Do you want to get me killed?" he demanded. "Now that's not funny. I'll keep our guest busy, and you put his official moniker on the folder. Understand?"

"Sorry," she apologized. "I was just trying to inject a little humor, but I guess it wasn't funny, huh? Honestly, look at that ridiculous title. Don't worry, I'll do it right away." He returned to his guest, relieved that he caught the "mistake" in time.

Down the hall from her office was a merchant from Poland. Anne had no idea what he did, but occasionally they met at the elevator, and she was struck with his wife's beauty. Toward the end of summer Anne was surprised to see a CLOSED sign on his door and a black funeral wreath. The newspaper report was all too familiar. He and his wife returned from a reception and dinner at about ten. He got out of his car to open the gate, a man stepped out of the shadows, shot him, and "fled the scene." There appeared to be no motive. For as little as five dollars a contract could be taken out on a person, and the originator was never apprehended.

One of the principal reasons we chose to rent Mr. Sun's guesthouse was security. He had four German shepherds, which were penned during the day. At night they were released to guard the compound, and we were warned not to leave the house without our maid, Sumsees. The dogs obeyed her. We had no phone, and occasionally a friend called our host's number and asked for us. We were expecting dinner guests one night when we got such a call, and Kedar, forgetting the warning, started to walk the fifty yards to the other house. When he was half way we heard a howl of pain when one of the dogs sank his teeth into his right calf and held on! Sumsee grabbed a big stick and ran out, waving it at the animal, screaming, *"Bai-bai-bai"* (Go-go-go). The dog slunk away as she brandished her weapon and went with Kedar the rest of the way. The guests wanted to let us know they'd be a little late. Fortunately the animals had received their shots. There was no major damage to leg or trousers.

We applied for residence permits for Thailand, but until they were approved, we had to leave the country every six weeks and reenter. We tried to arrange business trips to Laos or at least near the border so we could cross, get our passports stamped, and return. During Anne's visit we stayed over the weekend so she could see a little of the country.

Anne and Fran in Bangkok

One evening we were guests in the home of a Lao business associate. Drinks before dinner were served on the patio overlooking the quietly flowing Mekong River fifty feet below. It was delightfully cool, yet the mosquitoes were bold, seeming not to be fazed by repellents and curls of smoke rising from punk coils. A week later Anne called me at work to say she felt rotten and decided to stay home. At my suggestion she got a tuck-tuck, a three-wheeled taxi, and went to the Seventh Day Adventist Hospital to see a doctor. Before the day was over she had a dreadful headache and fever. When I got home she was in agony. Every joint was on fire and her temperature hovered around F 104 degrees. A blood test showed the poor child had dengue fever, big time. Rest was impossible. She itched all over, particularly on the palms of her hands and soles of her feet. For two days I gave her aspirin every four hours, kept ice packs on her head, and alternately bathed her with cool water and rubbed her with dry towels. When the fever finally broke she was as weak as a kitten, closed her blood-shot eyes and slept.

We met Paul and Betty Soderburg at the International Church soon after our arrival from Singapore. Paul worked

A Tale of Two Bamboos

for USAID, and Betty taught at the American School. Their three sons were about the ages of our children. David and Anne hit it off right away, which resulted in several weekend outings with their family.

Of the three boys, the most interesting was John.

"One day," Betty said, "when I opened the freezer I could hardly believe my eyes. Laid out neatly on a shelf was an eighteen-inch skeleton of a snake. John's into catching and studying them, but usually they end up in bottles, not with our food. When there's no more room for his specimens, he donates them to the Chulalonghorn University. He's recognized as an expert, second only to the foremost authority on snakes in Thailand."

"A friend called," Betty said, "to ask if John could identify a snake found in their yard."

"Bring it on over, and I'll take a look," he replied. The woman arrived carrying a Dutch oven, the only thing she could lay her hands on. Carefully lifting the lid just a crack, he peeked and quickly closed it again.

"Wow," he exclaimed, "Better be careful. That's a baby king cobra, and at this age they're extremely dangerous. They come in clutches of up to twenty, so you've more in your yard."

In John's senior year at the American School he went with a team from the CDC in Taiwan to the jungles of Malaysia. They were testing boots and other military clothing for durability and leach-repellence in tropical swamps. They asked him to go along to find and bring back several clutches of king cobra eggs. Soon after their return Betty took me to see them at Mr. Seeah's Snake Farm, one of Bangkok's interesting attractions. Enclosed in a glass-sided box were a dozen pulsing eggs. As we watched, a small rupture occurred, then a sleek little head protruded followed by an eighteen-inch body. It moved quickly all around the cage, and when Betty tapped the glass side, it shot right up to the screen cover. Instinctively we stepped back. I don't like snakes, but I'm thankful others do. And talking about snakes brings to mind a famous American-Jim Thompson.

Everybody knew Jim. His name is synonymous with Thai silk. He fell in love with Thailand when stationed in Bangkok at the end of W.W.II, and made it his home. At the time, the silk industry was small. He was fascinated with the exquisite fabric and dedicated his life to developing it into one of the country's major exports. Soon Thai silk was available in many grades and textures from dozens of manufacturers. Then cotton got into the act, turning out jewel-toned native designs by the millions of yards. It was a sewer's paradise. Jim Thompson returned much of his wealth to charities, and was considered a national treasure in his adopted country. He and several friends went on a vacation to the Cameroon Highlands in Malaysia. We made several weekend trips to those mountains during our stay in Singapore. It's a delightful resort, high enough to be cool, lush, and green, even in the steamy summer. A golf course is surrounded with private homes and small inns like the Tudor-style 'Ye Olde Smokehouse' where we stayed.

While on their visit, Jim Thompson disappeared! In the midafternoon while the others were napping, he went for a little walk and never returned. A chain-smoker, he left his cigarettes and lighter on the coffee table in the living room. Obviously he intended to be gone only briefly, but he never came back. There were all sorts of rumors about his being kidnapped and whisked off to China, or perhaps drug dealers had taken him, and would demand huge sums of money, but nothing, absolutely nothing produced a trace of him. For months the search continued without a clue.

I had my own theory. For years I've read accounts and heard stories of how pythons can swallow large animals such as pigs and cows, so why not a man? Once I saw a picture of one that died when the horns of a deer he'd swallowed pierced its body. After a big feed, a python goes to a cool place to digest its meal, such as a pond where it stays for as long as two weeks with only its head above water. They are known to slip into a deep crevice in the earth that will keep them from overheating. Sometimes they coil in trees and drop on their victms. I think that's what happened to poor Mr. Thompson, but nobody agreed until a reporter learned that it was the theory held by a local tribe of aborigines. To this day there has been no trace of him. It's sad.

The summer was over too quickly, and Anne headed back to college with several raw silk outfits that would knock your eye out and other Thai goodies.

Our 25th Anniversary

When we moved to Bangkok Kedar started drinking a strong Thai beer containing formaldehyde to produce a foamy head as it was poured. I often wondered what it would do a person's brain. Several times he suffered blackouts that scared him more than a little, but they weren't enough to make him think seriously about getting help. Our ride down the mountain was accelerating.

During this time I learned it could be dangerous to make him angry when he was drinking. Good friends from Singapore were visiting Bangkok, so we invited them to dinner. It wasn't a time Kedar felt the need to stay sober, and he was well in his cups when they arrived. As I cooked our sukiyaki at the table he became upset by a trivial matter and began to tell everybody off, calling our guests "a bunch of shitheads." I did my best to quiet him, but nothing helped. I don't know how we got through dinner. The adults obviously understood the problem, but the three little children couldn't believe their ears. They sat there with huge eyes and hardly ate a thing. I felt sick. As soon as dinner was over I drove them back to their hotel. Early the next day they were off to the States; we never saw them again.

By the time I got home I was boiling. Kedar was sitting there with another beer and staggered to his feet when I came in. Without a word I went upstairs to bed. He was so far gone there was no hope of any conversation. When he came into the bedroom I turned on him.

"You're just a damned, stupid drunk," I yelled at him. (Did those words come out of my mouth?) He didn't answer, but went to his dresser and took out a .22 pistol. As he clumsily checked to see if it was loaded, I managed to get it away from him and ran into the next room and hid it under the mattress.

"Where is my pistol," he demanded when I returned.
"I want it now."

"You can have it tomorrow," I told him. The next morning he was fine and didn't even remember what had happened.

I began taking it one day at a time, hanging on for dear life, but a terrible fear smothered me. There seemed to be no end to the agony that was getting worse with time, and I didn't know what to do about it. Even then I never

A Tale of Two Bamboos

considered leaving. I had promised to love him "for better or for worse". It just seemed that the "for worse" part was getting to be our whole life. I was afraid of what would happen to him in this foreign land if I were not there to look after him.

In the mid-1960s Thailand prospered. There were, however, serious problem with fires. Each year they were epidemic just before the lunar New Year. Areas of the city occupied by ethnic Chinese went up in flames. It is culturally correct to pay off all debts before the New Year or suffer the consequences. Whatever the sacrifice, all accounts are settled, otherwise the one to whom the debt is owed has a right, indeed the duty, to take revenge. A missionary doctor from China told us, "Every Chinese New Year we have a rash of cut throats. Sometimes we saved the victim, but most of the time we couldn't."

The Thai Chinese answer to the problem was to insure their houses, then torch them and collect. Many of the houses were flimsy wooden structures packed closely together, so when one burned, dozens, sometimes hundreds were destroyed. The huge loss of life and property was an annual disaster.

Mr. Twan, a high government official, decided the practice had to end. He announced in the press and over the radio that he would shoot anybody whose house burned down! The threat was widely publicized at the appropriate time, and he notified the fire department that he was to be told immediately of all alarms.

Sure enough, a week before the New Year a fire broke out in a shanty section of the city. Mr. Twan accompanied the fire truck to the scene, and there in front of the blazing house was a man, weeping, tearing his clothes, and cursing the gods for his great misfortune.

"Are you the owner of this house?" he asked.

"Oh, yes," he answered. "Everything is gone. Such bad luck. It's all burned up, woe is me."

"Didn't you see the announcement that there were to be

no more fires, that I would shoot anybody whose house burned down?" he inquired. Without waiting for an answer, he pulled out his revolver and shot the man! The curious crowd melted into the shadows until the fire was extinguished. The "bamboo wireless" began to hum. After one or two more executions, there were no more fires.

Mr. Twan was a colorful character. He had many "little wives", whom he favored one at a time, gifting each with a house or a Mercedes before moving on to a new conquest. Business benefited from his shrewdness. When large corporations which were vital to the health of the economy faltered, he took them over, infused government funds, and put them on their feet.

According to custom, his body was held for ninety days after he died, allowing his soul to rest before the cremation ceremony. When all rites were completed his will was opened, and lo and behold, nearly half the wealth and industry in Thailand belonged to him and his family! Not to worry–he wasn't a thief. He had kept all assets safe. Big corporations were returned to government control; smaller ones were privatized. The little wives were permitted to keep their gifts, and his number one wife and children were provided a comfortable income for life.

Pick up any travel brochure on the Far East, and you'll identify Thailand immediately by pictures of its golden-roofed temples and beautiful dancing girls with long tapered fingers, jeweled headdresses, and shoes with turned-up toes.

Thai are beautiful people. The men are handsome, but with their small frames, delicate features, and jet black hair, the women are the ones on whom to feast your eyes. Their movements are fluid, their voices soft and gentle as they talk in their multitoned language.

On the surface all was peaceful, quiet, and in harmony, but gradually we began to see another side of life in this golden paradise. Under a benign exterior lurked a violence that could erupt unexpectedly.

About the time of our arrival in Thailand, there was a robbery at a gold-merchant's shop in the Chinese section of the city. The owner and several customers were killed as the thieves made their getaway. In short order seven men were caught, tried, and sentenced to die by firing squad, but there was a problem. According to Buddhist teachings, it is wrong to kill any living thing, which made it improper to put them to death. Not to worry; such things can be worked out, and they were. Since it was not acceptable for the men to be shot, each prisoner was tied to a post, a tent put over him, and a big red dot painted on the tent in the area of his heart. On command the firing squad did its job, blazing away at the dots, not the men. After the first volley a doctor peeked into each tent to see if the murderer was dead. If he was not, the firing continued until the job was completed. Justice was done and traditions kept intact.

The custom of a man taking a "little wife" causes endless pain and strife. The husband may bring her into the home without giving up or divorcing his legal spouse. Though tolerated, she has no standing in the community. Her children cannot inherit property nor can they take their father's name. As long as she is pleasing she has a roof over her head, she and her children are well cared for, and she can be very happy providing she is willing to settle for a nonstatus life. She may stay or not as she chooses. The legal wife is still the boss and controls the household purse.

The daily papers have countless stories of problems related to the custom. One spoke of a woman who came home earlier than expected and surprised her husband and a young girl in their bedroom. The man, a police officer, tried to talk himself out of a tight spot as he and the girl stood on one side of the bed with the irate wife on the other. Protesting he was not doing anything wrong, he tossed his service revolver on the bed between them and said, "Well, if you think I'm such a bad guy, why don't you shoot me?" So she did!

Another account tells of a woman and her two children who moved back to her parents' home when her husband took a little wife. She was able to support herself with a good job at the headquarters of the Shell Oil Company. Soon her husband tired of the new girl, kicked her out, and wanted his wife to return. He picked up the children at school and went to the Shell offices to plead with her. They waited in the reception area until she arrived, and they sat down to talk. He insisted she come home that night, but she refused even to consider it. Just as the argument became heated, the woman was asked to take a phone call. When she got up to leave, the husband whipped out a revolver, shot her, the two children, and himself! People in rival Standard and Caltex oil companies jokingly accused Shell officials of resorting to extreme measures for a little publicity!

Others, with real or imagined grievances, found their own solutions. A story in the *Bangkok Times* is a case in point. There were two buses on the highway between Bangkok and Pattaya Beach. One was a big, air-conditioned tourist bus, and the other an open-air local. The driver of the smaller vehicle cut in front of the big one, causing it to pull over and stop. The uniformed driver got out to see what was the matter, only to find himself confronted by the operator of the local.

"You think you're so great, driving around in that big, fancy bus and wearing a uniform, cap, and white gloves?" he shouted. "Well, I'll show you what I think of you!" He pulled out a pistol and shot him. The assistant on the tourist bus ran to help the driver, and the enraged man shot him too! Both men died, and the driver of the local bus fled the scene, never to be found.

A Tale of Two Bamboos

In my job as secretary to the assistant director of Utah-Martin-Day, a joint venture construction company, building U.S. military facilities in Thailand, I came to know George Mendenhall, director of security. He spent most of his time at the several project sites. There were bound to be difficulties with employees that were best handled by the local police before they got to be big problems. He had a large entertainment budget and made sure all key Thai officials would be "helpful" if necessary.

His contacts served the company well when one of the engineers stationed in Bangkok fell asleep with a lighted cigarette in his hand. He got out safely, but the bedroom was gutted, and the rest of the apartment suffered smoke damage. George called in all his chips, got the apartment restored to pristine condition, moved the engineer to an up-country location, and breathed a silent prayer of relief.

George collected unusual weapons and had several made by the country people in the north. He sold one to me for twenty dollars but I promptly sold it back when I found out it was illegal. It was a very crude instrument made from a piece of pipe, with a chamber for a .22 caliber bullet, a cocking device, a trigger, and a grip. He said they were available everywhere up-country, and since they were homemade, there was no way the police could stop their manufacture.

One of the more interesting varieties was a front-loaded hand gun that the shooter stuffed with straw, set alight, and fired. A gun of that type had a tragic part in the tale of a country wedding.

According to custom, the entire population of the groom's village piled onto bull carts for the trip of several miles to the bride's home. In their enthusiasm some men shot their pistols into the air, sending wads of flaming straw skyward. Looking back a half-hour later, they saw the whole village aflame. The bamboo-and-thatch huts burned to the ground before they could reached them.

There was nothing to do but go on with the wedding, so once more they set off. After all, the astrologers had been consulted about the correct day and hour for the nuptials. Any deviation would spell doom for the union.

Because of the heat, cold drinks were served without stint, and inevitably some got roaring drunk. The ceremony ended up with the bride and groom seated on a platform, wearing woven crowns connected by a white cord. When they took their places, that was it; they were married. At that precise moment the shouts of congratulations began.

Enthusiasm mounted to the point where several then many took out their pistols and fired them overhead. If the tent filled with smoke, who cared? It was a time of celebration. But when the air finally cleared they found both bride and groom dead–shot through the heart!

While we were living in Bangkok in 1967 Edwin joined the Peace Corps and was assigned to Panchkura, a village thirty miles west of Calcutta.

On my return from the States to attend Jim's graduation from McCallie School and a family reunion along with Dee Dee Lampe's wedding, I stopped off to visit him. He took me to his village to see how he lived and what he did. During the train ride we went through a typical rural area, where people walked the narrow paths between rice paddies, shaded by black umbrellas with white hand towels hung from the struts.

"I remembered a similar scene from when we lived in Madras," he said, "and wondered why they ambled along so slowly, but now I know. I do the same, and it's amazing how you can stay quite clean and comfortable and get a lot done if you don't try to change the whole world in the next hour. In this heat, slow and easy does it."

A short walk from the station sat the mud-and-cinder block hut he called home. The walls were painted the standard creamy yellow color we'd seen in India ten years earlier. He had basic wooden furniture but little else. A woman from the village cleaned, did the laundry in a bucket, grocery shopped, and cooked.

He and another volunteer were there to demonstrate in the surrounding countryside the how-to of managing a small garden that would produce a variety of vegetables and legumes to provide a well-balanced diet. He distributed packets that included plans for laying out the plot, seeds, a planting schedule, and fertilizing instructions.

Along with the family pictures in his bedroom, Ed had a Scandinavian Airlines poster featuring a beautiful blue-eyed, blonde flight attendant. Under it he had written, "Lest We Forget." It reminded me of a remark made by a friend at a dinner party just before we left for Madras in 1955. She was concerned about her bachelor son who had been there for a year, and urged us to encourage him to seek the company of "our kind of people."

"You know how it is, Fran," she said as she rested her hand on mine. "After you've been away a while calico begins to look like silk."

Every couple of weeks Edwin went to Calcutta to get some "real food" (something other than vegetable curry and rice), shop, and enjoy the company of other Peace Corps volunteers, among them Peggy Macgruder. They fell in love and announced an October 1 wedding date.

Thailand's orchids are magnificent and very reasonable. They enthusiastically agreed when I offered to bring the bridal bouquet, which I ordered three weeks before my flight. Not wanting any trouble getting it through customs in Calcutta, I called the Indian embassy in Bangkok. I explained my request for a letter allowing me to take it into the country.

"That will not be necessary, madam," the clerk said. "There are no agricultural restrictions on taking flowers into India, and there will be no duty because it is not a commercial shipment, just a personal thing."

Knowing how petty officials love to throw their weight around, I wanted a letter of authorization, but they wouldn't give me one. All I could do was hope for the best.

On the way to the airport I picked up the bouquet from the florist. There were three huge white orchids with yellow centers, and from the cluster streamed narrow, white satin ribbons with small orchids and bits of fern knotted in every six or eight inches. It was stunning. The flight was under two hours, so there was plenty of time to get it refrigerated before the blossoms wilted.

At the customs counter in Calcutta I showed the official my suitcase and asked if he wanted to check it. When he spotted the box of flowers he immediately he went into action. "Oh, madam," he said, "It is not possible for you to bring those into India! Our agricultural laws do not permit it. I'm sorry. You must leave them here with me." So what did I expect?

"My son is getting married tomorrow," I answered, "and these are for his bride. I was informed by your embassy in Bangkok that I could bring them in without any difficulty whatsoever." He could see I had blood in my eye. "And I'm doing so. Will you please stamp this card, and I'll move along. By the way, what is your number?" I asked, looking closely at his badge.

"Yes, madam, thank you, madam." Suddenly he was all cooperation, doing his best to hurry me off. "I pray to God it will be an auspicious day for your son and his bride," he sputtered. "Yes, yes, madam, good-bye."

Thanking him, I folded a ten dollar bill under the customs slip–not a bribe, you understand, but a little baksheesh, probably more than he earned in a whole day. I gathered up my things, and trailing with more good wishes from the delighted official, rounded the corner and found two happy, smiling kids waiting for me!

 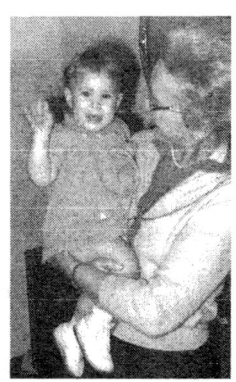

Peggy and Edwin Bryan   Katie & Gramma Fran

Ed and Peggy came to Bangkok the following Christmas for a delayed honeymoon. We wanted to give our new daughter-in-law something special, but what? They needed everything, but living in a mud hut in an Indian village, there was little call for modern conveniences, so we looked to Thailand's finest treasure-jewels.

Peggy wore her chestnut-brown hair short and sculptured to her head. Her delicate features precluded anything gaudy, so we searched shops for deep blue sapphire earrings. One night we stopped by the AA Jewelers in the Rama Hotel, one of the city's finest and most reliable merchants.

Weary from a long day, Kedar sat to wait while I examined tray after tray for the perfect pair. Fully engrossed with the task, I was startled when he said in a commanding voice, "Fran, come here," and pointed to the chair next to him. I sat down and wondered if something was wrong. "Look at who you were standing next to," he suggested. There, leaning over the counter was none other than Bob Hope, the Nose!

I returned the displays, found what I was looking for, and made the purchase at about the same time Mr. Hope made his. When he saw that I recognized him he smiled, offered his hand, and we chatted briefly. Never can tell who you'll run into overseas; President Eisenhower in

New Delhi, Prime Minister Nehru in Bangalore, and Bob Hope in Bangkok!

I was surprised to receive a letter from Edwin in the mail at work one Saturday morning. It was an airline letter written inflight and postmarked San Francisco.

Dear Folks, When you receive this I'll be in America for medical treatment. Two weeks ago I developed very sore glands on the inside of my upper right arm and ran a high fever. Aspirin didn't help, so we went into Calcutta for advice. Biopsies were sent to a local lab and one in Germany. The diagnosis is uncertain, but the one from Germany indicated I probably have some sort of cancer of the lymph nodes. We have authorization to go to the National Institutes of Health in Maryland for further examination. We'll keep in touch.

I was stunned. Kedar's office doesn't work Saturdays. He was out shopping and wouldn't pick me up until noon. I wanted to do something, but where should I begin? How could I find out what was going on. Who could help? A Presbyterian missionary doctor we'd seen several times, immediately came to mind. Fortunately he was at home.

"What can you tell me?" I asked Dr. Lewis after reading him the letter over the phone. "All I know about cancer you can put in your eye."

"There are several kinds that attack the lymph nodes," he said. "Some are easily treated, but others go through the body like wildfire. If you have any leave coming, I suggest you take it now!"

"Wow, that's a tough one," I answered as I tried to get my breath. "When we hear anything I'll let you know."

"Thanks."

"Perhaps I can help," said Ken Dixon, UMD's project manager. "I have friends among the military brass. Let me see if I can get one of them to check it out." I nodded my thanks and grabbed for a handful of tissues as the

A Tale of Two Bamboos

deluge began. In short order he enlisted the cooperation of an army doctor authorized to contact NIH directly.

"It's good-news day," Ken said on the phone the next morning just as we were leaving for church. "My friend accessed Edwin's file. I just received a cable which reads, 'All, repeat all, tests for cancer are negative, further testing continues.' So, Fran, you and Kedar relax and enjoy the rest of the weekend. See you tomorrow."

"Thanks a million," I said. "Bless you. This hot, humid day is the most beautiful of my life." Worship at the International Church that morning was a celebration. Our first-born was safe.

Letters came the next week filling in the details. When the first lab work at NIH showed Ed didn't have cancer, the team handling his case was stumped as to what could have caused those symptoms.

"We are sending you over to Children's Hospital for an injection," they said. "We think we know what caused your problem. The shot will confirm or deny it. We hope you'll have a whopper of a reaction. Keep in touch."

Ed had the shot, then he and Peggy went to Mother and Dad Bryan's in Arlington for lunch. As they ate, Ed's arm began to tingle and swell. It ballooned almost to the bursting point and turned a fiery red. He was having the hoped-for reaction.

"I knew it, I knew it, I knew it!" the doctor shouted triumphantly when Ed called. "You have cat-scratch fever. Come in tomorrow. We'll start you on an antibiotic and have you out of here and on your way back to India in a couple of days."

Wondering how in the world this could have happened, Ed and Peggy remembered that on one of their weekend trips to Calcutta, he found a tiny kitten in the gutter, more dead than alive. Having a tender heart for small, defenseless creatures, he picked it up and took it home. In spite of all the love and care they lavished on it, the poor little thing died. While handling the kitten it must have scratched or bitten him but not hard enough for him to notice. A few days later the swelling and fever began.

After everything had been sorted out and life was back to normal, I felt as if I had stepped off a roller coaster. Once again I was reminded of how very precious our children are, and how fragile life is. Ed, sensitive and gentle, with a delightfully dry sense of humor, is a very special son.

After two years in Bangkok we moved to Pattaya Beach, where Kedar managed a large automotive service facility located very near the U-Ta-Pao Air Base. Business was brisk as he negotiated contracts with the U.S. Air Force.

We found a bare-bones house right on the beach. It had been used for weekend parties but with a little money could be made into a comfortable home. The ground floor contained a large room that we divided with a curtain, using half for storage and the rest as a guestroom. Additionally, there was a maid's room and bath plus two showers and a large open area under cover. At high tide the first two of the four steps from the beach to the ground floor were awash.

Upstairs we converted a corner bedroom into a kitchen and added an eight-by-twelve-foot covered balcony on the oceanside. It was a delightful setting from which we enjoyed countless spectacular sunsets. We had a twenty-one foot cabin cruiser in Hong Kong and learned to love boating; so when we saw a nineteen-foot Lightning advertised, we bought it.

Several islands that we delighted in visiting lay within a few miles of our beach. All around them spread huge coral reefs teeming with fish, and pretty little coves sheltered by pine-topped cliffs welcomed us. On weekends we packed a cooler and with snorkel and fins set off to explore. Fortunately Kedar agreed with a strict family rule–no booze on the boat.

A Tale of Two Bamboos

The Lightning

On the day of the highest and lowest spring tides, we returned home late in the afternoon. The water was about half way in when we unloaded the gear at our steps and took the boat out to anchor it beyond where the waves broke at low tide. Knowing the depth of the water at high tide, I thought more line was indicated, but Kedar disagreed.

The sun had set by the time we got everything squared away, and cooled by a light breeze from the north, we sat down to supper.

"It looks like the boat has moved a little," I remarked.

"You have a very good imagination," he answered. I didn't argue and went to get our coffee. When I returned it was obvious that it was drifting toward our neighbor's boats to the south.

"You had better do something about it, and quickly," I said!

"You're right," he agreed. It was picking up speed. Few things would displease our friends more than having our boat crashing into theirs. Because it was such a warm evening, Kedar was wearing only boxer shorts. Without a second thought he sped down the stairs and dashed out, running along the street in the direction the boat was drifting, hoping to cut between houses to rescue it. I tagged along to see what would happen.

"Hey mister, that you boat?" two little Thai boys called out. "You no never mind. We catch. One dollar, okay mister, one dollar?"

"Go for it!" He waved them on. Within minutes they had the runaway in its place, securely anchored with plenty of line.

"Here you are, young fellows." Kedar congratulated them as he handed each of the dripping kids a dollar. "Good job, and thanks. You saved my bacon."

"Bacon, what thing bacon?" they asked.

"That's what we call our boat, Big Bacon." He grinned at them.

"Okay, Mr. Big Bacon, *Sa-wah-dee-kap*." We hugged and laughed together.

"This is probably the only place on earth where you can run down the main street of town in undershorts and have nobody bat an eye," Kedar chortled.

If there was anything that needed to be discussed, I had about a half-hour at breakfast. He was blacking out so often at night that he didn't remember a thing the next day. I was desperate about what to do when I met Vicki Baum. She and her husband, Lou, lived at the hotel, and she was just the person I needed. God is so good! We enjoyed studying our Bibles together, and as our friendship grew I was able to talk with her about Kedar. She knew exactly how I felt, as for years Lou had been a practicing alcoholic. She gave me invaluable insights into the family dynamic of the disease and how I could be a survivor. She had the AA Big Book, which I read from cover to cover, followed by others that literally saved my life. In a world where there was no AA or Alanon, I was about ready to go under, but this precious friend who prayed for me and the vital information I received gave me real hope that some day the agony would end.

On weekends Pattaya came alive. It was an R & R center for the U.S. military, but during the week it was just a sleepy little village. I got a job as head cashier/teller at the Base Exchange at U-Ta-Pao Air Force, Sataheep, Thailand. All my previous jobs had been secretarial, but nothing was available. Though I had absolutely no experience in handling large sums, a cashier was urgently needed. I figured I could count as well as the next, so I took the plunge. The only requirement was to have a balance at the end of the day equal to what was received in the morning–$28,600. Another young woman living near us worked there too, so we often picked her up in the morning.

Working in the cashier cage

She made other arrangements to get home after work because she could see that Kedar was drinking and was afraid to drive with us. I didn't blame her, but I had no choice.

With my eight-hour-a-day job and Vicki's encouragement I got through the year.

My job as head cashier/teller at the BX was never dull. I was one of a dozen or so American women working there along with some eight thousand officers and men of the U.S. Air Force during the Vietnam War. Life was anything but normal.

I was always treated with respect and courtesy. Rather than brown-bag my lunch, I liked to get out of the cage and away from the store for a little while, and since I was welcome at any of the on-base clubs, I enjoyed the variety. As I stepped out the door, without fail a jeep or taxi pulled up, and I was invited to ride to my destination. I never had to walk, and what a boon–most of the time it was extremely hot or raining.

The post office, however, was next door to the BX, so on breaks I often slipped out to mail packages and buy stamps.

"I always get to the deli shop just after all the dill pickles are gone, and I want a jar in the worst sort of way," a young postal clerk complained.

"If you'd like," I offered, "I'll get you some the next time they come in. How many do you want?"

"Hey, thanks a lot," he said with a grin. "Two to start with will be fine." I was able to deliver on the promise within a couple of days. After that I was a regular source for his pickle "fix".

Anne, in her second year in college, was writing a paper on Thailand and asked for books, pictures, and posters. They were easy enough to get, but heavy. Time was short, so I planned to send them airmail but hesitated when the package was weighed and I heard the cost. I decided to risk sending it by SAM (space available mail) and hope it reached her on time. My young dill-pickle friend was on duty. He stamped SAM all over the package, and I paid. "You know, it's funny the way some of these packages get into the wrong bag," he said with a wink as he tossed it into the one marked AIR MAIL!

There were times when things were slow, so I listened to a small radio tuned to the base station. Among the usual variety of programming, I couldn't figure out one that came on twice a day.

"Now here are numbers for today," the announcer said, and listed a dozen or so of three-digit numbers. A sergeant working at the station was a regular at my window. When he had a little free time he liked to browse through the BX and stop to chat. I came to count him a good friend.

"What in the world are the numbers they read out every day?" I asked.

"Ah, you don't want to know about that. It's really nothing you'd be interested in," he said giving my question an obvious brush-off. Of course it only piqued my curiosity. He kept telling me I didn't want to know, and I kept telling him I did, until he finally gave in and explained the mystery numbers.

As with most military bases, brothels flourished near the gates, and it didn't take long for a serious VD problem to show up. In an effort to keep contagion at a minimum, clinics tested the girls on a regular basis. Each was issued an ID card. If she was positive she was treated and told to stay out of business for a time. What they announced on the radio were the ID numbers of the girls who were infected. The men were urged not to have contact with any carrying cards with those numbers.

"It really doesn't help all that much, though," my friend said, "because the safe girls lend their cards to the ones who aren't!"

I met Caroline Bailey at Utah-Martin-Day, where she was secretary to the project manager and I secretary to the assistant manager. At the conclusion of the contract, Caroline went with another firm to Vietnam and couldn't take Gee Gee, her standard French poodle. We were delighted to have her.

After I started working at the U.S. air base in Sataheep, our afternoon routine was always the same. Gee Gee sat like a statue in the driveway waiting for us. When we opened the gate, she gave us a royal welcome and begged impatiently for a swim. She was dying to go, but in order to get in some real exercise, I had to leave her behind, walk down the beach a half-mile, and swim out about a hundred yards and back to the boat opposite the house. Then I called Lek, the maid, to open the gate. What a water dog Gee Gee was! Making funny little panting noises, she'd paddle out and nearly drowned me with her enthusiasm.

She loved to fetch, so I took a rubber shoe from the boat and threw it. I let her get a head start, and raced her. She was good, but I was faster and always got there first. If I didn't she wouldn't give it up for another throw.

"Come on," I said when we'd had enough, "let's go home." I turned her around, pointing her toward shore. Holding on to the fur of her hips, I let her pull me all the way to the beach.

Lek helped me give Gee Gee a bath by the cistern, then took her up to the balcony to dry and groom her.

After showering I passed them on the way to my bedroom, much amused to hear Lek talking as she worked. Most Asians prefer light skin to dark, and the Thai are no exception. As she combed the jet-black curly fur she'd said over and over, "Gee Gee number nung (#1) dog, Gee Gee no Negro."

Soon after we arrived at Pattaya Beach, my daily swim was straight out to the boat and back several times. The late afternoon sun reflected off the water in a way that made it impossible to see below the surface. One day I was ready to turn when I stroked right into the middle of an enormous jellyfish. It was like putting my hand in a pot of boiling oil! Stunned, I kicked away from it and screamed for help at the top of my lungs. Recent articles in the paper told of stings from some tropical fish that could stop the heart or cause temporary paralysis, and I didn't relish the thought of either.

A ski boat running near the shore came to the rescue.

They hauled me aboard, and though my arm was already beginning to swell, I had no trouble breathing, and my heart was okay. At home I didn't bother to shower or dress but just grabbed a wrap-around skirt. Kedar was at work with our car, so I caught a bhat bus to the army clinic a mile down the road. The "bus" was a little pick-up truck with a narrow bench along each side, and the ride cost a bhat (five cents) regardless of the distance.

As I walked in holding my arm, the nurse looked at me, and without a word reached for a bottle on the shelf behind her.

"Take these," she said as she shook out two little white tablets.

"What are they?"

"Just take them," she commanded. "We've had dozens of stings today. Evidently there is a whole mess of those nasties out there. It's not fun, is it?" I agreed, and took the medicine.

"Most of the poison is in the top layer of skin, so go home and with a sharp knife, scrape over the area to remove as much of it as possible, then bathe it in household ammonia. That will neutralize the acid."

All that day and night I paced up and down and applied cold compresses for relief. In the early morning, suddenly the pain was gone. I slept for hours, and when I awoke my hand and arm were enormous. The swelling extended from my hand to my armpit and down to my waist. I was back to normal within a few days, but it was six weeks before the big crusty scabs across my wrist, thumb and index finger were gone. After that I walked down the beach and swam back, moving at an angle that let me see what lurked below the surface.

"Listen to this, Daddy," I said during my early teen years. Putting the needle down on a new record spinning on our wind-up Victrola, I sang along with the words set to a combo beat, "Money is the root of all evil, money is the root of all evil."

"Sorry, but they've left out something important. The Bible says, 'The love of money is the root of all evil.' Look it up in First Timothy 6:10. There's nothing wrong with money, even lots of it. Problems arise, though, when money owns you. There is something strange about it," he went on. "If it's used well, everybody benefits; but misuse or carelessness attracts a stigma that's impossible to erase. The world forgives many things, but not when it comes to money. Above all," he warned, "be careful with it."

I thought about that as I sat in the cashier's cage. There I sat with stacks of money in the safe, but I felt no attraction to it. It might as well have been bags of beans. It just didn't tempt me.

The pressure came on paydays and the two days following. The BX and the bank were the only places to cash checks, and the line never ended. Enlisted men could draw up to five hundred dollars and officers a thousand. Extra money was on hand, but even so I made several trips to the bank for more currency. Over three hundred thousand dollars' worth of transactions took place in eight hours. Not a dime was ever lost.

It was just another routine day at the BX until an auditor came by my cage during a slack time. Leaning one elbow on the counter, he asked in a most casual way, "Did you make a loan to Tom Green for a party at the beach club last week?"

"I did. One of the hospital units was having a goodbye do for men returning to the States. It's standard operating procedure. Why do you ask?"

"Well," he responded, "there seems to be a problem. Are you sure Tom didn't return it?"

I didn't know where he was heading but liked neither the tone of his voice nor the look on his face. He seemed to be accusing me of something, and it was making me uncomfortable.

"Here," I said, showing him the signed receipt.

"Are you absolutely sure he didn't return the five hundred dollars and forget to pick up the IOU?" He was insinuating that I had taken back the money and kept the receipt! I couldn't believe my ears. I was stunned.

"There's nothing to do but check your balance and see if there isn't some mistake," he said.

Boiling with anger I shot back, "Well you just go ahead and check all you wish, but you can be sure I'm staying right here to watch everything you touch." When he finished, sure enough, the balance was correct and included the IOU.

"I'm sorry," he apologized, "but I had to be certain the money wasn't returned. Tom is a new employee, just out from the States and more than a little naive. The way I reconstruct it, he signed out the money from you and turned it over to the Thai staff at the beach club, neglecting to get a receipt from them. At the end of the day when he went to collect the advance to return it, they didn't know a thing about any funds he claimed to have given them. They had only the money generated from sales at the party, nothing more!"

Tom was in big trouble financially. He had come to the BX a few times during the two weeks he'd been at U-Ta-Pao, a nice young man and enthusiastic about his work.

"I left my wife and two kids in Seattle," he confided. "I had to take out a big loan to settle them and provide a little cash until my pay checks start coming in."

"Would it be possible for him to pay the money back over several months?" I asked the auditor.

"No," he answered without hesitation. "There have been disastrous results when American staff confronted local employees over shortages. You probably heard about the manager who was killed when he accused a Thai of theft. It was a grisly affair. Two masked men tied him up and emptied their weapons into him. From then on, whenever such an altercation seems likely, the American is packed up and sent out on the next plane. It's a-hard-and-fast rule. Tom will be leaving tonight. Everybody knew what had happened, but there was no way to prove it."

Outside main gate at U-Ta-Pao was a three-block strip of restaurants, barber shops, bars, massage parlors, and houses of pleasure. There were also thugs who preyed on unsuspecting GIs. Relieving them of their money was one of the lesser crimes. Many were brutally beaten, some died; and it was not just an occasional occurrence. It happened every night. The troops were warned repeatedly about the danger, but the carnage persisted until the base commander issued orders that nobody was to leave alone after 6:00 p.m. They were to go in groups of at least two, preferably more. Anyone ignoring the order could be in for strict disciplinary action.

The general was well aware that the mayor of Sataheep controlled all that went on and probably received a cut of the profits. However, the man did his best to maintain good relations so any problems could be resolved quietly. He claimed innocence and promised an end to assaults on the airmen, but nothing changed.

One afternoon what appeared to be a space man came to cash a check. As he lowered his head to write, I saw several two-inch round, bald spots across his crown and steel bars the size of a knitting needle protruding an inch from each cheekbone. As he pushed the check toward me, he neither spoke nor look me in the eye. There was no expression on his face, and he moved carefully as he took his money and left.

On the way home that evening, we picked up a dentist and a surgeon, who lived at Pattaya Beach. I asked if either of them knew anything about the man.

"Sure do," Dr. Fox answered, "Tom and I are the

ones who patched him up. Man, was he ever a mess! He's lucky to be alive."

Antonio was stationed there with the American Red Cross. One evening he wanted a loaf of bread, and ignoring the general's warning, walked just one block from the main gate, bought it, and started back. Two young men came at him with steel pipes. The first hit him on the head; as he fell the next one smashed him in the face just below the nose. They snatched his wallet and watch and fled. Nobody understood how he did it, but Antonio managed to crawl to the gate, where the guards saw him before he collapsed.

"It took most of the night to repair the damage," Tom Blain said. "The blow opened his skull, exposing the brain, showering it with bone fragments. The first order of business was to clean it up, close the membrane, then bring the skull back together and stitch him up. We shaved off small areas and attached suction cups to the scalp and linked them to a halo brace to keep the head from caving in. Then we tackled the injury to his face. That blow broke off his upper teeth at the roots and crushed the sinuses. The steel pin goes all the way through from one side to the other to hold up the roof of his mouth. His top teeth are wired together as are the lower ones. We attached little hooks for rubber bands that hold his jaws together. He's on a liquid diet but should he choke and need to open his mouth, he carries scissors in his pocket to cut them." The day I saw him the halo brace had been removed, but the steel pin was in place, and his teeth were still wired together.

"He's mending well," Dr. Fox said, "and will be okay. For a time we were concerned there might some brain damage."

For the doctors it was an interesting exercise in putting Humpty Dumpty together again, but for Antonio it was a long, painful ordeal.

The general had had enough. He closed the base from

6:00 p.m. to 6:00 a.m. until further notice. The airmen were not pleased, but the merchants were furious. For them it spelled economic doom. After a month the mayor went hat in hand to talk things over. With the promise of no more muggings or killings, the curfew was lifted, and "intercultural relations" resumed.

In a letter to the family I told about Antonio's misfortune. My brother, Jim Lampe, who was personnel director of the American Red Cross, Eastern Division, wrote back: "I wondered what was wrong with Antonio. A report came across my desk that he'd had an accident, and would be out of commission for a time, but no mention was made as to what had happened. The local office recommends we send him to another station, perhaps Korea." For Jim the mystery was solved. Antonio was a chastened, much wiser man.

With the slowdown of U.S. military involvement in Vietnam and the resulting lower expectations for business by Brownell/Lane, Inc., Lincoln decided to close out operations in Thailand. We had anticipated returning to Pattaya after a short home leave, and if that had been the case, would have rented our house with the understanding that the tenants were to employ Lek. She knew how to take care of things and would protect our property.

When we learned of the change, I needed to tell Lek, but my "kitchen" Thai simply wasn't adequate. I also wanted her to know that we'd do our best to get her a good job in another home. Well-trained servants were scarce, and I was sure I'd have no difficulty placing her.

Mr. Blake, a Baptist missionary, and several Air Force chaplains took turns conducting Sunday services for those on the Beach. After many years in country and speaking Thai like a native, Mr. Blake would certainly be able to translate for us and answer her questions.

The next time he preached, I asked him to have dinner with us and explain the situation to Lek. When he looked a bit puzzled I asked what was troubling him.

"Oh," he said, "I'll be glad to, but she won't believe you! She'll think you're trying to get rid of her, that you'll pack up and leave town, then return and hire somebody else. You see," he went on, "the Thai don't speak the truth to each other, even in the family, so when they hear it, they don't recognize it."

I could hardly believe my ears, but surely Mr. Blake knew what he was talking about after a lifetime of working with the Thai, yet how could that be?

"But," I protested, "Lek and I get on so well. She's learned quickly, and even with my poor command of Thai is able to do everything for us–cook, clean, launder, and iron to perfection. Her favorite task is washing windows, and you can see how ours sparkle. Surely she'll know we're being truthful."

"Well, let's hope so," he answered, "but probably not, though she'd never say so. When I translate for you, she'll weep real tears, kneel before your chair, and wrap her arms around your legs, but she'll not believe you."

"Mr. Blake," I asked, "how in the world have you been able to work here for so long if you know whatever you say isn't believed? What a way to spend your days!"

"You just hang in there," he answered. "In time, when what you say is what you do and you show that you can be trusted, then they do believe. My wife and I were here seven years before we made the breakthrough. It's still not easy. Every battle is fought on our knees and by loving them until we win them over."

After the dinner dishes were cleared away, I asked Lek to come into the living room. Mr. Blake carefully explained everything to her as I had asked. With sad eyes and tears running down her face, she did exactly as he had predicted. While I spoke words of comfort to her, I saw a look pass between Kedar and Mr. Blake. He'd been right about what she would do.

It turned out to be one of hardest moves we ever made.

There were no packing firms at Pattaya, which meant we had to do it all. Fortunately I was able to get the necessary packing materials on base, and trips to the Class-6 store provided a wealth of good strong boxes for china and other breakables. Every little thing had to be listed for export approval by the Fine Arts Department of Chullalonghorn University in Bangkok.

Each night from the time we got home from work until I fell into bed at around 2:00 a.m., I wrapped, packed, listed, and boxed. The legs of all the chairs and tables had to be protected with twisted paper and taped in place, and I made cardboard covers for tabletops. I listed every piece of clothing, linens, and bedding as it was put in trunks. I say "I" because this was a time of Kedar's heaviest drinking, and he was simply unable to do anything. It was truly a sad, difficult time.

When the moving company came from Bangkok with a lift van, I thought that was the end of it, but no such luck. Upon our arrival in the States following a trip through Europe, we learned that the shipment had been held up in Bangkok because certain items had been taken out for study at the university! The things in question turned out to be some Thai celedon, available in any curio store and a carved screen from Saharanpoor, India, that Kedar gave me for Christmas in 1960. Through the good offices of the shipping company they sent the van but kept the screen and celedon for "further examination." Within the year we received them and had the privilege of paying an extra $175 for their boxing and shipment. Oh, well, you can't win 'em all!

Chapter 10

Anne and Jim

Anne's romance with Gery Helsby began during her senior year of high school at Morrison Academy in Taiwan. He was the "hunk" in the class, and before Christmas vacation they were an item on campus. We went to her graduation in June and met the Helsby family, OMS missionaries in Taichung; then Gery came for a visit in Hong Kong on his way to the States. Anne was all aflutter when he gave her a pearl ring. She was going to Asbury College in Wilmore, Kentucky, and Gery to Roberts Weslean in North Chili, N.Y. It seemed to us unlikely the romance would survive. We should have known better.

Anne dated a number of boys at college, but there was no lasting interest in any of them. She and Gery corresponded and met a few times during vacations, but nothing she said hinted that they were getting serious about each other.

Anne wrote to ask for permission to transfer from Asbury to Roberts Weslean in January of 1968 in the middle of her junior year. We told her we could manage it financially if she could make all arrangements. With that it was as good as done, and she was one happy camper.

One day we received a letter from Gery asking if we could help him get a diamond ring for Anne. Wow! He worked hard during the summer on the New York Thruway and saved $350 for a wedding ring set and wanted a half-carat diamond if possible.

Everybody thinks that precious gems can be picked up for a song in Thailand, but it's not so. A good friend whose son is a geologist said that companies around the world who make good imitations send them to Thailand for the tourist trade. Knowing that, we were very careful about where we made purchases and took our guests.

But there was an answer. One of the young men at Utah-Martin-Day dated a flight attendant who regularly stopped off at Amsterdam and bought diamonds for friends. The next time she was in town we talked about the price of a half-carat perfect stone and where we should have it set. She also knew the most reliable merchants in town.

Within a month we had a beautifully mounted diamond in a Tiffany setting on a band of brushed gold with matching wedding ring, and fifty dollars to send back to Gery. Tell me I'm not a good shopper.

So now they were properly engaged but decided to wait to set a wedding date. Gery applied to the U.S. Air Force for pilot training and while he waited worked for UPS. Anne put in her application to teach and was accepted at a local high school.

The summer of 1967 I flew to the States to attend Jim's graduation from McCallie School. His diploma was blank because he lacked a few credits, which he could make up in summer school. He was such a nonstudent that it took him five years and two summer schools to finish, but at last it paid off, and he learned how to study. Miracles never end.

It was hard being so far away from him in Thailand and not able to talk with him. He seemed to lack direction or motivation, so Kedar urged him to consider joining one of the armed services and get that behind him. He agreed and signed up with the navy. At the appointed day he joined the others to be sworn in. They were all lined up when the officer in charged said, "James Bryan step out of line." He did. All the others raised their right hands and took the oath.

"Mr. Bryan," the man said, "you don't have a birth certificate because you were not born in the United States, so you can't join the navy. The army, yes, but not the navy."

"But I have a valid U.S. passport," he protested. "I couldn't have one unless I was a citizen, so what's wrong with that?"

"Sorry, son," he said, "what you need to get is a 'certificate of citizenship,' then we can take you in. It's a new law that says any Americans born out of the United States must have it to prove citizenship."

Poor kid. He was in deep yogurt with his paternal grandparents and father born in China and mother born in Korea! He had no interest in the other services, so he went to Springfield, Missouri, to seek the advice of my sister Molly and her husband, Dr. Harwood Sturtevant. He got a job with Litton Industries in the early years of manufacturing printed circuit boards and was hooked. He found an apartment and entered Southwestern Missouri State in the fall.

Taking the advice of the navy recruiter, Jim went to the courthouse and applied for a certificate of citizenship. He filled out the requisite forms, raised his hand and swore to their authenticity. They then were sent to the consulate in Bangkok. They called and asked us to present ourselves on a certain date and time. We were to go over the papers Jim submitted and then complete forms of our histories. That done, we stood, raised our right hands and swore that every word was true. A red ribbon woven through our forms and Jim's was fixed with a wax seal.

All was returned to the government office in Missouri,

and Jim was asked to read them carefully to make sure everything was in order. He again raised his hand and swore. We're not done yet! Back to Bangkok went the papers and had to verify the content of the large stack held together with the red ribbon and secured with the great seal of the United States. Finally we stood, raised our right hands, and swore that every word was true. Within six weeks Jim was issued his certificate of citizenship. We have first-hand knowledge of red tape.

One Saturday morning as we were finishing our breakfast coffee, we received a telegram from Jim. It was an urgent request for five hundred dollars to buy a 300 Honda Dream, such a bargain he couldn't pass up.

"The telegraph office is open til noon," I said, so why don't we go right away."

"What for," Kedar asked. "I'm not financing a motorcycle, for heaven's sake. If it's so urgent he can ask his Uncle Harwood. If he thinks the same way as Jim, I'll repay him." Kedar always had his head screwed on straight when it came to such matters, so I relaxed and went along with it. It turned out that Harwood, too, strongly disagreed with the whole idea. After seeing the disastrous results of motorcycle accidents in emergency rooms, he didn't want Jim to have one.

Eventually Jim earned enough to buy one but didn't keep it for long. On one of his outings a huge semi crowded him off the road. When Jim saw those enormous wheels come so close that they were sucking him in, he "got religion real fast," and sold his Dream. We gave a collective sigh of relief.

Jim and Christine met at the American School in Singapore. She was the daughter of R.B. and Avelon Cavaness, Assemblies of God missionaries. She was the prettiest thing you ever set your eyes on, a petite version of Marilyn Monroe, bright, and a gifted pianist. We were delighted when he took an interest in her and later wrote that they were engaged. They had school to finish and were content to wait until graduation to be married. Sounded like a plan to us. Just to be on the safe side I bought a beautiful navy Thai silk "mother's dress" in case there was a wedding while we were in the States.

Since there was no rush to get home, we decided to buy a VW camper in Germany and take a leisurely trip around Europe, looking at boats. Now that we'd had a little cabin cruiser in Hong Kong and a sailboat in Thailand, Kedar had a hunger for a more serious commitment to sailing.

For a time he was most interested in the trimaran, its comfort of space, ease of maintenance (just anchor it high on the beach and at low tide go to work), and speed. One owned by a New Zealander was anchored just a hundred yards from our house. One day he took us through it, and we were amazed. Each of the outer hulls contained a complete stateroom with double bunk, locker space, and head with shower. The center hull had all the controls, chart table, galley, and lounge. Encouraged, we sent to manufacturers all around the world for plans, and they looked wonderful; but then in quick succession two of the major builders in Australia were killed when their boats flipped over in high winds and seas. We decided to look for a monohull.

We made notes on yards all the way from Norway to England. There were beautiful old wooden ships you could buy for ten cents on the dollar and every kind of fiberglass craft, but the one that stole Kedar's heart was the Sailor Star in the Chechester Yacht Basin. The owner took us to see it. He lived aboard most of the year, and though Kedar was impressed with all the sophisticated navigational equipment, I wasn't. I couldn't see beyond the fact that it was dark and cramped. The guy was a lousy housekeeper, so it was a smelly mess. I couldn't wait to leave. Kedar had a big selling job ahead of him.

We sent the family an itinerary of our travels, so if necessary we could be reached. We went to the American Express office in each city to pick up mail and cash checks. When we reached Paris we had a frantic letter from Anne. Apparently we missed letters from her by a day or two and they were all sent on to Paris. She urgently wanted to know if it was okay for Gery and her to be married on June 24, two weeks after graduation. If so, she also needed five hundred dollars to get things rolling.

We cabled her our approval and the money before catching the ferry to South Hampton. We still had a week before the Queen Elizabeth II, sailed for New York, so we found the most convenient location for our camper–Public Parking behind Public Bath #12!

For two shillings we could rent a cubicle with a huge bathtub of hot water, a toilet, and dressing space with a long mirror. The wooden walls had a twelve-inch gap at the bottom but extended up eight feet. The enormous room had a vaulted ceiling and held dozens of cubicles. The room next to it had an Olympic-size swimming pool with a diving platform and a shallow pool for children. What a bonus. Bus and train stations were within a block or two. We could not have found a better location.

Since Anne was to be married soon, Kedar thought it would be nifty to have a fine British-made suit. We got an early morning train to London, and I took a tour while he set out to find a suit. We met at noon for another tour. It seems that there is no such thing as buying a suit off the rack, and they don't make them over night as they do in Hong Kong. To get a really good one meant measuring, one, two, and three fittings, and one hoped to have it within a month. An American suit would have to do.

We also booked space on the ship for the camper. We've done that several times, and without question it's the best way to go. All the stuff you don't want to use on the voyage can be left in the car, saving a lot of extra packing. You drive it to the dock a couple of hours before departure, and it's off loaded upon arrival at the other end. You get in and drive away.

We made a quick trip in Washington, D.C. to see Mother and Dad Bryan, and called Jim from there.

"We're here, son," Kedar said. "Do you have any solid plans to be married, or is it still on hold. We'd like to know before we head for North Chili for Anne and Gery's graduation."

"Good news," he answered. "Christine and I have been married for six weeks. We'll tell you all about it when you get here." We were taken aback but not really surprised. Jim had a way of doing things on his own timetable.

"Well," Kedar said, "that's two down and one to go."

Anne made arrangements for us to stay with Dr. & Mrs. Max Heath. He was the college physician and lived just off campus. Jean made us welcome while we completed preparations for the wedding. Anne had everything arranged pending our approval. Relatives and friends in the community pitched in to make it a gala evening affair with little cost or effort on our part. What a way to enjoy a wedding!

Anne borrowed a dress from a friend who had married two months earlier. She was just a tad thinner, so the waist was nipped in with a large running stitch on each side, which could be pulled out before dry cleaning. Her matron of honor took us shopping one evening. We found a perfect headpiece for all of two dollars and eighty-five cents in a hat, shoe, and purse store. The matron of honor cut up a long veil she didn't want to keep, and made a double fingertip veil for Anne.

The wedding cake was made by a classmate who'd lost a leg in an automobile accident and took off a year to bake cakes and pies while going through rehab. It was a beauty and cost all of thirty-five dollars. The flowers in the college chapel came from gardens of neighbors, and Anne's bouquet was made by the matron of honor. The bridesmaids each carried a large brandy snifter holding a lighted candle surrounded by blossoms. Ribbons and ivy cascaded down from the stem. Our hostess, Jean Heath, put on the rehearsal dinner, and Gery's relatives in town took care of the wedding reception.

Our boys couldn't come, but Mother and Dad Bryan came from Washington, and Kedar's sister, Alice Hondru, came from New Jersey. The Helsby clan was there in force, and it was good for the two families to meet.

The day before the wedding Mary and Heydon and their teen-age sons, Joe and Jim, were due to arrive from Pensacola, Florida, in their station wagon, bringing Daddy with them. He was scheduled to offer the prayer at the wedding. They were about a hundred miles from Rochester, New York, when they hit a rain-slicked place on a curve and began to slide out of control. They left the highway with a couple of complete circles but didn't turn over. Daddy was up front. Mary was lying down on the middle seat, and the two boys were in the back. Somehow in trying to keep from falling, Mary's upper arm connected hard with Jim's head. She was in such severe pain that they drove to the nearest hospital, where an X-ray showed her arm was broken. It required setting with a pin, so Heydon called us and asked us to meet Daddy, who was arriving on a Greyhound bus due in Rochester in a couple of hours. That evening at the rehearsal dinner he was there, calm as a cucumber. Word got around that he'd been in an automobile accident that very afternoon.

"Doctor Lampe," someone asked in surprise, "Is it true? Are you all right?"

"Yes, I'm fine," he answered. "I had my seatbelt on!"

It was my introduction to a wedding manager. He coordinated everything, taking out the worry of anything going wrong. He knew what was supposed to happen and when, and it went together seamlessly.

A Tale of Two Bamboos

At my turn to be seated he popped a mint into my mouth, taking away that awful dryness. What an inspiration. I swear it was the longest aisle in the whole world. Once I was seated the lights dimmed, and the wedding march began. The bridesmaids and groomsmen entered at both sides of the choir loft and moved down to the platform. When Gery, Daddy and Dr. Seamands came in and stood before the pulpit, the organ trumpeted the bride. She and Kedar were stunning as they approached. They stopped by me, Anne took a red rose from her bouquet and gave it to me with a kiss, before going up to join Gery. David Seamands conducted the service, and Daddy offered a prayer. How distinguished he looked standing tall with his head of white, wavy hair! At the end of the service Gery and Anne stopped across the aisle from us. She took the other red rose out of her bouquet and gave it to her new mother-in-law and kissed her.

We had the reception in the church parlor where pictures were taken. There were toasts, jokes and good wishes before Anne and Gery took off on their honeymoon, and the rest of us said our good-byes.

The next day with Daddy along we headed for Springfield, Missouri, to see Jim and Christine as well as Molly, Harwood, and their brood. It was a delight to have such a good hunk of time with Daddy, who was as surprised as we were that Jim and Christine were already married. They managed to keep it a secret from everybody.

As soon as we got in we called Jim to let him know we'd arrived and were eager to see him and his bride. Our happy anticipation turned to shock and disbelief when he gave us each a hug and announced, "It was a terrible mistake!"

"You're kidding, of course," I answered, knowing how he liked to do and say the unusual.

"No, not kidding," he said. "We need to talk before she gets here. She's coming as soon as her class lets out."

It shouldn't have surprised us. Jim always wanted to do things way ahead of schedule, but this was by far the most difficult to deal with. He began sneaking smokes when he was eight; he drove a company car down the street in New Delhi when he was nine and barely able to see over the dashboard and at twenty he thought he was ready for marriage.

Christine was eighteen. One problem was that both sets of parents were overseas and they had no one paying attention to what they were doing.

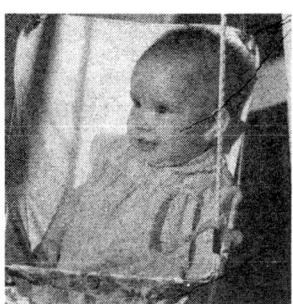

Lisa

David

Anne and Gery Helsby

Having just a few days with them, we tried to help them sort things out. After hours of listening, it all boiled down to immaturity, unrealistic expectations, and finances. We urged them to seek counseling, and with the promise that they would, we had hope for better days ahead.

Kedar was a man without a job, so once again we headed for Washington, to pursue every promising lead, and not many weeks later we got a good one. Premium Products Company of Portland, Oregon, needed a manger in Korea! Hot dog, we were on our way again and to the land of my birth. We couldn't have been happier.

Jim and Christine Bryan

Chapter 11

Korea

"Management is management is management," Kedar said when I asked about the new offer. He'd served with an oil company, automotive marketing, and as a manufacturer's representative, all overseas; and now he had an offer from the Premium Products Company of Portland, Oregon, that oversaw the production of the plywood purchased in Korea. "It's quite a spread," he admitted, "but the principles are the same, though priorities and methods change. It's exciting."

Korea was in the midst of postwar growing pains that reminded us of what boomtowns must have been like when our West was settled. Reconstruction aid was still pouring in, but the government was struggling with huge problems, not the least of which were tight money and a hostile neighbor to the north, just thirty-five miles from Seoul. Yet there was an air of excitement, and you could feel the energy that exuded from these people, newly set free.

We flew into Seoul in August of 1969. Housing was scarce, so we stayed in the Bando Hotel, not the greatest, but the best the city had to offer. New ones were on the drawing boards or on their way up.

The office was a short drive away. There were two engineers running the show, and Kedar was scheduled to take over management, allowing them to have more time at the mill.

The United States could use every sheet of plywood the huge plant turned out, but quality was often a problem. Premium purchased the finest grades used for home and office interiors.

Mahogany logs shipped from the Philippines and Indonesia, were off-loaded into ponds, where they floated until they were pulled into the peeling mill. After they were cut in eight-and twelve-foot lengths, huge grips attached to arms were clamped to each end. An overhead machine lifted the log parallel to the floor and moved it on a track to the peeler. Along its length the log was rotated next to a blade, yielding a continuous sheet of wood an eighth of an inch thick, down to a four-to-six inch core. While it was still moist and pliable, it was immediately cut into sheets and glued as the top layer of the plywood. It was then pressed, dried, cut, and trimmed before going through inspection. It's a fairly simple process, but a lot can go wrong.

Payment was made as soon as all mechandise was loaded, so there was always a rush to finish an order and get it aboard a ship. Korean companies worked on margins as low as 2.5 percent, so every day counted toward huge profits or if delayed, devastating losses.

After several shipments were refused by the final buyer, the company thought it was time for the engineers to make closer inspections. Thus Kedar's job opened up.

I was thrilled to be "home" again. Old friends were there by the dozens, and a whole new community of government and business people made up an American population of thousands.

Several couples we met were with the International Executive Service Corps. They were retirees who'd had a lifetime of working in an industry and were recognized authorities in their field. If a similar industry starting up in Korea needed a little help, an expert was invited to come as a guest of the company and the Korean government. His way was paid and that of his spouse, and they were given a generous stipend for living expenses. It covered such things as hotel, meals, laundry, transportation. The maximum stay permitted was three months, but it could be extended if necessary and all parties were agreeable.

I made friends with several, two of whom were particularly successful. The first was a man (we'll call him George) who'd spent his entire career as chief chemist for a major American cosmetics company. Yuhan, a Korean pharmaceutical company, had its sights set on providing a line of fine cosmetics to all of the Far East. Importing the base for lipstick, creams, and lotions was very expensive for an exchange-hungry nation. George was able to find all the necessary ingredients in-country, and showed Yuhan how to compound them. It was a good deal for all concerned.

Another was an engineer who was asked to check out a factory that produced Sanforized cotton cloth. It had brand new German machinery, yet shipment after shipment of the material sent to the States was rejected for lack of uniformity. He carefully inspected every step of the process and could find nothing wrong. "Okay," he said, "just get on with it, and I'll poke around. Don't worry, I know what to look for." So they did, and he observed every step. Everything was working perfectly.

One of the operations done to shrink the material in the weaving process is to send jets of steam onto the woof and warp as they came together. At about 11:30 one morning the steam was turned off, but the machinery kept right on going, disgorging hundreds of yards of improperly treated material. He went to see what happened and found that the man who swept the floor had diverted it to cook his noontime rice. I mean, what better way to use perfectly good steam than to prepare his meal? There

A Tale of Two Bamboos

was the answer. It was so simple but so important. I wonder what happened to the poor fellow.

In the middle of the night after a big Korean feast I woke up with a mighty pain in my belly and commenced to toss my cookies. I tried to sip some water, but nothing stayed down, and oh the hurt! When Kedar got up to go to the office I couldn't raise my head but urged him to go on. I could take care of myself. Whenever Daddy'd had such a problem he just sipped warm water for a couple of days until it quit. Thought I'd do the same thing and ordered a pot of hot water from the dining room.

Kedar stepped out in the hall and immediately smelled smoke. He came back in and called the front desk to report it. They were already aware of the fire next door in the Bando Arcade and demanded that all guests evacuate to the hotel lobby.

"What about it," he asked. "They tell me the whole arcade is ablaze, and since it connects to the hotel our building is in danger of catching fire."

"Well, when it gets really dangerous," I moaned, "I'll leave but not now. I just took my temperature and it's 103° F. If I go out it will be in an ambulance. Just tell them to let me know if we start to burn." I wished my head would quit pounding and that my sore tummy would quiet down.

"Mrs. Bryan," the telephone operator said when I answered on the second ring, "we are sending a man up to your floor to take care of your safety. He will sit by your door and help you escape if the fire comes here. Please be careful." I thanked them then called Gail Kinney to see if I could get a bed at her house if I had to leave. She wanted to come get me right away, but I was too miserable to go anywhere unless I had to. But it was good insurance in case the need arose.

It didn't. The arcade was a total loss; the hotel was saved. With a little help from medicine my case of food poisoning was neutralized, and I was back to normal in a couple of days.

The hardest thing in the world to come by was foreign exchange, and venture capital was equally difficult. For many companies it was a day-to-day boom or bust. Getting paid right on time so they could meet the bank draft was critical to survival. Any holdup was a disaster.

If one or both of our engineers could be persuaded to sign off on a shipment on time, it meant huge profits for the factory. Giving a little gratuity for the favor (which made their salaries look like pocket change) was an accepted practice. When the product was refused at the other end, however, Premium began to sit up and take notice.

The records were all too clear, and the engineers were in a tough spot. They had a really nice deal going, and Kedar was a threat. There was no way they could be easily replaced, so they sent an ultimatum to the head office–get rid of Bryan or we'll quit right now. They promised to be more careful with inspections, but Bryan had to go. So you guessed it, after just seven months Kedar's contract was terminated, and we headed for the barn. That was really a tough one, and all because he did the job he was sent to do.

Chapter 12

USA

Daddy had cancer. When diagnosed, it was too far advanced to hope for a cure. Treatment would only prolong the agony. He hadn't thought the evidences of colon cancer worth mentioning to Harwood, and it had spread to his liver before they knew he was sick. Thankfully, the suffering was minimal. He missed going to church just three Sundays before he died.

Molly and Harwood wanted to keep him at home, but they were beginning to wonder if they could. He needed constant care; the washing machine and dryer were going round the clock to keep up with his requirements.

"Daddy, may we pray for your release?" Molly asked him, knowing his time was short.

"Absolutely not," came the quick reply. "As long as I'm here the Lord has something for me to do." He clung tenaciously to that belief until one day Harwood challenged him.

"Dad, you've done it all. The Lord has nothing more for you to do. Will you please give us permission to pray for him to set you free to go home?"

"Yes, I guess it's time. You may pray the Lord to take me."

Three days later Dr. Dennis Bennett led the evening prayer meeting at St. James Episcopal Church. Molly wanted to stay with Daddy, but Harwood insisted she go; he would stay. Reluctantly, she went. At the end of the service Dr. Bennett asked if anyone had a special prayer request, and Molly spoke up.

"Yes," she said. "My father is dying of cancer, and we'd like to pray for his release."

"Is he a Christian?" the pastor asked. "If he's not, perhaps the Lord is keeping him here to give him the opportunity to be saved."

"That's not a problem," Molly answered, a number of her friends muffling laughs as she continued. "He's a Presbyterian minister and a missionary retired after forty years in Korea."

"Well, praise the Lord!" Dr. Bennett exclaimed, and lifting his arms he prayed, "Lord, take this precious child. Amen."

Soon after Molly left for the church, Harwood was startled to hear Daddy speak. His vocal cords had collapsed the day before.

"Glasses." Harwood found them and adjusted them on his face.

"Sit up," he said. Harwood gently lifted him into an upright position. His window overlooked a green lawn sloping down to a small lake complete with weeping willows and swans, and the early evening sky was bright with afterglow.

Harwood gazed at the scene then looked at Daddy, whose eyes turned a bright, shining blue, and rapture washed across his face. The view was as it had always been, but Daddy was seeing much more, a glimpse into glory. He closed his eyes and Harwood laid him down again. Knowing Daddy could hear, he repeated the Lord's Prayer, remembering to use "debts and debtors." He recited the Twenty-third Psalm, closing with, "And I shall dwell in the house of the Lord forever."

"Praise God!" Daddy spoke his last two words.

Molly and friends returned from church and joined Harwood, kneeling in a circle around the bed. His breathing was normal and his good, strong heart never missed a beat. It would take some kind of miracle to get him into heaven. Praying quietly, they touched him.

"Thank you, Lord, it's beginning to happen," Harwood whispered as they felt his spirit leaving. All but Leslie, their fifteen-year-old daughter, went out to the family room. In a few minutes she appeared saying, "Granddaddy isn't breathing anymore," They joined hands and sang the doxology.

Nathan flew from Dayton, Ohio, for the memorial service and I from Washington, D.C. Neither of us knew the other's travel plans and were delighted to be on the same flight from St. Louis to Springfield. Nathan was given a medical discharge from the Air Force because of a severe heart attack he suffered while in Germany. He was under out-patient care at the cardiac unit of Wright-Patterson Air Force Base hospital.

I asked if he had heard of Harwood's healing a few years earlier and was surprised that he hadn't. In a "family letter" Harwood wrote, "If any of you are interested in something extraordinary that happened to me recently, I'll fill you in." I could hardly wait to know what it was and called him. On the flight to Springfield I recounted the event to Nathan.

For several years running, Harwood had heart attacks at Christmas time. The EKGs showed greater and greater damage with each one. Molly began to dread the holiday's approach. In the middle of the afternoon the phone rang; it was one of Harwood's partners.

"Get to the hospital as soon as you can. He's in very poor shape. Hurry," he urged her. At his bedside in the CCU she was shocked to see the monitor tracing the pattern of massive heart failure. Panicked, she called their pastor and a friend who had the gift of healing.

"Come as quickly as you can," she pleaded. "I sure don't like the looks of the monitor."

Technicians attached discs to his head and chest and connected them to a little black box. Others drew blood as the team functioned like clockwork. Fear clutched at her. Within a few minutes the priest and her friend arrived. Not wanting to get in the way, they stayed less than five minutes but managed to give Harwood Holy Communion, anoint him with oil, lay hands on his head and chest, and pray. Two days later Harwood was dismissed with a perfectly normal EKG! He rested at home for two weeks before returning to work. His heart has been normal ever since.

"If you're willing, I'll see if those same two men will pray for you. How about it?" I looked hopefully at Nathan sitting next to me.

"Well, sure," he said, "if it wouldn't be too much trouble, with the memorial service and all."

"Do you suppose the two who prayed for your healing would do it for Nathan?" I asked the minute I could get Harwood alone.

"I'll call right away and see," he answered. It was arranged that we'd meet in the priest's office right after the 11:00 a.m. service. Nathan and I walked together into church the next morning, and I couldn't resist nudging him with my elbow.

"How does it feel to live just one more hour with a bad heart?" He smiled, shaking his head and giving me his "my-crazy-sister" look.

Not wanting to make a big production of it, only six of us were present. Nathan was asked to sit on a chair, and the rest stood around him.

"If there are any here who do not believe that Nathan can be healed, please don't take part in this," the priest said. Continuing, he asked Nathan for his full name and anointed him with oil.

We laid hands on him and prayed in low voices. It was quiet and peaceful until the priest began speaking in tongues. Several others joined in, and Nathan started moving, slightly at first, then violently. He seemed about to fall off the chair and I could hardly keep my hands on him. After thrashing around for a few minutes he became very still and opened his eyes.

"Wow," he said. "I don't know what happened, but something did!"

The room was filled with such inexplicable happiness that we were all laughing, with tears running down our faces.

Daddy's memorial service that afternoon was a celebration of a life lived in joy and fruitfulness. We were sad that he was gone, and we'd miss him; but what a privilege it was to have called him "Father".

Many people who have known miraculous healings are reluctant to talk about them. That was true of Nathan, too. Four years later came this letter:

"I had my six-month checkup this past week and because I had a new doctor, I was told to get an EKG and X-rays before I reported. He was a pleasant but intense fellow who told me, "I've studied your record carefully. The EKG and X–rays show no indication that you have ever had a heart attack. Tell me what happened to you back in 1972."

I had never been asked that by a doctor, and it sort of left me at a loss for words. I finally got it out.

"You know," he said, "I was very cynical about this healing bit until recently, but you never know what God will do."

He gave me a pretty thorough going-over and said I was in surprisingly good health. He thinks he knows Harwood too.

I'm to see him again in six months. The Big Man has certainly been good to me, and quite frankly I don't deserve it."

Just back in the States from Korea and with no job, we were urged by friends and family to stay with them. We tried it, but it didn't work. You know what they say-guests are like fish; after the third day they begin to smell.

We bought a Mercedes 250-C from an official in the Korean embassy. Diplomats can import foreign cars duty-free, so the price was right. Nothing like going first class when there's no income, but then that was Kedar, blessed with unlimited optimism even when there were massive layoffs throughout the government and business community. Daily there were tales of Ph.D.s flipping burgers to keep body and soul together, and others who couldn't take another rejection and ended their lives.

After the first couple of rounds of failures in his job search, Kedar began drinking heavily again. One evening he didn't come home after following up leads all day. We were staying with brother Jim and his wife, Peggy. We had dinner, watched a little TV, and they finally went to bed. Not a word from Kedar, and I was worried. Anything could happen, but all I could do was wait and pray. I finally went to bed too.

"We've just had a call from Kedar," Mother Bryan phoned. "We're picking him up at the jail where he's spent the night and will bring him home. We should be there in about an hour."

Jail! I was shocked, but so relieved to know he was alive and kicking that I didn't care where he'd been. He'd be home soon, and maybe learned a lesson or two. I wasn't against that at all, but I know how much it hurt his father, and he'd have to live with that.

It was another day of utter frustration so he did what all good alcoholics do, tried to drown his sorrows. Earlier in the day he cashed a large check and had a huge wad in his wallet. At about 10:00 p.m. he went into a convenience store to buy cigarettes. Moments before, the store'd heard that a white male had robbed a place not far away and made off with a lot of cash. The clerk saw the money Kedar was carrying and called the police. They had nothing to connect him to the crime, but clearly he was drunk, so they cuffed him and threw him into the tank with all the street bums. Oh, my. After he showered and slept we went to get his car, which was in a parking lot across the street from the store. The only thing missing, which he'd left on the seat was his gold Patek Philippe watch, the joy of his life. After his jail experience he was good for several weeks.

We had no idea how long his job search would take and didn't want to tie ourselves down with a lease and get too comfortable. For a while we rented a furnished efficiency until Kedar had an attack of wanderlust. Motels can be expensive, so we bought an Apache tent-trailer. Our mail went to Mother and Dad Bryan's address. They opened it and let us know of any promising leads. In the meantime we explored the East, found every good state and private campsite, and enjoyed a lot of peace and quiet.

Anne, bless her heart, was concerned for us, for me in particular. She didn't think it fitting that we were bumming around in such a rootless fashion and wrote an extremely critical letter, scolding her father for not taking better care of me! My answer was easy: "Precious child," I wrote, "don't worry. Sure, things are different just now, and I have seen better times; but you know what? I have a nice table for typing, sewing, eating, and reading maps, and I'm content. Your dad and I have lived in one-room efficiencies and mansions. We've vacationed in Kashmere on a houseboat, camped at Mt. Tulian, and climbed to its twelve-thousand-foot top. We've had a moonlight ride on the Nile. So if things are a little tight at the moment, it really is okay. We've never gone hungry, we've been housed and cared for wonderfully all these years; and I happily accept whatever he can offer."

Our camping came to an end with the arrival of winter. The Bryans had friends from Shanghai days who lived in Alexandria, Virginia, and were concerned about leaving their home unoccupied during an extended vacation. And our house sitting began.

We weren't concerned about making money. We needed a place to stay, and the owners wanted security for their property. They paid the utilities except for our long-distance phone calls; we could help ourselves to the food on hand. They agreed to give us at least two days' notice before returning, plenty of time for us to be out.

One opportunity led to another, and soon we had more such offers than we could fill, mostly in grand homes in elegant neighborhoods. Well concealed, they would have been prime targets for break-ins if left vacant. We never had an owner who wasn't delighted to come home to find it clean and cheerful with fresh flowers and the smell of the just-baked goodies overflowing the cookie jar.

Kedar's drinking was obvious to those who could spot an alcoholic–his face was flushed, he was getting a "drinker's skin," and his behavior gave the little hints typical of alcoholics who think they are covering up the problem. One day while we were having lunch with his mother and dad, they confronted him.

"I love you with all my heart," his father said with tears running down his face. "You are my only son, and I'm so afraid you're ruining your life and health with alcohol. Please promise me you will stop and never touch it again."

"Okay, Dad," Kedar answered, "but not even a little beer?"

"Certainly not," came the quick reply. Kedar promised; he was as good as his word and never drank again. He was not close to his father but there was a deep respect that was enough.

I could hardly believe it and for a long time just waited, thinking he wouldn't have the strength to stay sober. I was wrong. Glory and Hallelujah! The wonderful man I had married was again with me twenty-four hours a day. We could talk at any time, and he remembered. Little by little that knot of fear in the pit of my stomach melted away. The defenses I had built up to protect myself came down one at a time until I could breathe freely once more! Indescribable peace, joy, and confidence were mine. Truly, the chains of bondage to alcohol had fallen off, and I was made whole. Praise the Lord!

Aunt Bertha, a retired YMCA widow who had been Kedar's Sunday school teacher in Shanghai, asked us to stay at her house in Arlington while she wintered in Florida. Her son, Doak, was one of his playmates from sandbox days; they were in the same class at the Marine Corps's OCS; and though they went in different directions after the war, they had kept in touch.

We were making plans to move elsewhere at the end of her vacation when she became ill. Her children asked us to stay on to take care of her, and we were happy to oblige.

At first there was little to do, but as her health deteriorated much more was required. I've taken care of sick children, but bathing, shampooing, and cleaning up after a bedridden adult is a different kettle of fish. Aunt Bertha was a sweet, gentle lady, and I delighted in serving her. But I was more than a little irritated with her oldest son, Bob. Visiting his mother, he praised Kedar to the skies for taking such good care of her. He never even looked in my direction.

This period of hanging loose gave us opportunity to try new things. For years we'd heard about the Church of the Saviour, but had never gone there. One Sunday we ventured into this den of liberal Democrats (we are most definitely conservative Republicans) and didn't feel the least intimidated. The congregation was small, met in a brown-stone mansion just off Du Pont Circle, and everybody welcomed us. We particularly liked Gordon Cosby's sermon.

In the late 60s when hippies abounded, a few were there. Some had long, straggly, dirty hair, beaded head bands, dirty tee shirts and cut off jeans. We kept going and so did they. After a few Sundays we noticed that they were coming in clean clothes and to our middle-class eyes looked a lot nicer. This was typical. Everybody was welcome.

Beneath the gentle, warm atmosphere we found a tough, total dedication to pay any price to walk close to God, hear His call, and follow it no matter what the cost. Increasing their numbers was not a priority, and the challenges to newcomers were daunting. The School of Christian Living was held every Tuesday evening, starting with supper. You had to pass six of the core courses before you could be considered for membership. Likewise you had to be an intern member of a mission group for at least six months, have a sponsor, and among other things, promise to give five percent of your income; ten percent upon full membership. One person foolishly asked, "Is it a tithe of net or gross?" He was told, "You're not ready." Of course it was gross. Sounded pretty good to me. Daddy always taught and practiced tithing and his life was witness enough to me that you can't outgive God.

I began taking the courses and attended a weekend retreat at Dayspring, located on a farm in Maryland. Interestingly, to get there you take 270 north to the Road to Damascus exit. It was my first "silent retreat." After the evening meal nobody talked. The leader read devotional passages while we ate, and music was played in the meeting room lounge between sessions. There was a lot of time for rest, reading, walking, contemplation, and prayer.

Two-and-a-half days of saying nothing? After the first few hours it was wonderful. I met Jean Schnedl, later to become one of my dearest friends, and returned to Washington wonderfully refreshed.

Shortly before we left for Vietnam I was in a class of eight that looked at some of the customs of the early church that are not usually practiced in mainline churches. One evening we each brought basins and hand towels. We paired up and washed each other's feet. My partner did mine first then I washed hers. We were asked to sit on the floor and with our eyes closed, and ask the Lord to speak to our hearts. I was not expecting anything except perhaps a greater awareness of my constant need for cleansing.

He was there! His long white robe had a simple pattern all around the hem and up the front in dark brown and He had a hand towel over His arm. He looked at me so tenderly and said, "Trust me, Fran. Just trust me."

I was stunned, and when we were asked to share any insights we'd received, I couldn't. I was unable to talk, but left silently when the meeting was over. When I got back to Aunt Bertha's in Arlington I kissed Kedar good night and slipped into bed. I wondered, what was this message about? Was some big challenge ahead? In the months and years to come I remembered.

Jim's marriage to Christine lasted four years. Later he met and married Donna Gemeinhardt.

For several months Kedar began receiving calls from the personnel department at USAID. Although there was a job freeze on, they needed a man in Saigon with his qualifications, and if he was willing to go, they'd start the process of getting him onboard. At that point anything looked good, but they also stipulated that it was a key position which guaranteed my accompanying him. He was sold. I was thrilled.

The usual security checks were made, we were called in for physical exam and shots, and we were on our way.

"After you left for Vietnam," Doak wrote, "we had a series of caregivers for Mother, but none who had Fran's touch."

Jim and Donna

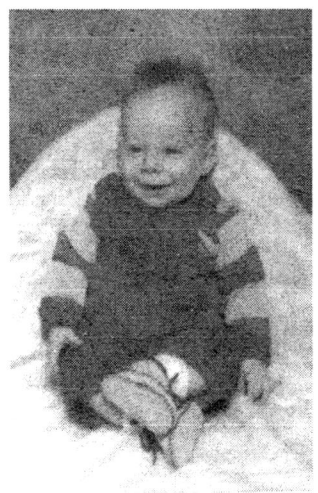

Christian Kedar Bryan

Chapter 13

Vietnam

While settling in and seeking employment, I had time to sample several opportunities for volunteer work and attend daytime social activities.

The next meeting of the American Women's Club featured several reporters, one from each of the news services, telling of their experiences covering the war. After each spoke, he took questions from the audience. Someone boldly asked why there seemed to be such discrepancy between what people witnessed and stories in the papers.

Soon after arriving in Saigon I began to wonder about articles appearing in Stars and Stripes. I happened to be downtown just outside the USO when some teenage boys began hurling stones at parked cars. Police spotted the trouble and came running, blowing their whistles. They went after the boys, threatening them with billies. Cameramen arrived out of nowhere with lights blazing and film rolling. It was over in less than five minutes.

Two days later the incident was front page news headlined, "Children Brutally Beaten by Viet Police." The write-up had little similarity to the event I witnessed with my own eyes. The only way I could identify it was by time and location.

The answer was enlightening. Unless they were on a special assignment, all reporters daily received an official military briefing. They wrote the stories and submitted copy to their U.S. principals. From there the items went out over the wire to buyers. The next day a posted comeback listed the services that picked them up. The one whose story on a given event got the most takers won that round of friendly rivalry. It's not hard to add up: in the competition to sell their pieces, more blood and guts meant more buyers. Never mind telling it like it is; they had to eat too. O truth!

Much of our orientation to living in Vietnam under the U.S. Department of State's umbrella had to do with the customs of the country, language, and health. Kedar and I had lived in the Orient most of our lives, so adjusting was easy for us. It was our first experience of being government employees abroad, however. Having PX, Commissary, and APO privileges was a real boon. In no way was it a hardship post, though so designated. No complaints–we were happy to receive the associated 25 percent bonus.

We'd had all physicals and shots required before leaving home but, in Saigon we were urged to take three anti rabies injections. The disease was rampant. If by some misfortune we were bitten or even licked by a rabid animal, they would greatly improve our chances of survival.

We lined up to start the series and were told to remain for twenty minutes afterwards to make sure we didn't have a bad reaction. Silly, I thought. I'd never had one with anything except typhoid, and that happened only once. A stick in the arm, a little stinging; that was all. We sat down to wait.

Almost immediately I had a tingling sensation on the top of my head. It spread down over my face and neck. Perspiration gushed from every pore. I was turning beet red, and my heart pounded so hard it felt as if it might burst out of my chest.

"What happens when you have a reaction?" I asked the nurse who had her back to me. She didn't respond, so I asked again a little louder.

By this time the symptoms progressed down my arms and had reached my waist, and I was having trouble breathing. At the urgency in my voice, she turned.

"My God, come over here quickly." She and Kedar helped me lie down on the table, and she rushed out to get the doctor. He loosened my clothing, took my blood pressure, and peered into my eyes. The strange sensations continued down my body right to the soles of my feet, and then as quickly as it had started, it was over.

By now I looked as if I had just stepped out of a shower! My hair hung limply around my face, all makeup was gone, and my clothes were wringing wet.

"Young lady, don't you ever get in contact with a rabid animal," the doctor said as we left. "You can't take the shots."

I used to pet cute little puppies or kittens in the market, but no more. I intend to live to be at least a hundred and eight!

We sat propped up in our bed watching the AFVN-TV feature of the evening, a Jaques Cousteau under-water adventure, "The Truk Lagoon." In 1972 the curfew lasted from 10:00 p.m. to 6:00 a.m. Dinner parties ended at an early hour because you most definitely didn't want to spend the night in a Vietnamese jail. Even though we were both employees of the U.S. government–Kedar as an AID officer and I as a swing secretary at the embassy, it didn't exempt us from the law if we were on the streets after hours.

The show was of a swim-through of Japanese ships at the bottom of the Truk Lagoon where they were sunk on the morning of February 17, 1944, by a United States

Navy air attack. Altogether forty ships went down, and thousands of men lost their lives. It was one of our first big successes of World War II in the Pacific.

Moving through several ships, the commentator explained what we were seeing, and always in the background there was the hiss and gurgle of the diver's scuba gear. Along with the audio from the TV there was an occasional muffled ka-boom of an out-going shell from the nearby Tansanoot Airfield.

Toward the end of the program a diver swam over to one of the ships to clear algae off its name. "This was a former passenter/cargo vessel that was converted for cargo only," the commentator said. "It was the *Heian Maru*."

"Did you see that?" Kedar said, as we both sat bolt upright.

"Can I believe my eyes?" I said in awe. The *Heian Maru* was the ship on which we met in Yokohama harbor the summer of 1940!

In the May 1976 issue of the National Geographic, the feature article is Truk Lagoon. A map shows the location of all the ships that were sunk, and right in the middle is the *Heian Maru*.

I'm convinced that when things are tough, God raises up special people to face the challenge. One such person I had the privilege of meeting was Gene Ainsworth.

A former police officer, he had two years under his belt as an MP in Vietnam. Upon discharge from the army he joined World Vision with a special mission to the "street boys" of Saigon.

They were everywhere–on the corners encouraging all comers to have a shoeshine, mixing with the crowds to pick pockets, begging food from the noodle-shop owners, or catching a few zz's in a doorway. Most of them ranged in age from six to sixteen, had at least one parent, and for a variety of reasons found home life intolerable. When Gene found a boarded-up building that had once been a

A Tale of Two Bamboos

French gambling casino, he talked the city fathers into letting him use it free of charge. They were willing to do anything within reason to rid themselves of these pests who were potential criminals.

The casino was one big open room, about seventy-five by one hundred-fifty-feet with a thirty-foot lofted ceiling. Bathroom facilities were located in one corner.

Gene had numerous contacts from his army days and was skilled at scrounging excess military materials. In short order he had things shaping up for his boys. He set to work with lumber and a few willing GIs on leave. Twelve feet above the floor they built a fifteen-foot-wide platform with a railing that ran the whole length of the building. Two rows of bunk beds accommodated one hundred boys with Gene's bed right at the head of the stairs. He called it his command post.

The area below was divided up into office and storage space whose walls were made of two-by-fours and chicken wire to accommodate the flow of air. Saigon is hot and steamy, and every breath is welcomed.

Gene took me on a tour of the facilities. As we walked around he explained his philosophy of managing the boys.

"There's no way to regiment a hundred free spirits, but there are strict rules by which they're required to live," he said. "The slatted front door is locked at 11:00 p.m. If they're not in by then, tough beans, they spend the night on the street. If anyone doesn't make bed check three nights in a row, he's out. Another boy will have his bed and locker. The locker is, incidentally, sacred territory. Nobody else can get into it. For most, it's the first time they'd ever had space to call their very own, and they control it. The key is proudly worn on a string around the neck. Almost every night," Gene said, "I see little faces at the door, looking longingly at their beds. It takes all my strength not to get up and let them in, but they have to learn."

"We don't provide food," Gene continued. "There

are no facilities for cooking, and I'm not about to add that burden. Instead I've made arrangements with a nearby restaurant to supply meals in exchange for special coupons we issue to the boys. None of these kids has seen the inside of a school for years, so we encourage them to attend a regular or a trade school if they have a special talent, and I do my best to reunite them with their families. Often the boys change their names, so we keep a book of mug shots," he said, pointing to the fat, battered album on the table. "It helps parents find children if they're here, and it assists the police when they come looking for somebody who has committed a crime."

Each bed had an army blanket on it, but except for a few cold nights in January, they were just too hot to use. "Some sort of washable covering, a little heavier than a sheet, would be wonderful," Gene said, pointing out the problem.

The U.S. embassy maintained several hundred apartments and villas in Saigon, and the turnover of personnel was constant. Every time a residence changed occupants, the new arrivals had the option of keeping the current draperies or having new ones made at government expense. Most opted for new ones. The old ones were taken to a warehouse, where they were ripped up to use as rags by the cleaning staff. One night at a cocktail party I was introduced to the man in charge of that operation, and I questioned him about the discards. "Most are made of a loosely-woven cotton, and there is a whole pile of them in the warehouse," he said.

"Sounds like just what I need," I told him. "I want to make cotton quilts for the street boys' home and can probably use all I can get my hands on."

"Be happy to oblige," he said with a chuckle. "Give me your address, and you'll have them in a couple of days."

When I got back from work later that week, the house

girl met me at the door, very agitated.

"I think so one big mistake," Juanita said, leading me to the spare bedroom. There, stacked from floor to ceiling, was an enormous pile of filthy curtains, far more than Juanita and I could manage alone. I called four friends who lived in the building and asked them to help. Each agreed to take several pairs, rip them apart, wash, iron, and hold them until I figured out what to do next.

In his work with USAID, Kedar frequently dealt with H. P. Jen, the owner of a cotton mill that had huge contracts with both the U.S. and Vietnamese armies. Mr. Jen invited us to his home for dinner, and we entertained him and his wife in ours. Bold as brass one day, I called him.

"Mr. Jen," I said, "I wonder if you could help me."

"I'll try," he answered. "What can I do for you?"

"I understand in manufacturing your cloth there are usually end pieces that are discarded and sometimes materials that can't be sold because of some minor flaw, even though it's perfectly good fabric." I told him of my project and asked, "Could you give me two hundred yards each of cotton flannel and blouse-weight cloth?" I was delighted when he said, "No problem" and within the week I had more piles of material crowding the bedroom.

Fortunately, most of the draperies were of nice bright colors. I matched them up with soft cotton printed fabric for the backing. With an inner lining of cotton flannel we made quilts that would keep the boys warm but not cook them to death.

The most time-consuming operation in making the quilts was tying them every four inches with embroidery floss, but that was accomplished by our house girls while we were at work. Each of us made twenty-five, finishing them within a month. I wish I could have had a picture of Gene's face when we delivered one hundred coverlets to the home. He and the boys were ecstatic. But it seemed they needed something more.

"Most boys have only the clothing they stand in," Gene said, "so if you can find some shorts, it will make a wonderful Christmas gift for the season just ahead."

Again I called Mr. Jen, and he produced yards and yards of very nice summer uniform material. Bless him! We didn't try anything fancy, like zippers and belt loops, but made boxer shorts in three sizes with side and back pockets and elastic in the waist. Just before Christmas Kedar and I loaded them into the back of our car and took them over. One of the youngsters was a budding tailor, and for a fee accommodated some of the older fellows who wanted fitted shorts.

Gene wanted us to see the kids wearing their new clothes (we had also gotten a whole bunch of tee-shirts from willing donors) and invited us to attend their Christmas party. For the occasion a small stage had been erected to accommodate a combo of several instruments and a mike. As we walked in the door, one skinny youngster was singing his heart out with the volume turned up as high as it would go. I thought for sure we'd be deaf before the evening was over.

"I want to tell you about him," Gene said, pointing to the vocalist. We collected our Cokes and sat down at a little table to talk as best we could over the racket.

"When Duc first came to us he was very quiet. He didn't mix with the other boys and never asked for food coupons or made friends. He was a loner, out at seven in the morning and back just before eleven at night. I tried talking to him, but the conversation was all on my part. One night I made a point of being there when he returned and asked him to come into my office. He still wouldn't say where he had been or what he did all day. I had him show me both of his hands, palms down. Slowly, reluctantly, Duc placed them on the desk, never taking his eyes off of mine. Fear darkened his face, and I thought he'd run, but he didn't. Sure enough there was the telltale trademark of a thief—the nail of the index finger allowed to grow as long as the end of the middle finger, making it easy to lift wallets!"

"So, you're a pickpocket. Are you good at it?" Looking not the least bit ashamed, he made a quick, affirmative jerk of his head. From that moment on, he began to change. I didn't beat him up, call the police, or throw him out. A big load seemed to be lifted off his shoulders now that his secret was known. I didn't tell him it was okay, but I put my arm around his shoulders and suggested there were better ways of making a living; I was ready to help him whenever he was willing. Poor kid, I thought. What has his life been like? Anyway, very soon he was mixing with the other boys, going to meals, and now he's in school, too. Just look at him! Six months ago he wouldn't have been celebrating with us. He's one of our miracles."

There was just one more thing that Gene needed–a dryer. Washing their clothes was no problem. Each boy did his own, but getting things dry in Saigon's humidity was something else. It took forever.

Every Friday the embassy published a paper. One section was a "swap-shop" where people could list items for sale and inquire about needed ones. I entered my request for a free (sometimes if you ask, you'll get) dryer. Within a day I had a call from a man being reassigned. He had one for me, but I'd have to figure out how to get it to Saigon from where his wife lived. It turned out to be very close to the home of my brother, Heydon Lampe, and his wife, Mary, in Bangkok. A retired navy chaplain, he was running the Christian Servicemen's Center there. I arranged with him to pick it up and get it on a military shuttle Sunday morning at 8:00 a.m. Gene was ready with his truck to collect it and got it installed, all for free. The Lord must have wanted those boys to have dry clothes.

Gene and two of his boys

One of World Vision's important ministries was a clinic/ halfway house for orphans. A three-story building, it was jammed among others in the industrial part of the city. Newborns and preemies in incubators were on the top floor. The second floor housed those from three months to a year, and the ground floor had children of a year and older.

Those babies couldn't survive in government orphanages. If a child was healthy he could usually manage, but with the shortage of staff, any who were ill or in need of special attention died. The management was reluctant to let its charges go because the government paid so much a head, but out of compassion, the sick were sent to World Vision. Volunteer doctors from the Third Field Hospital donated several hours a week.

One day I was invited to go with others to "love the babies." After visiting each floor, we chose a place to help out for a couple of hours. Most of the time I went to the second floor. The little ones were in cribs, usually standing up hanging onto the railings, bellowing for attention. At first I picked them up one at a time and tried to comfort them, but there were too many. I put all of the noisiest ones down on the clean tile floor. Sitting on a pillow with my back against the cool wall, I could love about twelve at a time. The ones who cried the most were held the most, but for the others it seemed to enough just to touch my arms or legs or snuggle up close to receive a caress every now and then. It was a long two hours but a time I cherished.

"Will you come to the third floor to help a special baby?" asked a staff member I met in the hall one day. I had never seen a three-month-old like him. He had the face of a man, not a baby. It was perfect in every detail, and without expression. He was absolutely quiet, with no movement of his arms and legs. His eyes were open, but unfocused. Nothing invited his attention.

"Here's his bottle," she said. "Feeding him will be a challenge." When I picked him up, his back arched and his head went back. He thrust out his legs and arms and clenched his fists. His whole body was rigid. There was no way he could swallow in that position, so I sat down, put my left arm under his head and pressed his hips with my right forearm until he was at least straight, then jammed the nipple into his mouth. He fought me with everything he had, but gulped the milk at an alarming rate. Four ounces were gone in no time. A big burp came up, and the next four ounces disappeared.

I put him over my shoulder to get the final burp, but again his back arched. His eyes told me nothing. He didn't whimper or cry. I stood up, forcing him to conform to my body as I walked back and forth. Singing lullabies I had sung to my own three babies, I patted his back, and stroked his limbs. Finally the burp came, but he was still as stiff as a board. I kept walking, singing, and talking to him. Little by little everything relaxed, his eyes closed, and his tiny hands lay open on the blanket.

"What made him that way? What happened to him?" I asked the nurse after putting him into his crib.

"He was okay until he went to a huge orphanage with over two hundred children," she told me. "With the shortage of staff, he was left lying in his bed day after day, crying. Nobody ever held him, poor little thing." After that I always went to the third floor.

"The little man is waiting for you," the nurse called out when she saw me. It was a battle of the wills, but guess who won. One day he wasn't there.

"Where's my date?" I asked.

"He got sick, so the doctors took him to the hospital," she answered. "He survived only three days. He must have been too sad to live." I think she was right. Sad babies die. Fortunately most of the others were adopted into European and American families where there was no shortage of love.

Prewar Saigon was a city of wide boulevards, elegant clubs, and gracious homes. As the war raged on hundreds of foreigners and hundreds of thousands of refugees flooded the city. The streets were jammed with cars, trucks, scooters, and bikes, and the air was blue with exhaust fumes.

Shoeshine boys were on the lookout for opportunities to relieve the unwary of unguarded valuables. Pickpockets mixed with the crowds on sidewalks and in the markets. They skillfully lifted treasures from pocket or purse, completely unnoticed.

Cowboys cruised on motor scooters. The one in front drove, and the one riding pillion snatched. They were highly feared because frequently victims were injured. Their modus operandi was to roam until they spotted a target–usually someone carrying a loosely swinging shoulder bag or one tucked casually under the arm. Alleyways ran between and behind large buildings. The miscreants stayed level with the mark, and just as she crossed an alley, drove in just behind her and snatched the loot. Moving so quickly they were seldom caught.

One morning an American businessman in his chauffeur-driven car happened to glance down a side street. He saw what looked like a "splash of pink" on the ground. It didn't seem right, so he asked the driver to stop. Going back on foot, he noticed a crowd had begun to gather. There on the cobblestone pavement a few yards from the street was a woman in a pink dress, groaning, trying to get up. Obviously she needed medical help, so he picked her up in his arms, carried her to his car, and took her to the hospital.

"Never again," Mary Anne Johnson told me later. "When those miserable wretches snatched my purse, my reaction was, oh no you don't, and I held on. Big mistake! They dragged me about fifteen yards before they realized I wasn't going to let go and dropped me. The whole side of my body was black and blue. The hair was scraped from that side of my head, my glasses were smashed, and there were deep cuts on my jaw and cheek. See," she said, tracing the scars with her finger. "Since then I don't carry a purse. I've had pockets put in all my dresses and skirts and advise others to do the same. I learned a painful lesson–if they snatch anything, let them have it. Taking that kind of beating just isn't worth it."

Another encounter didn't turn out so badly. Cynthia lived near her office, so she walked to and from work. Every noon she went home for lunch with her husband and a rest as Saigon still observed the French custom of a midday siesta. She took the same route at the same time every day, which she admitted was not wise.

"When you are a foreigner you stick out like a sore thumb," she said, "and if the bad guys have evil intentions, your routine makes it easy for them."

The tree-lined side street on which her apartment was located was quiet in the early afternoon. Fifty yards from her door, she was suddenly surrounded by several men.

She didn't see where they had come from—they were just there.

"Don't make any noise, or I'll cut you," one of them threatened. Looking down, she saw a wicked-looking knife poised at her waist! "Just take off your earrings, rings, and watch," he ordered, "and put them in this bag." She did as he asked, and as quickly as they had appeared they were gone.

Cynthia was shaken but relieved not to have been hurt. She felt sorry about her wedding band, but it could be replaced.

The same men reappeared two days later at the same place. Before she even had time to be frightened, the man with the knife addressed her.

"How dare you? It was fake, all of it except the wedding ring. How could you be so cheap!" With that he slapped her hard on one side of the face and backhanded her on the other. And again they disappeared!

Our government abroad makes regular contact with U.S. citizens locally incarcerated. We received mail for the inmates and checks or cash, which we converted to piasters. Without funds to supplement the dangerously limited prison diet (thirty-five cents a day), survival was difficult.

Not long after I started working as a swing secretary, Consul Tom Carter asked if I'd like to accompany him on his weekly visitation to the Chi-Wah Prison, called the "Hilton" because it was so much better than the Immigration Jail.

We notified Mr. Nguyen, warden, of each visit, giving him time to arrange a meeting with the three prisoners on our list. We weren't permitted to see a fourth man held under tight security because of his connection to a big international drug ring headquartered in Thailand.

They were nice looking young men, probably in their early twenties, who had served a year in the army in Vietnam before being honorably discharged back to the States. Knowing how to board a MAC flight illegally they returned to Vietnam to make an overnight fortune selling drugs to the troops. Their very first contact happened to be an undercover agent. Tried and convicted, they were beginning a four-year sentence. I was sorry for them, but they were getting no more than they deserved. They wanted to make a killing selling misery and death to others; now they were paying the piper.

Mr. Nguyen served us tea in his office.

"Mrs. Bryan will accompany me on our regular visits to Chi-Wha. When I'm unable to come, she will represent the consulate on my behalf," Tom said, introducing me. A tall, nice-looking man in his fifties, Mr. Nguyen spoke excellent English, smoked cigars, and prominently displayed pictures of his wife and children on his desk.

"Mr. Nguyen, I'd like to see where the prisoners live," I said after the usual pleasantries. "Can you arrange it for our next visit?"

"Yes, yes of course that can be done," he answered, looking rather startled. "Please let me know the day before."

Ahead of time I bought a big box of the best cigars the PX had to offer for Mr. Nguyen and Whitman's Sampler chocolates for his wife. He seemed to have forgotten about my request until I gave him the packages and reminded him of his promise.

"Yes, yes of course," he said at once. He ordered the young men in question returned to their cells, and invited us to follow him.

The Chi-Wha is a large hexagonal building, five stories high. The center is open, divided into pie-shaped areas by a steel mesh wall topped by barbed wire. Prisoners from the different sections who didn't admire each other can thus enjoy safe recreation out of doors.

"Mrs. Bryan," he said, "you walk right behind me; and Mr. Carter, you stay close behind her. The guards will follow." It sounded quite ominous.

He stepped into the dimly lighted hall, lifted his arm in a Hitler-style salute, and in a loud voice shouted, "Ha." Immediately the many prisoners milling about in the corridor fell back against the walls remaining there until we had passed. We processed through three sections of the prison, and each time it was the same. Three flights up we entered the foreign section, where he left us in the care of the guards and went on to more important matters.

I was surprised and delighted with what we found. The three men shared a suite of rooms whose floors, walls, and ceilings were painted a light yellow. One large room accommodated beds and chairs for each; the bathroom had a basin, shower, and toilet (a hole-in-the-floor squatty-pottie) complete with flush. A tiny kitchen held a table with hot plate and a small sink. Ceiling to floor on the side facing the courtyard was covered with wire mesh. They were required to maintain their place, and not having a lot to do, kept it neat as a pin, free of odors and bugs.

They badly needed food such as tuna fish, fresh fruit, and vegetables that were safe to eat, and anything else that came in one-meal containers. There was no refrigeration for leftovers. The prison daily provided each man with a small loaf of French bread and four ounces of rice. Prisoners aren't expected to live on it without support of family and friends, and these three were showing the effects of a poor diet. Nor had they mosquito nets, and Saigon is definitely malerialand.

I recruited the help of the women of the International Church to meet their needs. As time went on we found other things. One man had a bad tooth, so we arranged for him to go under guard to the U.S. Army 5th Field Hospital for dental care. All of them needed cholera and tetanus shots. On another visit I took along an army nurse to do immunizations and brought a supply of basics like vitamins and aspirin. When the holidays came, we got hot turkey dinners from the Red Cross and delivered them to the prison. With someone to show them a bit of human kindness they might eventually be open to the gospel message and become changed men.

A group from Teen Challenge came to speak at the International Church. They had all been drug addicts, had gone through treatment, and were ready to help others. The army brought them to Saigon and took care of all their expenses as they went from base to base talking to the troops. Drugs were a big problem for the military in Vietnam. The hope was that these youngsters would make a difference. On one of my last visits I took three of the team to see our protégés at Chi-Wha because I was pretty sure they were still using. Even those so carefully controlled could get drugs. It was interesting to see how they worked. Each took a prisoner aside and talked quietly with him–no loud preaching or lecturing, just calm, personal contact. They left literature and suggested getting in touch with me any time they wanted another visit.

Within the year Saigon fell to the Vietcong. I have often wondered what happened to those three young Americans.

The consular section of the embassy paid similar visits to American citizens held in the Immigration Jail, where inmates of many nationalities were detained until their governments got them transported home or they went to trial in the Vietnamese courts. A lot depended on the nature of their crimes. Illegal entry or overstaying a visa was a common offense.

The difference between the Chi Wha Hilton, and the Immigration Jail was striking. The latter resembled a zoo, with three large cage-like rooms on an open courtyard at the back of the administration building. Each was about thirty feet high, thirty feet long, and twelve feet wide, with the ubiquitous wire mesh from ceiling to floor on the courtyard side. Four tiers of bunks were attached to the far wall. The cement floor, regularly hosed down, was not well drained and usually wet. The men had absolutely no privacy except for the toilet at one end, identifiable by its odor even from a distance. Little breeze relieved the heat and humidity or the intense sun. All wore only undershorts.

Most of those charged with minor crimes were released into our custody if we put them on a plane bound for the States, preferably nonstop so they couldn't get into further trouble in another country.

We tried to find out if their families would send money for their passage home. Contrary to common belief, consulates don't provide stranded citizens with a return ticket. There is no such item in the budget.

Unfortunately, they lied constantly. When they filled out information on their SSN, DOB, names and address of parents or responsible next-of-kin, that habit often served to invalidate the search. Week after week the computer came back with the same answer–no such person. Sorry, but they had "misremembered" something. So we'd try again, and again, and again. On top of it all came a drumbeat of complaint: the government didn't care about them. After years of paying taxes, they got no service. What a paradox!

Each time I made the jail run, a Vietnamese driver took me in a staff car and never left my side. I was immensely thankful for that large, strong man who was prepared to protect me from harm.

The authorities provided the office where I interviewed the prisoners brought in by a guard. One day Tom Carter asked me to talk to two men who had been playing games with us for months. The Vietnamese were anxious to get rid of them. Bill Simpson, who was white, and Tommy Blake, who was black, came in together. Tommy called himself Buddha. He was properly shaped with a nice round belly, and a gold front tooth that shone beautifully in his broad smile. Both were in their early twenties. Formerly in the army, they had overstayed their welcome. Bill was the spokesman and immediately demanded to see Mr. Carter. He was not interested in talking to me, a mere woman without official rank.

"I'm sorry," I informed them, "I am the only person from the consulate you'll see this week, so if you have anything to say, you have to say it to me."

"Mrs. Bryan," he said, giving me a haughty look and clasping his hands behind his back, "I don't want to talk to you. You tell Mr. Carter to come down here (pounding his fist on the desk) today, not tomorrow. Buddha and me, we don't give a damn about you or the government. We're militant up to the max!" I had a hard time keeping a straight face.

Poor boys. I hope they got home before Saigon fell a few months later.

One of my duties as secretary to Consul General Pete Halum was to file all incoming mail on personal affairs when it related to the responsibility of the consular office. One such letter came from a Mrs. Barton in the States. Her husband, an army colonel, had served two years in Vietnam. He then resigned his commission and was back in country working with a construction company.

"My husband wants to adopt a little Vietnamese girl, but I really don't want to," she wrote. "We already have two teenagers, and it's all we can do to provide for their ever-increasing demands. I just didn't see how we can take on another child. I don't want to hurt his feelings, and I'm sure he's very generous and kind to the poor little child, but I'll deeply appreciate it if you can put some roadblocks in the way of his plans!"

I sympathized with her, but there was nothing our office could do but provide any and all assistance to those seeking to adopt Vietnamese children. I set up a file under her name and thought nothing more about it.

A week or two later there was a big ruckus in the front office, where people came for information. A moment later the door to my office was jerked open, and before me stood a tall, nice-looking man who appeared very upset.

"I want to see the consul general," he demanded rather brusquely. "Those idiots out there don't know from nothing."

"Please wait a moment while I see if Mr. Halum is free," I responded and called him on the intercom. "It's okay," I said, indicating the door to his office.

Not more than two minutes passed, and again there were raised voices and pounding on the desk. Above the din I heard him roar, "But I promised her!" The guest stormed out past my desk and through the other door, slamming it so hard the walls shook.

"Remember the woman whose husband wants to adopt a little Vietnamese girl?" Mr. Halum was holding his sides, laughing.

"Of course. How could I forget," I answered, wondering what could be so funny.

"Well, that's the husband. I had a hard time convincing him that the maximum adoption age is fourteen. It seems the "little girl" is thirty-two!"

I maintained files on all Vietnamese women in the process of fulfilling the requirements of both governments for going to the States to be married. If things progressed normally, it took about six months to complete the paperwork, plus three thousand dollars for legal fees and a round-trip ticket. If the girl didn't marry her American sweetheart within ninety days, the law required her to return to Vietnam. If they married she could cash in the unused portion of the ticket.

Consulates and embassies have very strict rules about responding to certain letters. Those from a senator must be answered within forty-eight hours and from a con-

A Tale of Two Bamboos

gressman within seventy-two hours. One morning two flagged letters arrived, one each from a senator and congressman concerning the same woman. An impatient GI was hot to get his fiancée out of Vietnam and into his lovin' arms. Six months had long passed, and he was sure we were responsible for the delay.

I pulled her file and called and asked the lady in question to bring the paperwork to see if we could help. I was not prepared for what I saw the afternoon she came.

Tee-tee (her nickname which means "little") was tall and slender with waist-length, dyed hair of a greenish-yellow hue that framed her dark-skinned, hard-looking face.

"Tee-tee," I said, "Your fiancé is very anxious to have you come to the States and has asked us to help you complete your processing. Have you had trouble with any part of it?"

Reluctantly she handed me the documents, which were attached to a legal-size sheet of paper listing all the requirements. One of them was police clearance. She couldn't qualify because she'd been arrested for prostitution. She had passed the TB test but not serology because she had VD. She hadn't paid her taxes. There were other minor problems, but those were the big ones.

There was nothing to do but present our findings to the senator and congressman and hope the young man would console himself with a sweet young thing back home.

The four-story apartment building where we lived on the third floor was built in the shape of a ladder. The two outside parts contained the apartments, and the joining "rungs" were the stairways and elevators. There were airshafts onto which the bathrooms were connected, and on occasion if conditions were just right, conversations in any of the seven other bathrooms on a unit could be heard quite clearly. We were very careful about what we said.

Early one morning while Kedar was still in the States, I went into the bathroom half-asleep, but I came fully awake at the sound of loud, angry voices. A woman was screaming and crying, and a man shouted, "No, you can't do that. Now just calm down. I said you can't go, and that's final." There was a pause and I thought the fight was over.

"No, Mamma, no," a man yelled. There followed a very loud bang and dead silence.

A pistol shot? A door slamming? I didn't know, but I was terrified that somebody had been hurt. Frightened but curious, too, and not wanting to be a target, I crept out to the balcony off the living room to see if I could find out what was going on. Nobody was shooting, so I stood up and looked around. On the driveway three floors below lay a woman in pajamas. A man in his bathrobe ran out and knelt beside her. Within minutes an ambulance arrived. They placed her on a stretcher, put her in the vehicle, and drove away.

Word spread quickly. By 7:30 a.m. when I boarded the minibus to work, all were talking about the Korean woman who had fallen to her death from a fourth-floor balcony.

I listened to the conversation of those who knew the couple. They married when he was stationed with USAID in Korea twenty years earlier. They had several children in school in the States, and she was deeply concerned about one of them. She wanted to go to help that child, and her husband was saying "no." She had also been drinking a lot and was given to fits of temper and extravagant spending.

Orientals, particularly if they are not Christians, often consider suicide an acceptable solution for a difficult situation. If she had been drinking, her decision to end it all was predictable.

They always investigated deaths of this sort, so I felt I should speak to the authorities. The one most likely to be accused if anybody thought there had been a murder was the husband, and I truly believed he was innocent.

When I got to the office I called the MPs and told them I had some knowledge of the accident that took the life of a woman at 259 Trung Quok Yung. Within minutes three officers arrived at my door. It felt a strange to be closely questioned, but I could tell them only what I had overheard and the conclusions I had drawn. They left as quickly as they had come,

I was pleased to learn that the death was called a suicide and the husband cleared of any suspicion. Shortly thereafter he was transferred to another post.

Kedar started smoking as a teenager. It wasn't considered dangerous at that time. He began with a pipe–he thought it looked very sophisticated, but soon switched to cigarettes. When I met him in 1940 on the way to college, he was smoking two packs of Camels a day.

During World War II free cigarettes were given by the millions to men serving in the armed forces. The smell of smoke became a permanent part of our life. It hung in the air, permeated the draperies, our clothes, everything. It was the same in the majority of American homes.

For years Kedar had a "smoker's cough". In spite of it he was very healthy, hardly ever missing a day of work. In 1969 when we were in Springfield, Missouri, visiting Molly and her husband, Harwood Sturtevant, he X-rayed our chests and found something a little "irregular" with Kedar's film. He advised that it be checked out by our family physician.

Kedar was unemployed at the time, and he felt well, so we did nothing about it. In 1971 he was hired by the U.S. Department of State to go to Saigon with USAID. Before departing we both went through thorough physical examinations and received clean bills of health. We thought that whatever it was that Harwood saw on the X-ray must have corrected itself or wasn't of any great significance. We were just glad to have a good job and to be on our way again!

In 1972 I became concerned with Kedar's cough. It was a constant problem, particularly the first thing in the morning. He jokingly said that he was reacting to his toothpaste. I finally talked him into going to the embassy doctor. On the side I urged the doctor to order a chest X-ray, which he did. I began to wonder if this "irregularity" Harwood had seen a year earlier needed attention.

As Kedar and I pushed through the swinging doors into the X-ray department of the Fifth Field Hospital, Saigon, I had a strange feeling that our lives would be forever changed from that moment on. Indeed, the examination showed that the aorta didn't go straight up as it should but was making a half circle around an obstruction. Within a week arrangements were made for Kedar to go to Bangkok for further examination, and I would follow if surgery was indicated.

We called Harwood right away and asked him to mail to us the X-rays he'd taken so the doctors would have some basis of comparison. They arrived two days after Kedar departed for Bangkok. I called the office that schedules the routine Saigon-Pnompenh-Bangkok flights. "May I beg a favor," I said.

"Sure, what can we do for you," came the answer. I explained the situation.

"Would it be possible to take them tomorrow morning?"

"Glad to oblige," they said, "and they will be hand-carried to the hospital as soon as we land in Bangkok." As the plane left Cambodia, it received ground fire from "unfriendlies" which shot away about a third of its right wing! The sturdy little plane kept going. Fortunately, it was not far from Bangkok, and literally landed on a "wing and a prayer." As promised the film was rushed to the hospital. The doctors had it in their hands fifteen minutes before they met to decide on Kedar's treatment. It looks

A Tale of Two Bamboos

like the Lord really did want them to have that bit of information.

None of the tests gave positive information on the "things," so open chest surgery was recommended. I flew to Bangkok the day before it was scheduled.

Kedar was very upbeat figuring nothing could be any worse than the bronchoscope he had endured the day before which left him with a low pitched, hoarse voice. It was before the day of fiber optic devices the patient could swallow without distress. His was the old fashioned kind– a round, rigid tube that was forced down the throat.

"I wondered who these hefty men were standing against the wall dressed in green gowns and caps," he said, "but I found out when I was asked to lie on the table on my back with my head over the edge. They held me down while the doctors rammed the instrument down my throat. It was extremely painful and frightening. I couldn't breathe. I was sure I'd die."

The operation was the first thing in the morning. I was on hand to see him being wheeled into the operating theater and waited to see the surgeon when it was over. I had a peek at Kedar before going into the doctor's office. He was still asleep, and looked just fine.

As kindly as he could, the surgeon told me that they had found a malignant tumor on Kedar's bronchus right at the point where it branches off to the right and left lungs. It was not possible to remove the tumor, but that they had hung some little staples on either side so that in the future it could be easily identified during treatment.

I was perfectly calm as he talked to me. I remember feeling the wood at the edge of the desk with my hands. It was polished and smooth. The desk was real, I was real, but nothing the doctor was saying had anything to do with Kedar or me. He was talking about somebody else, not us. Kedar was fine. I had just seen him. The doctor was saying things that would profoundly affect the people involved, but it had nothing to do with us.

I thanked him and went to the snack bar to get a cup of coffee and something to munch on. I wasn't hungry or thirsty, but it was just something to do until Kedar would be awake and we could talk. I found a seat and watched people as they entered the lobby below. Everything was so normal. Women came in leading children by the hand, or carrying babies in their arms. Others were leaving having had their appointments. People were busy. They had a lot to do. They were coming and going. As I watched, my coffee grew cold, my snack was tasteless, and a deep pain began to spread. There was no longer anything "normal" about my life, about our life! Kedar had cancer that they couldn't get rid of. I had read the statistics. What were they for those involving the lungs? Two percent? Yes. For those who had that kind, only 2 percent would survive for five years. Kedar was strong and had enjoyed good health all his life, but those were lousy numbers, and they were talking about us!

Suddenly the full impact of it all hit me. The dam broke, the flood came, and I was helpless. As I struggled to control my tears, a nurse walked by and noticed my difficulty. She urged me to come into her office where I could have a little privacy, and that was good, but soon even that was not enough. I needed someplace where I could be completely alone. Bless her, she found an empty bedroom where I could lie down, closed the door, and hung up a "Do not disturb" sign.

I cried, I prayed, and cried some more. There was no way I could stop it. Wave after wave of grief overcame me, and when I thought I had nothing left to cry with, another flood washed over me. Everything I had loved and counted on was crumbling around me. Since Kedar's sobriety a year before, we had grown closer than I had ever thought possible. I had the best of everything with that man, and now God was going to take him away from me. How could I face life without him? He was the center of my life. Without him all I could see was a deep, dark hole, and I was about to fall into it. All I could pray was, Oh, God, help me. Please help me! I felt no peace. I knew that feelings have very little to do with reality. They come and go without my consent, but I did know that my Heavenly Father was always true to His word, and that although I knew nothing but unspeakable pain, I could give it all to Him, and He would carry me through this valley. I remembered what He'd said, "Trust me, Fran. Just trust me." I clung His words with all my life. If this was not the truth, nothing in the world mattered. I slept.

Within the week Kedar was strong enough for us to return to Saigon for a few days on our way to the States for radiation therapy. I was given a round-trip ticket to accompany him as his "non-medical attendant." As soon as he was settled and established in his routine, I was to return.

Two nights before departing for home, Charles Long, the pastor of the International Church, called us. He is a missionary with the Christian and Missionary Alliance who had served for many years in their Bible School in Cam Ran Bay. Because of the war and the city's occupation by the U.S. and Vietnamese Army, they were sent to live and work in a safer place.

We had come to know the Longs quite well, and were fascinated with tales of their experiences with the new Christians, the Montainyards in particular. Theirs was such a new and unhindered faith that they believed what they read in the Bible without question. As a result they saw many miracles of all kinds, particularly healing the sick, many of whom were completely healed when Charlie prayed for them.

The hour was late, and soon everybody had to be home because of the curfew, but Charlie asked if we would like to have a prayer for Kedar's healing. He needed to ask only once! I got some oil from the kitchen. We knelt, he anointed Kedar's forehead, laid his hands on his head and prayed. It was not a long prayer. He got to his feet, gathered his things, wished us a safe trip, and left.

I knew a man named Chuck Motley in Washington, D.C. He, too, had the gift of healing. At the Church of the Saviour I had seen with my own eyes a woman's severe curvature of the spine healed in a moment. The dress she wore, which was fitted to accommodate her twisted back, suddenly hung strangely on her straight frame! Remembering this, I called Chuck as soon as I could and set up an appointment for him to see Kedar and me.

After making us comfortable, Chuck asked about Kedar's illness, and said that before he did anything he needed to ask some questions.

"I have given up healing as a full-time ministry," he said. "It was wonderful to see so many restored to health and energy, but most were sick again within a short time. I have found that those suffering with cancer have a problem with unforgiveness of somebody very close to them–spouse, a parent or child." Then he turned to Kedar and asked, "Do you have any area of unforgiveness of somebody in your family?" Think carefully. This is very important."

"I can't think of anyone," Kedar said, "except for a fellow Marine who jumped into my fox hole in the Solomon Islands during WWII, leaving me exposed to enemy fire," Kedar said. "That was the only person I can think of that I haven't forgiven."

As gently and kindly as he could Chuck said he could not pray for Kedar's healing unless and until he could forgive completely. I was devastated because I immediately figured that I was the culprit. I had been pressing him for months to give up smoking, but he was just not able to do so. He was completely helpless in his addiction to tobacco.

The daily radiation therapy was difficult. Kedar was in good spirits and was most optimistic, but he was having a lot of burning on his back, and had no appetite whatso-

A Tale of Two Bamboos

ever. These would be hard days, but worth it when he was cured.

Kedar urged me to get back to my work in Saigon. I went to the State Department travel section to make reservations for the trip, stopping off in Great Falls, Montana, for a quick visit with Anne, Gery, and Lisa, then on to Seattle and an overnight in Fairbanks, Alaska, to catch to New York-to-Tokyo flight early the following morning.

I survived a couple of stand-bys in getting to Seattle then ran into trouble. I was booked on Pan Am all the way, but the flight from Seattle to Fairbanks was a domestic, and the ticket showed I should be on an international flight. We discussed, argued, consulted schedules, and pulled our hair until finally the clerk decided to get me on the domestic flight. My relief lasted until they asked what hotel I was registered for in Fairbanks. I gave her the name, whereupon she told me it had burned down the previous winter! I could just see myself sitting in the airport all night, but she was able to get a room in another hotel. I began to wonder about the information the State Department travel office was getting!

All was set when we departed Seattle until we had engine trouble a half-hour out and returned for another plane. What next, I wondered, but from then on the trip went without incident.

Charlie gave me a call when I got back. He apologized for having left so quickly after praying for Kedar, but I had thought nothing of it.

"I have prayed for the healing of many people, but that was the first time I had such an experience," he went on. "As I prayed, a deep chill went through me that left me so drained it took all my strength to just get to my feet and speak. I was completely spent. It lasted for several hours and was so strange that I asked the Lord to reveal to me what it meant. During the night the answer came. 'Kedar will come to the place where he will give all honor and glory to God, and he will be healed, but it will take a long, long time'." That thought comforted me. The battle would be a tough one, but Kedar was going to be healed. Praise God!

Our first boat was a twenty-one foot cabin cruiser in Hong Kong. In Thailand we bought a nineteen-foot Lightning. We were bitten. A vague wish to own a larger boat evolved into the hope of actually buying one on which we could live and sail the seven seas. Boating people were the greatest, and the joy of sailing, regardless of tough times when we were in trouble, convinced us to make life on the water a big part of our future plans.

On the Eastern Shore of Maryland we haunted yards making ferrule cement boats. Sound impossible? Barges of that construction made during WW I are still in use, and very practical, too. If a bottom is "holed," all it takes is a little chicken wire and cement to make it good as new. Slow but steady, with the best price, perhaps that was what we should investigate.

The search for just the right one continued as we avidly read boatyard announcements. Before departing for Vietnam we spotted a builder in Thailand and wrote to the owner. At the first opportunity we flew to Bangkok and found Terry Allen's thriving business up a klong just outside the city. He, too, was building ferrule cement boats of several sizes and designs. For forty thousand dollars we could have a fifty-foot motor-sailor, small enough to qualify for Lloyd's of London insurance and not too big for the two of us to handle. We had found our boat, and we were excited.

Two months later we made another trip to Bangkok with our four-hundred-dollar blueprints from Australia and money for the first payment. As work progressed over the months, reports and statements arrived frequently. When the initial funds had been exhausted, we dispatched yet another check. Terry gave us a list of fittings we could have sent from the States by APO. He'd order the mast from Australia and a Perkiness engine from England. It would be grand to sail home, but neither of us was a seasoned yachtsman, so we decided to ship our prize to Baltimore.

The hull was finished, cured, and had five coats of fiberglass before Kedar was diagnosed with inoperable cancer. In a flash all our plans lay dead in the water. We couldn't continue, and according to our contract with Terry Allen, in spite of all we had paid so far, the boat was his. We were disappointed but not crushed. Our whole attention was directed toward Kedar's treatment, and we hoped, a cure.

Chapter 14

USA

Kedar returned to Saigon looking wonderful. He'd lost a few pounds, the cough was gone, and the radiation burns on his chest and back faded quickly. His energy was high, but darn it, he was still smoking! I could hardly believe it. His favorite brand was unfiltered Camels, the strongest you can buy. I kept telling myself I was not this doctor, and no amount of begging on my part ever got me anywhere.

Kedar's replacement was due in six weeks, so he picked up where he'd left off; and I gave notice that we'd be leaving in early January. Christmas in Saigon was always festive with thousands celebrating in the streets, but the New Year came with the announcement of more troop withdrawals. We were glad to be leaving while there was time to depart in an orderly fashion.

We broke the trip in Hong Kong to walk memory lane, see a few friends, and shop. Kedar was usually careful in his spending but he wanted the things he used every day to be the best. He bought a new camera and insisted the Leica on sale at twelve hundred dollars was a bargain. Couldn't prove it by me. I was beyond arguing and bit my tongue when he also bought a solid gold DuPont lighter, a gold Cross pen and pencil set engraved with "Kedar", and a gold Patek Philippe watch. I breathed a sigh of relief when we boarded the plane for the States.

He was due to begin work in the Rosslyn office of USAID within a month. Mother and Dad Bryan found a nice three-room apartment for us in Arlington Towers just across the street, and as soon as we were settled I went job-hunting. There were three to choose from, and because of its location I took the one with the USDA Forest Service in the building next to Kedar's.

He had regular visits to the Georgetown University Hospital doctors and all was well. The tumor was greatly reduced, and in fact at one time it couldn't be found. Things were definitely looking up.

"Let's find our boat," Kedar urged. We attended boat shows, haunted marinas and checked out those for sale but nothing triggered a "yes" until we went aboard a thirty-five-foot *Rasmus* from Sweden. It was much like the *Sailor Star,* but this time I agreed it was our dream come true. It had a center cockpit, fore and aft cabins, the usual head, galley, and salon, with the interior beautifully crafted in mahogany.

Aboard the *Kedarnath*

We didn't own the boat; it owned us! Everything we did was related to the *Kedarnath*, which means Kedar's Place. We signed up for power squadron courses and attended them three nights a week from 6:00 to 9:00 p.m. We started at the beginning and went straight through, one after the other.

We rented a slip at the end of 2nd St. in Annapolis, Maryland, and as instruction continued we felt comfortable in taking trips farther and farther afield.

When we began studying marine electronics I knew I was in for a challenge. I didn't understand anything, not even the terms used such as "base vs. noble metals." What the heck were they, but as they say, "The only stupid questions are the ones you don't ask." So I asked and asked and asked some more. The instructor was very good in making everything clear.

We had a fifteen-minute break half way through the evening. I had to laugh because so many men came to thank me for getting answers they needed, but didn't dare raise their hands for fear of looking stupid. It provoked Kedar no end because I usually made better grades on the tests than he did, but then I worked harder too.

We learned all about the sudden, sharp storms in the bay. The water is so shallow that when a strong wind blows up suddenly it turns the water into a boiling caldron, and it's scary. One Sunday afternoon we were on our way home after an overnight on the Eastern Shore and stopped in a pretty little bay to have lunch and a swim. Several other boats were nearby. It was a picture of peace and tranquillity when all of a sudden the sky turned black, the wind whipped up huge waves, and the air sizzled with lightning and crashing thunder. We put out a second anchor, thanked the Lord for the lightning rod at the top of the mast, then huddled together in the cabin while we were tossed around like a toy in a bathtub. It was over in fifteen minutes, but it was exciting while it lasted.

After a few months we found a small marina on the Patuxent River where the rent was reasonable, and the owner, a retired marine sergeant, kept a keen eye on our boat while we were away. Other renters became good friends, and we'd frequently sail out together for a weekend of exploring the bay and raft-up together at night. That's where we met Buddy and Sarah (pronounced Sa-rah) Newman, who'd lived all their lives on the bay and knew everything about it, including folklore going back to the beginning of time. Buddy knew all the knots and helped me tie them correctly; he also gave me a pipe and taught me how to blow it when we were making the turn in the river to alert Dave (the owner) that we were coming in and could probably use a little help getting berthed, especially if there was a crosswind.

I learned how to catch big crabs too. It was easiest the first thing in the morning when they were resting on the pilings; if they were "doublers" that was even better, especially at night with a bright light on the water. Dave provided a pen to keep them until we were ready to cook them.

Some days we'd spend hours and hours polishing and fixing (that's what you do when you have a boat) and at about five o'clock Dave called out, "Miss Fran and Capt'n Kedar, come on up for some hush puppies and crab." That was an invitation we could never refuse. M-m-m.

Jim and Donna, who were living in Delaware, frequently came for the weekend and thoroughly enjoyed life on the bay. I showed her how to catch the crabs then went over to chat with Sa-rah. Donna was a quick learner and soon had some huge blues. Holding a big one by the back fin she came over to show it to us.

"That's a beauty," I said, tapping it on the shell. Out came the claws which had been folded in.

"Don't wake it up," she exclaimed, almost dropping it, but the crab couldn't get to her hand, so she held on tight and dumped him into the cage. After a day with her on the boat, we had a bounteous evening feast.

In the spring of 1974 Kedar's tumor began to grow again. It was wrapped around the bronchial tube. It finally penetrated and continued growing inside. At first it was only a minor irritation, but before long he was having trouble breathing, which was more than a little frightening.

Kedar'd had all the radiation he could take, so he was admitted to Georgetown University Hospital for further evaluation.

"Please come in this evening," Dr. Katz said. "We need to talk about your husband's treatment options."

Hunkey was in town and agreed to go with me. It was another one of those times when I felt detached from reality. Kedar, Hunkey, and I sat in a lounge and listened to the doctor. He was saying some pretty awful things about his prospects and the best hope for his future, but I couldn't relate it to us. Every day, every week, the news was of a new breakthrough in the treatment of cancer. Surely one of them would be just what Kedar needed. At the last moment he was going to be snatched from death, restored to perfect health and vigor, and by golly, we'd sail around the world!

After a while we took Kedar back to his room. He was tired, so we kissed him good night, tucked him in, and returned to talk with Dr. Katz.

"I'm sorry," he said, "but his prognosis is very poor. We keep trying all sorts of drugs, but more and more it is believed that the best cure is to build up the immune systems so that the body can fight off the disease. That is the greatest hope for the future.

"I recommend that your husband be moved to the Veteran's Hospital. They work closely with the NIH and have the latest information on all possible treatments. They will carefully follow his case. He's a veteran, isn't he?" he asked.

"Yes, but he's been out of the service for years. I don't know if he's eligible or not," I answered. We have a friend in the House, and I'll see if he can help us."

"Good, good," he answered, "and Mrs. Bryan, when you're with your husband, don't hold your feelings in so tightly that he doesn't know that you're hurting too. One wife comes in here every day, all smiles and laughter, and her poor husband thinks she doesn't care at all that he's sick."

"I understand," I answered. "He knows how much I love him, and I'll be honest with my feelings without making them too much of a burden for him."

We thanked Dr. Katz, shook his hand, and peeked into Kedar's room before we left. He was sound asleep. We went out the door on the second floor and were going down the outside stairs to the parking lot when all of a sudden the full impact of the evening hit me and I was overcome with grief. I clung to the railing, unable to move as a primal cry from deep within my soul surged up and gave voice to my agony. Hunkey urged me to move on, but I couldn't. She stood there holding me while it poured out. People passed us, but I was all alone with my sister. All I could cry was, "No, no, no!"

Utterly drained, we made our way back to the car and drove home in silence. At the apartment Hunkey undressed me, put me in a warm shower then tucked me into bed. I knew nothing until the sun filled the room with light and warmth. It was a workday, so I called in to let them know I wouldn't be there. Fortunately my boss was on a trip, and I'd not be greatly missed.

Not wanting to delay Kedar's move to the VA hospital, I put a call through to John Jarman's office at the House, asking if he could meet me in Kedar's room in the Georgetown University Hospital. His secretary arranged a late-afternoon appointment, and he showed up right on time. Man alive if he wasn't the best looking thing in long pants I'd ever seen! Although we'd never been to Oklahoma we claimed him as our congressman. I told him of Kedar's needs.

"But we'll need help to get him in. Do you think you could pull a few strings? It's pretty full, and perhaps others will have priority over Kedar."

"Don't you worry," he answered. "I'll get on it the first thing in the morning."

That settled, I had to ask him about his switch from the Democratic to the Republican party.

"Ruth taught me everything I know about politics," I said, "and you two were staunch Democrats. She'd role over in her grave if she knew you were a Republican. What in the world made you change?"

"It wasn't easy," he answered, "but I had to leave the party I'd served in for many years because they are totally irresponsible with the nation's treasure. For too long they've had a majority in the House, and if something isn't done to stop them, they'll spend us into bankruptcy. I had to try to shift the weight a little in an effort to bring about fiscal soundness." I wanted to stand up and cheer, but poor Ruth! What would she have said?

John was as good as his word and called the next day with the news that Kedar was to be admitted to the Washington, D. C. VA hospital in two days. It was a long hike to the other side of town, but without doubt it was the best place for him; and we were grateful.

Every day I went straight from work to the hospital and stayed until 10:00 p.m. There was no time limit for those visiting cancer patients, but I needed my rest for another working day. At that time of the night the parking lot was nearly empty, so I always asked a guard to walk me to my car. He stayed right there until I was locked in and on my way. As soon as I got back I called the nurse's station. They let Kedar know I was safely home. It was a routine he counted on.

Kedar was able to be up a good share of the time and came home for weekends.

Jim and Donna drove down as often as they could, and we went out overnight on the boat and sailed with

Buddy's help. Kedar was more realistic about his condition than I. All I wanted was to be with him and suggested I quit my job, but he was vehemently against it.

"Absolutely not," he said. "The day will come when you'll need a reason to get up in the morning, so whatever you do, don't give up your job."

I could see that every week he was losing ground but refused to believe he was dying. After all, didn't the Lord show Chuck Long he'd be completely healed and totally give his heart to the Lord, but that it would take a long, long time? Weren't new cures for cancer being discovered almost every day? Surely one would be just right for him.

Anne, Gery, and the children were stationed at Clark AFB in the Philippines. She wrote that they could afford for her to come home for a week's visit, so I told her to come as soon as possible. She was able to stay with Kedar during the day, which was great; and that weekend we went for one of Kedar's last sails on the bay. Jim and Donna came, too, as did Edwin and Peggy from Baltimore. I made a point of stopping whatever I was doing, even for a moment, and soaking up the blessing of being together, seeing him and the kids, talking and joking. My eyes feasted on them. My heart ached but was still full of hope. It was the last time we were all together.

Our last sail together

In his final six weeks Kedar told me stories of little things in his childhood that bothered him. It was almost as if he was dealing with troubling memories and confessing them. Again and again he said, "My life would have been so different if only my mother had lived." I didn't understand it, but the repetition made me wonder.

The last story he told was of a time the family was summering in Pei Tai Ho in northern China. Shanghai in the twenties and thrities wasn't blessed with air conditioning, so in July and August families fled to the mountains or seashore to escape the deadly heat and humidity. The village market was much like a flea market with stalls offering numerous wares, many of them hanging, making good places to hide.

Kedar, age seven and Peggy, four, decided to shop one Saturday morning after receiving their weekly allowance. Kedar spent his right away; then as they continued to browse, asked Peggy to buy him a cold drink.

"No, Kadie," she protested, "you had your own money. This is mine."

"Oh, come on," he coaxed, "I'm thirsty. Do you want me to stay here with you, or shall I just leave you and go home?"

"Course not, but this in my money and I want to buy something." When her back was turned he slipped away from her and hid in the middle of some hanging merchandise. She went on a step or two before realizing he was no longer with her.

"Kadie, where are you! Please don't hide from me. I'm afraid. Please, please, Kadie, come back and stay with me!" She wandered from stall to stall looking for him, but he remained hidden.

"I'm afraid, Kadie. Please come out and I'll buy you a drink, I promise." With that he jumped out and with a big grin held out his hand for the money.

"There she stood, poor little thing," he said, "with the tears running down her face. I felt like such a bully, but I let her buy the drink for me. I'm so sorry I did that to her."

Almost daily he told me things he was thinking about.

"Will you please wear my favorite peach-colored dress," he asked, "and the good pearls I bought you, not the cheap ones? I want to think of you all day tomorrow in that dress, wearing those pearls and high heels. Will you do that for me?"

"A little dressy for the office," I said, "but of course I will."

"When I hear your step in the hall I think of a peanut," he said another time as I sat beside his bed reading the mail.

"My goodness, why a peanut?"

"Because that's how we fit together, perfectly, just like two halves of a peanut."

A week before he died, Kedar came home for a while. Sitting up in the car was agony. It was hard for him to breathe unless he was in a certain position on his left side. Mother and Dad Bryan were driving us in their car, and I sat in the back with him. As we approached Key Bridge he gasped for air.

"I don't know if I can make it or not," he said. "It's so hard to breathe."

"We're almost there," I said, "hang on and we'll be home in a few minutes." He didn't say anything more, but the struggle was for his very life. When we stopped in the garage by the door to the hall on the level with our apartment, he got out quickly. I took one of his arms and Mother took the other, and I was surprised at how fast he moved. When we entered the hall he shook both of us off and lay down on the carpeted floor.

"What can I do for you, Honey," I said, kneeling beside him.

"I just have to stay here for a little," he gasped. "Just let me rest." I hurried the few feet to our door. Two or three young men were coming toward us, so I asked if they could assist us.

"He's quite ill," I said, indicating Kedar there on the floor. "Would you please help me get him into our apartment?"

"Glad to," they said as they lifted him in his prone position, carried him into our apartment, and laid him on the bed. Normally I don't ask favors of complete strangers, but this time I didn't hesitate.

"Thanks so much," I said as they left.

"No problem. Glad to help," they said, waved, and were gone.

As soon as he was settled we brought in a big bagfull of pills to take, the schedule, and all the paraphernalia that accompanied him every time he came home. Several weeks earlier a tracheotomy had been performed to ease his breathing. The hospital provided me with a suction device on a stand to keep it clean and clear, along with a supply of sterile tubes to use and discard and a box of disposable latex gloves to wear during the procedure. Another large apparatus delivered cold vapor to the opening in his neck to ease his breathing, supplied from a bottle of distilled water. I was amazed that each time we brought him home, all that equipment was supplied to us at no cost, and it was brand new. When I return it at the end of the weekend it was dumped into a large plastic container. I wondered if they tossed it out, and if so, what a terrible waste of money. That stuff had to be expensive.

"Fran," Kedar said after we'd set everything up, "get a note pad and pen. There are some things I want you to write down." Years before, I'd turned over all family finances to him and kept completely out of it. It worked best for us that way, but now he needed to tell me where everything was. He listed bank accounts, and the name and address of the manager of our portfolio. He wanted me to know what I needed to do when he died. I took it all down, but even faced with the evidence of his illness I was in denial. I just knew that a wonder cure would come in time for him. It had to. I believed it with my whole heart.

After Kedar'd had a little nap, he called and asked me sit close to him. He patted the bed and moved over a little to make room for me.

"I have something to tell you," he said, "and I think it's important." It was another of those moments frozen in time. I can clearly see the dress I was wearing, the blue flowered apron, and the dust cloth I had in my hand.

"Last Wednesday afternoon I had a vision," he said.

"Oh, you had a vivid dream?" I asked.

"No it wasn't a dream, it was different," he insisted. I was transported to outer space. All around it was light blue, like the heart of a glacier. I saw my body. It was in a sitting position but wasn't sitting on anything. I was over and above the body that was bright and shining. Then it shifted a bit, like the leg of a chair shipping off the edge of a rug onto the floor, and I was in that body; I was warm. There was no more pain, and I knew I was right where I belonged. What do you think it means?"

"Well, I don't know," I answered. "I'll have to think about it," but I did know and wasn't ready to accept it. I think he did too. The vision was very precious to him, and I heard him retell it several times, word for word. The last time was to Gordon Cosby when he came to see Kedar in the hospital two days before he died.

Early Saturday morning Jim and Donna came, and we spent the day with Kedar. By this time he'd been moved into a private room, another step toward the end. He was restless and couldn't get comfortable.

"If it's not going to get any better than this," he remarked, "then I don't want to go on. It's too hard."

"Oh, honey," I said smoothing his hair back from his face, "I know it's tough, but who knows what the NIH will have for you when they come on Monday? It might be just the thing they've been looking for. Hang in there. Remember that Chuck Long said you would be completely healed."

Before leaving for the night I put several notices up on the door and the wall giving the phone numbers where we could be reached in case he had a bad night. Confident that he'd be fine, we left for some Chinese food at our favorite restaurant. A plate of jaud-za and a bowl of rice could cure nearly anything.

September 8 was a beautiful bright morning, and we were all set to leave for worship at the Church of the Saviour in Washington, but thought I'd call the hospital and check on how Kedar'd done during the night.

"He's had a very hard time of it," the nurse answered, "and is quite apprehensive." I didn't wait any longer to ask if she hadn't seen the request I'd put up all over his room to be called, but told the kids to hurry, we had to get there quickly. With little traffic we crossed town in record time. Jim pulled up at the front door. I was out and running before he stopped.

The nurses were just leaving after giving him a bath and putting on a fresh gown, but already it was soaked with sweat. His breathing was labored, his eyes were wild, and he thrashed from side to side as he gasped for air. I felt sick with anguish just looking at him. He extended his hand when he saw me and we held on to each other while he struggled to survive. After the doctor came to check on Kedar I went with him into the hall.

"Isn't there something you can do to ease his suffering,?" I asked.

"If I gave him anything at all," he answered, "it would probably result in immediate death. He's only semiconscious because he's getting so little oxygen, but he's really not suffering all that much. The body puts up a huge fight, but he's not in as much agony as it appears. We expend about 2 percent of our energy to breathe. He's using about 98 percent of his. It's only a matter of a short time now. Go on in there and be with him." So saying, he patted me gently on the back, and I went. Soon Jim and Donna joined me.

"Take off my watch," Kedar said. I wanted to resist, telling him he'd need it when we left, but I didn't.

"It'll be right here in the drawer," I said slipping it off his wrist. In a few minutes he grew quiet, taking a deep breath every few minutes. His eyes were closed and I could feel that his hands were growing cold. I knew from what I'd read that he'd be able to hear me until the very end, so I talked to him.

"Honey," I said, "I want you to know how precious you've been to me all the nearly thirty-two years we've had together. Nobody could have been a better, more loving husband than you, and I cherish every thing about you. Please forgive me for the times I've made you angry or disappointed. I'm so sorry. You've been so good to me, never raising your voice or getting rough. What a tender, passionate lover you are, and I'm going to miss you terribly."

Donna talked to him too, kissing him on the cheek and holding his hand.

"Honey," I said, remembering his vision, "You've already seen your new body. Now you can go and collect it. Tell Jesus how much we love Him, then see Mother and Daddy and your mother, hug and kiss them for me. Find my precious friend Ruth and tell her how much I've missed her."

I was so caught up in what was just ahead for him that I was full of joyful anticipation. All of us were crying, laughing, and talking.

"Dad," Jim said, "you've been a wonderful father. I hope that if I'm fortunate enough to have a son, I'll be half as good a dad as you've been. I know I've given you a lot of grief, but I appreciate your patience, and I ask your forgiveness for the times I've disappointed you." He reached over and put his hand on Kedar's head.

"Take Jesus' hand," he said, "and walk over to the other side. It will be so easy." Kedar took one last breath and was gone.

Good-bye, precious one.

Edward Kedar Bryan 1921-1974

Chapter 15

Widow

Kedar died at 12:00 noon on Sunday, September 8, 1974. This date, a cold fact, refused to stick in my mind as I signed papers, responding as a robot to requirements of the moment. Was it "8/9/74" or "9/8/74?" I couldn't seem to get it right.

Hunkey came to see me through the next few days. She made me drink a lot of water, eat, and sleep. She kept track of phone calls, food that was delivered, who sent it, and a thousand other tasks.

She went with me to the hospital to receive the post-mortem report.

"We expected to find the cancer metastasized all through his body but it was not so," the doctor said. "There was just one tumor about the size of your thumb, and it was all in the wrong place."

The memorial service was conducted by Gordon Cosby at the Church of the Saviour. The sanctuary was filled with friends and family, who said many kind, comforting things to me; then it was over. I felt empty.

Although I had known for the past three months that he was dying, I had still clung desperately to the hope, even the belief, that some miracle would happen. But it didn't. Kedar was gone. I guess that is what they mean when they say, "He was healed on the other side of Jordan."

For weeks after his death, I moved through a daily routine without effort. It was almost as if I were detached from the real world. I went to the Forest Service office and did my job. I packed Kedar's clothes and gave them away. I wrote thank you notes to those who donated to the cancer fund on his behalf and sent food. I completed a myriad other tasks without thinking, without feeling. Once in the office Ruth, a fellow secretary, told a joke, and when I heard myself laughing I thought, it really does happen. One day it will be normal rather than unusual. It felt good.

Seventeen days after the funeral I had a call from Edwin's mother-in-law, who managed the building where he had an apartment. He and Peggy were separated; he was struggling with alcoholism and depression, stumbling from one episode to another.

"Ed's a basket case," she said, "and needs to be in a hospital. Is there any way you can help him?"

"I'll get there as quickly as I can," I said. "I'll see if my brother can come with me." Jim could, and in fifteen minutes we were on our way.

A very strange thing happened: the heavy weight suddenly lifted from my chest and the dull ache at the back of my head was gone. I could leave my sorrow behind and focus on Edwin, and it was liberating, almost like getting a new lease on life.

I had never seen him in such bad shape and thanked God Jim was there to help. An official at the national headquarters of the American Red Cross, he knew the buttons to push and strings to pull to get Edwin into Johns Hopkin's Hospital psychiatric unit. What a relief! For the moment he was safe. I'd worry about his future another day.

A Tale of Two Bamboos

On the way home we stopped for a burger and coffee. When Jim eased out in traffic he was a little late in making a left turn and we were hit on the back, left fender by the car that had the right-of-way. Both cars were operable, so we exchanged insurance information and went on our way. I suffered whiplash that didn't hurt much that night, but oh, the next morning! Ouch.

I drove over to see Edwin three to four times a week after work and on weekends. After a couple of days of good food and no alcohol he looked wonderful. The nurses began to count on him to help them with other patients who were difficult to control. We had lots of time to talk, and he shared his determination to go back to school to prepare for counseling. He wasn't cut out to be a captain of industry or in the military. He had a gentle spirit, and I always thought he should have been born a girl. After three weeks he was released into my custody, and I drove him to a halfway house on a farm near Quantico, Virginia, where he had a place to live, work, attend AA meetings, and get on his feet again.

It was the first of many false starts. Without fail, as soon as he was on his own he was able to get an entry-level job, earn a few dollars, and find the nearest ABC store.

Once he contacted the doctor who'd treated him at Johns Hopkins and convinced him he needed Valium to deal with stress and depression. That man needs to go back to school and learn about alcoholism! He gave Edwin a big bottle of the pills and guess what? Cheap wine was all he needed, so he got a supply and was off and running.

I was almost as bad. He was able to convince me several times that if I'd loan him rent money for one month he would pay it back in no time because he could get a good job once he had a roof over his head. Well, I needed to go to school, too.

I lived for open AA meetings on Friday and Saturday nights where speakers told of their fall into that deep, dark hole. When they'd had enough, with the help of friends, AA, and a few swift kicks in the pants, they found sobriety and lived happy, productive lives, one day at a time. If it could happen for them, surely it could for Edwin, too.

I was beginning to believe life wouldn't be so hard after all, when suddenly the bottom fell out of my world. I was in church. I don't remember the subject of the sermon, but somehow the reality of Kedar's death, my total and complete separation from him became real. I was devastated. Tears coursed down my face as silent sobs shook me. I tried telling myself, now this is enough. Don't do it here. Dry up and listen to the sermon. I wiped my eyes and blew my nose. I bit the inside of my cheek to focus on something else, but it didn't work. The dam had broken, and there was no way I could stop the flood. I went through every Kleenex in my pockets and purse. Finally I didn't possess another dry thing except a scarf, yet still the tears came.

At the end of the service I covered my face and fled. I wept most of that day. As my mourning had finally begun, so had my climb out of the mindless grief I'd been living in. I didn't expect that those who professed to love me most would be those who kept me chained to that mourning. I had become a widow, half of a couple, an odd person out at every gathering, and a constant reminder of life's ephemeral nature. I was shunned–politely, of course–and forced continually to realize that I was now a single in a world made up of couples. I began to feel that there was something wrong with me.

The ache for Kedar never left. I missed his voice, his beautiful smile, and, oh, the loving expression in his eyes, the way he always reached out to touch me as I passed, his ability to cheer me up even when he suffered awful pain and frustration. He was gone. He really was gone, and the thought ached in my bones. Some days the pain was so intense that I couldn't think beyond small bits of time. Five minutes was all I could manage.

I was strongly attracted to the Church of the Saviour, a unique faith community, its disciplines, and its outreach in service to the poor in our nation's capitol. Kedar and I'd always received a warm welcome, and I met several members with whom I felt a particular kinship. One of them was Jean Schnedl. We met at a Dayspring retreat several years before Kedar died. Short, a little on the plump side, bright blue eyes, and blond hair, she could be serious and reflective one moment then break you up with her humor the next. I liked her immediately, and as time passed and we had further opportunity to share experiences in classes in the School of Christian Living, I looked on her as one of my best friends.

Whereas Jean is a jubilant, effervescent person, Ed, her husband, is quiet and reserved. I categorize him as a deep thinker, not given to small talk and aimless chatter. Ed gives you the gift of his full attention, looking at you, listening, and being fully present to you. So a few months after Kedar's death when I decided to join the church and the time came to choose a sponsor, it was easy for me to ask that sensitive, gentle person to be my shepherd.

During Kedar's last month, he warned me several times to be careful not to make any big changes in my life for at least a year.

"Don't change jobs," he said. "Don't move, sell your investments, or make any major purchases. I've seen too many women make foolish mistakes in the first few months of their widowhood thinking that change would relieve their agony. They are prey to all sorts of unscrupulous people who take advantage of a time of shock and grief to fleece them of their treasure. Just sit tight," he warned me, "and carry on as normal a life as you can. Give yourself a little time."

"Normal" for me is being with people, so it wasn't long before I began inviting friends to lunch or dinner. I loved to be with those who knew Kedar and felt comforted by their happy memories of him. Almost immediately I became aware of a difference in our relationship. I couldn't quite put my finger on it, but it was there. On the surface all was fine, but the warm-hearted acceptance I had known before was gone. Almost without exception, my invitations were politely accepted but not returned. When I was invited to dinner, it was always with several other women–not with the couples we had socialized with before. Familiar, comfortable social structures were gone, and I resented being forced into the new mold of "widow." I felt inadequate, incomplete, and separated without Kedar. My friends' attitude only made it hurt more.

Ten weeks after Kedar's death, his father died. A few days later Mother Bryan reminded me I wasn't included in Dad's will. She was the beneficiary of his estate, but upon her death, it was to be divided equally among his surviving children–or in the event of the death of a child, the grandchildren in that line. The spouses of deceased children would receive nothing.

I understood the conditions of the will. It was Dad's estate, and surely he had every right to dispose of it any way he wished, but it reminded me once more that my status had changed drastically.

I loved Mother and Dad Bryan and always felt an important part of the Bryan clan. Yet now that Kedar was gone, I didn't seem to count any longer. As his wife I had a place in the family. Without him, I didn't matter. It wasn't logical, but logic didn't stop me from feeling discarded, thrown away. As Mother Bryan settled her affairs, she reminded me several more times that I would not a recipient of Kedar's share of Dad's estate. Each time it cut a little deeper.

One night when I got home from an evening of working at the Potter's House in the District, I turned on the TV for the comfort of a friendly sound. A dramatization of *Widow* was playing. I was tired so I sat down to watch it for a few minutes. The widow was frustrated and in anguish over life's difficulties.

"Sam died, but I got sent to hell," she said. It was all I needed to push me over the edge. I sat in the middle of the bed and bawled my eyes out.

The phone rang. It was Molly and Harwood in Springfield, Missouri.

"How are you doing?" they asked.

"Well, if you really want to know," I sobbed, "just horribly. I feel like I've been thrown into a deep well, the lid's been put on, and there is no way to get out."

"I'm so sorry," Molly said. "Is there anything we can do? I wish we could be there with you."

"We know it's tough," Harwood said, "but you've got to keep a stiff upper lip and know the Lord will see you through."

"Oh, for goodness sakes, Harwood," Molly exclaimed, "would you please shut up? What do you know about what she's feeling? I do, and sometimes things are so bad you can't even pray.

"Remember the time you had that last heart attack and I rushed to the hospital to be with you? I was horrified when I looked at the monitor that showed a picture of massive heart failure. You were completely relaxed, expecting to go to heaven any minute, and I was frantic with fear. I called our pastor and a special friend to come and pray for you, and they did, and you were healed; but I couldn't pray. I was too frightened. So Fran, you go to bed now and rest. We'll stay up and pray for you, okay?" They did, and I had the best sleep in months. What a wonderful sister and brother to do that for me when I was helpless with grief.

That old feeling kept cropping up again and again. I

had begun to win back some self-esteem by entering a course of study at George Mason University. But just when I was beginning to feel good about it (I knew Kedar would be proud of me), I overheard a friend in a Bible-study group remark, "I wish we could have a group of couples only. I think I'd prefer it to what we have now."

There it was again. The remark went through me like a knife. The bad feeling was there, right under the surface, and it took so little to expose it. No matter if I got ten academic degrees, I would never be a valid person again. I was a widow!

I was growing and changing, but still I was in chains. In the two-and-a-half years since Kedar died, I bought a condominium, cut my hair (a big step after wearing it long and in a bun for thirty years) started dating, joined the Church of the Saviour, and started back to college to complete my degree. All during that time the social side of my life remained difficult. I continued to feel at a frigid distance from all the friends who knew Kedar and me. They were such good friends before he died, but they kept me at arm's length afterwards, and a subtle but persistent accusation at the back of my mind suggested that there was something wrong with me. I was convinced that without Kedar, I'd never again be an acceptable person.

Some places were better than others. When I learned that Edwin was an alcoholic, I began attending Alanon and open AA meetings. There I met people I hadn't known before, and wonder of wonders, to them I seemed to be a whole person, not the sorry remains of a couple. Together we shared a common problem and the struggle for serenity within it. I yearned for such acceptance among the friends Kedar and I had shared.

Along with the Schnedles at the Church of the Saviour, I belonged to the Wednesday Night Potter's House Mission Group. We met for an hour and a half each Wednesday night for worship and sharing at the Potter's

House–a coffeehouse in the Adams-Morgan area of Washington, D.C. Then we waited tables when the doors opened to the public later in the evening. Working and worshipping together, we became a close-knit family. They helped me understand that accepting loss is to accept the reality of it, and that I must allow myself to lean into the pain. Only then could I come to terms with its meaning. Doing so is vital if the spirit is to continue to grow, and to survive.

As I groped my way along the path to wholeness, the mission group was there to comfort, council, or scold me. More often than not I needed it pointed out that I wasn't dealing with my problems but having a pity party.

Recalling that Chuck Motley refused to pray for Kedar's healing, I carried the thought for a long time that I was responsible for his dying of cancer.

Chuck was so insistent that the person whom Kedar was unable to forgive had to be very close to him–a parent, spouse, or child–that I was sure I was the one. For years I tried to get him to stop smoking, convinced that it caused his bad cough. More and more evidence on the killing effects of tobacco was being published. He smoked three packs a day of unfiltered Camels. He inhaled deeply and held the smoke for a moment before exhaling.

Several times when Kedar wanted to buy something I objected to, he promised to stop smoking if I'd agree. He was absolutely sure he could quit. So I agreed, believing that no price was too high, even if it took our last dime, to get him off that filthy weed! The last time we went through the exercise was when he wanted to buy a Mercedes Benz 250-C. No question about it, it was a good car, safe, with good road-handling qualities, the color I liked, and with excellent resale value. (Can't you just hear the sales pitch?) For a man without a job, paying twice the price of another good used car, sure, that's what we needed like a hole in the head, but it came with the promise to stop smoking. I believed he really meant it, and I'm sure he did; but his addiction was much stronger than his resolve. In a couple of weeks he was smoking again, and I was not happy about it. I got over the disappointment, and put it behind me.

After Kedar died, however, it came back to haunt me. Had I made smoking such a difficult issue that he was unable to forgive me? It stuck to me like flypaper.

During an exercise in one of the courses in the School of Christian Living at the church, we were required to write in detail about some recent traumatic event in our lives. I wrote about Kedar's last days and the conversations we had. In doing so, I recalled that over and over again during his final weeks he remarked, "My life would have been so different if my mother had lived."

I thought about it a lot. She died when he was four years old, so he had very few memories of her except that she was tender, cuddled him a lot, and that she was very pretty with golden hair.

Gertrude Barndt, a math teacher in the Shanghai American School, became stepmother to three lively children, Alice, Kedar, and Peggy, a baby when their mother died.

Gertrude was a good mother and ran the household efficiently. She loved the children and saw to all their needs, but she was not a soft, tender person. Kedar was very affectionate and needed a lot of touching.

One of his earliest memories of Gertrude was when a friend came to call.

"And Gertrude," she asked, " how are you getting along with the discipline of your ready-made family?"

"We understand each other very well, don't we, little fellow," she said, picking up a ruler and shaking it at him. They all laughed, but that gave a good picture of how they got along.

Reading over what I had written and recalling Kedar's words, I began to see that it was not I but his Mother whom he had been unable to forgive for dying! If only she had not died, he would have had the tenderness he so desperately needed as a child. Something within him wasn't filled up. A raw wound was left unhealed and pushed down in his subconscious where it wouldn't hurt so much.

I felt sad that his needs hadn't been met but tremendously relieved to have the puzzle solved at last.

I was introduced to Bibles for the World through Cliff and Betty Robinson, friends since our days in India. Their purpose is to get the Gospel in the native language into areas where they are not readily available. In 1976 I took a week of vacation to attend their annual conference at Willowbank in Bermuda. Of the several personal testimonies given, one was particularly significant for me.

Tom and Brenda Alexander told their story; it changed my life forever.

"We were fair-weather Christians," Tom said. "We went to church if there wasn't anything more interesting to do, and that was about the size of it. We have three children. When Brenda was carrying Tommy, the oldest, she contracted rubella in the first trimester. He was born with terrible problems, and from the day of his birth, he was a patient at Johns Hopkins. Every month we took him in for treatment, but nothing got any better.

"When Tommy was six, the doctors began to plan open heart surgery, the only option left to save him. So far he hadn't talked and could do very little for himself. He attended a special school for challenged children, but his prognosis was poor.

"One Saturday we were out shopping and sort of half-listening to a radio program about a person who had the gift of healing. It interested us, as there seemed to be little hope for our son. We listened for the name, but just as it was given the kids in the back seat were making such a noise that we missed it.

"A social service worker at the hospital tracks patients who are in long-term treatment, and if things looked grim, he invites to go with them in his van to a weekly healing service in Pittsburgh conducted by Katherine Coolman. When he asked us we both remembered that was the name of the person we'd heard about!

"Yes, we want to go, but we'll have to follow you in our car. Tommy needs so much attention." When the day came we left very early, yet it was still dark when Brenda carried Tommy into the church and the doors shut behind them. It was full. Not even I could get in.

"They were taken to the lower level to watch the service on a closed circuit TV. I was finally admitted when I told the guard that I had Tommy's medicine, and he'd be in a lot of trouble if he didn't get it on time. An usher came and told us it was our turn to go up. Katherine Coolman asked about Tommy's problems, she prayed for him; we thanked her and left. There were no bells, whistles, or warm fuzzies. That was it. We went home.

"Very slowly Tommy began to change. Teachers at his school sent us notes saying he'd done this or that for the first time, and we saw him change, too. The hospital postponed the heart surgery. Things that had been impossible for him were beginning to be normal. We were astonished and thrilled. Little by little he was being made whole.

"The day Tommy said his first word I was due to go to a meeting but decided not to. It was blustery and cold, and I was tired. After Brenda bathed the kids and heard their prayers, Tommy took a deep breath, sighed, and died. Brenda called frantically for me, and I gave him mouth-to-mouth resuscitation while she called 911. He came around for a few seconds, then slipped away again. It kept happening. We couldn't stabilize him. The paramedics did no better, so finally I had to tell them to give it up. He was gone.

"The next morning, three people who didn't know each

other called to say, "I had such a strange dream. I dreamed that Tommy was walking away holding Jesus' hand. Every few steps he turned around and waved bye-bye!" Three people and they all had the same dream!

"The hospital called and asked if they could do a postmortem on him and send his vital organs to their lab in Texas, because they were absolutely baffled about why he died. We gave permission, but knew what the results would be. We buried a shell of our child and in time the report came–he was perfect in every way. It was just Tommy's day to die."

Their story comforted me. Kedar was just fifty-three and too young to die, but who's to question God? Isn't it written that our days are numbered even before we are born? I was able to accept that September 8, 1974 at twelve noon was Kedar's time.

I was so glad I'd was with him at the end because it helped me to bring closure to an important part of my life. I believe our three most important dates are the day we are born, the day we are reborn into the kingdom of God, and the day we die.

The next year I went back to the conference in Bermuda.

"Fran, how's your life?" Ro asked as we gathered on the patio before tea.

"It's good, but it's still lonely."

"Come, come, come," he said to all, reaching out his arms and motioning us all together. "Let's stand in a circle, hold hands, and pray for a 'man for Fran!' " We laughed as we did so. I couldn't believe that man, but his heart is made of pure gold and he prays mighty prayers. The rest is history.

About the time I was beginning to feel like a whole person once again, that life was good as it was given, Jean and I decided to go to the "Faithful Friends Event" at Dayspring, a three-day retreat to study and learn the meaning of deep and honest friendship. I like the quotation from Ecclesiastics 6:16, which is the basis of this sort of friendship, "A faithful friend is the elixir of life, and those who fear the Lord will find one."

By lot we were paired off to study and discover the real meaning of that kind of friendship. I had thought we'd be able to select our partners and wanted to be with Jean. Out of thirty participants, I thought it impossible that we'd be together. I was overjoyed when our names were drawn as teammates! I can remember thinking, before the foundations of the world, the Lord knew we would be together for this event.

Over the three days there were times of silence, meditation and prayer, and sharing with the partner what had been given to us through selected readings.

The last morning of the retreat Jean was quiet and thoughtful as we read Douglas V. Steele's "On Being Present Where You Are." One passage states, "In all areas: personal, ecumenical, educational, racial, political- to be present, really present, is to be vulnerable, to be able to be hurt. And when pain is in prospect, it is so much easier to be elsewhere than where we are."

In the hour before lunch, Jean sat beside me on the sofa; her forehead creased in a frown, and tears ready to spill from her eyes. "Fran," she said in a choked voice, "I have to tell you something. It isn't easy, and I don't want to hurt you; but I must say it, more for my own sake than yours because it's something I have to deal with. It's been hard for me to listen to you tell our mission group about your problems in adjusting to widowhood. I know it has been rough, but hearing about it made me unconfortable, uneasy." She blew her nose and dried her eyes. Twisting her handkerchief in her hands, she continued. "But today, reading this passage for the Faithful Friends, I see why I felt that way. I saw in you the very thing I fear most in my own life–losing Ed."

We sat in silence. I was shocked and saddened to think I had caused her pain. Had the others in the group felt the same? Had I dumped on them problems I should have kept to myself? But that's what the mission was all about–being open with each other, vulnerable to hurt, ready to confront when necessary. They were my new family, and I loved them. Was I kidding myself that they loved me in return?

We reached out and held hands and as we prayed, Jean's words came back to me: "Sometimes I have wanted never to see you again because I saw in you the thing I fear most–losing Ed." Now I heard what she said! She had a problem with fear. I didn't have the problem, she did! I could hardly believe it. There was nothing wrong with me after all. I really was an okay person. Perhaps others had that same fear and couldn't handle it. Had I been carrying a burden all this time that didn't belong to me?

In my stomach, the very spot where so many times I'd had that awful twisting sensation when I felt condemnation, a warmth began. It was like a blessing that spread to every part of my body. My shoulders relaxed. I breathed deeply, and uncrossing my legs, felt the firmness of the smooth, polished floor under foot. I was smiling.

Our prayer ended, we stood up and hugged. She went toward others who were coming for lunch. I walked to the door and stepped out onto the terrace into one of the first warm days of spring. The apple orchard on the hillside sloping away from the building was in full bloom and humming with bees. The air was clean and sparkling. Everything seemed brighter than life. Joy poured over me. The world was so beautiful, all that bound me for years fell away. Life was good as it was given, and open-ended once more–I was set free!

Epilogue

A year and a half after Kedar died, his sister Peggy also died of cancer. Of the original Bryan family of five, only Alice was left.

My brother Jim never lacked for female companionship, but one young lady was of particular interest. Peggy Leinbaugh was originally from Lewiston, Illinois, where Heydon pastored the Presbyterian church for several years. Her family were members. Peggy was a gawky kid Molly's age, and her older brother, Bud, was in my class at Knox.

After Peggy's husband, Bob Jones, died of a malignant brain tumor, her mother wrote saying that Pastor Lampe's brother, Jim, was living in McLean, Virginia, and it would be nice if they met. Peggy wasn't the least bit interested, being much involved in making a success of her boutique, Top Drawer. Eventually they did get together, and both were smitten. In due course a wedding date was set for May 16, 1976.

Peggy and Bob Jones, Milley and Harley Grimm, and Babe and Pete Peterson were the best of friends in the Air Force. Babe had died very suddenly two years prior, and Peggy and Milley thought it was a good idea for Pete and me to meet; so he was invited to the wedding.

Remember the prayer Ro Pudiate prayed for "a man for Fran?"
Well, it turned out that Pete was the one, but early on I wasn't so sure. The first time I saw him he was puffing on a cigarette. Oh, no, I thought, I'm not going there again. Nevertheless, things do change, and exactly eighteen months later we exchanged our vows at the Church of the Saviour in Washington, D.C.

The Eagle and the Egret is the story of our years in Florida, getting our fill of the good life, but before long we had an itch to do more. Two summers we took our young people from Trinity Presbyterian Church and others from the St. John's Presbytery to Haiti to help build a school in Pele, a slum of Port au Prince. We spent the better part of two years in Thailand with COSIGN (Church of the Saviour International Good Neighbors), working with the Lao, Cambodian, and Vietnamese refugees. Then it was off to Taiwan with IESC (International Executive Service Corps), and on to Korea, first with VIM (Volunteers in Mission) of the Presbyterian Church, USA, and with OMS (Oriental Missionary Society), International, as honorary missionaries. What a blast! All our life experiences seemed to have prepared us for this time, and we thoroughly enjoyed it.

So come join us in our new adventures!

Blessings, Fran.